T0290447

THE DEAL: ABOUT FACE

ALSO BY ADAM GITTLIN

The Men Downstairs

The Deal

THE DEAL: ABOUT FACE

A Novel

ADAM GITTLIN

Oceanview Publishing

LONGBOAT KEY, FLORIDA

ISBN: 978-1-60809-107-2

Published in the United States by Oceanview Publishing,
Longboat Key, Florida
www.oceanviewpub.com

2 4 6 8 10 9 7 5 3 1

PRINTED IN THE UNITED STATES OF AMERICA

For Hunter

ACKNOWLEDGMENTS

I want to thank Pat and Bob Gussin, Frank Troncale, David Ivester, Susan Hayes, and everyone at Oceanview Publishing. I'm fortunate to be with such a fine house, a group that believes in, and backs, their authors to the fullest. Pat, you're an awesome editor and a key component in this latest Jonah Gray installment. God bless the technology at our fingertips, allowing us to work on a manuscript without me having to keep track of which corner of the globe you're visiting.

Mom and Dad, thanks as always for your support. Mom, your artistic sensibilities and the love of stories you passed to me are two of the reasons I'm once again writing an acknowledgments page. You're always one of my first readers, giving valuable insight as to what's working, and what needs to be better. Watching your dedication to your painting has shown me the kind of fortitude I need to put forth toward my writing. Dad, you're the reason I took such an interest in commercial real estate, thus why I have subsequently found this world such a fascinating thriller backdrop. You have been a constant champion of my writing since the beginning. You are my top commercial real estate resource for each Jonah Gray installment. I'm appreciative of, and hope you will continue to be, both.

Thanks to my sister Gail, Larry, T, and all those who remain part of my initial reading group. Your suggestions and criticism always prove valuable. And a special thanks to Jay—Dr. Jason Auerbach—also a member of my trusted reading group, one of my closest friends, and my medical go-to.

Thanks again to Gary Rosen, Howard Tenenbaum, and Andrea Soloway. My days working with you three, as well as so many others in the New York City commercial real estate community, remain a driving force behind Jonah Gray and these stories.

Dave, Annemarie, Richard, Pat, Matt, Amanda, Geralyn, Elliot—and, of course, all the little Plotkins. Some of Jonah's finest moments have come to life in your summer home. You all gave that to my readers.

A special thank you to Rachel Tarlow Gul, George Foster, and Ivan Roos. Your contributions to *The Deal: About Face* are both significant and appreciated.

Lastly, thank you to a certain girl with long, dark hair. You are beautiful and glowing inside and out, and throughout the process of writing this book were the muse who seemed to always show up at just the right time.

THE DEAL: ABOUT FACE

PROLOGUE

A hand from behind reaches over me and grabs my chin like a vice, pulling it back as far as it will go. I groan in agony. My eyes stare at the ceiling. A drop of filthy water hits me dead center on my forehead. Seconds later, my torturer's blue eyes meet mine from no more than two inches above.

"*Gereed om te spreken? Of jullie nog denken jullie wipen enigerlei handeling held?*"

What language is that? I think, his spittle spraying my skin. And why do I understand it? Given my restrained circumstances, my reflexes still function, and I attempt to shake my head. As I do, my assailant repeats himself. This time I hear it in English . . .

"You ready to speak? Or you still think you're some kind of action hero?"

. . . As I recall why I now process everything I hear in two languages.

He gently traces my face with his fingertips, like a blind man seeing something for the first time.

"My God, Jonah. Look at you . . ."

My thoughts are distorted, but I recognize the voice. Andreu Zhamovsky, my dear half-brother. My head slowly bobs back up. Then, in an instant, bright, beautiful colors flash across my mind. There are jewels—splendid green emeralds, luscious red rubies.

There is gold, silver. Subconsciously or consciously, I can't be sure, I squint from their sheer brilliance. I look forward. I could swear *Danish Jubilee Egg*, the one of the eight missing Fabergé Imperial Easter Eggs I had been saddled with years earlier in New York City, is suspended in midair. I think of how I had kept it—a true, rare treasure—out of harm's way. I smile.

"I have something you want, Jonah. And we both know what you have to give me first to get it."

My mouth fills with blood again. Instead of spitting it out, afraid of the ensuing pain from such force, I part my lips and gently push the deep red liquid down the front of me. Its warmth feels strangely comforting against my raw chin, my freezing chest.

"Why don't you uncuff me and face me like a man?" I ask.

In one swift motion a vodka-soaked rag is crammed into my mouth. The burning of my bleeding tongue and cheeks is off the charts. A clear plastic bag is pulled over my head. Trying to move is of no use. I simply can't. My heart is racing so fast I think it might explode. The unmistakable scratching sound of duct tape pulling away from its roll fills the room, though I can barely hear it. The plastic is thick. The noise seems distant. The tape is being wrapped around my neck, securing the bag to my skin. Moments later, breathing my own warm, recycled breath solely through my nose, the bag starts crumpling in and out. It won't be long until I'm dead.

He's bluffing.

He's got to be.

CHAPTER 1

It's dusk. Sleepy light sneaking in around the edges of my bedroom window blinds tells me so. My eyes, wide and alert, stare at the ceiling. Without adjusting my line of vision, I reach my right hand out for the other side of the bed. I'm feeling for Perry's arm. Once I feel her soft skin, I'll go straight for the crease on the inside of her elbow, one of her more sensitive spots. A handful of twelve-hundred thread count Egyptian sheets are all I get. My head rolls right. No Perry. She's gone.

Walking through the all-white master suite, past our walk-in closets and his-and-her changing areas, I head to the bathroom. I drag my index finger tip up a sensor on the wall where a switch undoubtedly used to be. The light zips from dim to blazing. As it bounces between the white marble walls, I can't fight the sense of surprise, even after all these years, of what I see when I catch myself in the mirror. I see a man I don't recognize. I don't mean figuratively, I mean a man who literally looks nothing like the man who fled the United States—more specifically, New York City, my home— nine years earlier. I still can't tell you what I used to look like. To do so would illustrate what I don't look like now. That alone tips the odds in your favor. What I can tell you is the eyes staring back at me belong to the Jonah Gray I remember. Everything else belongs to Ivan Janse. Like always, a PowerPoint presentation of my life plays out in fast-forward across my brain like it's rolling across a six-story IMAX screen. Within seconds I look at my hands, my fingertips, remembering I no longer even have fingerprints. More on all this later. We'll get to it soon enough.

Deciding I'm not yet ready for reality, I turn the lights back off and get in the shower. With the turn of a nozzle, water falls from the wide overhead fixture like the heavens are opening up. I savor the warmth as the water coats my body. And can't help but ask myself if it is me who has life by the throat, or if it's the other way around.

Like most days, even for a few minutes, I'm thinking about the summer of 2004. That's when a childhood friend from Moscow named Andreu Zhamovsky came calling in New York City. I was a commercial real estate power broker on one of the most dominant teams in Manhattan. Andreu was the son of one of my father's "friends in high places" scattered around the globe. What happened over the course of three weeks that summer became the impetus for every second I have lived since. Those events, and more importantly the outcome of those events, are what consume me with every breath I take.

The bottom floor of my five-story canal house on Keizersgracht Straat—ultra-contemporary and white aside from the brushed steel fixtures and artwork, same as the four stories above—is strategically lit for evening with a soft glow. Dressed in a solid navy Canali suit, white Armani button-down shirt open at the collar, and brown tie-up Ferragamos, I enter the kitchen. The room, like all rooms in our home, is state-of-the-art from the décor to the appliances, though I had no hand whatsoever in the design. In fact, I didn't even purchase the home. It was given to me, something else we'll get to. A second before I open the refrigerator, I hear a distant jingle. It's the bell on Neo's—long since renamed Aldo—collar. He's awoken from a nap on his favorite chaise in the living room. He realizes it's time for his dinner.

By the time he struts into the room, his short nails lightly clicking on the white, polished marble underfoot, I've moved the plate
of grilled chicken our housekeeper Laura prepared for him from the
fridge to the counter and uncovered it. Neo looks at me without
breaking stride. His mouth is open a bit. The spots where his lips
meet on both sides of his face have receded giving him an appearance of smiling. Not as spry as he once was and unable to leap into
my arms, my favorite white long-haired Chihuahua stops at my feet
and extends a paw up to me asking for a lift. As always, I happily
oblige. But before putting him on the counter, I hold him up so
we're nose to nose. Excited, he licks my face. Even in the white fur
of his adorable face I can see graying wisps. Again, as is the case
multiple times a day, I'm reminded of the time that has passed, how
my life has changed. I reciprocate his kisses with kisses of my own
to his nose and face and place him next to his plate for his feast. I
uncork a bottle of Brunello and spend a few relaxing moments with
my precious friend as he eats.

I'm about to cross the threshold between my home and the
Amsterdam evening. Before I do, I grab my keys. The simple sterling silver key ring has six keys on it: two for this house, one for my
office, and two for another residence on Herengracht, which we'll
get to later. The sixth key, I've just acquired.

And it's not for a home or an office.

My eyes catch a silver-framed photo on the side table just to the
left of the front door. It's of Perry, Max, and me—not the Perry,
Max, and me that ran from New York City, but the new version of
us—three years ago on the beach in Mykonos. I touch my fingers to
my lips, then to the photograph, and leave.

I head west on foot. It's a typical spring night in the Netherlands:
drizzly, a bit windy, a touch chilly. Before arriving here, I'd never
been to Amsterdam. All I'd heard about was the legal pot smoking
and prostitution. I envisioned some tired, crumbling, dirty little
European city with pubs and gas lamps lining the streets. Some borderline, irrelevant place stuck in an earlier century. Not the case.

This place is rich with history and wear, but it's also lively, forward thinking, and romantic, commerce driven, cosmopolitan, even a little spicy. I had no idea it was built on water much like Venice, only with streets as well as the four main half-moon canals that make up the heart of the city. Amsterdam is an inspiring, beautiful mixture of past and present.

I eventually turn on to PC Hooftstraat, the city's most upscale stretch of retail. Hermès, Zegna, Cartier, D&G—it's got them all. My destination is a watch store called Tourbillion. I look at the Audemars Piguet on my left wrist, a gift my mother gave my father and my only tie to my previous life. My mind drifts back to the summer of 2004, to Andreu Zhamovsky. Our fathers met in 1979 with Communism on the precipice of crumbling. Alexander Zhamovsky, Andreu's father, was in control of most of the Soviet Union's natural gas resources. He was attending New York City as part of a series of secret conferences with the purpose of strong American business minds teaching our Cold War counterparts about the finer points of Democratic capitalism, a win-win for both sides in the ultimate game of what all governments want most regardless of their actual political views: making money.

Andreu and I connected, clicked. We became fast friends. Though we lived on opposite ends of the globe, we remained tight. Our families traveled together. If my father and I were overseas—business or pleasure—we'd try to all meet up for a day or so. Andreu and I would write. We were like pen pals. As we got older, we drifted somewhat but only in terms of length between communications. If a week or a year passed it didn't matter, the next time we spoke it was like we had just done so five minutes ago. Like we were family.

In four days, I'll be making my long-anticipated return to the United States. The last thing I can allow to happen, after all these years being so careful and with much unfinished business, is for someone to put together who I am because of a hunch and an image of me caught on film at Newark Liberty International Airport the day I left with the Audemars on my wrist. Crazy paranoid? Maybe. But like I said, I've got unfinished business. And here's my reality.

When I'm driving, I stop farther than necessary behind the car in front of me at a light in case I need to make a break for it. When I walk into a restaurant—or any public place for that matter—I first scout all possible escape routes then survey every set of eyes in the room to see which might be the ones looking to arrest, or kill, me. When I sleep, I always do so with a gun within reach. When I fled America, I did so a wanted man. I was wanted by the law for inadvertently killing a crooked New York City cop and for taking the matter of my father's murder into my own hands. I was wanted by a very powerful Russian family for denying them the storied eight missing Fabergé Imperial Easter Eggs that are in fact not missing at all. Did I do some things I still, to this second, regret? Definitely. Were all of my actions, in my mind, justified? Absolutely.

I reach address number 72 and enter the store. The walls, like my home, are white, and the floor is darkly stained, wide, hardwood planks. There is a quaint sitting area comprised of four modern, cubelike brown leather chairs around a rectangular glass coffee table. In the center of the table is a vase with fresh white roses. The rest of the space is occupied by glass display cases filled with expensive timepieces. Realizing it feels like eons since I've shopped for a watch—or a trophy as I sometimes called them back in New York, since I usually bought one following the close of a deal—I can't shake the feeling of nostalgia that passes through me. I can't deny the sense of entitlement, wanted or unwanted, that hard-earned wealth brings.

I know, I know. Right now you're thinking, "Hasn't this guy learned his fucking lesson?"

The answer is yes.

I have.

I understand better than anyone that millions of dollars ensures only two things: a roof overhead, food in the mouth. Nothing else. Not love, not happiness, not faith, nothing. But I also know that in the big play of life, I've been cast in a new role. And this role, like my last part, calls for a certain level of wardrobe. At my core I'm fine with a Timex or Swatch. But all this would do is bring questions from those who surround me, successful professional types not very different from my old associates back in Manhattan. And questions, for me, bring one thing. Unwanted attention.

"*Dag*," the statuesque, brunette saleswoman says to me.

"*Dag*," I say back.

The true sign of a Netherlands native is the ability to speak either Dutch or English on a dime. Something I have been able to do for years now.

"*Bent u zoekt...*"

"*Perregaux?*" I cut her off.

"*Natuurlijk. Juist deze manier.*"

She leads me to the case holding the Girard-Perregaux watches. Like I said, the watch I'm buying is more prop than anything else. Therefore I don't need to spend much time browsing, especially since I have somewhere to be. The moment I learned I was going home, and that I needed to leave behind the watch that is the only connection to my mother who died when I was five, a Girard-Perregaux World Time jumped into my head. It was next on my list of desired timepieces back when I was a commercial real estate power broker in New York who still cared about extravagant bullshit.

She hands me the watch. It is large and heavy. The rose-gold case is forty-three millimeters in diameter. The face is white with a cream inner bezel where the chronograph dials are located. It tells time in all twenty-four official time zones around the globe and has an exposed backing, allowing the handcrafted movement to be viewed as it works. I slide it on. The crystal backing glides silkily over the skin on my hand. The smell of the fresh leather strap fills my nose.

"*Hoeveel?*" I ask.

"*Zestien duizend, negan hindered negentig vijf Euro,*" she responds.

A little more than seventeen thousand Euro, or just under twenty-four thousand American dollars. To tell time.

I wear it out of the store.

CHAPTER 2

It's Saturday evening. The cool air feels refreshing. My destination is 23 Kerkstraat, which is just off Leidseplein—"Plein" meaning Square—one of three main Pleins in the city. Once I reach the Van Gogh Museum, it's only about another five minutes. I turn right on Kerkstraat, a quiet old cobblestone road. Old street lamps with energy-saving bulbs on top where a gas flame used to be supply the night light. I look at the two opposing rows of coach houses. When I arrived nine years ago, part of me was still so angry, so bitter, I saw these houses as nothing more than simple lines of four or five-story buildings that seemingly ran in to one another, like the townhouses of Manhattan's Upper East Side can look at first glance.

Today I see these buildings for what they are: a twenty-four-foot-wide, five-story, red-brick coach house with red moldings and three tall ground-level windows; followed by a thirty-foot wide, four-story, brown-brick coach house with white moldings and what appears to be a single-windowed attic, or smaller level, on top; followed by a thirty-foot-wide, five-story—you get the idea. The houses, in actuality, are similar but far from the same. Even the pulley—each house has a pulley centrally located on top to hoist objects up since the internal stairways are so narrow—is different in quality and characteristics upon inspection from one to the next. Attention to detail in my constant battle to remain free of my past life, as if I'd shed that life like some spent reptilian skin, has been my greatest ally these past years. Just as it has been my greatest ally in becoming a professional success all over again from scratch.

I enter the restaurant. A happening bar and restaurant catering to Amsterdam's young elite throbs before me. Architecturally the space begins and ends with crisp lines. The colors—mostly browns and creams—are earthy yet rich. Although the space is packed, square mirrors running the entire shell of the rectangular bar give an odd illusion of a sea of legs. Slicing upward from the bar, beginning in the center of one of the rectangle's short sides to the second floor is a golden staircase.

Abeni, the striking, six-foot-tall African hostess with a shaved head, is mobbed. I wait for her eye. On sight of me, while mid-sentence with a patron, she smiles and motions me upstairs.

I reach the top, the main restaurant. A waiter points me in the right direction. Cocktail hour is well underway. In the far corner, enmeshed in conversation, is Cobus de Bont. Cobus is my boss. He is the founder of de Bont Beleggings—*Beleggings* means Investments in Dutch. De Bont Beleggings is one of the largest and most successful private investment firms—and the single largest private owner of commercial real estate—in the Netherlands. The dinner party is in honor of his wife, Annabelle's, fortieth birthday.

Cobus, chatting with local real estate player Martin Gemser, sees me. He waves me over. I pass through the crowd, shaking hands and kissing cheeks.

"*De heer Ivan. Hoe we vanavond gevoel?*"

Cobus, who also more readily chooses Dutch over English, just asked me how I'm feeling tonight. From this point on, to make things easier, I'll go with English in all cases.

"Feeling great, actually, I even managed to get in a nap this afternoon," I respond.

"You know I meant to ask," Cobus continues, "how was your

excursion to Hamburg last weekend? How was your visit with your friend from university?"

Was I in Hamburg?

Yes.

Was I with a friend from university?

Not quite.

"The weekend was great. It was a lot of fun catching up. Where's your beautiful wife?" I change directions. "Has she arrived yet?"

He points. Annabelle, a gorgeous, smart, blond fashion photographer, is across the room giggling with others at some guy's story. A waiter approaches, asking if we need cocktails. Before I can answer, Cobus tells him I need a Belvedere over rocks with a twist.

Yes—I even changed my drink of choice.

"Three buildings." Martin continues their previous conversation. "Forty-four Utrechtsestraat and Sixteen Muntplein definitely. Possibly also Eighteen Damrak. Utrechtsestraat and Muntplein alone could be stolen at a seven cap. Easily. We all know how Henrik Bosch markets property. These buildings should have occupancy levels much higher than seventy, seventy-two percent. Because Damrak—"

"How much?" Cobus interrupts.

"I—maybe—eighty-five; perhaps a bit—"

"Where are the rents today?" Cobus continues. "Where should they be?"

"For which property? I mean—if—"

"I need to cut you off, Martin. And I apologize in advance if I sound disrespectful. I know you think you're giving me information. But each time you do this—each time you present me with a potential property minus the meaningful numbers—all you're really doing is wasting both of our time."

"I'm not sure why you say that, Cobus. Even looking at the scenario in general terms—"

"I don't do general terms, Martin. You know why?"

Martin Gemser is a local real estate player with bigger dreams than bank accounts. He's in nowhere near Cobus's league and neither of us particularly like him. Unfortunately, Annabelle's sister is married to this guy. Martin stares back blankly.

"Because numbers don't lie. People do. Now, I'm not calling you a liar, Martin. What I'm saying is that, intentionally or unintentionally, people can paint the wrong picture when it comes to real estate. People's accounts can be—disputable. Not the numbers. The numbers do not—cannot—lie. The numbers, Martin, are indisputable. The numbers are irrefutable."

Martin takes a sip from the whiskey-filled lowball glass in his hand.

"You want to bring me a deal we can make?" Cobus goes on, "Here's the way I suggest you do it—"

Martin is too dim-witted to realize he's about to get a gift. Most individuals anywhere near the commercial real estate game in the Netherlands would kill to hear what Cobus de Bont needs to take a potential deal seriously.

"Numbers. Nail down every last number. Rents, occupancies, depreciation, commissions to be paid, operating expenses, capital improvements—I want every pertinent line item of the true financial run in front of me so I can see the financial landscape down to the last penny. Include conservative forecasts. Include aggressive forecasts. Include explanations of where the numbers might be improved and include explanations about which numbers may not be as appealing in the years to come. Don't worry about things like Bosch's ability to market a property or why a particular building may be a sleeper in terms of the retail space—I'm fine to evaluate all remaining tangible and intangible aspects on my own. All I want from you is one thing."

Cobus sips his glass of Chianti.

"Numbers," Martin says.

"Not after a deal is presented—before," Cobus goes on. "E-mail them to me. This way, to be frank, we'll both know if a discussion is even going to take place."

"Numbers first," Martin says again, gently nodding his head.

"Wrapped in a bow."

Cobus smiles. He takes another sip.

"Get me the numbers for the three buildings. If I like them, we'll talk."

This is one of the things—Cobus's respect for others—I respect most about Cobus. Real estate evaluation, from Amsterdam to New York City to anywhere else for that matter, is a multifaceted undertaking. But anyone with half a brain who plays in property understands clear as day that a deal begins and ends with the numbers. In this same situation another guy of Cobus's stature might have spoken down to Martin, in some way made him feel inferior. Not Cobus. In typical fashion he used the opportunity to enlighten Martin, to teach him. Knowing Cobus as well as I do, I clearly understand there are two reasons for this. Number one, he genuinely cares for, feels for, people. Number two, the buildings Martin speaks of may, in fact, work for him.

Martin walks away. Cobus leans over the table next to us. He grabs a toast point and scoops on some steak tartare.

"Eat something," he says before taking a bite.

I look at the table filled with appetizers. There's caprese with tomato, mozzarella, cucumber, mint, and feta. There's a rouille— rust sauce—based bouillabaisse, as well as the steak tartare. There are frog's legs sautéed in a fine fruit sauce paired with crisp, sliced potatoes to be dipped in a chili-pepper mayonnaise. After surveying my options, I, too, drag a toast point through the raw seasoned ground beef.

Cobus puts his arm around my shoulders. As I chew he takes a sip of his Chianti. Six-feet, two-inches tall with thick, dark hair and dark skin to match his chestnut eyes, Cobus is dressed like always. Black suit, black shirt, black tie. The clothes are perfectly tailored, every edge from hem to collar knifelike. Since the day I met him, I don't recall him wearing anything else. Summer, winter, morning, evening—doesn't matter. He says he has a rare skin condition called Solar urticaria. Exposure of his skin to sunlight results in painful, burning lesions. Hence the ever-present, perfectly manicured five o'clock shadow completing his more Mediterranean than Nordic look. This may be the case, but part of me can't help feel Cobus doesn't mind his affliction. His approach to clothes means more time—even a few precious moments a day—to focus on the important matters at hand: Business.

"Tell me about Willem," he says to me. "He's been with us for eight years, Ivan. He's one of the best in this entire city."

Willem Krol. Chief building engineer of Astoria, one of the oldest office buildings in Amsterdam, located on the corner of the intersecting Keizersgracht and Leliegracht canals. Best known for its copper-plated roof, the six-story home to numerous companies is part of the de Bont Beleggings portfolio.

"It has recently come to my attention Willem Krol may be fabricating some overtime. I still need more facts. But it's not looking good."

Cobus sighs and drops his chin. The waiter arrives with my Belvedere. We clink glasses and each take a hearty sip of our drinks.

"How about—"

I answer Cobus's question before he's done asking. His tone alone tells me he's changing direction.

"Harkin Aeuronautic accepted the higher security deposit and signed the lease. I made it clear the option for another term at their discretion wasn't going to happen. Staying on the Vinoly Building—"

The official title is Mahler Four Office Tower, but because of its world-renowned architect—Rafael Vinoly—it is simply referred to as the Vinoly Building. It is one of the most prized office properties in Amsterdam's highest-end commercial market—the South Axis. It is here one can find modern skyscrapers like those found in New York City or London or Sydney, only on a much smaller scale.

Completed in 2005, the Vinoly Building is a twenty-four-story rectangular glass L. The bottom six stories make up the base, and the rest of the floors make up the high backstop. It is a sleek, refined structure that appears, oddly, to have a crack running down, around the edge of the tall backstop. Vinoly carved an external fire stair-case into the building's shell. The goal was to incorporate Amster-dam's innovative spirit into his design. The result is a property that helps define architectural vision.

Cobus bought the building last spring for forty-four million euros. It is one of three he owns in the South Axis. Our offices are on the top floor.

"Jaap Jan de Geer let me know CCM Global will not be renew-ing. They'll be out in six months, which is more than enough time to market the space. I'm not sure if you recall but their build-out is really high-end. We're talking about—"

"Do you two ever tire of talking business?" a female voice asks from behind us.

We turn around. It's Annabelle. Wearing a tight, sleeveless, lau-rel-green embroidered dress with a black leather belt and high black heels, she's an image out of one of her own photo shoots.

"Sorry, boys. It's time for Cobus to toast his best girl."

Wasting no time, Annabelle grabs a random empty water glass and begins clinking it with a spoon.

"I appreciate the update," Cobus says to me, "but that's not what I was going to ask."

"What then?"

"If you still think New York City over Berlin is the right move?"

Ninety minutes later, as we're finishing dinner, I receive a text. The name pops up with the number. It is from Scott Green. After a few seconds I place the contact. He's in-house counsel—someone I've spoken with only a handful of times—for the Manhattan-based firm with whom we're about to make a deal.

CONFIDENTIAL, THE TEXT BEGINS. IVAN—NED TO SEE YOU. IN TOWN HAMMERIG OUT DETAILS WITH YOR LAWYERS. MUST SEE YOU IMEDIATELY. TELL NO ONE.

I look around. Both confused and intrigued, I return my eyes to my iPhone and read it again. I can't help but be a bit thrown off by all the misspellings. I've seen numerous complicated, detailed legal documents drafted by this man. Scott Green doesn't strike me as such a careless texter.

I look at Cobus. He's whispering in Annabelle's ear, and she's grinning ear-to-ear absorbing the tender moment. Figuring it's most likely a fire I can squelch on my own, I decide not to bother him.

OF COURSE, I write back. AMSTEL HOTEL?

This, the finest hotel in the city, is where I recall members of the "Seller's" team stayed during their last trip to Amsterdam.

NO, he replies almost immediately. NIEUWE PRINSENGRACHT. HOUSEBOAT. NUMBER 030. CONFIDENTIAL. TEL NO ONE.

CHAPTER 3

Standing in the center of a thirty-five-meter-wide, cast-iron foot-bridge, I look down the narrow canal that splits Nieuwe Prinsen-gracht Straat. Both sides of the water are lined with houseboats. Beyond the houseboats, on each side, are diagonally parked cars and bicycles followed by the street then the sidewalk. Canal houses tower above all, like bookends mindfully containing the life below.

The neighborhood is quiet. I hear a baby crying from above through an open window. Barely audible remnants of the weekend crowd enjoying the bars, shops, and restaurants graze me from near-by Rembrandt Square. There's a cool mist in the air. The lights on the next footbridge up ahead are muted, like a fuzzy photograph.

I start toward the canal houses to my right. As I get closer, I can see some of the numbers on them. Even, which means I chose cor-rectly. Even-numbered canal houses mean even-numbered house-boats. After a few steps, at the end of the bridge, I turn left.

The second houseboat down is number 030. This is one of the city's newest, more like a doublewide trailer home on a mini-barge as opposed to an actual boat. Aesthetically it isn't much to look at—it's a white, rectangular box. But unlike the relics of the sixties and seventies moored around this city, what the new generation houseboats lack in character they make up for with running water, electricity, gas heat, and an attachment to the municipal sewer system. Plus, they're twice the size.

As I descend an eight-step ladder from street level to the dock, I hear music coming from behind the front door. I can see through a large picture window into the brightly lit living room. I notice the finishes are more upscale than I might have imagined. There are beautifully polished cherrywood floors, a plush, L-shaped chocolate leather couch, a matching square ottoman, and contemporary light fixtures. Then I notice that the room—or what I can see of the room—is empty.

I knock on the door. The rap of my knuckles nudges it open an inch. "Hang Me Up to Dry" by the Cold War Kids blares much louder than I anticipated. I recognize the music. My young, robotically efficient assistant Angelique is the reason. She listens to this music constantly at her desk, which is just outside my office.

I find it odd a guy in his fifties would be listening to an American alternative band favored by twenty-somethings. I slowly push the door open. The rest of the living room unfolds to my right. Two steps up lead to the dining area and kitchen. Scott, standing in the latter at the counter next to the sink, pours himself a tall glass of what appears to be scotch or whiskey. He notices me. He gestures for me to close the door, which I do.

Scott Green is about five foot ten. He's got a full head of curly gray hair. His wide shoulders and build suggest at one time he was athletic, his potbelly suggests not so much anymore. His nose is a bit large, made to look larger by a poorly selected pair of smallish, round, tortoiseshell glasses. He's wearing black slacks that strike me as the bottom half of a suit and a half-open light-blue button-down shirt showing more of his chest than I care to see.

I smell weed in the air, something else I find odd. Green doesn't strike me as a man interested in Amsterdam's coffee shops. He offers me a drink over the music by lifting a glass in my direction. I shake my head no, and mouth "no thanks."

He picks up his glass and heads in my direction. With only one step I see he's hammered. After a couple more, he stops. He holds up the index finger on his free hand and a blank look glazes over his face. He turns back toward the counter and looks for something. He fumbles, then picks up what appears to be a remote control.

As he stumbles again in my direction, he points the remote at the tuner sitting on a shelf behind me at the end of the room. The volume quickly lowers.

"Ivan. Ivan...you're a good man," he slurs, nearly losing his balance as he navigates the two stairs. "You're a good man."

"A little different from the Amstel," I say, not exactly sure where to start. "When did you get in?"

He throws the remote on the couch and takes a gulp of his booze.

"I got in...um...I got in when, uh..."

We shake hands. He changes gears as if our hands touching triggered a different thought pattern. His cheeks are rosy, his palm sweaty. He's overheated.

"It is definitely different from the Amstel. Yes. Without question. But, you know, it just—it's a nice change of pace. This way I can just unwind and, I mean, I've got the whiskey and I'm fine and I'm here and—"

His alcohol-saturated breath warms the air between us.

"It just—"

He looks around like a proud farmer gazing out over his acreage.

"It just *works*."

He swings his face back to me fast, a man trying to appear sober, but failing.

"Can I get you something to drink?"

"No, thanks," I say, not bothering to point out he'd already offered.

Awkward silence.

"So, Scott, I was surprised to receive your text," I say.

"Oh, I can imagine," he responds. "But when—please, please, sit down. Please, come in and—"

His sentence and thought vanish into thin air. I take one of the two seats opposite the couch.

"I got in just this morning," he says, going back to the first question I asked him. "But I'm always just—it's just, I'm always just working. So it's the weekend, so I figured, I'm just—"

He clumsily moves toward the couch. The whiskey sloshes violently in his glass. He falls into the leather, facing me. He takes a long, sloppy sip of his cocktail. Some of the liquid never reaches his mouth and runs down his chin instead.

I can't help feeling frustrated. There's a ton riding on this deal. About six months ago a few of the larger, global firms in commercial real estate expressed interest in acquiring the commercial real estate portion of de Bont Beleggings's holdings. Cobus turned them down. He wasn't interested in selling out. But he did agree that it was time to take the firm to new heights.

Indeed, Cobus decided, it was time to make our first foray into another market. Since that moment, he's been looking for the right property. It now came down to two deals—one in Berlin, the other in New York City. Cobus wanted to go with Berlin. I convinced him to go after New York City.

We're close to the end. That's why Green is here. Our attorneys have done the bulk of the flying lately. As an act of good faith, the seller in Manhattan—a firm called GlassWell—sent their counsel over for what should be the last serious round of legal discussions surrounding the language in the documents as we move toward closing in the coming days.

A lot of people will be watching de Bont Beleggings's entrance into a new market. The Berlin opportunity seems to have found another suitor. The last thing I need is a problem.

"The text you sent me this evening—," I say.

He points to the ottoman. There's nothing on it but a silver pen.

"Please," he says. "The pen. Take it."

Confused, I lean forward and pick it up.

"I know that you and Mr. de Bont are headed to New York in a few days," he continues. "Just make sure you, when you're there, just be sure to pay attention. When it's time, just, with, just make sure the pen is straight. You know, straight forward. Straight. Because you'll think you're done. But looking closer is—to look closer—"

I look at the pen. It is sterling silver, long, slim at the tips but fatter in the center and has lengthwise grooves. It doesn't have a cap. It looks like a pen from a desktop set. The butt is flat and engraved with the letter *D*.

"I'm sorry, I'm not clear," I say. "What does this pen have to do with our deal?"

Green leans forward, resting his elbows on his knees. His hands dangle, the one holding the drink so limp he's about to spill. His glassy eyes suddenly become serious.

"That pen has everything to do with this deal," he responds. "That pen, my young friend, is everything."

He sits back again.

"I like you, Ivan. I know, when, I know we've only met a couple times but with certain folks you know they can, there can be, they can be trusted. I feel okay to count on you."

"Count on me?" I ask, hoping to elicit some clarity.

No answer. With his free hand, he takes a half-smoked joint and small, blue plastic lighter out of his pants pocket. He manages the dope cigarette into his mouth and fires it up. In doing so, he barely misses singeing one of his eyebrows. He tosses the lighter onto the ottoman.

"Wow," he says as he exhales. "I never knew what I was missing."

He extends the joint my way. I remember the old days, when I would have been happy to join in, but I pass. He takes another hard pull. He lays his head back, then spews smoke straight into the air.

"Scott, why exactly did you ask to see me tonight?" I ask, growing impatient. "Is there a problem with our deal? Is there something I need to be told?"

"It has been so many years—" he slurs after a pause.

He props his head back up. His eyes don't meet mine, as his line of vision is just left passing over my shoulder.

"So many years working so hard. And for the most part they've been . . . law, dealing with the law, legal, dealing with all those battles for the most part I've enjoyed it."

He throws the last gulp of whiskey down his throat. He balances the empty glass on the ottoman and sits back.

"I grew up in a place called New England. Do you . . . have you ever heard of New England ever, Ivan? New England in the United States? A state called Maine?"

I decide to forego any further effort to lead the conversation.

"Perhaps," I lie, "but I can't be certain."

"I grew up in a place called New England. A place called Brewer, which is a little town in Maine. My family was, in New England— my family never even thought about something like college. They worked in paper mills. I was first. I was the first to make it to college. I made it, took it all the way, made it to New York City. I was a corporate trial attorney, I was . . . I was a lawyer from a town of nothing. It was, then, to go to New York City, I was like a local hero."

He awkwardly slides down to his right into one of the couch's pillows. I think he's passing out, a notion quickly dispelled when he slides back into an upright position and his right hand emerges from behind the pillow holding a shiny, silver pistol. His hand can barely grip the thick handle. The barrel is huge.

My heart skips a beat. The last time a man sat across from me with a gun, I shot him dead. Only, this time, I don't have a gun of my own.

I barely know this man. What does Scott Green think I've done to him? My mind starts swirling. Who is this man really? What does he want from me? Am I being set up? Why am I here?

Here.

Shit. No one knows I'm here.

Or do they?

"I wasn't supposed to be anything," he continues. "I did it right.

All those years, living, working—working—I did it right. Trials. Then, threw my hat into the real estate ring. Private business. In-house counsel. Big business. It—the excitement—I did it, you know, I did it because I was sick of dealing with lowlifes all the fucking time. What do I exchange for—"

He burps.

"What do I get for it? In exchange for it? Same shit. I go from defending corporate scum to working side by side with it. I wish I could have known it would only lead to darkness. To people like Ryan Brand. To people like you."

First he's counting on me. Now I'm paired with the enemy? I have no idea what's going on. He drags the loosely held gun onto his knee. His eyes drop. They focus on nothing. They're searching, like he's seeing the thoughts he's trying to articulate, but can't.

"That's why I did it to myself when all the darkness began," he says, almost in a whisper. "Talking—you know—darkness. But it makes sense. I know how to do it. One was elsewhere, the—covert, but I learned how to do it. I—for proof."

"Proof of what?" I ask, my eyes locked on the gun.

Green lifts his eyes again. He doesn't answer. Instead he abruptly stands up. He starts toward me. My mind takes off. Is he really sober? Is this all an act to soften my guard? Should I jump for the door? No—can't risk it. Drunk or not, he may start firing. He trips, but keeps his footing. He's coming. His bloodshot eyes are focused on me. Every muscle in my body flexes at the same time. Finally I find my place of unbelievable commitment. I find that place in my soul I haven't gone in a long time, a place reminding me I'll maim, ruin, crush anything I must to remain standing.

"Get what you need," my father always said. "Clean up the mess later."

My psyche offers a visual pep talk—I see my fingertips gouging like spears into the skin covering his forehead and peeling his face forward as if manipulating fruit. He's two feet away. I stand up. I grip the pen hard, ready to jab it deep into his neck. I gird myself for chaos.

He stops.

"I miss being a kid. I miss Brewer," he says, his voice sad. "It's my favorite place anywhere. This world. I think of it every day, a time when I was just me. Just a boy."

He reaches down to his left and plucks the remote from the couch with the same hand holding the joint. He returns to his original spot on the couch. He takes another pull. His eyes settle on mine.

"How have you lived, Ivan?" he asks, his voice straining as his lungs hold the smoke.

"I'm not sure what you mean?" I ask back.

He exhales. A plume of smoke hangs in the air between us.

"I mean, how have you, have you—how many people count on you? Love you?"

My chest tightens. I think of Perry and Max. And Neo. I say nothing.

"If you were to die right now, in this room—" he goes on.

He raises the gun. He points it at me lazily, casually, like it's just another finger on his hand.

"Would anyone miss you?"

Talk about a loaded question. Nine years ago I disappeared from New York City. A few people—my best friend since I'm a kid L, my senior partner Tommy Wingate, my partner Jake Donald—knew what was going on, why I was leaving. But for others, from colleagues to friends to clients to thousands of readers who learned about me in all the prominent business publications, I simply vanished from the earth.

"I like to believe they would," I answer.

Emotion starts bubbling in my host. He starts getting choked up. Tears form in his eyes.

"Me too," he says softly.

The gun starts shaking. But now he's holding it more firmly.

"Tell me something honest," he says.

Fighting to maintain my composure, keep my breathing steady, I ponder the question. For nine years I have lied every day—to everyone I know, about every aspect of my background—to protect my freedom and probably my life. An unanticipated feeling of gratitude warms me, comforts me in the moment. I welcome the opportunity to say something meaningful.

"All I do, every day, is for those I would miss if something were to happen to them," I say. "Everything else is just noise."

He gently nods his head up and down, as if satisfied by my answer. The volume of the music begins climbing. The song has turned over. I'm swallowed by Percussion Gun's "White Rabbits." Green's sight is still locked on me. The surging fright within has me frozen. The growing anger inside me forces another nugget of honesty to shoot through my mind.

You better be a good shot, you crazy, drunk fuck. If you're not—I'm going to reach down your throat, rip out your tongue, and stuff it straight up your ass so far it's licking the back of your eyes.

The music is so loud I'd literally have to scream for Green to hear me. He drops both the remote and joint and grabs the handle of the gun with his second hand as well. Tears start falling from both of his eyes. He's questioning himself—I can see it. But he's determined. I see that too.

Instinct tears me from my chair. My ass lifts from the seat. Instead of firing at me, I see out of the corner of my eye he's turned the gun on himself. I stop, face him. He puts it so far down his throat I see him gag.

"No!" I scream.

I can't even hear my own voice.

He squeezes his eyes shut, no doubt hoping to see all he cares about one last time. Then he pulls the trigger.

I nearly choke on my own breath as the back of his head explodes. The world freezes for a second, like a snapshot. A sunburst of blood, skull, and brain, most dense in the center, starts dripping down the wall. Some pieces of tissue roll down end over end as gravity takes hold. Others fall to the floor undoubtedly with a squishy splat.

Shock-ridden, bug-eyed, I stare in disbelief. Both of Green's arms hang slack at his sides. His eyes remain closed. A ribbon of smoke rises from the gun, still in his right hand. I can't move.

The pen drops from my trembling hand, pulling me from my stupor. I pick it up, place it in the inside pocket of my suit jacket. I take a step toward the body. I stop almost as quickly as I started. The mess on the wall reminds me there's no reason to check for a pulse. My eyes transfixed, I run my hand through my hair, stopping at the top of my head.

What the fuck just happened?

I put my hands out in front of me, palms down, like I'm trying to keep my balance. I nervously scan the premises, like someone's going to jump from a closet or the refrigerator and try to pin this all on me. My eyes catch the canal outside one of the windows behind my dead associate. A shimmer from the streetlights above blankets the calm water. I leave through the front door doing all I can to remain collected, normal, should I encounter anyone.

I close the door behind me. As I climb the steel ladder back to street level, still able to hear the music, I fight off an image of Scott Green on the couch as I just left him. Relief that his eyes remained closed postblast washes over me. I still have nightmares of the dirty cop back in New York's left eye staring back at me once I put a bullet through the right.

I turn right on Nieuwe Prinsengracht Straat. A cool breeze confronting the thin layer of sweat I feel coating my body under my suit sends an icy chill up my spine. Conscious of controlling my gait, I let my eyes wander a bit without moving my head. The quiet neighborhood remains still around me, unaware of what's just happened. Both questions and answers start flowing, like a dam containing them in my brain has broken.

Could I have prevented this? Were there signs this was about to happen—this nut was about to blow his head off—or have I gotten so used to protecting my own ass I missed a chance to help calm this guy down?

Reality sets in with a thud: it doesn't matter now. Besides—the guy had a gun in my face. At least I think I understand some of the

elements of the scene now. The joint, the booze—courage en-
hancers. The music so loud was to mask the blast.

But why do that? Why worry about the neighbors when your
head's about to be hamburger?

And why me? Why have me there?

How would a guy like this score a weapon within hours of being
in the Netherlands?

I reach inside my jacket pocket and touch the pen, as if to confirm all of this really just happened.

I only know Scott Green because of the deal we're both involved in. Is the deal relevant?

Or is the only relevance my arm's-length relationship to this
man? Does this have nothing at all to do with the deal?

My name, as I said, is Ivan Janse. My soul is still Jonah Gray. In
four days, I'll be returning to New York City. Make no mistake—
I've been planning for this trip a long time. Sure, I have a deal to
help close. A deal that means a great deal to Cobus, to my firm. But
little does anyone know I'm a man on another mission. A wanted
murderer intent on clearing his name, a fool by my own half-brother's hand still seeking answers about some of the rarest treasures
ever crafted by human hands.

Nothing is going to derail me.

Nothing.

CHAPTER 4

The de Bont Beleggings Gulfstream G550 lifts off from Amsterdam Schiphol Airport at five p.m. The plan is to touch back down again on this very airstrip in a little over three days' time. Which means by the time we're in New York City I'll have roughly three days to get to the bottom of what happened to Scott Green, determine the fate of Perry, help Cobus make sure this deal falls into place properly, and once and for all, get down to the real meaning behind the lost Fabergé Imperial Easter Eggs.

The jet has a black exterior, Cobus's color of choice. Soon the corporate aircraft, powered by flawless Rolls-Royce engines, is cruising over the Atlantic Ocean at more than five hundred fifty miles per hour, though it remains still as if grounded. The interior is a beautifully conceived hybrid of efficiency and luxury. There is a conference area and there are single seats for those needing to spread out individually. There is a state-of-the-art communication center as well as tons of functional lighting options. The finishes ooze richness, from the soft, caramel leather seats to the polished cherrywood tables and moldings.

I look out the window, my mind meandering. Alexander Zhamovsky, Andreu's father, had been brutally murdered in a Russian subway station in 1998. That's when Andreu had assumed control from Alexander of Prevkos—the largest natural gas conglomerate in Russia and one of the most powerful companies in the world. Andreu had called me that fine morning in 2004 because, so he said, Prevkos was looking to diversify in order to throw off risk and they felt New York City commercial real estate was a safe bet. He came to me looking to spend a half-a-billion-dollars' worth of his shareholders' money on commercial office property in Manhattan.

Only he never had the intention of buying any buildings.

Within days of Andreu calling me, I discovered one of the world's rarest treasures in my briefcase. Ever hear of Fabergé Imperial Easter Eggs? There were fifty of these treasures made between the years of 1885 and 1916 as gifts from Russia's Czar to the Czarina. Each is a one-of-a-kind handcrafted tribute of precious gems and metals to some aspect of Russian history. And today, each is valued at around forty million dollars. Now, as legend has it, eight of these fifty treasures went missing during the Russian Revolution. Two were found under a barn in Russia in 1979 and auctioned off; one of them—Danish Jubilee Egg—was the one planted in my briefcase. The other six? Never found.

Or so the world thought.

And still thinks.

I think I mentioned Andreu and I had a connection that felt like family. That's because it turns out we are. His mother, Galina Zhamovsky, also met my father during those secret seminars and the two had an ongoing affair from the moment our fathers met. Turns out Andreu's father is Stan Gray, not Alexander Zhamovsky. Andreu is my half-brother. And Mommy Dearest, an artist who also goes by the name "Ia," is also someone who will do anything to get her hands on the missing Fabergé Imperial Easter Eggs—including selling out her own son. The shareholder money Andreu was using to supposedly buy Manhattan commercial real estate? All a front. It was a ploy to get funds into the United States to ultimately buy the missing eggs. And not just the two the world knew had been recovered.

All eight.

Half a billion dollars.

The Gulfstream seats sixteen. Today it is just Cobus, Arnon Driessen, and myself. Arnon is in-house counsel. He's a tiny little, bald, sixty-something-year-old man who can't weigh more than he did in sixth grade. But whatever he weighs, I'd swear half that poundage is his brain. Arnon is one of the brightest commercial real estate law minds I have ever been around—New York, Amsterdam, anywhere I've ever been. And he eats, breathes, and sleeps de Bont Beleggings. Arnon, the first and only in-house counsel Cobus ever brought in, has been with him for years. He's seated toward the front of the cabin entranced by one of the documents he's reviewing related to the deal in Manhattan. Cobus and I are in the back of the cabin discussing the deal.

"Did you ever find out what the rift is between GlassWell and the minority partner?" asks Cobus.

GlassWell Holdings Inc. is the seller. They are a private commercial real estate firm that owns thirty-two office buildings, half of the portfolio in Manhattan and the rest in Boston. The target, our desired property within their portfolio, is one of only two New York City buildings they own with a partner.

"Just the basics. Apparently, the partnership is a long-standing one. GlassWell is of the mind-set of spending on their buildings—capital improvements, system upgrades, whatever enhances both value and the tenants' experience. They like to spend on their buildings and they have the cash on hand to do so, both very much like us. For the minority partner, a small-time family player, this is one of their biggest holdings, and they are finding things like three-million-dollar roof replacements too big a burden. Simply two different philosophies, and the minority is starting to threaten legal action—claiming GlassWell is spending unwisely and trying to drive them out of the building. Classic example of a partnership gone sour, and GlassWell simply finds it all to be occupying too much of their time. So they want out. This is one of the main reasons I find the target so attractive. The building is in phenomenal shape and in the hands of a very motivated seller."

"It will be interesting to meet Ryan. He seems to be a quality individual, a very smart fella," Cobus says, referring to Ryan Brand, Director of Acquisitions for GlassWell who's been at the helm of this deal for them.

"Seems to be," I respond with a slight shoulder shrug.

Ryan Brand is smart as they come—Cobus is right about that. But he's also a real estate animal. He must be around fifty now, and will creep into your bedroom in the middle of the night and snuff you out with a pillow if it means getting his deal done—a buy, a sale, a refinance, whatever. He has the rare combination of self-control and aggressiveness they probably find in serial killers, masked with an unbelievable poker face. Ryan is good looking, confident, well dressed, Yale educated, ice in his veins, and out for blood. Before this deal I had never known him, and in putting this deal together we'd only dealt with him over the phone. But back in my days at PCBL my team had placed a number of tenants in Glass-Well-owned buildings. And at the height of my career in Manhattan, I knew as many people in the real estate community as anyone. I had heard the stories about Ryan Brand.

"You love that Annex," Cobus says. "You just love that aspect of the target."

Cobus was now talking about the actual building itself.

"I do. I can't help thinking it is about as unique a property as I have seen. And in one of the best submarkets—from what I understand—in all of New York City."

The situation is surreal. We're discussing a property I've made deals in and know like the back of my hand. As if it's a new building sitting in a new market in a new city—all of which I'll be experiencing for the first time.

The target property is 120 East 52nd Street, a building known as the Freedom Bank Building because of the retail component of the property—a huge, wide-open, three-story high-ceilinged bank from the 1920s that today is one of the preeminent catering halls in all of New York City. The bulk of the property is an eighteen-story, two-hundred-and-thirty-thousand-square-foot Class A commercial office building above the retail space. The Freedom Bank Building is a special property for a host of reasons. It is a perfectly located, high-rent office property that is never less than 95 percent leased. The pristinely maintained, ornate, predominantly gold-appointed original lobby with arched, vaulted ceilings painted to resemble an afternoon sky takes you back to one of the great ages of prosperity in our country's history. The retail component—today called "Alessi NYC"—is run by the world famous Alessi restaurateur family and is one of the most desired event spaces in The City.

But the property is also special because of The Annex.

A thirty-thousand-square-foot, double-edged, real estate sword.

The office tower is on the north side of 52nd Street. Directly east, attached to the property, is another smaller property called The Annex. At the time the Alessi catering hall was Freedom Bank, almost a century ago, The Annex was where the corporate employees of the bank were housed. It is comprised of five stories, each six thousand square feet and change. There is a spiral staircase in the center of the building spanning all five floors, as well as a single elevator bank at the back of the property that goes from the basement to the top.

These are tough floors to lease if a landlord has to do so individually. They don't have great amenities for single floor users, as two of the five floors are underserved in terms of restrooms, there is only one elevator, the central staircase would need to be slabbed over, among other issues. On the other hand, there are hundreds—maybe thousands—of firms that need in the ballpark of thirty thousand square feet. How many of them get to have what is essentially their own Midtown building?

"Let me ask you this, Ivan," Cobus continues, "would we be flying to New York right now if Enzo Alessi hadn't made the Annex deal?"

"Irrelevant question." I respond.

The question is far from irrelevant—more like moot for the time being. And the answer is most likely no. Something I would never tell him.

"He made the deal," I continue. "The entire Annex, fifteen-year lease, rent starting at sixty U.S. dollars per square foot and escalating to seventy-two dollars per square foot by year fifteen. The perfect headquarters for the Alessi Family to run their American operation. And at—again, from what I understand—above market rents."

Aimee, our cute blond flight attendant appears. She places a bowl of fresh fruit, a plate of assorted cheeses and sliced Italian meats, and a pitcher of ice water and two tall glasses in front of us.

"Perhaps a cocktail or a glass of wine, gentlemen?"

We decline. She pours each of us a glass of water.

"Haven't we already been through this, Cobus?" I say, taking a long drink of the cool water, parting my lips just enough for a bit of crushed ice as well. "I believe my initial comprehensive analysis of the property covered all potential scenarios in substantial depth. As my analyses always do. No?"

"Yes, we've been through this. And, yes, your analysis was thorough, one of the reasons we are purchasing the target. I just like hearing you flex that intellectual real estate muscle. You've become quite convincing over the years, Ivan. Sometimes I like to hear things a second time to make sure I didn't rely too heavily on your instincts the first time around. Makes me feel like I'm still important around here."

You want to be humored? Then humor you I will.

"Yes—the Annex accounts for thirteen percent of the overall space. And yes, having to market the floors individually would certainly be a challenge. But what's to say it would ever come to having to market them individually? I said it before, I'll say it again. How many users of this size space get their own address in New York City? If it weren't Alessi, it would have been someone else. A boutique marketing firm, a tech firm, a small, local law firm—this is sexy, flexible space that can work for many potential users."

Though the words sound convincing as hell as they roll from my tongue, I'm far from convinced myself. The reality is this Annex—though appealing for all the reasons mentioned—has a number of drawbacks. I've mentioned a few but add to that the natural lighting sucks. The back wall of the Annex essentially faces another building so there is only one wall—the front wall—allowing sunlight in. There's no dedicated service elevator. The list goes on and on. If I was the broker for a tenant shopping for thirty thousand square feet—back in my days at PCBL—and the Annex had been available, I would have most likely steered my client away.

"The Annex is prime for a user like the Alessi Family. Not only is their headquarters literally attached to one of their most important entities, their U.S. operation is growing exponentially. They have a new event space opening in Miami in three months, as well as a new restaurant in Chicago in just a couple weeks."

"In Manhattan they have five venues," Cobus says looking to confirm his knowledge of the tenant. "Two event spaces, two restaurants—one Midtown, the other Downtown. Plus a new cutting-edge restaurant-slash-art gallery concept spot opening in Midtown."

I nod my head as I answer, "Correct."

Cobus touches a button on the wall next to him. The shades throughout the cabin slowly descend. He hits another couple buttons, and with each one touched another block of the cabin lighting goes dark. Without even looking up, Arnon enacts his personal lighting toward the front of the cabin, lighting that only touches his immediate space. He knows the drill all too well.

"Okay, enough about the Alessi family for now," Cobus continues. "Let's discuss some of the other tenants."

I pick up my iPad, and with a couple taps of the screen, a small projector in the wall of the cabin is enabled. In front of us, floating in the air, a 3-D hologram of the target appears—the Freedom Bank Building. From the tablet in my hands I can manipulate the image as desired—I can rotate it, separate it into pieces, flip it—whatever we need. Each tenant is identified by a different color, which allows us to see the exact make up of the property in terms of who has what space.

"Let's touch on the specifics of Lazaar & Dutchess first," Cobus says.

Lazaar & Dutchess, a law firm, and one of the two largest tenants in the building.

"They have just under eight years left on their lease if I remember correctly," he goes on. "They're paying pretty solid overall numbers. The majority of the space was taken at then-market rents, maybe a bit higher. They added to their space a couple years later at numbers that were a bit soft as they saw good timing in terms of both their needs as well as deteriorating market conditions."

"That's right."

I tap the iPad. The canary yellow portion of the hologram identifying the Lazaar & Dutchess space—the top two and a third floors—separates from the rest of the property, doubles in size, and moves in front of the rest of the floating building so it can be examined more closely.

"Up here," I go on as I stand and point, "is where they tend to place the associates. Apparently Jessie Jordan, the principal partner who runs the show, likes them as far away from his office as possible."

As we continue to discuss each tenant in painstaking detail for the duration of the flight, all I can really think about is one thing: I'm really on my fucking way back to New York City.

CHAPTER 5

The moment I realized I had no choice but to flee the United States, I knew where I'd be going.

The South of France.

Throughout my life I have been fortunate to have traveled frequently. For business, for pleasure—I have been on five continents, having done everything from eating fugu in Tokyo to sailing in Auckland to attending the Winter Olympics in Lillehammer. The traveling began when I was young. My father—a prominent New York City office-building owner—was also a huge believer in diversification. A savvy international investor, he put money in all sorts of business and financial instruments with roots all around the world. Though I can't even remember all of the places I've visited once, there is one place I've gone a couple weeks every August since I was a boy. The Côte d'Azur or French Riviera.

I left the U.S.—with Neo as my travel companion—under the alias Roy Gordon. Courtesy of my best friend since childhood, L, real name Tanqueray Luckman, I had both an authentic Alaskan driver's license as well as a valid American passport that spoke to this as my true identity. My temporary destination was St. Maxime, France, via a direct flight to Nice.

I wasn't the only one with false documents back then. I had secured them also for my three business partners: Tommy, Perry, and Jake. The three were definitely going to take major heat—NYPD, FBI, the works—because of my actions. I wanted each of them to have an out—as well as the sizeable chunk of change left in Swiss bank accounts under each respective alias courtesy of my father's ridiculous life-insurance policy payout—should they want it. They probably wouldn't, as I made clear, *need* it, as the fact was none of them had any idea what I was up to, or what kind of hell I had been dragged into. I just wanted them to be covered should others prejudge them as they had me. And because I felt so guilty about fucking with the lives they had all worked so hard to carve out.

Before leaving, I told one person where I'd be temporarily. Perry York. Even though we worked together and had never even kissed, she was the true love I had always sought. When I told her I was leaving, she asked if I could live knowing even the dream of us being together was dead. I said I couldn't. Right there, on the spot, she told me she'd run with me. Not just to protect her young son, Max, from her crooked, vindictive husband, but because, deep down, she was in love with me too.

I told her I'd be in St. Maxime, France, and that leaving together would be simply too dangerous. If she followed, once she arrived, she should call every hotel and ask to be connected to Roy Gordon's room. I told her I wouldn't be there long, three days tops.

Once the plane was in the air, and Neo and I were officially on the run, I passed out. I hadn't even realized how exhausted I was. The previous three weeks had felt like years. At wheels up it was sunny out. When I awoke hours later it was pitch black. I remember looking in Neo's carrier, which was strapped into the window seat. He was sound asleep on his side, all four legs extended straight out. His little belly expanded then retracted with each breath. At that moment, my new reality stole my own breath. I was, justifiably or not, a fugitive.

I was terrified. I had no choice but to embark on a completely new life. None of the same people or places ever again. How was I going to make this work?

Could I make this work?

Do I spend time worrying about what I left behind? Or do I strictly focus on moving forward? I had always felt like the roughest guy in the room, the man with no fear. Nothing in my life had ever felt potentially insurmountable.

Until now.

After seven and a half hours in the air, we started to descend. More mixed emotions. I was excited by the prospect of getting off the plane, ridding myself of this confinement. But I was petrified by the possibility that I hadn't been as smart as I thought. And that I was about to be greeted by cops waiting with stun guns and hand-cuffs.

As soon as I saw the glimmer of lights along the coastline in the distance, like scattered diamonds on black glass, I squeezed my eyes shut. I forced myself to say good-bye to everything I had ever known. I did everything I could to fight back tears. Through the vent on top of his carrier, I saw Neo stretching. The house lights coming on and passengers preparing for arrival had awoken him.

I knew the terminal well. Once inside, I stopped in the duty-free store. Like all duty-free stores, the joint was a hoarder's wet dream—everything from alcohol to chocolates to fragrances to apparel to toys and everything in between. I hit the electronics area for hair clippers and batteries and a prepaid, disposable cell phone, then grabbed a pair of jeans and a couple of dark, solid t-shirts. The next stop was only a few meters past the store, a counter where I was able to convert a bunch of cash to euros. From there I hit the men's room, discarded the hair clippers' packaging in the garbage, and locked myself in a stall.

Another fucking bathroom stall, I thought to myself. Just a cou-ple of weeks earlier, in a stall just like this one in my office building in Midtown Manhattan, I first discovered one of the rarest treasures known to man—*Danish Jubilee Egg*, one of the eight missing Fabergé Imperial Easter Eggs—had been planted in my briefcase. A replay of the chaos that ensued tried forcing itself into my brain. I shook my head hard to shake such thoughts away. I needed to keep moving. I was literally at the starting line of a race with an undetermined finish line.

Without a thought I sheared off my hair, watching it hit the water only to settle on the surface for a few seconds before sinking. I did it quickly, methodically. Once the first pass was done I did a second. This time there were sprinkles instead of the clumps. The third pass produced nothing. With toilet paper I scrubbed the clippers clean of my fingerprints. Then I ditched them underneath the rear of the toilet bowl, almost perfectly out of sight, and flushed the hair and paper away.

Wearing the Yankee cap I bought at Liberty International earlier in the day—to help hide my eyes as TVs throughout the airport flashed my picture—I exited L'Aéroport Nice Côte d'Azur and headed for the Hertz car rental lot across the way. The air was crisp. A hint of Mediterranean breeze welcomed me back. Behind me, and beyond the structure now at my back, I heard another plane take off. My right hand held Neo's carrier, my left hand had my briefcase. Slung over my shoulder was a small gym bag stuffed with a few crumpled suits, ties, underwear, and socks, all I had time to grab before escaping my own apartment.

I let Neo out of his case for the longest pee of his life, which he did on the tire of a black Mercedes, and a quick poop. Then within minutes Roy Gordon was traveling south on the Bord de Mer, the famous road hugging the southeastern coastline of France from Monaco to St. Tropez. I was in an Opel Astra. The compact, four-door sedan was perfect for the region's tight, windy roads. Having driven one all my life, whether in the United States or Europe, the manual transmission's stick shift was like second nature. I rolled the windows down and headed south.

Though the Côte d'Azur was my given escape route, there were still obstacles to be considered. The towns I knew the best were actually off limits. Cannes, Antibes, Juan-les-Pins, Saint-Jean-Cap-Ferrat—the hot spots for me could unfortunately prove exactly that, too hot. This was summer, high time. The chances were strong that I knew people—from business associates in Manhattan to other vacationers or locals I'd met over the years—in each of them. The best bet for me was a simple one. I had to pick one of the sleepier, tier-two towns.

Local time was about midnight. The road alternated between one and two lanes. The thirty-five-mile-per-hour pace was just right, fast enough that I was moving yet slow enough I was able to breathe, think. A steady stream of warm, salty air flowed through the car, down my shirt. Each town I passed through—the ocean on my left, beachside bars and restaurants to my right—reminded me of a happier time. I had never imagined being on the Côte d'Azur in the pursuit of anything other than topless, tanning women and an endless party.

About an hour later, still a good twenty miles or so north of St. Tropez, I rolled into St. Maxime. I didn't know St. Maxime for shit. Which meant it was perfect. I had passed through it almost every time I'd been on the Côte d'Azur, but never stopped. It was almost an afterthought. Now I needed a remote nook in the world, but I couldn't fight the paranoia that comes with living in the information age. A portrait of the cop I killed in New York had already been on CNN before I left. Had I already been flashed across CNN around the globe, along with other news outposts, as well? Had the whole world already learned who I am? If yes—how many people are really paying attention? How many people could possibly spot me?

Was I really ready to find out?

Due to the late—or early, depending on your habits—hour, traffic was light. It was easy to maintain my pace and scope my surroundings. After a few minutes I slowed on the sight of the La Belle Aurore. It looked to be a small, clean, quiet hotel on the cusp of calling itself a resort. It was understated, dim. It looked to be the perfect place for me to lay up as I got my head in order.

As I pulled off the road, up away from the beach, within seconds I was faced with the easiest decision I had to make in what felt like an eternity: valet or self-parking. Valet was to the left, so like a robot I stayed right. I scoured the lot, scanned every single space to see which made the most sense. The answer was easy. One of those closest to the main road should I need to break in a hurry.

I pulled into the third spot from the entrance and turned the key, silencing the engine. There was an unexpected, eerie sensation, like I had closed the lid on the box holding my past. All I could hear was the gently crashing surf on the opposite side of the street, the interspersed passing cars, and my thoughts. Anything and everything, each breath that would pass through my lips from here on out, would be about my future. I was shocked by how distant a life I had left only half a day earlier could seem.

The lobby was beachy, comfortable. It was also empty. A thin, rust-colored rug held yellow couches that surrounded iron-framed, glass-topped coffee tables. One of the tables had a sterling silver bucket in the center filled with water—no doubt previously ice— and a spent, overturned bottle of cheap champagne floating in it. The corners of the room were adorned with assorted potted plants. The wooden walls held a few simple lithographs of scenes of the Riviera. The solid white ceiling was smooth and undisturbed aside from a couple small spotlights.

I walked up to the reception counter. I placed my briefcase and Neo's carrier at my feet. I was greeted by a forty-something female with bobbed red hair and fair skin wearing a navy pants suit with the La Belle Aurore logo on her blazer.

"Bonjour," she said. "Comment je peux aider ce soir?"

"Bonjour," I responded.

I had picked up a good amount of French from all my time spent here, but again, I'll go with the English version to make things easier.

"Unfortunately, my plans changed at the last minute and I don't have a reservation this evening. I'm hoping you have something available."

She looked down at her computer and began typing.

"I do, in fact, have something Mr.—"

I paused. She looked up.

"Gordon," I said, hoping she didn't see me swallow. "Roy Gordon."

Boarding an airplane as Roy Gordon was one thing. Referring to myself as Roy Gordon was another.

Her eyes returned to her computer.

"I do have a few available rooms, Mr. Gordon. Unfortunately, they're all suites. Will this be okay?"

Little did she know I would have settled for the basement. Or a cabana.

"Sure—that will be fine."

"Terrific," she went on, "The rate is five hundred seventy euros per night, plus tax. And how many nights will you be staying with us?"

"I'm not sure," I answered.

I needed to come up with something, and quick. Not having a clue about how long I was staying would seem suspicious. Or would it? This was all so new.

"My current plans tell me three nights. But it may be a bit longer, depending on how some business affairs fall into place."

That's the fucking spirit.

"Will that be okay?"

"It will be just fine," she answered, fingers still typing. "I have a beautiful suite with a magnificent view of the gulf."

After a few more seconds, her head popped up again.

"You're all set, Mr. Gordon. The last thing I need from you is a major credit card to keep on file."

I had practiced the upcoming conversation in my head at least twenty times.

Confidence. Always.

Own every word that comes out of your mouth.

"Unfortunately, I don't have one on me," I said as I reached into my front pocket. "I lost my wallet somewhere in all of my last-minute-preparation-for-departure errands."

I took a wad of euros out of my pocket. Her eyes caught it immediately. I started counting out bills.

"Anyway, American Express is sending a new card. I have been promised it will arrive no later than the day after tomorrow. So why don't we just handle it this way? You said five hundred seventy euros per night. I'm happy to give you twenty-five hundred euros, which should cover the three nights I'll definitely be staying as well as any taxes. Sound good?"

"Well, unfortunately, we require a major credit card for reasons other than just room-rate considerations. There are liability issues that—"

Improv time. Her name tag read Brigette. I smiled and cut her off. "Brigette, I absolutely understand your situation. I really do, you guys have rules. But you don't have to worry about me trashing the room. I promise you I'm probably the most boring guest you'll have in here all summer—and I don't make much noise. If it makes you feel better, I'm happy to give you my passport so you can make a copy for your records."

The door closed behind me. We were in the living room. I let Neo out of the carrier for good and tossed his carrier, my gym bag, and my briefcase on one of the two yellow couches. The only light fell from a lamp on a white wooden desk. The desk had been positioned between the French doors leading to the terrace and the entrance to the bedroom. The suite was mellow, actually charming. The walls were the same yellow as the couches. The rug and curtains were the same orange hue I'd seen in the lobby. An antique-looking armoire I opened, white-painted wood like the desk, revealed an older, chunky TV. The coffee table matched those found in the lobby as well—iron-framed with a glass top.

Neo immediately went to work sniffing out the entire suite. I zeroed in on the television. I powered it on and went straight to

CNN's international channel, the only station I had ever really watched outside of the United States. Charles Hodson was in the middle of a financial report, first discussing the results for the day on the American stock exchanges followed by those of exchanges around the globe. I sat on the end of the bed, my eyes glued. After a couple of minutes he seemed to be nearing the end of his report. I literally inched forward, only to have him flow right into a story about banking powerhouse J. P. Morgan's impending merger with Bank One.

Dejected, antsy, I stood up and walked over to the French doors leading out to the terrace. I went out. The whispers of the Riviera, the gentle crash of the surf below, softened the sound of the reporter's voice. Fragrance from the fruits and flowers of the Maures Mountains, hovering behind, rolled downhill and filled my nose, my every pore. I stepped outside, right up to the ledge of the waist-high, top-floor terrace. I looked out over the dark, moonlit waters of the Gulf of St. Tropez. Taking a deep breath, I wondered if Perry was going to follow me.

"An unbelievable situation is taking shape in New York City—"

I ran back inside. International correspondent Becky Anderson was reporting from London. As always, her angular jaw was perfectly framed by her cropped brown hair. Her thick British accent that could make the weather sound dire added to the intensity of her words.

"In a storyline seemingly ripped from the world of fiction, two headline news stories seem to be crashing into one another. Just last Saturday morning, prominent Manhattan real estate figure Stan Gray was gunned down on the stoop of his townhouse on the Upper East Side—one of the city's most posh neighborhoods. Thus far, there have been no arrests."

And there wouldn't be anytime soon, I thought, exterior footage of my childhood home filling the international airwaves. Lloyd Murdoch had covered his tracks well. The only reason the prick is still breathing, after taking my father down like a dog as a message to me over a deal that was all bullshit, was because I hadn't killed him—though I certainly came close. The only reason I hadn't turned him in was because I hadn't had time.

"Meanwhile, in what seemed like a completely unrelated matter, approximately forty-eight hours ago a New York City police officer was pulled out of Manhattan's East River. He had sustained a single gunshot to the head and his body had been stuffed postmortem in a duffel bag. Few details are being released at this time, the one individual the authorities are seeking in relation to this crime is…"

A photograph of me—taken from my father's house—filled the screen. The picture was snapped at his sixtieth birthday party.

"Jonah Gray. Mr. Gray is a successful commercial real estate broker in New York City and the son of Stan Gray. That's right—the same Stan Gray whom we just mentioned gruesomely murdered on—"

I grabbed the remote and clicked it off. I decided right then and there to never look again. It simply didn't matter anymore. Everything had gotten so fucked up. Now I was running for my life. Unknown to the rest of the world, the cop whom I had killed wasn't some sympathetic figure, but a crooked lowlife who had violated every oath to serve and protect. He was a greedy, loathsome miscreant, shaking me down for *Danish Jubilee Egg*. And, if you recall, I didn't mean to actually shoot him. The gun went off accidentally. My father, animal that he was, was killed because of a deal I was involved in that turned out to be a ruse created by my half-brother Andreu Zhamovsky to get Prevkos shareholders' money into the States. Money that he and his crazy fuck mother would use to get their hands on the coveted missing Fabergé Imperial Easter Eggs.

What's worse? What's maybe the hardest part of the whole sick scenario to swallow? *Danish Jubilee Egg* ending up in my briefcase was never part of Andreu and his mother's original plan—it was a contingency plan that went sour. I was simply somewhere the egg was to be parked for a day or so—a middleman. Only I wasn't having it. In the process of safely returning the rare treasure for transport to the U.S. Capitol where it was headed for display, I managed to piece together the location of the other six believed missing since the Russian Revolution. They were with a man named Pavel Derbyshev in Baltimore. Pavel Derbyshev is a direct descendant of a man named Piotr Derbyshev. Piotr Derbyshev, though a master stone carver in the House of Fabergé, but never previously in the driver's seat when it came to their creation, was mysteriously asked by Maria Feodorovna to oversee the creation of these particular eggs.

Now why would the czarina of the Russian Empire ask a certain man who worked in the House of Fabergé to craft the eight eggs that would ultimately go missing?

We'll get to that.

Same way we'll get to the fact Galina Zhamovsky—Ia—is a direct descendant of Czar Alexander III: Maria's husband. And the fact these eggs may hold secrets that will ultimately alter the course of history.

For almost thirty years, when it came to things such as the secret of Andreu as well as the truth about the missing Fabergé Imperial Eggs, Galina would communicate secretly through artwork sent to my father that then hung in our home.

My mother's home.

It all still sickens me.

Anyway—none of this mattered now. I had to worry about me. I had to keep moving, and thinking, forward.

I tossed the remote on the floor and lifted my palms up in front of me. My hands were shaking. The last few weeks had been so crazy I doubted it was simply nerves. Was I hungry? No, even though I couldn't remember the last time I'd eaten. Was it some kind of withdrawal? These last days I'd shunned the cocaine and weed in exchange for a clear head, but had these substances been more engrained in my being than I ever realized?

I opened the minibar. Figuring a little alcohol would dull the edge, I grabbed a Heineken, popped the cap with a bottle opener, and headed back outside. I fell onto a lounge chair and took a long, savoring sip of my beer. Neo, having concluded his surveillance of the place, leaped into my lap and curled up so tight his head rested on his tail. He was spent, like me, from our journey. The difference is he fell right asleep. Scared of what sunrise would bring, I could only focus on the stars.

I thought I might never sleep again.

CHAPTER 6

Neo's sandpapery tongue swept over my lips. When I opened my eyes, the sunlight was so intense I could only squint. We were nose to nose. He was on his hind legs, his two front paws using my chest for balance. It took me a few seconds to remember where I was.

I grabbed Neo under his stomach and put him on the ground. I sat up. I looked at my watch, at the Audemars my mother had given my father. I touched it, remembering all the times she made me smile before she died just days before my fifth birthday. The watch was still on New York City time. The 2:00 a.m. I was looking at translated to 9:00 a.m. local time. I stood up and walked over to the edge of the terrace. The sky was solid blue, like a reflection of the sapphire water below. The gulf was teeming with life. Boats of all colors and sizes drifted about. Down below were scattered people sunbathing at the pool, as well as on the beach just beyond.

I thought about Perry. How much I missed her, hoped she was safe. I wondered if I'd ever see her again. I thought about my father, who I knew I'd never see again. I became choked up. I thought about Jake and Tommy, too. Sure, they were my partners, but they were also two of my closest friends. I feared they were being pressed about things they knew nothing of, and I was sorry for that.

I walked into the suite, into the bathroom off of the living room, grabbed one of two lowball glasses next to the sink and filled it with water. I walked back out to the terrace, put it on the ground so Neo—following me at my heels—could enjoy it in the warmth of a beautiful morning. I returned inside. It occurred to me that water was one thing, food was another. I contemplated my options. I could order room service or venture out. Either way I would have direct contact with someone new. I decided the farther away this person was from this location, the better.

I walked into the bedroom for the first time since I'd arrived. I stripped off the suit pants and button-down shirt I'd been wearing for almost twenty-four hours, leaving them on the floor. I headed for the door in the far left corner leading to the second bathroom.

With a flip, I turned on the single light in the center of the ceiling. With a counterclockwise twist of a knob, I ran the shower. I tested the water with my hand. Cold, but beginning to even out. My eyes caught the mirror, my bald head. To my palm it felt stubbly and was a touch itchy. It dawned on me that aside from food for Neo, I needed other items. I needed food, toiletries, and casual beach wear that would help me maintain the identity of someone living a normal St. Maxime life. Someone who blends in.

After toweling off, I grabbed the gym bag off the couch in the living room and brought it into the bedroom. I took out the plastic bag containing the clothes I'd picked up at the airport, as well as a pair of underwear and socks. As I slid into the jeans, it occurred to me I had no idea who made them. I chuckled to myself. Days earlier, the only jeans allowed to touch my body had trendy labels and couple-hundred-dollar price tags. Now I was just happy not to be in a jail cell. Or dead.

I put on a black Hanes t-shirt and Yankee cap.

Fuck.

Shoes. All I had were the Ferragamos. The fact that they didn't

exactly match my outfit wasn't the issue. The fact that such a mis-
match might stick out was.

I was stuck and could do no better than wait until my first
opportunity to replace them. The issue at hand was Neo. Did I
leave him here in this room? Even though I didn't plan on being
long, what if I got held up? Or my plans called for quickly changing
course? I needed to be agile. He didn't even need a leash as he
always stayed right at my feet. Still—what if we had to run? What if
he couldn't keep up, or we got split up? I exited the hotel, Neo
slung on my shoulder in his carrier. I pulled my Yankee cap as low
to my eyes as possible without interrupting my vision. The previous
evening, I recalled, I had passed St. Maxime's main port, and center
of town, only a couple of kilometers before La Belle Aurore
appeared. I turned right on Boulevard Jean Moulin, the portion of
the Bord de Mer that brought me into town the night before and
headed back the way I'd come.

Outside the day was warm, drawing eager, ritzy beachgoers to
the hotspots. Music blared from convertibles—everyone within
eyeshot was getting loose while I sharpened my senses like a knife.
Traffic crawled and every couple hundred yards I turned around to
see if I was being followed. After about ten minutes, I decided, for
the time being, I was alone.

Ten minutes after that, twenty in all, I came upon the main
port. It was vast, orderly; a grand parking lot, only on water. Unlike
the more chichi ports along the coast, most of the boats here were
of average length. A couple vessels trickled through the inlet, no
doubt a no-wake zone. In the distance, out in the gulf toward St.
Tropez, I could see a number of mega-yachts scattered in the water.
Most likely they were owned by wealthy visitors without a slip right
in St. Tropez. Therefore they'd be using motorboats to get to shore
for over-the-top, Domaines Ott-soaked lunches at haunts like
Cinquante-Cinq and La Voile Rouge.

My black t-shirt was sticking to me. I could feel my socks wet
inside my dress shoes. Up ahead I saw a thickening crowd. The last
thing I wanted was exposure, but a morning market in the South of

France in the center of town meant for one-stop shopping. Using my time expeditiously, I wouldn't have to venture out again to shop until I had some direction.

Just past the port was La Plage des Elephantes, or the Beach of the Elephants. It's named this because Jean de Brunhoff, creator of Babar the Elephant, wrote his first Babar book in St. Maxime—so a sign told me. The place was buzzing. Bikinis were flat-out everywhere. Unfortunately, this is Europe, which doesn't limit this last statement to gorgeous women. We're talking women, men, young, old—you get the idea. Up ahead a bit farther I could see my destination: the morning market, or Les Puces.

I stepped over the curb, into the fold. The crowd was dense. Body odor, perfumes and colognes, the smell of sweat—it all rolled together into one pungent aroma of life.

Perfect.

There seemed no order to the booths lining each row, and I was immediately reeled in by the smell of sweet crêpes, gripped by the hunger I hadn't felt since jetting from New York. I chose one with Nutella for me and a strawberry one for Neo. I dropped my little partner's sweet treat in his bag and let him go to work. I stood there, people jostling me, and inhaled mine, nutty chocolate sauce running down and between my fingers. Then I ordered a second and did the same. My hunger satisfied, I started moving again with the crowd. Fruits and vegetables were next. I bought fresh blueberries, blackberries, and raspberries. I stocked up on dried fruit such as apricots and prunes figuring they would keep better. I got broccoli, cauliflower, potatoes; I got lettuce, tomatoes, onions, and carrots figuring I could make salad. My plan was to remove every item in the minibar, which would serve as my refrigerator, and simply replace them upon my departure. Which wouldn't be more than sixty hours from this moment.

No matter what.

I could not stay longer.

Perry or not.

Moving on, I peeked in Neo's carrier. He was finishing his

crêpe. He looked at me, his warm eyes glowing with appreciation. Strawberry was all over his white face. He looked like a peppermint candy. He licked his chops. Satisfied.

The next few stations were of no use. Fancy soaps, kitchen items, women's shoes. Next were toys. Surprising myself, I stopped. I wanted to have something ready should Perry and Max appear. I bought a couple of Transformers books, something I imagined all boys liked and something that also made me feel close to home. I moved on. Flip-flops! Ideal? No. Better than my dress shoes? Absolutely. I bought a pair, replaced my Ferragamos with the flip-flops, and continued on.

More stations of no use—costume jewelry, tablecloths, tobacco products, Provencal fabrics. Then I ran into a string of booths that worked for me. Bathing suits: bought one. Charcuterie: purchased some hard salami and pâté. I eyed some bacon and sausage but reminded myself I needed to stay away from things that needed cooking. Freshly baked breads: grabbed some fresh croissants and rolls. Sunglasses: bought two pairs for a combined twelve euros.

As I tucked my change in my pocket and positioned the three medium-size brown paper bags I'd accumulated in my arms, I noticed I had hit the jackpot. Casual shoes and sneakers. As I moved toward them I noticed something else. A pair of eyes seemed to be watching me from two aisles over.

They belonged to a young guy around my age—mid to late thirties. He was tall, fit, wearing jeans, and a hunter-green short-sleeve polo shirt. His skin was light and freckled, he had red hair, and a matching goatee. My pulse quickened. I turned away casually like I hadn't seen him and headed to the sneaker booth. The owner welcomed me, and I began browsing. I picked up a pair of Puma running shoes, pretending to look at them as I strained to keep tabs on my new friend with my peripheral vision.

I thought I saw him make a move. I looked up. He hadn't. As I made eye contact, he slipped on sunglasses. He didn't pretend to look away, but kept his focus locked on me.

I dropped the sneakers and began walking, clutching the paper bags against my torso. The crowd had grown thicker, and I wasn't sure exactly where I was. Using the bags like bumpers to nudge past people, I contorted my body to minimize jostling Neo's carrier, and I headed in the direction from which I thought I'd come.

Who was this guy?

How long had he been following me?

A couple folks had words for me as I squeezed by, but I paid them no attention. When I got to the end of the aisle, I checked for my pursuer. He, too, was making his way through the crowd.

Under the scorching sun, I kept pressing. With each step, the absurdity and seriousness of the situation became more apparent. My sense of reason told me to maintain a decent pace as not to attract unwanted attention to myself. My survival instincts, which I had come to rely on so heavily these last few weeks, suggested barreling through people to create as much distance as possible between me and Red.

Through the flimsy rubber soles of the flip-flops I now felt every ripple, every pebble, of the uneven earth of the outdoor market's floor. Every few steps one of my ankles threatened to roll. The thought of having to outrun this guy was a daunting one.

My senses went into overdrive. I honed in on the foot traffic patterns all around me. Tommy always said the best leaders know when to let others lead. I identified a young couple a few people away to my left at exactly nine o'clock that seemed to be in a hurry. In only seconds they had made it to eleven o'clock.

Locals.

I pushed myself forward diagonally, falling in behind them. Their approach was one of anticipation from obvious experience, an understanding of where tiny holes would open in the crowd right before they did, most likely due to booth location. Their route was anything but straight, more like an ambulance moving through parking lot traffic in Midtown Manhattan.

After about a hundred feet, a sign above the sea of heads in front of me, off to my right, caught my eye.

"Salles de Bains."

Bathrooms.

I looked behind me. No immediate sign of Red. Pretending to look for something I'd dropped, I crouched down and shooed legs away left and right as I moved forward. I made my way to the edge of the crowd. I sprung from the fringe of Les Puces. I raced toward the sign.

I rounded a corner and entered a hallway leading into a small, sandstone building. Straight ahead was a door that had a small plaque on it with a charcoal drawing of a woman twirling, her summer dress fanned out. Jutting off left just before the ladies' room was another hallway. On the wall before the turn was an arrow and another plaque marked with a charcoal drawing—this time a guy in a seersucker suit.

Two steps into the hallway I stopped. I leaned against the wall, closed my eyes, then lifted up my t-shirt and wiped the sweat off my face. I hadn't even been in France twelve hours. Was I nothing more than a fugitive, foolish to think I'd ever get a moment's peace again?

I tapped the back of my head against the wall, snapping myself back into the moment. I needed to make my move now. If Red had kept up with me, he'd already be upon me.

I sucked in a breath. I peeked around the corner. There he was.

No more than twenty feet away.

With speed and precision, I placed the bags down. Then Neo's carrier. The idea I might have to run flashed in my mind. I kicked off the flip-flops, deciding I'd be better off barefoot.

Red turned the corner. Before he could react to my presence, I wrapped my right hand around his neck. I dug in, placing my left forearm across his chest and slamming him to the wall. His sunglasses went flying. My thumb and index fingers were so far up under his jawbone I could feel his larynx. His wide eyes confirmed we were thinking the same thing. That I could crush it.

"Who the fuck are you?" I snarled, right up in his face.

No response. His eyes were steely, hard.

I grabbed his shirt with my left hand. Never moving my right hand, I pulled him a foot forward then drove him back into the wall. I could leave no question as to who was in charge. I had already learned the hard way: the second anyone gets an inch they become a wild card.

"I mean it, motherfucker," I growled. My own fear had me squeezing tighter. "I need to know who you are. Right now."

He wasn't gasping, but I could tell he was having trouble breathing. Trying with everything he had to move forward, he took a swipe at me. I fended off his right hand by lifting my left elbow as I kept him pinned to the wall. Nonetheless, as his fist opened into a reaching hand, his fingernails raked the front of my face. The sting of the instant, shallow wound was sharp.

Our faces were so close we could feel, hear each other's every breath. My forearm felt his wildly beating heart. I squeezed harder yet. I was officially choking him. The sooner this guy accepted I was in control, the sooner I'd reward him with just enough air to offer his identity. I felt a streak of blood running into the corner of my mouth. I stuck out my tongue and lapped it up.

I was a warrior now. Not because I wanted to be. Because I had to be.

"I don't want to hurt you," I pushed out through clenched teeth. "But I will. Last chance. Who are you?"

I felt Red's body start to weaken, to relent. He raised his hands in surrender. I eased my grip just enough to let in a swallow of air.

"Michel Bourdoin," he said, raspy. "Michel Bourdoin," he repeated.

"What do you want, Michel Bourdoin?" I said, no space between his last word and my first.

"Your cap," he said.

I was confused. My head twitched as I searched for words. My thoughts started going wild. My cap? Could there be something hidden in my cap? Was this another *Danish Jubilee Egg*, another plant job of some sort? How? I had bought it randomly at the airport in the States before my departure.

"What about my cap?" I asked.

"It is zee Yankees—no?" he asked with a heavy French accent. "Zee New York Yankees?"

"The Yankees," I answered. "Right. So?"

"I have never been to New York. My son, he ees six years old. He loves zee American baseball, especially zee New York Yankees. I am sorry if I—"

I didn't believe him. I couldn't.

"Bullshit!" I barked right in his face, tightening my grip again and purposely spraying spit in his face. "Who the fuck are you? Who the fuck are you working for?"

"Please! Please!" he pleaded, his straining neck taut against my palm. He forced his arms farther in the air. "I am Michel Bourdoin. Take out my wallet and see for yourself. Please! I mean you absolutely no harm, I was—"

I slammed him into the wall again.

"First you watched me. Then you followed me."

"I know. I'm sorry. It's just that—eef—I, I just figured that—I can't ever find a New York Yankees cap around here. Please—I'll give you fifty euros for it. Seventy-five! I don't make much money, but—"

The sincerity in his voice caught me off guard. He *had* watched me. He *had* followed me. Both of those acts could have been about exactly what he was proclaiming. At that moment, something about my new reality slapped me across the face. As long as I remained Jonah Gray, anyone and everyone I would ever come across again would be the enemy until I could prove otherwise. I couldn't trust anyone.

Anyone.

God, that feeling sucked.

I could have crushed this guy's windpipe. Either he could act on the level of De Niro or all he genuinely cared about was getting this cap for his boy. In a heartbeat my fear turned to envy. I couldn't help acknowledging what a special love that must be.

Did my father ever feel that way about me? Ever?

His words tapered off. I backed off. Mortified, without another word, I gave him the hat. Even though I had straight-up assaulted this guy, he still tried to give me cash, which I denied. I could barely look him in the eye again. I picked up Neo's carrier, then the stuffed brown paper bags, and was on my way.

Twenty minutes later I was back in my suite. I hung the "Privacy" sign, locked the door behind me, let Neo out of his carrier, pulled everything out of the minibar and restocked it with my fresh booty. Over the course of the next thirty-six hours, I did little more than eat salad and crudités with fresh lemon juice as dressing out on the terrace as I watched the boats move around the gulf endlessly, like pieces on some giant chessboard. The more I tried to devise a plan, the more I realized I had no idea what to do, or how to think like a criminal on the run. Without any sleep day had run into night, then well into day again. And all I had achieved was an enormous headache.

CHAPTER 7

The shades are down, the cabin dark, as the wheels touch the ground. Cobus and I are still steeped in our discussion. I'm listening, but I don't hear him. All I can think about is what waits outside. I can feel the goose bumps all over my body.

I'm home.

After all the running, all the scheming, all the strategizing, all the lying, all the re-creating, all the research, all the misunderstanding, all the gratitude, all the guilt, all the fighting, all the questions, all the answers, all the choices, all the soul-searching, all the trusting, all the dreams, all the nightmares, all the praying, all the clawing, all the scratching, all the gains, all the losses, all the struggling, all the remorse, all the determination, all the grief, all the yearning, all the sorrow, all the pain.

I'm home.

I want to jump from my seat, blast through the door, and race toward everyone and everything I left behind. My partners. My best friend since childhood, L. I want to find Perry. I have no idea if she's alive or dead but I need to find her. I want to seek out Detective Morante and give him the real story behind the dirty cop pulled from the East River. Animal that he was or not, I want to visit my father's grave. "Fuck all of you," I want to scream, then steal the first car I can get my hands on and head to Baltimore to get a look at the missing Fabergé Easter Eggs.

I reach inside my suit jacket, into the inside right pocket, and touch the silver pen Scott Green gave me before blowing his own head open. It's in the same pocket as my iPhone. As well as a state-of-the-art Swiss-Axe, Triplet Hawk, 10x jeweler's loupe.

So much to do. So little time.

"Where's the little guy?" asks Cobus, breaking me from my thoughts.

"What?"

"The little guy. Aldo. Who's he staying with now that Tess and Johan left?"

After Perry and Max's abduction, I told Cobus that Tess had left me. That I was too focused on my work and she needed more. Turning my back on what happened to Perry was one of the hardest choices I ever made. But I was in no position to start explaining things to people, nor did I want her husband to get wind of what had happened to her and their child if he wasn't involved—as he was the one she was running from.

Were Perry and Max taken as a message to me? Was this the work of her husband? Someone else? Are they safe? Are they dead? I have no idea. But I also knew I would be better served to wait until the day I made it back to the States so Jonah Gray could find out as opposed to Ivan Janse starting with the Dutch police.

"He's home with Laura."

I hate leaving the little guy behind. But God only knows what awaits me on this trip. I've put him in harm's way enough over the years, and he's remained loyal as ever. My little trooper, no longer a spring chicken in the world of dogs, has earned his time for drama-free relaxation.

And I fully intend on seeing him again. Soon.

"Right. Laura."

I hear a whir as the shades slowly ascend. The early evening,

American light fills the cabin. It washes over us, over me, as if welcoming Jonah Gray and his new confidant Ivan Janse with open arms.

Customs officials board the jet, and we clear immigration on the tarmac. We exit the Gulfstream and walk down the stairs. There are two black Escalades waiting for us.

"I arranged for a separate car before we left," Arnon says, a bulging briefcase in each hand. "As you know, Mr. Green's unexpected death set us back some these last few days. We're at too critical a stage in this process and there is much work to be handled as we move toward closing. I was able to talk opposing counsel into foregoing this evening's dinner party in the interest of making headway, to which they agreed."

"Absolutely," Cobus says. "Great. Then we'll see you downstairs for breakfast in the morning before we head to GlassWell's offices."

"Of course," Arnon replied. "Enjoy the evening."

Arnon walks to the second Escalade. After the driver opens the doors to the first, Cobus and I climb in.

Like a bullet from the barrel, The Queens-Midtown Tunnel shoots our Escalade out into the heart of New York City. Looking out the tinted window away from Cobus, part of me—the old me, Jonah Gray—can't help from letting a slight sneer find my face. These buildings, this city, it was all mine once. Mine to manipulate, mine to build, mine to conquer. This is the city I was raised in, the city where I learned to work people over left and right to get everything I needed, wanted. I feel a pang in my gut. Suddenly, I'm ashamed of the sneer on my face.

These buildings, this bustling, thriving city all around me—I had been given one of the greatest gifts of all in life. To be born and raised in New York City. The greatest city in the world. Fair or not—cursed, damned, or simply victim of my own destiny—I was forced to leave not only my home, but the place everyone in the world hopes to get a chance to make it to for one reason. To shine.

If there was anything I'd learned from losing this city it was one thing.

Lose the fucking sneer.

And remember every second it's been replaced with unmatched resolve.

I hit the button on the door and the window goes down. I can feel Cobus looking at me.

"Warm," I say, my attention still outside.

The tinted glass disappears. The city comes to life. The sounds, the smells—it all rushes back in through every pore on my body straight into the core of my soul. Pizza place, dry cleaners, Starbucks, bank, McDonald's, hardware store, yogurt joint, nice-looking restaurant—the city passes by, block by block, same today as it was when I left, albeit with a bunch of new franchises and what seems to be a whole bunch more of them locationwise.

Whatever broker's representing Starbucks in this city must be killing it, I can't help thinking.

As we make our way uptown, I look up at the office towers, the skyscrapers. I feel like I'm being reunited with old friends. I want to reach out, slap them, like we're high-fiving. I sense the buildings feel the same way, like they want to pat my back, tussle my hair. And say welcome back.

As we turn left to head west through Central Park, Cobus also puts his window down. The crisp, fall air flows freely through the car.

"So? What do you think?" asks Cobus, both of us still focused on the city as it passed beyond our respective windows.

"About what?" I respond, my eyes still on the passing gray stone wall bifurcating the park for Sixty-Sixth Street to run through.

"About New York City?"

What do I think? I think the best burger in Manhattan is probably still Corner Bistro on West Fourth Street.

"Big," I say. "And just as busy as I imagined it would be."

Soon we roll up to Fifteen Central Park West.

"Beautiful," Cobus says, looking up at the limestone façade tower. "Supposedly Mr. Spencer lives in one of the finest buildings in Manhattan."

Mr. Spencer is Gary Spencer—one of the two principals of GlassWell. He's a seventy-three-year-old titan in the real estate world, and between his property and other investments, one of the wealthiest men in the United States. As far as the building he lives in—fine is an understatement. Fifteen Central Park West is one of the most prestigious residential addresses in New York, if not the entire world. The property is separated into two buildings connected by a glass-enclosed lobby—a nineteen-story tower on Central Park West known as "The House" and a forty-three-story tower on Broadway. Finance moguls, actors, athletes, diplomats—residents include or have included the likes of Denzel Washington and Bob Costas to Russian oligarchs and Sting. Only the most fortunate in life ever even sniff a building like this.

We pull into the private driveway, an amenity of the building designed to keep paparazzi out. Once inside, the lobby is gorgeous. White marble under foot, brown-and-white swirled marble columns line the English oak panel enclosed space.

We step off the elevator on one of the penthouse floors, into a small, white foyer. There is a small, contemporary, brown table. On it is a glass cube holding water. Floating on the water is one huge brown rose. Next to the table is a solid white door. No number. Apparently, Mr. Spencer's apartment is the entire floor.

The door opens, and we're immediately swallowed by luxury. The foyer flows into a monstrous living room overlooking what seems to be the entire island of Manhattan. One wall of glass faces Central Park, another faces downtown. As the sun sneaks away, the sky resembles one continuous, panoramic sheet of cobalt and violet marble. The wood flooring is wide, diagonally intersecting Peruvian walnut planks. A portion of the floor—underneath the glass coffee table and surrounding plush, white couches and chairs—is covered by a huge, white area rug. Three striking contemporary pieces of art hang on the walls. The closest one to us upon our entrance immediately grabs my attention. It's a large picture—it has to be at least eight feet tall—with what looks like four black-and-white photographs of older Chinese women in geisha garb scattered about. Under the photographs are Chinese words. Covering the piece are streaks of blue paint.

"Julian Schnabel," says Ryan Brand as he approaches us. "In fact, all three of them are," he goes on gesturing toward the others. "Guess you've done something right when you have three Julian Schnabel pieces hanging in your living room."

He extends his hand to me. We firmly shake hands.

"Ryan, nice to meet you in person," I say. "I'm Ivan. And this is Cobus de Bont."

Ryan Brand is sharp as the edge of a piece of broken glass. He's taller than I remember—then again, I don't think I ever stood this close to him. He's got long, thick, slicked-back salt-and-pepper hair. His facial features are well proportioned and strong. His eyes are hazel, his skin is well tanned and implies long stretches of time in beautiful weather. He's most certainly not an off-the-rack guy as the stitching on his navy suit, as well as the precise fit, tells me Ryan only goes custom.

Brand takes his hand from mine and moves it to Cobus.

"Mr. de Bont. It's fantastic to meet you."

"Please. Call me Cobus. The pleasure is ours."

"So, Cobus, Ivan," Brand goes on, "we've got work to do. The goal is to close this up and ensure the Freedom Bank Building is your firm's first property on American soil. But that's for tomorrow. Tonight, we enjoy ourselves. It's not every day one gets to mingle with Gary Spencer's inner circle at a dinner party in his home."

Brand looks into the room, which prompts us to do the same. Upper-crust guests are floating around, as are white-gloved servers with trays of hors d'oeuvres. Lots of suits, lots of slim, beautiful, over-exercised and underfed women in knockout cocktail dresses, lots of gems shimmering from the combination of interior lighting mixed with remnants of the day's sunlight coming through the glass as dusk sets in.

Across the room, telling a story to a few of his guests, is Gary Spencer. He's a slender man no taller than five foot seven or eight, dressed so tight I feel like the large, perfect knot in his silver tie must be impairing his breathing. He looks younger than his years, like a man who takes pride in taking care of himself. Ryan takes us over and introduces us. The meeting is quick. It's like he's Mick Jagger or the president and we're promptly, subtly, ushered onward.

"Follow me," Brand says, "the bar was set up in the kitchen. You boys have had a long day. My guess is you could use a cocktail."

We follow Brand out of the living room and down a hallway. I've seen a lot of impressive New York City apartments in my day, but this place is simply off the grid. Both to my right and left, what seems like every ten or twenty feet, there's another door leading to another room. A dining room, a large den, a study, bathrooms—seriously, between the living room and not yet even the kitchen, I feel like I've seen three bathrooms—a small den, a library, a—

"Is that entire room a humidor?" I ask.

"It is," Brand responds. "Gary is quite serious when it comes to his cigars."

You think? The humidor is bigger than many Manhattan studio apartments.

Finally, we get to the kitchen. The floor in the kitchen is hardwood like the living room only the planks are linear and lighter in color. The walls are white. The cabinets all have borders but are glass in the center as to be able to see what's inside. All the appliances are top shelf—Viking stove, Sub-Zero fridge—like the liquor bottles standing at attention on the black, marble surface covering the huge island in the center of the room.

Behind the island, tending bar, is a man in a tuxedo. But it's the woman he's pouring champagne for who captivates me. I see her from the side, just her profile. She's tall, probably five foot nine but at the moment easily over six feet because of the sky-high heels of her Sergio Rossi patent leather platform pumps. The shiny shoes are beige, the color perfectly matching the tight, predominantly viscose form-fitting Alexander McQueen dress she's wearing. The perfect combination of classy and slinky, the tea-length dress beautifully hugs her body then flares at the bottom. It has a jewel neckline and cap sleeves. She's tall and thin, bordering on too thin but not quite there. Her skin is light, as is her long straight hair, which is pulled back in a ponytail. Her cheekbones are high. Her nose, though I'm only seeing it from the side, is perfectly sized for her face and nicely rounded at the tip.

"Ahh—one of the people I wanted you both to meet," Brand says. "Cobus, Ivan, meet Julia Chastain."

I immediately recognize the name. Julia Chastain leads the team that oversees all GlassWell leasing for five of the firm's Manhattan properties—one of which is the Freedom Bank Building. We've spoken a couple times over the last few months. She's been directing the forwarding of all sorts of documents to me at Brand's direction from the building's current leases to Midtown occupancy/vacancy reports to updates on negotiations with tenants whose leases are soon turning over. Just as she takes a swallow of the champagne, Julia turns to greet us. When she does, I'm struck all over again.

On the left side of her face, the side I hadn't been able to see, is a red-wine birthmark. It starts at her hairline. It doesn't extend very far into her face but is a few inches wide and runs straight down covering her ear, the top of her jawbone, the side of her neck, then down into her neckline where I imagine it also covers a portion of her shoulder. Its shape reminds me of the country Chile.

Shit—I think I'm staring. Not because of the birthmark. Because Julia Chastain is one of the most beautiful women with whom I've ever been in a room.

"Julia Chastain," she says, extending her hand to Cobus.

Her voice is a bit raspy, sophisticated, sexy.

"Cobus de Bont."

"It's nice to meet you."

"You, as well."

Her eyes move to me.

"Ivan," I say. "Janse."

She moves her hand to mine. She has long, slender fingers with perfectly French-manicured nails. Her shake is firm.

"Of course. Nice to meet you, Ivan. I always enjoy putting a face with a voice."

We both pause. I could swear we each just sucked in a breath. Our eyes are locked, as if we each see something we didn't expect to see.

"I appreciate your attention to our requests," I say to keep us moving forward.

"Of course," she quickly replies, withdrawing her hand from mine.

"I know it's a lot, but we like to be thorough," I add.

She now addresses all of us, not just me.

"Please, it's our pleasure. Mr. de Bont, I understand this is your firm's first acquisition in the U.S."

"It is."

"Exciting," Julia goes on. "Are you current in terms of all you need from my team, or is there anything else you're waiting on?"

Cobus turns to me.

"Ivan has really been the point man on this deal, in terms of all due diligence. Ivan?"

I look at Julia.

"I think we have everything at the moment."

"Um, Cobus, I actually wanted to ask you something about the European market for a moment if I might," Brand says, grabbing Cobus's attention.

Brand and Cobus break into their own conversation.

"So what are you drinking, Ivan?" asks Julia.

I look at the bartender.

"Belvedere on the rocks please. Twist."

"This must be exciting for your firm," Julia says, "your first foray into the American property market. De Bont seems to have grown quite fast. And you seem to have put your stamp all over that growth."

"What makes you say that?"

"I do my homework, Ivan. I always find it helpful to know all I can about who I'm—who GlassWell—is dealing with. Cobus de Bont is one hell of an impressive man. But it is hard not to notice the more articles you read surrounding the explosive growth of these last few years, the more your name pops up with regard to acquisitions and how de Bont handles property as a whole."

"Is that right?" I say.

"It is."

"Well, I admire someone who understands the true value of information," I say, as I nod thank you to the bartender handing me my cocktail, "almost as much as I admire someone willing to use words like 'foray' and phrases like 'explosive growth.'"

Julia giggles.

We clink glasses.

"To closing," I say.

The corner of her mouth, ever so slightly, turns up.

"To closing," she mimics.

We each take a long sip of our drinks. Damn, that cool vodka feels and tastes good sliding down my throat.

"Long journey to the States?" Julia asks.

Talk about a loaded question.

"You might say that," I reply.

Julia takes another healthy sip, almost completely draining the flute.

"Bit of a long day on your end as well?"

"This time of year is always crazy as we move toward year's end. Now throw in the sale of a building on top of that to an overseas buyer who needs an inordinate amount of hand holding—"

I raise an eyebrow.

"Kidding," she says before I can even answer, revealing a smile that shows her perfect teeth. "I actually have a couple deal-related questions. Why don't we freshen these up and head out to the terrace? It feels a bit stuffy in here."

New drinks in hand, I follow Julia through the apartment toward the terrace that is off the living room. Watching her from behind is a sight every man should be allowed to experience just once. Her shoulders are a touch broad, perfectly complementing her flawless posture, making for a commanding, model-like presence and gait. The dress is so clingy I can see certain muscles in her back. Her thin waist runs seamlessly into her exceptional ass. Her legs are long, perfectly contoured. There's a knot in my stomach. The more I admire her exquisite form, the more I think about Perry. Even though she's been removed from my life for a couple years now, I still miss her, and love her, every day.

Every eye in the house, male or female, checks out Julia as we move through the crowd—some because she's a business acquaintance or associate, others simply because she's so damn hot. We stop intermittently as Julia handles a couple of work-related odds and ends and introduces me to a few worthwhile people. Soon we're outside. The terrace, overlooking Central Park, is probably about twelve hundred square feet. The sun is almost gone.

We walk to the edge of the terrace. Aside from us, there are only a few other people outside.

"Sorry about Mr. Green," I say, just before we stop. She turns to me. "That must have been a big shock for everyone," I go on.

"Yes, it was," she responds. "It's always sad when someone dies too young."

"Did you know him well?"

"No. I mean—a hello here or there, but essentially we only spoke on legal issues as they pertained to leases or deals. That's really it."

She changes directions.

"I know I sent you all the specifics on where we are with the Lorgan negotiation—"

Lorgan Engineering is a tenant in the Freedom Bank Building whose lease is about to turn over.

"But they're resisting the numbers harder than I thought they would. They're a twenty-thousand-square-foot user, so while it wouldn't be the end of the world if they walk, I'm doing my best to keep them. Even at a dollar or two lower per foot, I think it's the better move for the building. Hence, for de Bont."

"I agree. And I appreciate you filling me in."

We each take a sip of our drink.

"Inside you mentioned you like to do your homework on people GlassWell is dealing with," I go on. "Now, I don't mean to overstep, but why would this be of interest to you? I mean—why wouldn't you simply care about the leasing elements to a deal like this? Why would you be interested in who de Bont is? Or who any buyer is for that matter?"

"You're an astute man, Ivan Janse. It turns out I'm a bit closer to the situation than being one of the leasing directors for the firm."

"Closer how?"

"My best friend growing up here in the city was Chloe Spencer. Mr. Spencer's daughter. Chloe and I were together literally from the time we went to nursery school all the way until the end of high school. At that point we split up when we went to different colleges."

"Are you still in touch?"

"Very much so. We speak on the phone once a week. She's a dermatologist in Los Angeles. And for her father, who has always been like a second father to me, it worked out perfectly. While Chloe was always the science-oriented one of us, I was the nerdy business type. When I graduated from Duke armed with a business degree, and not a clue of what I wanted to do with it, Mr. Spencer couldn't have been happier to bring me in. It was like he was able to give me the spot he'd hoped Chloe would fill. I think it did something for each of us."

"So you feel an obligation to look out for the company," I say.

"I do."

It's getting colder. I notice Julia shivering ever so slightly.

"Hold this," I say, handing her my drink.

She takes it without a word. I start taking off my jacket.

"Oh, Ivan, no. Really, I'm—"

"Please," I cut her off without altering my actions. "It's my pleasure."

She doesn't contest further. I slip it over her shoulders and take back my drink.

"Besides, I can't have you getting sick on me. We have a deal to close."

The raspy giggle.

"So," I go on, "I guess the family connection explains something else for me."

"Which is?"

"How a woman as beautiful as you ended up in this male-dominated world of commercial real estate."

I'm not sure which of us is more surprised this just came out of my mouth.

"I'm sorry," I continue, "Not sure that presented itself as intended. Was actually kind of a stream-of-consciousness thing, I believe."

"You don't need to apologize."

"No?"

"No. The answer is, I like it."

"Real estate?"

"Being called beautiful."

Once back inside I excuse myself to find the bathroom. I have a general idea where a door is that leads to what looked like a study. I find it. I casually take a sip of my drink and look up and down the hallway. Looks clear. I step into the room. When I do it's like I've crossed over into an entirely different apartment. The walls and ceiling are dark, rich wood. The carpeting is equally dark brown if not darker. The walls are lined with full bookshelves. In one of the corners there's a small table topped by an antique chessboard. In the center of the room is a rustic, teak coffee table, a dark-green velvet couch on each side. In the far corner of the office is a massive oak desk. I walk toward it.

There's a small fire glowing in the fireplace. This and the dimly lit ceiling lights provide the only illumination in the space. Everything in the room appears as an outline, but as I get closer to the desk I see stacks of papers, a desktop computer, the backs of standing picture frames—there isn't what seems to be an open inch on the desk's surface. Finally my eyes locate a desktop pen set. It has a rectangular sterling silver base with a glass globe the size of a baseball positioned in the center. On each side of the globe is a holder for a pen. To my disappointment, a sterling silver pen is resting in each one.

"Julia mentioned she saw you head this way," a voice startles me.

Brand.

"Something I can help you with?"

Shit.

"I was looking for a bathroom," I shoot back.

I start walking toward the fireplace slowly, to make it appear I'm just casually wandering around.

"The fireplace caught my eye as I walked past. Once I peeked in and saw the chessboard, well—" I go on.

Brand looks down to his left at the small table with the chessboard on top, as if to make the point it's all the way back toward the doorway. So why had I crossed the entire room?

He looks at me again.

"You a big fan of the game?"

I've never played once.

"I am."

"Me too," Brand counters. "Perhaps we can square off one day."

"Perhaps we can," I respond.

"Come on. I'll help you find a bathroom."

I follow Brand out of the study.

CHAPTER 8

The phone rang. Neo, who had fallen asleep on the lounge chair next to mine, sprang onto all fours like a cartoon character. I pulled my eyes from the gulf waters glimmering with orange light from sunset. I looked at the Audemars—1:38 pm in New York, which meant 7:38 pm on the Côte d'Azur.

I walked back inside. On the fourth ring, I decided not to pick it up. Hopefully, it was housekeeping telling me because of the "Privacy" sign they hadn't been able to make up the room. My stomach dropped after ten seconds of silence when it began ringing again. Now it occurred to me—if the hotel personnel knew categorically I was there, my not picking up would be suspicious.

"Hello?"

"Good evening, Mr. Gordon. It is Brigette from reception. I had the pleasure of checking you in two nights ago."

"Of course," I replied. "Good evening."

"How has your stay been thus far? Are you finding everything that you need?"

"I am. Thank you."

"I just wanted to check with you regarding your credit card," she continued. "According to you at check-in, American Express said you would receive your replacement card today. Unfortunately, there is no record of any packages arriving for you today."

"Oh, you know, you're right," I countered, a touch of surprise sprinkled into my voice. "I've been so preoccupied, I must have subconsciously blocked out anything whatsoever that has to do with responsibility."

I had hoped for a little laugh. Which I didn't get.

"I am happy we were able to accommodate you upon arrival," Brigette went on, "but it is strict hotel policy that we must keep a card on file for all guests. Now I'm—"

"Brigette—say no more," I cut her off. "I'll call American Express right now, and get back to you."

"Thank you, Mr. Gordon. I appreciate your assistance."

I hung up. Still staring at the phone, concocting my next credit card story, it rang again.

"Yes, Brigette?"

Silence. There was a long pause. Was this it, I thought? Was it already time for my next big play?

Do I say hello again? Or do I hang up?

Just as I was about to speak, the first word about to leapfrog the back of my tongue, I heard a voice.

"Jonah?"

I sucked in a swallow of air.

"Perry?" I said, in a near whisper.

"I'm here," she went on, her voice stern. "We're here."

Max. Her son.

She stopped. I heard a sniffle. She continued.

"We're in St. Maxime. We just got here. What room are you in?"

Hearing her voice shocked, awed, relieved, and confused me. I was stuck in no-man's land. My previous life was freshly behind me. Yet after what happened at the market it already felt a thousand years away.

"I . . . I, what—"

"Don't even *think* of cracking on me now, tough guy," she blasted me.

She called me out for being at an unusual loss for words. I half smiled. Knowing her strength was intact was comforting. But I hated myself for putting her and her young child in a place where her voice could ever sound this nervous.

I closed my eyes, collected myself.

"Cinquante-douze. Five-twelve."

Fifteen minutes later, there was a knock on the door. I opened it. Perry, wearing jeans and a tight-fitting white cotton tank top, stood with her hands on the shoulders of Max who stood in front of her. He too was wearing jeans, and he had on a blue t-shirt with the Superman S. Both were in Nike running sneakers. There was one small, black rolling suitcase standing upright next to them.

The second our eyes met I wanted to pick her up by her waist and swing her around. For a fleeting moment, all the circumstances surrounding our meeting here, now, were gone. That changed when I looked down, as if Max's gaze was pulling at mine.

I squatted down so Max and I were face-to-face. He had just turned eight years old. He had a full head of dirty-blond hair and his cheeks were a bit flushed. He had a peaceful yet dazed look on his round face. The look of a confused boy in new surroundings who just completed a long journey, but did so unquestioningly because of the faith he has in, and love he has for, his mother.

"How are you, Max?" I asked.

Sure, I knew Max. But overall my experience with children was minimal, and from an emotional standpoint, it was zilch. I stuck out my hand. I was surprised by how small and soft his palm was against mine when he shook it.

"I'm okay," he answered with a shrug.

"Did you have fun on the airplane?"

His brown eyes looked tired. He rubbed them.

"I guess."

I stood back up, looked at Perry again. Then I reached out and grabbed their suitcase.

"Why don't you both come inside?"

Max entered first. Immediately, he perked up upon sight of Neo and dropped to his knees to greet him. Always the friendly one, and never of mind to turn away a belly scratch, Neo flipped onto his back. Perry followed Max in and stopped in front of me. Without a word, her eyes briefly taking in the scabbing scratch from Red, she placed her hand on my cheek. I only wanted to touch her back—feel her smooth skin, run my hand through her flowing brown hair. With our eyes we absorbed each other. As usual, she barely had on any makeup. And, as usual, she looked gorgeous.

"Mommy, I *really* need to go to the bathroom," Max said, his gaze still on Neo. Apparently, he had found a good spot on my little partner. Neo's left hind leg was twitching out of control as his tail wagged wildly.

"There are two," I responded as I closed the door. "There's one right here and another in the bedroom."

Max stood up and started for the one off the living room.

"Baby, use the one in the bedroom," Perry said taking her hand from my face. "Mommy needs a minute alone with Jonah."

Max listened and headed off. As he did, neither of us said a word. We just stood there, face-to-face, staring into each other's eyes. After a few seconds we heard Max close the door behind him.

Perry stepped closer to me. She reached up with both hands and grabbed the sides of my head. Then she pulled me into her and kissed me deeply. I let go of the suitcase and wrapped my arms around her waist. Between her pulling up high and me pulling down low, lifting her into me, our bodies were pressed against each other in a way that I'd previously only imagined. Her stomach was as tight as her grip. Her breasts were firm and her hard nipples sticking into my chest were driving me crazy. I wanted to tear her clothes off. The only thing stronger than my urges was the reality Max would be back any minute.

Perry pulled her lips from mine. We both froze.

"I'm so happy you're a good kisser," she said. "Talk about potential for the utmost disappointment."

We went back at it, our hands now moving over each other wildly. I could feel my testosterone rising at a rate it never had before. Yes, this was a moment with Perry I'd dreamed of, but it was more than that. It had come at the time in my life—the *second* in my life—I most needed to lose myself.

I unraveled my tongue from hers, moved my nose into her neck, and took a deep sniff.

"Ahhh," I exhaled, "you smell so good. Like, like—"

We heard Max open the bathroom door in the other room. We jumped apart. Staring at each other still, we straightened our twisted shirts.

I called Brigette and told her Amex had screwed up. That they had sent my new card to my address back home and promised one to me at the hotel by the next evening. Then, once we had Max and Neo situated on the terrace having some fresh fruit together, Perry and I sat down on the couch.

"How bad are things at home?"

"You have no idea. You weren't kidding when you said people would be looking for you," she said. "Police, FBI—two mornings ago, after seeing you the night before for the last time, they swarmed the office like yellow jackets."

"I was skeptical that you'd actually meet me here," I changed directions. "I mean—I know we decided we'd do this together, that you wanted it for Max as much if not more than for us. And it's not like I consciously doubted you. I just—still—"

"You know I'm a woman of my word, Jonah. And you also know I'd do anything for Max. Anything."

I also remembered exactly what she said just a few nights earlier outside Acappella in Tribeca. I had just let my three partners know that the deal presented to us by Andreu Zhamovsky was a sham, simply a ploy to move a large sum of money into the United States.

I could still feel her warm breath on my skin as she whispered into my ear.

"Are you really prepared to let even the dream of us being together die?"

To which, I replied, no.

"You're sure this is best for him?" I asked, immediately sorry I'd let the words slip past my lips.

What was I thinking? Did I want to scare her? Send her running back to the U.S. before they even settled in?

"I am. I was sure when I told you the other night. I was kicked in the ass when I received notification from my ex-animal's attorney that Max should immediately be turned over to his father's full-time care as a result of those with whom I'm associated."

"Jesus," I said softly. "I'm sorry."

She looked down for a second, then back into my eyes.

"Who's the cop they pulled from the river? Why are they looking for you?"

"It's not at all what you think. Not even close," I replied.

"I know that." she said reassuringly. "I do. But I need to know what's going on. Everything. I mean—your father being murdered, Zhamovsky using us to round up these Fabergé eggs, the cop—I need to know what the hell is going on."

Over the course of the next couple hours, I took her through every hour, every minute, of the previous three weeks.

"You still haven't explained why you're tied to the cop," she eventually said.

I explained to Perry that I accidentally shot him. And that Mattheau, my father's chauffeur and a man with secrets of his own who viewed me as a second son, clumsily disposed of him. I also told her I was still struggling with the memory of watching his life—dirty bastard or not—drain from his body right before my eyes.

CHAPTER 9

For almost the next twenty-four hours Neo and I remained in the room. While Perry and Max spent most of that time with us, her not being a fugitive with her image plastered all over the news enabled her to take Max into the pool midday and get a bite at the hotel restaurant. Both activities were more about not letting Max sense anything too peculiar and less about enjoying the Côte d'Azur.

Around five fifteen p.m., all four of us took a stroll down to the sand as the sun began waving good night by painting the sky with purples and greens. We brought some fresh fruit from the minibar. Max ran down to the surf while Perry—for keeping up the appearance of a true vacationer—spread out on a lounge chair next to me in a purple bikini. After chewing and swallowing a nice chunk of pineapple, Neo jumped down from the lounge chair to my left then up on to Perry's glistening stomach. She gently began petting his back and rolled her head to the left. My eyes moved from Neo, and Perry's awesome body, to her eyes. She stared at me, but said nothing.

"What?" I asked.

"When do we need to leave?"

I shrugged.

"Not exactly sure. Pretty new at all this."

"But soon," she continued.

I nodded.

"Real soon."

"After all this talking, all this strategizing, is there actually a next move?"

Fifty-two hours and counting. So much pondering, thinking, questioning, hypothesizing, querying, evaluating, postulating. The incident back at the market had been gnawing at me since it happened. Being scared for Neo and myself was one thing. Perry and Max on top of that was another. At first glance of them walking into the hotel I thought it would only add to the blizzard in my mind. But their appearance had worked in the exact opposite manner. Adding Perry and Max to the mix seemed to be the precise kick in the ass I needed. Having a next move wasn't an option now. Would never be again. As a broker, I always snapped into my next move. As someone living a one-hundred-mile-per-hour double life the last few weeks, I always snapped into my next move. Now, as a worldwide fugitive on the run with an innocent woman and her child, this had to be the case more than ever.

Take the facts. Take your gut. Snap into the next move.

I clenched my teeth. I turned my head and looked out again over the gently rolling water.

"There is."

About quarter to seven we all walked back into the room. Max walked out onto the terrace eating a piece of cantaloupe. Neo followed him, hoping for some sharing. Perry headed straight for the bathroom. Just as she closed the door, the phone rang.

"Shit," I whispered to myself.

"Good evening, Brigette," I began. "I just got off the phone with American Express and it—

"Bonjour, Mr. Gordon. Good evening. This is Monsieur Acelin Bernot. I'm the manager of La Belle Aurore. I trust you are enjoying your stay?"

Acelin Bernot definitely had a French accent, but his English was perfect.

"I am, Monsieur Bernot. Thank you."

"Fantastic," he went on, "we certainly aim to please. Now, I understand there has been an issue with your credit card. Our lovely Brigette has filled me in on the situation and at this point we need to have the issue resolved. According to Brigette it was supposed to be finalized last night."

This guy was no-nonsense.

"I, yes—she—"

I pulled my mouth away from the phone, covered it, and took a deep breath.

"That's correct, sir. My card was lost, and instead of forwarding me a new one here as I had requested American Express sent it to my home in the States."

"I understand this, Mr. Gordon. Thank you. I also understand it was supposed to have arrived by this evening, but, unfortunately, it has not yet. Now, I am sorry to bother you—but I would appreciate it if you might join me in the lobby so we can call American Express together. Due to the fact all deliveries have usually been made by this time, it is imperative we take this step if you'd like to continue your stay."

"I just got out of the shower," I countered. "Why don't I give American Express a call and see exactly what's happening. If there is in fact a problem with delivery, I could have them call you directly and—"

"I apologize, Monsieur Gordon," he cut me off, "but I would prefer you to join me in the lobby."

Huh. I could understand his concern, but such urgency? Something didn't feel right.

"I understand, sir. Of course. Let me get dressed, and I'll be right down."

The toilet flushed, the faucet ran, then Perry emerged from the bathroom as I was hanging up.

"What's going on?" she asked.

Remain calm.

Own your fear. Or your fear will own you.

"I need to go downstairs to check on something. I'll be back up in a few minutes. In the meantime, I need you to get dressed and get our things together."

"Should I be nervous? Is something happening?"

"Maybe. Or maybe not. Either way, it's time to go."

CHAPTER 10

The commute to the hotel following the party at Gary Spencer's abode is a quick one—about thirty feet by foot. We're staying at the Mandarin Oriental, located in the Time Warner Center—a monster real estate endeavor comprised of retail, office space, condominiums, and our hotel across the street from 15 Central Park West. Cobus and I grab a nightcap in the Stone Rose, a low-lit, swanky cocktail haunt on the fourth floor of the Time Warner Center, and discuss both details of our deal as well as the players we just met. Then we head into the hotel, check-in, and retire to our respective rooms for the evening.

Half an hour later, I'm back downstairs. I walk outside, hail a cab, and jump in. Jose Aceveda, my Latin-blooded cab driver who doesn't look a day over sixteen, is listening to mariachi music so loud I could swear the band is sitting in the front seat with him.

"Sixty-Eighth between Second and Third," I borderline scream.

I'm barely done saying the address and Jose tears away from the sidewalk like he's just been given the green flag in the Daytona 500. I'm headed to Perry's building. At this point, with all I've gone through, where I've been, paranoia and being ridiculously careful have become so intertwined I don't even bother trying to differentiate any more between them. My thinking until this point has been simple. Everything about my life, as well as Perry's, since we left nine years ago must be under constant surveillance—phone lines, our homes, our bank accounts, anything directly linked to our lives. That's why I never called her after she and Max were taken. On my cell, from my office, at a pay phone in Amsterdam—it hasn't mattered to me. Whether I'm crazy or not, I've been influenced by the possibility such a call would lead back to me. A chance I simply can't take.

Could Perry even possibly be there? I mean—even if she is okay, could she possibly just be residing at her Upper East Side condo as if nothing ever happened?

I've been through every scenario imaginable. Yes, perhaps, if it was her husband who found her and literally dragged her back to the States. Maybe he took Max, told her if she just accepted she had made the decisions of an unfit mother, she could quietly go on with her life with minimal visitation rights to see her son. Something he wanted for Max—a mother—instead of letting her rot in jail.

On the other hand, if this was somehow related to the authorities finding her, they would have never just let her back into life after what she had done—what she knew—without getting all they could possibly need on me first. And Perry never would have given me up. Anymore than she would have tried to contact me for fear of leading anyone my way.

The ride is quick. Perry's building is mid-block, but I have Jose drop me off on the corner of Sixty-Eighth and Third. It's dark. It's a strange sensation; I grew up in this neighborhood yet as much as it feels like I never left, it feels like a lifetime since I've been here. The neighborhood is quiet, calm. I start down the street, looking at the townhouses lining both sides, thinking of the one I grew up in just ten blocks or so from here. The townhouse where my father was gunned down.

An image of his bullet-popped head on a gurney flashes in my mind.

I don't even flinch from it. I've seen it so many times.

About fifty feet from the entrance to Perry's building, I stop and wait. Though I'm no longer Jonah Gray to the world, for reasons just mentioned I don't need to be caught on the building's security cameras as Ivan Janse or anyone else who's coming looking for a girl who ran with a wanted fugitive years ago.

I stand silently in the night, pretending to speak on my cell phone. A few people walk by, some of them with their dogs. Every few seconds I glance toward the front of the building waiting for my chance. Finally, it comes. A town car pulls up to the front of the building, and the doorman scurries out to open the door. He's been drawn from the property. He's still no doubt on camera. But this doesn't mean I need to be.

A middle-aged woman gets out of the car. The two exchange pleasantries, then she steps in front of him and heads for the building.

"Excuse me," I say.

The doorman turns around.

"Good evening," I continue.

I take a few steps in his direction then pretend to roll my ankle. I stumble and partially crumble to the ground. The doorman, concerned, makes his way over to me. He helps me up.

"Are you all right, sir?" he asks.

I grimace, swallow my first few words, play the part.

"Ahh—yes, I think I'm okay. Thanks," I push out.

He gestures toward the building.

"Would you like to—"

"No, no, really." I cut him off.

I gingerly take a few steps, "walking it off" in a circle.

"Really. I think it's fine," I go on. "I was actually just looking for someone who lives in the building, Perry York. Is she in tonight?"

The doorman doesn't answer. He is clearly surprised by my inquiry.

"Perry York?" I say again. "Is she home?"

"You'll have to forgive me, sir, it's just been a while since anyone mentioned her name. No—Ms. York is not here. In fact, she doesn't live in this building anymore. She hasn't for many years."

"Is that right?" I say, casually as possible. "Huh. Her office must have given me her old address."

The doorman is looking at me as something more than a European guy with bad information. I want to ask more questions: What happened to the apartment? Who lives there now? What happened to Ms. York? But my danger sensors have already kicked into higher gear. Time to move on.

"Anyway, I'll take it up with them tomorrow," I continue. "Sorry to bother you this evening."

I extend my hand. The doorman takes it.

"No bother," he says. "I hope that ankle feels better. I'm sorry— I didn't catch your name."

That's because I didn't give it to you. But nice try.

"Alphonse. Alphonse Bakema."

Instead of hailing a cab, I head uptown on foot. The Upper East Side is quiet. I can hear the leaves rustling on the few interspaced trees dotting the sidewalks. The cool night air is refreshing as it fills my lungs. Ten minutes, and ten or so blocks later, I'm standing across the street from the brownstone I grew up in. I see the structure, the windows, the front door. But it's the memories I see that wash through me, and take my breath away.

I remember the commotion in front of the home the day my pop was murdered. I can see myself all over again running toward the yellow police line. I see a lifeless body that turned out to be my gunned-down father covered with a blood-soaked sheet. Images and memories are flying now in no particular order, without any rhyme or reason. It's like a montage of my life—Jonah Gray's life— is being projected onto the entire front façade of the four-story townhouse. I see my mother whom I've missed every day since she died when I was five. I see my youth. I see myself at all ages coming and going with friends, girls, Pop. I see the beautiful dining room. I see Galina Zhamovsky's—Ia's—drawings lining the staircase wall. I see my father's study.

I see secrets.

So many secrets.

Secrets that led to me being set on so many different paths at once.

Secrets that led me to perhaps giving the world the true meaning behind the lost Imperial Fabergé Easter Eggs.

Secrets that led me to murder.

Secrets that killed Jonah Gray and gave birth to Ivan Janse.

I feel so much I barely feel anything.

Or is it the other way around?

I ball my hands into fists and clench my jaw.

I hail a cab and head to Times Square. Before going back to the hotel, I stop in one of the electronics stores and buy—as always, with cash—a disposable cell phone that can handle domestic and international calls and texts, photos, attachments—all the capabilities I'm going to need.

CHAPTER 11

St. Maxime, France
2004

I closed the door behind me. Instead of getting on the elevator, where Bernot would more likely be looking to see me coming, I decided to use the stairs. Once on the ground floor, I opened the door a crack. I peeked out to get my bearings. I could see the front entrance. Immediately, I realized I was around a corner from both the front and concierge desks, by a nook where both pay phones and house phones were located. I exited the stairwell and picked up the closest phone to the corner I needed to peer around.

Pretending to speak on the phone, I took a casual look, exposing only one eye. The ground floor was rife with activity. People were coming and going. There was a rowdy group sitting around one of the glass-topped tables, enjoying cocktails and champagne. At the front desk I saw Brigette and a tall, dark-haired man wearing horn-rimmed glasses I assumed was Bernot.

And they were talking with two cops.

"Okay," I said upon entering the suite. "Everyone ready to get moving?"

Perry was in the final throes of getting our bags together. Max and Neo were playing tug-of-war with a sock.

"Tell you what," I said, taking her suitcase from her hand, "why don't you let me handle these?"

Our eyes were locked. Perry didn't need to say it. She was nervous.

"Max," I went on, "why don't you take Neo onto the terrace for one last breath of the ocean air?"

"How do you deal with this feeling?" she asked when they were out of earshot.

I was dying inside like she was. I hated that she had to know such uncertainty, a feeling of fear that threatened paralysis. It was at this moment, I vowed, I would never let her see that from me. Strong as she was, I would always be stronger. Especially, when she needed that from me most.

"Not now, Per—we don't have time. Here."

I handed her the car keys.

"We're driving a silver Opel Astra. It is in the third spot from the entrance, as close as possible to the main road. I need you to take Max and Neo, pull the car out, and wait for me. Can you drive a stick?"

She was having trouble focusing.

"When . . . when will—"

I put my hands on her shoulders.

"Perry, there are police downstairs and they are no doubt looking for me. I know this is all becoming much more real than you ever imagined, but I need you to focus. You need to trust me."

She nodded her head yes.

"Can you drive a stick?" I asked again.

"Yes."

"Good. Take Max and Neo—I'll give him to you in his carrier—and walk out of the building casually. Like I said—there are police downstairs so try not to look at anyone for too long, especially them. You never checked in, but people may be able to recognize you as having been with me, so don't draw any attention to your-self. Can you do that?"

"Yes. Yes. Got it. Take Max and Neo, get the car, wait for you."

"What kind of car?"

"Silver Opel Astra."

"Where is it?"

"Third spot from the entrance. Near the street."

"Good girl."

"What about the bags?"

"They're coming out the back with me. I don't want anyone knowing you're leaving."

Dusk was upon us. Our three bags next to me—Perry and Max's suitcase, my small gym bag stuffed with not only the items I grabbed in New York, but my new casual items as well, and my briefcase. I looked over the terrace. I was on the third floor. We'd been in a cor-ner suite. I looked around the corner, around the side of the build-ing back toward the street in front. There was a story-high stone fence separating the rear portion of the property from the begin-ning of the parking lot area. Which made my life a lot more diffi-cult, as once on the ground, I'd have to completely circumnavigate back the other way around the entire property where I knew I could get around the building.

Pool deck area life below had thinned out, but still had life nonetheless. I picked up the bags and moved with them from the long edge of the terrace to the farthest possible east corner of the terrace. I leaned over as far as I could to survey the situation below, then reached down, grabbed my gym bag, leaned over again—swayed my arms to-and-fro a few times to get the right directional momentum—and dropped it on to the terrace below. I waited qui-etly for a second to see if perhaps the occupant of the room belong-ing to that terrace noticed a strange bag falling from the sky.

Nothing.

Next was Perry and Max's suitcase, then my briefcase.

Now it was my turn.

I looked back at the pool area. Evening around me was getting darker by the second. The remaining people were either into their poolside cocktails or gathering up their children and belongings. Most important, none of them seemed to be looking up in my direction.

Moving around the terrace like I'd been put on fast-forward, I bounced yet again back to the short side. I leaned over. What was the best way exactly to do this? I put my leg up on the rail—but the position didn't feel right. Going forward meant I was going straight to the ground. I brought my foot back down. My breathing was gaining rapidity. I stepped up again, this time turning around as I did so. I stepped completely over with my right foot, placing it just under the rail on the other side but still on the top of the terrace wall, then my left. Now, hands holding the rail, I was facing the building. I was in a crouched position. My feet were only inches below my hands. I turned my head as far as it would go while looking down. The outside of the terrace was smooth, which meant there was nowhere else to put my feet until the next terrace below.

I was in a stare with the ground below when I heard a door slam. Fuck—was it my room? Had the cops entered my room? Time was ticking. Was Perry clear—or had she run into trouble? I needed to go. At that moment. No more thinking.

I took my feet from the top of the terrace wall and let them slide down below. As I dangled, I removed my right hand hoping to dip down just enough to gain a visual for even one second that might give me an idea of what to grab. Then I heard another door slam and lost my grip completely. As I sped past the top of the second-floor terrace, I stuck my stiffened arms out. I did my best to muffle a scream as my forearms slammed into the top of the railing. My right one bounced right off, but with the will of an Olympic gymnast on the uneven bars I managed to keep my left—post-bounce—close enough to the bar to get one more shot. My left hand grabbed the railing, and in a millisecond my right was back on it as well. I hoisted myself up and over.

My breathing ragged, I grabbed both of my forearms. The pain was shooting, and especially sharp in the right. I looked over, down below. All was still as clear as I could hope. I dropped the three bags over the terrace to the ground. One story I could handle. I got up over the railing, faced forward with both feet on the top of the terrace wall, and jumped.

My timing was right, and my knees gave at precisely the moment I needed them to as I fell into a semicomfortable roll forward, breaking the fall. Quickly I slung the gym bag over my shoulder, picked up the suitcase handle in my left hand, and my briefcase with my right. I headed for the pool deck.

Look natural.

A guest having a last look at the property before departing.

Keeping my gait steady I decided to use the outermost path around the area, the route that took me along the two-and-a-half-foot wall separating the deck from the rocky shore leading to the Mediterranean. Everything was calm. I looked at the building, glowing against the impending night. Hearing the breaking surf, I looked to my right. I wanted one more look at the white foam, which by now I could barely see.

About halfway around the deck, I heard a new French-speaking voice enter the mix. It was somewhat distant. I looked back toward the building. One of the two cops had appeared. And he was speaking with a bikini-clad male guest.

Without a thought I quietly slinked over the wall. The rocky ground below was more uneven than I'd thought. As I placed the bags down next to me snug up against the wall, the suitcase tumbled about fifteen feet away. I wanted to go after it, but didn't want to risk being seen moving beyond the wall.

For a few moments, my back against the wall, I sat silently. The two were still talking. After a few more seconds, their conversation ended.

I had no idea where the cop was now or where he was going.

As I gathered my nerve, about to peek over, another conversation started. This time it was the cop and a woman. I listened. Where were they exactly? It sounded like he had walked a bit east on the deck, but I couldn't be sure. Lifting nothing more than my eyes past the crest of the wall, I looked. I was right. He had walked east. He was about a hundred feet from me. When the conversation came to an end, the cop seemed to be turning in my direction.

Eyes wide, I retook my place, back to the wall. I looked up. The stars were beginning to pop. I listened. I waited.

Thirty seconds later—nothing. He hadn't initiated another conversation, or at least one I could hear. I had no idea where he was. He could have left. He could have been right upon me. Either way, I needed to keep moving. Perry, Max, and Neo were waiting for me.

And I wasn't about to leave them waiting because my guard had fallen.

I looked over again. The cop was walking around, surveying the area. He was west of me now, but closer to the wall, no more than thirty feet away. Like a fox lying in wait, I watched him. I registered his every move, breath. If he only came back east, then past me, I could continue in my intended direction along the outside of the wall. But until then—until he was well past me in the opposite direction—I couldn't risk him hearing me navigate the challenging terrain.

I watched. I waited. Finally, it was happening. He was circling back, heading to the east side of the deck. His vision was forward. As he was about midway, directly in front of me now, a large wave crashed behind me. The cop looked toward the ocean, toward me.

Then he stopped walking.

I dropped back down. And at that moment, my line of vision now exactly the same as his, I realized he hadn't seen me. He was looking at the suitcase fifteen feet in front of me.

Which meant he was on his way.

I braced myself for battle. There was no escape now. Chaos was upon me. Quietly as I could, I swung my legs left to put them as close to the wall as possible and keep myself out of sight for as long as I could.

I could hear his footsteps. They were getting faster. Adrenaline shot through my body so intense I thought my head might explode, but I managed to remain still as the rock I was sitting on. My lips were slightly open to make sure even my breaths were silent. Then, as I had anticipated, it happened. Slowly the cop's head and upper torso appeared above me.

And I was ready to go to that place I'd learned to go.

Like Carmelo Anthony exploding toward the rim for a jam, I lifted off the rock, grabbed a fistful of his uniform chest-high with my right hand, and flung him over the wall. The pain in my forearm was over the top, but I welcomed it. I appreciated the reminder of the kind of pain I needed to inflict.

The cop let out a yell when he landed on the ragged backdrop, tumbling end over end. As he rolled, I was already after him like an animal. When he stopped, I was already pouncing. Before he could even comprehend what happened, I was on his chest. Under the night light I could see blood on his face. I didn't care. Before he could speak, I pounded him with two massive rights across his jaw. He tried to look up at me but went limp. I started to get off him, blood trickling from my knuckles, but as I did he started flailing his arms and legs as human nature kicked in. I pinned his chest down with my knees again. Then I gritted my teeth, loaded up, and gave him another right that laid him out.

As I rushed up on the car, Perry, who had thrown on jeans and a white wifebeater, slid across to the passenger seat. I dropped the bags in the back next to Max then jumped in. As I grabbed the stick and released the clutch, Neo—in his carrier on Perry's lap— poked his head out, leaned forward, and licked my bloody knuckles.

My breathing pace somewhat restored, I embraced what had just happened, let it seep into me. Because it was confirmation the plan I was about to put into motion was not just the right one, it was the only one.

"We ready?" I asked, rolling all the windows down.

I needed to be able to hear the first note of a siren.

Perry swallowed. Then nodded yes.

I pulled out on the Boulevard Jean Moulin portion of the Bord de Mer and headed back toward Nice.

CHAPTER 12

At eight forty-five a.m. the following morning we settle into a conference room in GlassWell's headquarters. Their executive offices take up floors forty-six through fifty of 1112 Avenue of the Americas, one of their most impressive holdings. The property, a one-point-five-million-square-foot white travertine façade covered beast, stands almost six hundred fifty feet in the air. We're hovering at around the six-hundred-thirty-foot mark on floor fifty, overlooking Bryant Park.

The conference room is one of the longest I have ever been in. It's contemporary, sleek. The conference table is unusual, imposing—a mahogany-framed rectangular slab of chocolate-and-white swirled Italian marble that could probably seat fifty. The kind of table my father once taught me firms use to gain subconscious advantage. A couple-ton piece of rock that needs to be craned into a building so people can have somewhere to write and a place their coffee lets you know you're dealing with people who like to win. The carpet underfoot is a matching chocolate, the walls are beige, the ceiling is white with perfectly placed white Luxo Silvy hanging light fixtures. As everyone says their last "good mornings" and grabs coffee, fresh fruit, and bagels from the platters on top of the beige Vox credenzas, I take my seat with just ice water. Our team had already huddled over breakfast at the hotel.

If the table is a football field, we're seated at around the twenty-five yard line facing the windows—me on one side of Cobus, Arnon on the other. Next to us, going toward the closer end, is the beginning of GlassWell's team—in-house counsel, some operations people, some property management people.

In-house counsel.

I could have been sitting next to Scott Green at this very moment.

An image of his brain splattered on the wall flashes in my mind.

The string of GlassWell corporate starts opposite us with leasing, then stretches around and heads back our way with acquisitions. Leasing and acquisitions. I catch Julia's eye across from me just as she's about to sit down.

"Good morning, Cobus, Ivan," she says.

"Good morning," I say back.

Cobus waves cordially as he's finishing a call with Europe.

"Sleep well?" she went on to me directly through the surrounding conversations.

You mean with one eye open? As I do every night of my life?

"Like a rock," I answer.

I can't help noticing how great Julia looks even when dressed for the boardroom. Gray Armani silk/linen fitted ruffled jacket with matching straight-leg pants over a white stretch jersey tee. Julia's two for two. There's something just incredibly sexy about a woman so stylish she can light it up no matter the situation.

The only thing sexier?

A woman who knows it.

"Let's get to it," Brand says as he takes his seat.

We jump in. The conversation begins with some legal issues regarding international transfer of title. Arnon essentially gives GlassWell's in-house counsel a lesson in the matter. Soon we move on to some housekeeping. When it comes to the closing of a property deal, the last issues often center around—big surprise—money. Who's going to pay for what unforeseen items following the closing, last-minute price adjustments because of further repairs or improvements that need to be done, whose responsibility undetected building code violations buried within the Department of Buildings database are, things like that. I'm entrenched in reviewing some language with Arnon and Cobus regarding preexisting environmental issues arising post closing when a discussion in the room turns to the property's HVAC system.

"That's right. The building is serviced by two five-hundred-ton chillers, three Worthington Centrifugal pumps and two five-hundred-ton cooling towers on the roof," one of the GlassWell property management cronies says. "But I believe the chillers were installed in 2003. And they have been—"

"The chillers were installed in 2001," I chime in, my eyes still on the legal language we're reviewing. "And I believe some of the other specifications you were just discussing were off a bit as well. The electricity in the property is not two-hundred-twenty volts, but in fact two-hundred-*forty* volts to go along with seventy-five-hundred amps and six watts per usable square foot. And it isn't just the fourteenth floor with increased height—"

My eyes still on the document, my right hand, pen extended, motions from the ceiling to the floor back to the ceiling.

"The seventeenth floor is fourteen feet slab to slab as well."

My brain switches gears.

"Arnon, why is this sentence worded like this?" I ask, pointing to the page.

No response.

I look up at Arnon.

That's when I notice he, as well as Cobus, the property management team, Julia, Brand, and others, are just staring at me.

Shit. Jonah Gray knows this building better than GlassWell does.

But Ivan Janse shouldn't.

"Anything else about the specifications of our property you'd like to correct me on?" asks the property management crony.

Yeah, I'm thinking, you forgot to mention the façade of the building is landmarked also—not just the lobby.

"Just looking to be thorough—um—"

"Roger."

"Roger. In fact I've been known to overdo it a bit when it comes to things like research, fact-checking, reviewing—no need to take it personally."

I stand up.

"Excuse me. Which way to the restroom?" I ask no one in particular.

I start down the hallway. It, like the offices and interior bullpens I pass, is of the same contemporary furnishings, style, and colors as the conference room. I reach my right hand into my left inside suit jacket pocket. I remove the disposable phone.

I dial information, and within seconds—after receiving a text containing the number I just requested—I'm being connected to the office of gynecologist Dr. Brian York. Perry's asshole, low-life husband.

"Doctor's office," a pert female voice answers.

"Hi," I jump right in. "This is Richard Everton from the Department of Education. I'm calling with regard to Max York, as this is the phone number on record. We're in the process of compiling statewide results based on this year's student performance, but unfortunately an administrative error on our end has caused some confusion with where Max is currently enrolled. Now we're showing he's at—"

"I believe Max is enrolled at Columbia Grammar," the voice cuts me off. "Hold on and I'll double-check."

Thirty seconds later she's back.

"Yep—Columbia Grammar. Upper West Side."

Without breaking stride, I thank her and hang up. I place the phone back in my left inside pocket. A cute, African American girl with short hair dressed in a smart black pantssuit is coming toward me.

"Excuse me, I think I'm a bit lost," I say to her, "can you possibly point me in the direction of Ryan Brand's office?"

Brand's assistant has her own office next to her boss. I peek in. She's on the phone. She'd been in the conference room earlier. We recognize each other.

"I think I may have left my phone in—" I start, doing a half-whisper talking thing as I point toward Brand's office so as to not disturb her.

She waves me on while continuing her conversation as an "of course" expression crosses her face. I step next door. The corner office is bold, just like the man. As I walk in, in front of me, is a sleek set of four timeless brown Knoll Barcelona chairs surrounding a small glass-top coffee table. Diagonally from where I'm standing, in the corner, where the two back walls that are essentially all windows meet, is Brand's desk—a leather-finished minimalist piece by BassamFellows. Nice. Humanscale Freedom Headrest chair behind it. Also nice. Dude knows his furniture.

To my right, wrapping around beyond where one can see when entering the room, the windows run into another perpendicular wall holding a huge flat-screen on CNBC. Under the TV, like the wall to my immediate left upon entering, are framed articles about and pictures of different GlassWell properties.

I step in and, like someone's watching, pretend for a second to look for my phone. I reach my left hand into my suit jacket's inside right pocket and touch the pen. After a quick look by the chairs and coffee table, I head straight for the desk. Files neatly stacked, iPad charging, desktop PC, family photos—one thing is for sure. Brand is an organized guy.

But there's no sign of a desktop pen set of any kind.

Damn.

A pen from Scott Green.

I remember his words.

"That pen has everything to do with this deal," he said. "That pen, my young friend, is everything."

Why?

Whose pen is it?

My mind searching, calculating, organizing, shuffling, I walk out of the office. I poke my head back into Brand's assistant's office.

"No luck," I say doing that half-talk, half-whisper thing again. "Where would I find legal?"

I walk down the internal staircase to the forty-ninth floor, and hook an immediate left. Realizing I'm close to the point people will be wondering what's taking me so long my gait picks up, stopping just short of becoming suspicious. Thirty yards down the hall I see a name on the wall outside an office with the lights off.

Scott Green.

I quickly look around. No eyes in my direction. I step inside. I close the door and turn the lights on. The feeling is eerie. It's like the office is just sitting and waiting for Green's return, like he'll just walk back in here and pick right up with whatever is open on his desk waiting for his attention. It's quiet. Unlike Brand's office, this one is a mess. All the same fixtures, colors, and carpet, but that's it aside from a few family photos on the walls. There are stacks of files everywhere—the desk, the couch, the floor, everywhere.

I walk over to the desk. It's a disaster, like someone just walked over with arms full of files, pens, pencils, staplers, an older model desktop PC, calendar, cans of Diet Coke, Tums, Post-its, rubber bands, bills, magazines, newspapers—and just dropped it all. In the chaos I do see a desktop pen set.

Both pens are in their spots.

And they're brass.

Damn.

What am I missing?

As my mind starts flying again, my eyes search the top of the desk for anything. And they stop on an envelope. It's a cable bill. It's addressed to Scott Green: 166 East 30th Street. I take out my iPhone, type in the address, and place the cell back in my suit jacket's right inside pocket. Just as I do, and I'm heading back toward the door, I hear the doorknob turning.

The door opens just as I'm upon it. Two men, dressed casually but nicely in pants, button-down shirts, and sport jackets, are in front of me.

"Oh, I'm sorry," the one who opened the door says. He's white, athletically built with a shaved dome, has sharp, green eyes, and chiseled facial features. "We were looking for…"

He cranes his neck backwards and looks again at Scott Green's name on the wall outside the office.

"No. It's me who's in the wrong place," I jump in. "I was looking for my phone and I wandered into this office. I got lost."

"Detective Lovell," he introduces himself. "Do you work here?"

I notice the shield on his belt.

"I don't," I respond. "My firm's doing a deal with GlassWell. We're in the office today for meetings."

"Got it. Do you know Mr. Green?"

Interesting. They're referring to him as if he's still alive. Must be in their DNA. After all, I am in the guy's office. And he did die under what one might call suspicious circumstances, to put it mildly.

"Who?"

"Mr. Green. The man who's office you're in."

"Ah, right. Sorry, no. Can't say that I do. Like I said, I was wandering around and, well, this seemed like an office I had previously been in, but—"

I start to move forward.

"Anyway, I'm going to get back, so—"

"Of course."

The detective steps aside. I walk between him and his Asian-

American counterpart, a man who looks like he's either the most serious man on the planet or is actually in the process of shitting his pants.

I'm three steps past when Cue Ball speaks to me again.

"Oh, Mr.—"

I turn around.

"Janse."

"Mr. Janse. Good luck finding that phone."

CHAPTER 13

New York City
2013

At two p.m., following five hours of working toward a close on the Freedom Bank Building, we exit 1112 Avenue of the Americas. The plan is for me, Cobus, and Arnon to head to the target property for a walk-through. I need to lose them.

"Nice work, boys," Cobus says. "We're almost there."

He looks at his watch.

"Let's get moving. Where's the car?"

Just as he asks, an Escalade comes rolling to a stop in front of us.

"*Doorgaan*," I blurt out, which is "go on" in Dutch. "You two go ahead."

"What's up?" asks Cobus.

"Roof documents," I respond.

All of which are in the briefcase I'm holding.

"Specs, past as well as the most recent inspection reports, my notes—I left all my roof-related materials in my room. I'm not sold the north portion doesn't need to be replaced from taking the brunt of winter's weather. I want everything with me when we walk it."

The hotel is out of the way. It's back west and we're standing only fifteen blocks from the target. I put my arm up for a cab.

"Mike O'Grady is the chief building engineer," I go on. "He'll be waiting for you in the lobby to take you through. I'll catch up with you in a bit."

"Our schedule is tight," Cobus says. "If possible, I'd like to meet Larry Elman for a drink before dinner."

Larry Elman oversees retail leasing for all GlassWell properties. Cobus wants to talk about the target's retail tenants, as well as retail in the surrounding submarket as a whole. Dinner, as he's referring to it, is with the GlassWell team at Del Posto.

"So try and be quick about it," he goes on.

A cab on the far side of the street slashes through traffic on a dangerous sixty-degree angle to pick me up. It's like the driver can sense my urgency. Other cabs, a bus, civilian cars, all honk furiously. I jump in.

"Let's head toward the Upper West Side," I say to the cab driver. He or she could be Santa Claus for all I know as my nose is already buried in the disposable as I access the browser. I go to Google, and type in "Columbia Grammar NYC."

"Ninety-Third and Central Park West," I continue, as we head up Sixth Avenue.

My eyes hidden behind gray-shaded turquoise Gucci lenses, I walk east along the south side of Ninety-Fifth Street toward the park. I hear kids laughing, playing, and screaming. I walk toward the joyous, youthful voices. As I get closer I can start to see a red brick building come into focus across the street: Columbia Grammar and Prep, a prestigious private school for children grades kindergarten through twelve. Straining my eyes, I do my best to glance while maximizing my shades and peripheral-vision skills.

My timing is right-on. It looks like school just let out. Kids are everywhere. Black, white, Asian, Latin, every ethnicity under the sun seems to be represented within only a hundred square yards of Manhattan sidewalk.

Near the main entrance, on the stairs, a bunch of boys toward the older end of the spectrum are talking. Apparently they're cracking jokes or discussing something funny as they all keep bursting into laughter at the same time. Only one of the boys isn't laughing.

Max.

He's staring right at me.

I stop.

Thank God. Max. He's safe.

I swallow hard. My eyes well up. My legs feel weak. Like if even for just a few seconds I want to collapse to the ground, let all the worry that's been bottled up for these last years spill out of me onto the sidewalk.

I also feel an overwhelming sense of hope.

If only a safe Max means a safe Perry.

I know my window is small. I quickly scan the area and notice the strategically placed adult supervisors because of the younger children. I look back at Max. I cross the street and head toward the school. He takes the cue and begins toward me.

He wraps his arms around me. I squeeze him back.

"Max," I say. "Oh, man. I'm so happy to see you. I missed you."

Window.

I pull my face back. I take him by the tops of his arms, by his shoulders, and separate us just enough to face each other.

"Are you okay?" I go on. "Are you safe?"

He nods.

I look him up and down.

"My God," I say, realizing he's almost as tall as me, "you're a man now. You look like you even shave. College in the works?"

"I'm going to Syracuse next year."

"Syracuse," I repeat. "Good for you. Great school. Look, I couldn't—" I change direction, stammering, "I couldn't . . . I mean, I didn't . . . or, I didn't not want—"

"I know," he said, surprising me.

"You know what?"

"That you've been worried. And that we wouldn't have been there with you if my mom didn't think it was the right thing."

I move my right hand gently from his arm to the side of his face.

"You're so smart. And so brave."

In all of this, I still have zero idea why they were taken. How they were found. What went down.

"How about Mom?" I go on. "Is she okay too?"

"I don't know," Max responds with a shrug. "I hope so."

"What do you mean? You haven't seen her?"

"Uh-huh. Not since that day."

"That day," I repeat. "You mean—"

"That day. The last day we saw you."

I feel like I'm going to vomit. Or pass out. Maybe vomit then pass out. Or vice versa.

What the fuck is going on?

So many questions.

Window.

"You haven't seen her—but have you talked to her?"

"Uh-uh. Dad said she went away. And that she isn't ever coming back."

"Is that right," I respond to this interesting nugget. "What else did Dad say?"

"That sometimes the stars align when we least expect it. That's how I made it back to him."

Out of the corner of my eye, I sense something. I look, and a heavyset, thirty-something brunette is headed my way.

Time for one more.

"How about me? Did you ever tell your Dad about me?"

He shook his head no.

"I've never told anyone about you. Mom whispered in my ear not to when—"

The teacher reaches me.

"Excuse me."

"Hi—Ken Millman," I say, extending my hand. "I'm Brian York's cousin."

We shake.

"I'm in from Connecticut, and even though we're all having

dinner together, I figured I'd swing by and say hi to Max since I was doing a little uptown shopping."

I turn to Max and tussle his hair.

"I'll be seeing you later."

I jump in a cab.

"One Sixty-Six East Thirtieth," I say to the cab driver.

CHAPTER 14

While en route, the salty Côte d'Azur air surging through the car as we hugged the coastline, Perry called Rail Europe on the disposable cell I'd purchased at the airport. Little more than an hour after leaving La Belle Aurore, we were on the 8:52 p.m. train from Nice, getting in to the Lyon Part-Dieu station at 1:10 a.m. where we'd be picking up our connection—the 3:50 a.m. from Lyon Part-Dieu arriving in Geneva at 5:36 a.m. We were on a TGV, one of the fastest trains in the world. Perry purchased four premier class tickets in cash.

The premier cabin was basically empty, for which I was thankful. Upon walking into the cabin, solo seats were to the left and duo seats—two per row next to the window, as opposed to one—were to the right. An older couple occupied seats 12 and 13, the first duo row. A thirty-something woman was sound asleep in the third solo seat. There was no one else. We took the last two duo rows, seats 62 and 63 followed by 65 and 66.

The lights were low. The main illumination was from the bright night sky blanketing the passing French countryside coming through the windows. Within minutes Max was fast asleep in seat 62, and Neo was out on his side in his carrier in 63. We were behind them. Perry was in seat 66, the window, and I had the aisle, seat 65. I took the disposable from Perry and dialed. As she sat next to me, we stared into each other's eyes as it rang. She had no idea who I was calling.

"Hello?" asked an older gentleman's voice on the other end.

Gaston Piccard. He was one of my father's closest friends and our financial consultant based in Geneva. Gaston had overseen every aspect of our portfolio overseas since my father started making real cash back in the day. He managed not only our Swiss bank accounts, but he'd helped us devise every aspect of our financial portfolio both domestic and foreign as to how best shelter us from what some Americans might see as "unnecessary" taxes. Not only was he one of the most respected, sophisticated, and loyal bankers in Switzerland—if not the world—reaching this level in life clearly told me he must also be one of the most resourceful.

And for the plan I was looking to put in play, to say I'd need serious resources was an understatement.

"Gaston. It's Jonah."

He didn't respond.

"Gaston?"

"Yes—yes Jonah. I'm here. I'm just—I'm so sorry about your father."

"I appreciate that, Gaston."

More silence.

"I'm in Europe. I'm just leaving—"

"Jonah—your father and I—we certainly go way back, and I have the utmost respect for him, for your family. But I just—I'm just—"

"Gaston—please. I need your help."

"Jonah, I'm sure I don't have to tell you but you are serious international news right now! I mean—"

Gaston, becoming more anxious with each passing second,

reeled his voice back in. "I mean, according to the news you are an international fugitive. And they're saying you may be tied to your own father's murder."

"I know, Gaston, I know what they're saying. But it's not as it seems. Please. You need to believe me."

More silence.

"I know you believe me. You've known me my whole life. You've known me since I was a little kid. I'm a lot of things. But I could never be who the cops or FBI think I've become. You have to believe me."

I heard a sigh on the other end. I kept going.

"I promise I will tell you everything. But, for now, as I'm running for my fucking life, I have no one else to turn to, Gaston. You have always been one of the most trusted members of my father's inner circle. If my father were still alive—and I needed his advice on who to call right now, at this very moment—he'd be telling me to call you."

"Okay, Jonah, okay."

"You've been so loyal to us, Gaston. I'd never want to put you in harm's way. But this is literally my life we're dealing with here."

"Where are you?" he asked.

"On the train from Nice. I'll be in Geneva first thing in the morning."

"How did you get to the train station?"

That was the question I wanted to hear. It was the question that meant Gaston wanted to know how I'd been covering my tracks. Which meant he was now invested in my survival.

"Rental car from the airport. I left it in the middle of the parking lot."

"What did you do with the keys?"

"I took them with me."

"Good. Give them to me when I pick you up. I'll deal with the car."

Just as I suspected. Resources.

"What time exactly do you get in?"

"We get in at five thirty-six a.m."

"We?"

"Like I said, I promise to tell you everything."

"Silver Bentley Mulsanne. Five thirty-six a.m. Till then."

I hung up the phone. Perry pulled her eyes from the passing countryside and buried them deep into my own. She reached up, put her hand on my face. Without a word, we spoke to one another. I put my hand on hers, moved her fingers to my mouth, and kissed them.

Perry started to stand up. As she did, I grabbed her hips firmly, and helped her straddle me. We kissed each other slowly, deeply, passionately. All we could hear were our choppy, nervous breaths against the sound of the train slicing through the night. My mouth moved to her right shoulder. As I savored the taste of her bronzed skin, I lifted her wifebeater up to her neck. It wasn't long until my lips tasted her chest and her right breast was in my mouth. I wanted every inch of her, had wanted every inch of her for years. Chills shot up my spine as she ran her fingers through my hair. Every stroke, kiss, breath from each of us was strong yet laced with restraint. We wanted to tear each other apart. But our boys were sleeping soundly in front of us.

At 5:36 a.m. on the dot our train stopped in Geneva. My senses on overdrive, the four of us quickly got off and followed signs for the exit. The dawn air was crisp, invigorating. Immediately I noticed Gaston though I hadn't seen him in years. Not simply because there were so few cars waiting to pick up passengers at this hour, but because he was memorable. He was a tall man—around six foot three—with a full head of bushy silver hair and strong facial features. Inside Gaston Piccard was a swirl of brilliance and bigheartedness. Outside he had a big head, big nose, big hands, an imposing figure.

Gaston was in his silver Bentley. As we walked toward it, I saw the trunk pop. I threw in our bags, put Max and Perry in the backseat, and jumped in the front with Neo's bag on my lap. Gaston nodded hello, and we pulled out. My eyes wandered as we did, and noticed from the fine automobile's details we were not only in Bentley's top-of-the-line model but a Mulliner commissioned one, or essentially a custom-built Bentley. A serious car for a serious man.

It wasn't long until it was clear we were leaving the city limits.

"Where are we going?" I asked.

He put his hand out. I gave him the rental car keys, which he dropped in the inside pocket of his blazer.

"Somewhere safe."

He looked in the rearview mirror at his backseat passengers.

"Tell me everything, Jonah. And don't leave anything out."

Perry handed Max his mini-DVD player, put headphones on him, and pushed play for whatever video he'd been watching. For the next four hours, I filled Gaston in on everything from the moment I found *Danish Jubilee Egg* in my briefcase until my call to him the night before and everything in between. Accidentally shooting the dirty cop bastard trying to shake me down, the real story surrounding my father's murder, the Fabergé egg situation, the connection between Galina Zhamovsky, my father, Andreu Zhamovsky, me—all of it. At times I wanted to blast my fist through the windshield. Other times I wanted to crumble from the weight of reliving it all again.

We rolled into the beautiful Canton of St. Gallen, Switzerland, into the town of Valens. Our heads were all on swivels. There were lush green fields and scattered farms. We were so high up in the rolling mountains it felt like we could reach up and grab the unencumbered, low-hanging blue sky. For the first time in what felt like an eternity, I could breathe.

I felt safe.

We pulled into the driveway of a huge mountaintop chalet. We walked inside. The open space footprint was bathed with light from every angle. There were windows everywhere. The foyer and "Great Room" immediately in front of us must have been three-stories high. All of us were drawn toward the rear wall of the home—a solid wall-to-wall, ceiling-to-floor piece of glass—like a magnet was pulling us. We slowly walked toward it. As we got closer, it felt like we could fall out of the back of the house like it was a cliff. We were so entrenched in the view of the Tamina Valley, I could feel myself almost losing my balance. Once up against the glass all three of us put our hands out as if to make sure there was really even a window there. Neo put his front paws up on it as well and stood looking out with us.

"Perry, Max—why don't you take, um—"

I turned around and looked at Gaston. He was looking at Neo.

"Neo," I said.

"Why don't you both take Neo out for a walk. Explore the property a bit."

Perry looked at me.

I nodded.

"It's a good idea. Gaston and I need to talk."

As Gaston gave Perry a verbal lay of the land, I continued to look out into the valley. I heard them behind me, but not really. I was consumed with the wide-angle lens view of the world in front of me. I started thinking about my father. I remembered what he looked like the last time I saw him. In a coffin.

The door slammed. I turned around. Gaston took a seat on a huge, white couch adorned with what seemed to be a hundred brown throw pillows.

"What comes next, Jonah? What do you want?"

"I want a new identity," I said.

"Passports, ID—let's say I can handle documentation needs for all three of you. Then what?"

"I didn't say passports, Gaston. I said a new identity."

I walked over and sat down a few feet away from him on the couch.

"I want to literally change my identity. Become a different person."

"What are you talking about?"

"Plastic surgery. I don't want to look like Jonah Gray again. I can't. Not if I'm going to keep on living. Not if I'm going to go the places I need to go. Not if I'm going to get a chance to clear my name."

"Jonah, that makes no sense. What you need is time, which you can take here. Time to get all the facts in order, put the missing pieces together, clear your—"

I started shaking my head.

"No," I broke in, "it's not that easy. Too much has happened. It's not like I can just turn myself in and say, wait! Please! This is what really happened."

"Why not?"

"Because there is evidence against me on one side. And people who want me dead on the other."

"Jonah—"

"I can never go home, Gaston—"

At least, not yet.

"Even trying to clear my name will take time. I have no choice but to forge a new path. As a new person. I have thought long and hard about this. There simply is no other option."

What I wasn't telling Gaston was that clearing my name was only part of the mission. I had to find out the true mystery behind those eggs. What they meant. If I didn't, everything that had led to this exact moment would have been for nothing. There was no way I could leave Valens, Switzerland, as Jonah Gray. Jonah Gray was a wanted man the whole globe over.

And with all that had gone on, I had way too much unfinished business.

"I told you about the insurance money. Cash will never be an issue as my existing accounts never need to be touched. The first order of business is accounts being set up in numerous tax-shelter countries aside from Switzerland. The second order of business is turning this place into a plastic surgeon's office."

"Forget it," Gaston said. "I simply can't be party to this, Jonah. I know you are in trouble. And I genuinely believe you have been dragged into something you didn't ask for. But I have a lot to lose here—a family, a career, my whole life. I can give you this chalet to take a little time to get this situation sorted out. But that, unfortunately, is all I can give."

"Gaston, please. We both know I have the money, and you have the resources."

"Jonah, I'm sorry. I have too much to lose. More than you could ever know."

He stood up from the couch. He looked down at me.

"Like I said, my home is your home for a bit of time. And I'll be happy to provide whatever essentials I can in the meantime, as well as what you might need once you leave."

He turned and started to walk toward what looked to be the kitchen.

"That's it?" I said. "Years of loyalty as a family, numerous clients sent your way that probably accounted for a good portion of your business, and that's it?"

Forget that we were a good part of Gaston Piccard's ability to own a country chalet, this was life or death. I may have been surrounded by luxury, but I needed to remain in survivor mode.

Get what you need. Always. Leave the mess for later.

"My father and I talked about a lot of things, Gaston. We talked about you."

He stopped in his tracks.

"You said it yourself, Gaston. My father wasn't just a client, he was a friend. And friends talk. I know about your clients—who they are, which tax havens they prefer. How much money they are avoiding taxes on."

He turned around.

"Bullshit, Jonah. I don't buy it."

"The Lowensteins hide family money behind numerous shell corporate entities in Luxembourg and the British Virgin Islands—

about a hundred million in each jurisdiction. The Berks, who own—shit, I forgot the name of it—that big-box chain of home-repair stores all over the world—anyway, they've got closer to a billion spread out around Gibraltar, Belize, and Vanuatu."

Silence.

"Buy that? If you'd like, I'm happy to keep going. In fact, I think there may have been a story or two involving some celebrities."

Gaston took a defeated breath and returned to the couch.

CHAPTER 15

The cab comes to a stop on Thirtieth Street between Park and Madison. I pay and get out. As I hear the tires pull away from the curb behind me, I look up and notice the sky has gone gray. I look at number 166 and think Scott Green must have been a smart, sensible guy. Beautiful brownstone, no doubt a strong property as far as the buy. Great neighborhood, without great neighborhood pricing. Probably three or four million for the townhouse. Upper East or West Side would be double that.

I don't have a game plan, aside from assessing the situation once the front door opens and devising a game plan. The building is interesting. It looks to be prewar, but some of the architecture suggests a facelift around this last turn of the century. The basement and parlor-floor-level facades are limestone. Above them the building rises in red Philadelphia brick, four stories in all, and is topped off with a copper mansard roof.

I head toward the wide staircase that gracefully fades left leading up to the porch and entrance. When I take the first step, I'm surprised when the front door opens. A sixty-something couple exits. All of a sudden I hear voices behind me. I turn around. Two men who appear in their forties are approaching the house.

What's going on?

I keep moving so as not to look suspicious. The couple exiting leaves the front door a couple inches ajar for me. I push it open. Off to the left, just past the entrance foyer, is a small table with a tall candle burning on it. Beyond that I can see into the dining room. The long table is covered with cakes, pastries, bagels with all the trimmings, pitchers of water, juice, and coffeepots. Immediately I get it.

Scott Green was Jewish.

And I am apparently now making a shivah call.

I slowly move through the downstairs floor. Unlike a party where people are looking to introduce themselves, socialize, this is obviously different. Everyone around me is keeping to their own, quiet, respectful. I decide floating around silently, looking to seamlessly blend in and find Green's home office, is the way to go, but I'm apprehensive. What if the widow or some family member finds me snooping?

I find my way into the living room, a high-ceilinged, warm room with a predominantly deep-red theme. The walls, the couches, the area rugs over the dark wood floor—all deep, rich red like blood at the exact moment it comes through skin. Old World, wrought-iron chandeliers with candles hang from chains above.

It doesn't take long to identify Green's widow. She's sitting on a plush, burgundy love seat. She's a slight woman, pretty. Her hair is brown and straight past her shoulders. She's wearing black pants, a matching black blouse, and comfortable black Tod's Ballerinas on her feet. Her face is sad but shows a forced half smile as she speaks with some people offering their condolences. Her eyes are also dark, focused. She's sitting gracefully, legs crossed. In the moment she strikes me as strong, confident, and sweet.

I walk toward her, unsure of where to begin. Time is thin. I overhear the conversation she's having end with, "No, really, I'm fine to get it myself. I need to stretch my legs."

I move in.

"I'm truly sorry for your loss," I say, extending my hand.

She takes it. Her hand is tiny and even more delicate than I would have guessed. Though her grip is bordering on firm, I can't help noticing I could crush her fingers like dried leaves.

"I appreciate that," she replies, now fully standing. She can't be taller than four foot ten inches.

Her expression can't suppress her puzzlement.

"I was wondering—" I continue, stepping left away from the immediate people around us as she takes her hand back, "if we might just speak for one second. You see—"

"I'm sorry," she cuts me off, "and I apologize if I should remember your name. There have been so many people coming and going, and, well, as you might imagine—"

"Of course. I understand. This must be a really difficult time."

She's waiting.

"I knew your husband through work. We were involved together on the Freedom Bank Building. It turns out—"

"You work at GlassWell?" she interrupts, her eyes hardening a bit.

"No. I work with a different firm. We're in the process of purchasing this particular property, and, well, if we might—"

Whether it was the mention of knowing her husband from work, or this particular deal, her comfort level with my presence changes right before my eyes. In a blink, she's pissed. Her face goes sour.

"How dare you?" she seethes. "You have the nerve to just walk into my house? My husband's house? Like all is fine and well?"

Tiny Woman becomes aggressive. She starts toward me like she's going to make a move. Like perhaps she's going to reach out—for her, up—and grab my balls as hard as she can. Or take the closest hot coffee she can find and throw it in my face. I actually start backing up.

"I apologize. I certainly have no intention of upsetting you," I respond, my hands up slightly in front of me in a conciliatory manner. "If we can just speak for a second, maybe—"

"Really? If we can just speak? You people—you people are responsible for him being dead!" she goes on, her voice elevated.

I look around. We're now making a full-blown scene.

"You get the fu—" she starts before reeling in her voice. She comes even closer. "You get the hell out of this house," she snarls.

I take a deep breath.

"Please. Mrs. Green, I know you're upset. But if you'll just take a couple moments to speak with me, I think—"

A burly middle-aged guy stuffed into a suit a couple sizes too small walks over to us. He gently touches Green's widow's arm.

"Is everything okay?" he asks her, but looking at me.

"Everything is fine, Richard. This gentleman was just leaving."

She turns her back on me and starts off.

Shit.

Not good.

I need answers. I need to see Green's home office. I can take my chances and head upstairs. By the time the cops are on their way I'll already have my answer, and I have no problem taking care of who-ever gets in my way.

But do I really want to cause all-out chaos in this poor woman's home? With all she's going through?

And what if I find something useful?

What if the pen really did come from here? What if I need this woman on my side?

Less than three days.

"Please," I call after her one last time. "Please, Mrs. Green, if you'll just speak with me maybe together we can—"

She doesn't even turn back. Burly Man puts his hand on my shoulder.

"You heard her," he interrupts.

Running on sheer instinct, surprising both of us, I rip his hand off me.

"Who the fuck do you think you're touching," I growl.

Looking into his eyes, without a word, I let him know the next time he touches me, his hand comes off. Realizing I have already drawn way more attention to myself than I'd like, I turn and leave. I retrace my steps through the first floor, and open the front door. It's raining now. Inside, next to the door, is an antique-looking, hand-painted umbrella holder. I grab the tallest one, a blue-and-white golf umbrella.

I may be exiting. But I'm not going anywhere.

I descend the staircase. At the sidewalk I turn right. After thirty feet, I stop. I face the Greens' brownstone again.

The rain is heavy, like a flash flood. The umbrella is huge. A smaller umbrella and I'd be getting soaked from the thighs down. A steady stream of heavy drops pelts the taut nylon overhead so hard it's loud.

My iPhone rings. I check the number and pick up.

"What's keeping you?" asks Cobus.

"I've been in the bathroom. I went up to grab the file, and let's just say I never made it back down. Must be one of those sandwiches they served."

I hate lying to Cobus.

Then again—technically—every single word ever spoken between us has been a lie.

"Ouch," he responds. "Great timing. Not to be insensitive, but where's your head at? You down for the count?"

Jonah Gray?

Ivan Janse?

Down for the count?

Are you serious?

"Just a germ or two running through me. Not even close."

"Good to hear—because I need your eyes and ears. I'll forge ahead with Arnon, then we can get back to the target tomorrow to review any items we still have questions about. I seem to be on schedule to meet Elman before dinner. You going to make it?"

"Hard to say, but I'd rather play it safe. Why don't I shoot for the restaurant at eight."

"Right then. Feel good. Get yourself back together. Ivan?"

"Yes?"

"Why are you outside?"

Shit. He hears the rain behind me.

"Ran out to get some milk of magnesia," I hear myself say, immediately wishing I could catch the words before they make it out the other end.

Milk of magnesia?

Really?

This is the best I can come up with?

Silence.

"Gotcha," Cobus responds after a pause. "Why not just have someone from the hotel fetch it?"

"Tried that. They were taking too long, so I decided to handle it myself. No big deal."

"Got it. Get yourself right. See you at eight."

He's gone.

I wait outside for what feels like a month. The rain and umbrella keep me shielded from most passersby. I nod cordially to those who happen to catch my eye. I wait. The rain stops. Twenty minutes later it starts again. I look at the new rose-gold Perregaux strapped to my wrist—6:50 p.m. I decide though people will still be coming by for a few hours, many more in the last little while have gone than come. Sensing a lull in the action inside, I head back to the house and up the stairs.

I look at the doorbell but opt for a semi-gentle knock. Nothing. I knock again. Just as I do, the door opens. It's Green's widow, and she's shell-shocked by my presence. She goes to slam the door.

I raise my hand and catch it so strong, so easily, there's zero give. She's so light she loses her balance a bit. We stare into one another's eyes. Again—sour face. She's searching for words she can't find. She's so pissed I think either the throbbing vein in her neck is going to explode or she's going to scream as loud as she can.

"Who do you think you are?" she pushes through her teeth.

"Please. I need to speak to you."

"How dare you!" she forges on. "Do you have any idea—"

"Your husband contacted me before he died," I cut her off.

I take a second and let her absorb my words. She's confused. Her expression unwittingly softens.

"Please," I continue, "the last thing I want to do is cause you more pain. I'm not trying to hurt you. I simply need to talk to you."

A glimmer of the strength I saw in her face hours earlier when we met returns. She turns back into the doorway, surveys the immediate area inside, then closes the door behind her. She steps under the umbrella with me. A cylindrical sheet of water falls all around us; it's like we're in a fairytale standing under a waterfall but not getting wet. We're face-to-face, my chin down a bit, her chin up.

"What do you mean, he contacted you?"

"He left me with something. A message, I believe."

I decide this is the better way to go than telling her I watched him splatter his own head on a wall. At least for now.

"A message? I don't understand. What kind of message?"

"I'm not sure. And it might not have to do with you or your home. But I believe your husband—"

"Scott."

"—Scott was trying to tell me something. Something that may be linked to his death."

"What do you need from me?"

"Did Scott have a home office?"

We head back inside. As I guessed, the crowd has thinned for the time being. A couple of eyes from the dining room catch us as we cross the space, but nothing more.

I follow her up the wide, wooden staircase, some of our steps in unison, others a far cry from alignment. Once we hit the second-floor landing, we make a left and head down a narrow, navy-blue walled hallway lined with beautiful black-and-white photos of nothing but trees and leaves. At the end of the hallway we come to a door.

She's hesitant to turn the doorknob.

"I haven't been in here since I lost him," she says, her back still to me. "Some officers came by to have a look—"

Shiny Dome Lovell, I imagine.

"But I just pointed them upstairs."

"Would you rather I go in alone?" I ask.

She pauses then gently shakes her head.

"No."

She turns the knob. Past her I see the office. Like the one at GlassWell, it's a complete mess.

She takes a couple steps inside and stops. I walk past her. Outfitting the wall to my left, facing Green's desk, is a large wall unit holding family pictures, a huge flat-screen in the center, stacks of what appear to be golf magazines, and paperweights commemorating certain real estate deals. The wall behind the desk is lined from floor to ceiling with bookcases stuffed with all kinds of materials. There are law books, real estate books and publications, you name it. I even see some novels in the mix—Silva, Coben, King, and Berry among other top names. I look across to the far wall where the windows are and walk over to them. Through rain-streaked glass I get a distorted look at a dark, soaked Thirtieth Street. I turn back in and face Green's widow. Then I take a few steps toward the weathered, black leather chair behind the old, nicked, black-painted wooden desk and I stop. I gesture toward the chair.

"May I?" I ask.

"Sure."

I sit down in the chair and scan the desk. Just like his desk at GlassWell, it's a heap of files, Diet Coke cans, rubber bands, Tums, pens, pencils, and newspapers. In the far center, at the rear of the desk's surface farthest away from me, I notice a pen set holder. The base is unique. It's a raw, rough, rectangular chunk of white onyx about ten inches wide, six inches deep, and an inch thick. It sits in a sterling silver frame holding it about a centimeter off the desk. On top are two translucent holders.

Only one holds a pen.

The one on the right.

It's silver.

The butt, sticking up, is flat and engraved with the letter W.

I move my eyes again to my host. Her eyes take in my gaze; she's anxious. Without blinking, our vision locked, I reach into my inside jacket pocket and pull from it the set's match. As she catches a glimpse of it, she covers her mouth. When she does, I feel my heart race. The nerve endings on my neck and arms have my skin so sensitive I want to rip my shirt off.

I place the pen back in its rightful spot, an action that brings an unexpected sense of accomplishment. The pen has been on quite a journey, a cross-Atlantic-and-back odyssey that happened solely for the purpose of it finding its way back to this holder, right where it started, simply to tell me something. In the moment, I feel connected to Scott Green. And looking into his widow's eyes, I feel infinitely sadder for him.

A muffled choke, cry, sniffle thing escapes through her fingers. I look at the pens, the matching set.

"*D* and *W*," I say.

"David and Wendy. Our children," she responds. "Why do you have that?"

"Because your husband gave it to me."

"When? Why?"

I leave the first one word question alone. The less she has about me, or the situation, the better. But I need to offer something to keep her believing in our newfound trust.

"I have no idea," I say, responding to the latter.

David and Wendy.

Their children.

And?

I don't get it. I look around the desk again for nothing in particular, for no particular reason. Then again back at Green's widow.

"Are either of your children involved in real estate? Are they somehow connected to what your husband does?"

Shit.

"I'm sorry—did?"

"It's okay. No. Not at all."

"Why did you get so angry once I said I knew your husband through business?" I change directions.

"Because his work is what killed him. Somehow, in some way, it's because of those people at GlassWell he's dead. My husband was a strong man, a man who loved his family. He would never take his own life. I don't care what the authorities say. Somehow, in some way, they did this."

"Why do you say that?"

She takes a second and draws a deep breath while collecting her thoughts.

"Scott always dreamed of being in-house counsel for a big player, for a company that really mattered in the big picture. Since he started at GlassWell the workload has always been immense. One deal that required his undivided attention ran into the next, but these last few months were different."

"Different? How?"

"It all got to him unlike it ever had before. The stress, the calls. Scott always liked a cocktail, but lately it had been different. I've never seen him drink in all the years we were together like he had been lately. He was definitely trying to escape something."

"Calls? What kind of calls?"

"Calls that would happen at odd times. Late, early, whenever. I'd ask who it was. All he'd do is bark at me 'No one. Just work.' All I know is he'd been literally having nightmares lately. He'd wake up sweating and shaking in the middle of the night."

My gut feeling tears my ass from Green's chair. I lean forward and lift the penholder. It's heavy, solid rock. I sit back down with it. I remove the pens and place them on the desk. I start to manipulate the base in my hands. I immediately feel the rock and sterling are two pieces. I separate them. I closely examine each piece. Nothing. I shake each piece, as if hoping to hear something rattle inside. Nothing.

I don't get it.

I decide to start from scratch. I reassemble the pen set holder, then I replace the pens. I stare at the set.

The pen.

I remember Green's words:

"That pen, my young friend, is everything."

I take the pen from the set again. Noticing a thin line running around the circumference of the center, I decide to unscrew it. When I do, it separates into two pieces. And something falls out of the top half.

I hear Green's widow suck in air as I reach down and pick it up.

"What is that?" she asks.

"A Micro UDP-chip," I say, "or the world's smallest flash drive."

"Flash what?"

I recognize the technology. It is the latest and greatest in electronic file storage—a USB flash drive so small it measures only three-quarters of an inch by a half inch, and is a millimeter thick. But this discovery leaves me with another question.

Why give it to me hidden in a pen?

Why not just hand it to me?

I think about running it right now in Green's desktop computer, but decide against it. God only knows what it contains. And I have no idea what this woman can or cannot handle, or really who these people even are.

I stand up and walk toward her.

"Thank you, Mrs. Green, for—"

"Anne," she corrects me.

"Thank you—Anne—for trusting me. Now, I need you to keep doing just that—trusting me. You can't tell anyone about this. In fact, you can't tell anyone at all I was even here."

"I don't understand? What was—why?"

"The only way I can hopefully find the answers you're looking for is by working on my own. Answers about your husband."

"Why not just go to the police?" she asks.

"Because if it were that easy, your husband would have done so."

CHAPTER 16

Over the course of the next five months, Gaston Piccard's country chalet became our entire world. Within a week, our physical transformation began. A world-renowned plastic surgeon who happened to be one of Gaston's childhood friends was secured. I was told he never knew any of our names or identities. All he knew was he'd be making a small mountain of cash for a few days work.

The attic of the four-story home was transformed into a wild contrast of rustic wood and state-of-the-art medical equipment with a couple small windows overlooking the lush, storybook countryside. The white-and-silver machines seemed so sterile you could drag your tongue across them, while at the same time the thought of walking in the space barefoot screamed "splinter."

My surgery was hardcore. I was a full-out global fugitive, therefore I couldn't take even the slightest of chances. Changing an identity is all about the face. Altering the body surgically is both unnecessarily agonizing and pointless. If someone looks the same but has broader shoulders or they're a couple inches taller, they're still toast. But if a serial killer on the FBI's "America's Most Wanted" list were to brush shoulders with law enforcement with the same exact bodily proportions but with a few strategic facial alterations they'd probably never recognize him.

In my briefing before we got started it was explained that in the world of plastic surgery there are two choices: to enhance or take away. For example, let's take the eyebrow line. We each have a certain projection of our brow based on cell tissue thickness and the proportion of our skull. If the brow starts out as protrusive, you can reduce, or make even more protrusive. If the bone starts out weaker—not dominant in terms of appearance strength with regard to a certain feature—you can build upon it: bone grafting, injection fills, or silicone implants.

All options have their pros and cons. Injections can be effective, but whether right under the skin like Botox or the deeper shit like Restolin, you're talking like six months before it has to be done again. Bone grafting while truly appearance altering requires bone to be taken from somewhere else—either another part of the body or a third party. Silicone can also be insanely effective in terms of changing one's look, and you'd be surprised to learn implants don't simply come in perfectly round bags for fake tits—they come in all crazy-shaped, small derivations made to be stuffed up into your face to change your cheekbones, eye sockets, you name it. But, this stuff can leak. The language of plastic surgery is a complicated one. Understood, it seems, only by those who perform it and upper-crust women who elect to put themselves through it.

The tip of my nose—do you think I went with more of a point or the exact opposite which left it looking like a little ass? Or what about the angle of how my nostrils attach to my face?

Doesn't matter. I was a ghost to you when this all began, now I'm just a different ghost. But I will tell you this:

I look forward to nothing more than the day I can reveal myself.

The day I am both exonerated and ultimately enlightened.

Free from both the law and my past.

What I can tell you is that my surgery ran the gamut: both the tip and bridge of my nose, brow line, eye sockets, cheekbones, chin, lips, even my ears. They even touched on my neck a bit. Injections were bypassed. With regard to enhancements I intended on this lit-tle makeover sticking permanently. There were implants and reshaping; there was bone grafting and bone shaving. All of this was done in three different surgeries spread out over ten days. Once the bulk of the swelling for the first stage subsided after about three days, we moved into stage two, then the same process for stage three.

When I awoke, even in my drug-induced haze, I held my hands up because they felt funny. There was gauze around the tip of each finger.

"There is something else. Something we hadn't discussed," the doctor said in English weighed down by a heavy Western European accent.

"Like what?" I asked through barely parted, burning lips.

He reached down and gently took hold of my right wrist. He lifted my arm up so my hand was in front of my face.

"I was contracted to give you a new identity. So that is what I did."

I was confused. Drugs like morphine and Vicodin were racing through my system.

"No matter how we change the way we look, there is one thing we can never change. Our eyes. And there will always be a special few that no matter what you have done to conceal your birth face will always be able to recognize your eyes. My guess—those people will not let you know they have identified you until it is too late."

The doctor let go of my wrist. He stood up. My hand still in the air my eyes followed him.

"I don't understand. What does—what do my eyes—"

"What it means is that in my estimation there is little chance anyone could ever recognize you again. But should someone be able to—someone really looking for you, should someone or someones like that exist—because of your eyes, what I have given you is an absolute last line of defense. My team removed each of your finger-prints starting from the joint seam where such a procedure would be hard to identify for even the most trained of eyes."

He placed his open left hand in front of me. With his right hand he pointed to the line where his left index finger creased at the joint below his fingertip.

"It was done with a cutting-edge procedure that uses both lasers and acid. Dual effectiveness, you might say."

My eyes moved back to my hand.

Or should I say the new hand that belonged to the new person. "Holy shit."

I could feel a slight, unexpected smile come across my face. I couldn't help being inspired by the doctor's ambition. And I appreciated his desire for me to get where I needed to go. It was either that or this guy saw me in the news—whether he told Gaston or not—and wanted to ensure he could never be linked to me.

Either way, I didn't care. It was genius.

"Whomever you were when you walked in here—that person has officially been wiped from the face of the earth."

For the next two weeks, all I did was sip smoothies through a straw and stare out into the Tamina Valley. Even with all the medication, the pain was extraordinary. Even so, I couldn't help playing back every second of the previous month—Mattheau, my father, Murdoch. The Ia drawings. Detective Morante. I thought of how much I already missed Tommy, Jake, and L—and how the size of that hole in my heart was only sure to grow with time. Every second felt like an hour. I still couldn't tell if I was being punished or spared. If a higher power was looking out for me, or simply ensuring that I suffer.

Two weeks later, sitting up in bed and looking in a mirror for the first time, I stared at what looked like a mummy from the Syfy network. Perry and Gaston were in the room along with the doctor. The doctor, sitting on the edge of my bed, started to unwrap the gauze. My eyes, wide as the moment they saw the world for the first time, never blinked. With each layer removed, the underlying white, stretchy material became more blood and pus stained. Finally, the last piece was removed.

I heard Perry suck in a breath, shriek. My peripheral vision caught her covering her mouth. The sensation of looking at myself in the mirror, and seeing a man I had never seen before, was a fierce mix of raw emotions that had me trembling. There was relief that the face being sought around the globe no longer existed. There was rage for those who drove me toward such measures. There was a sense of tremendous loss; a sense both of my dead parents would have been disappointed I had let the one face they gave to this world slip away. There was determination unlike any I had ever felt before to move forward. The transformation was complete. All that was left was to top it off with a new hair color and style.

Perry's transformation was less drastic as she was not a fugitive. A little bit of work on her nose and eyelid shape—both things she claimed she wanted anyway. Her long, beautiful brown hair was chopped and changed to an auburnish red bob, which was actually quite hot considering her face is so beautiful. As for Max, the beauty of children at this age in this situation is that they seem to be changing every day in terms of appearance. Nonetheless, Perry made it into a game and told him as a special treat he could do whatever he wanted with his hair. He said he wanted a Mohawk.

Done.

Perry was concerned about Max, and rightfully so. The father she took him from was certainly an animal, but I could see in her face her questioning if she had done the right thing every time I saw her look at him. We discussed what she should tell him about my transformation. She decided that she didn't want to lie to him; she told him I had to do it because people were saying I had done something very bad that I didn't do. And I had to make it right before they could find me.

Like I said, Perry was concerned for Max. I was achingly concerned for both of them. Max kept saying he wanted to see me. Once I was truly on the mend, Perry and I decided it was time. As he entered the room, Perry remained by the doorway. I was sitting in a chair by the window overlooking the valley I could by this point draw from memory. Funny, he didn't even pause or break stride in the slightest upon sight of me. He walked right over and stood in front of me.

He studied my face. He started to put his hand up, but put it back down, probably thinking I was still in pain from some of the residual bruising.

"It's okay," I said. "You can feel it. You won't hurt me."

He reached out and touched my cheek lightly. Then he ran the tip of his finger across my brow line.

"I like your chin. It looks cool."

"Thanks."

He put his hand back down to his side.

"Did you do it?"

I was taken aback.

Did I do what? Did I accidentally murder a dirty cop? Did I inadvertently get my own father killed? Did I run from the police, and put everyone I know and love back home in harm's way?

I looked at Perry. She shrugged. I knew she hadn't given specifics.

"Did I do what?"

"Whatever it is the people you are hiding from say you did."

"No. I mean—anything I did, it was accidental. Or was done to someone who deserved what they had coming. I would never do anything bad to anyone or hurt anyone on purpose."

"Good. Because you're nice to me. And you're nice to my mom."

Then, surprisingly, he moved into me and hugged me. A tear ran down my new face. Perry, smiling wide, started to cry.

"Can you go outside for a walk yet?" Max asked.

"Absolutely. Time for some fresh air."

In discussions with Gaston, we decided that Amsterdam would be the right place for us. Not only did he work closely with some high-ranking Netherlands' government officials, meaning we'd easily obtain authentic ID, he knew a lot of people there, a number of whom were owners of real estate. Getting an apartment would be easy. As for what I would do professionally, I thought it was probably best to start fresh here as well—perhaps another area of business, or something far more low-key altogether—but Gaston felt otherwise. Commercial real estate was still the way to go. Not only did I know and love the business of buildings, thus giving me the opportunity to start working straight away, I had learned about and worked at the highest level in the industry in the world's most comprehensive market—New York City. Another plus—one doesn't need a real estate license to perform as a real estate agent in The Netherlands. Once in Amsterdam—a city of seventy-five million square feet of office space as opposed to the half a billion I was used to—I would lay low for a few weeks and literally walk the streets, learn the lay of the land, scope out the product. From there I would find a firm and start at the bottom as a junior broker showing space.

For the next couple months all we did was learn to speak Dutch—Gaston brought in a teacher twice a week in order to ensure our being out of his hair for good once we were gone—perfect our backstories, and learn about the Dutch culture. What Dutch people liked to eat, do for fun, what they valued; where Dutch people vacation, about their work ethic, what they typically spend money on. We devoured books and information online. We absorbed anything and everything Dutch. Did you know the Dutch are the tallest people in Europe? Or that when Dutch schoolchildren pass their exams, they hang the Dutch flag and a schoolbag outside their homes?

My background? I was born and raised in The Hague, the second largest city in The Netherlands. I attended the University of Groningen and graduated with a degree in economics. Once in Amsterdam, the plan was for me to literally take a day trip to Groningen in order to take notes and photographs to study should I run into others who attended the school, a scenario that was more than likely. My father was a simple man who worked for the State Department—most of The Netherlands' government departments are located in The Hague—while my mother was a waitress. We were a hardworking family of modest means. I was an ambitious boy, an only child, who wanted more. We developed a similar back-story for Perry and Max. The story would go that Perry—a single mother who had never been married—and I met a couple years earlier while vacationing in Tenerife.

We also got my finances in order. Once we were gone, the goal was for me to never have to check back with Gaston unless there were extreme circumstances. In order to achieve this, we needed to strategically set up bank accounts in tax-safe havens around the world; the plan was to spread out my thirty-seven-point-five million dollar share of my father's life insurance payout. While Gaston had access to my U.S.-based accounts, obviously these funds couldn't be touched. What *could* be touched was the account for the life insurance trust. The payout of the trust was set up to hit a completely segregated bank account—an account based in Switzerland—where at this point my portion still resided. Once ready to roll, we created many anonymous accounts all with benign balances that would never raise any red flags in the usual spots like the Cayman Islands and Bermuda along with places like Dubai, the Channel Islands, Lichtenstein, Andorra, Cyprus, and Grenada. Some of the accounts were personal, others were corporate shells, depending on jurisdiction. Four hundred fifty thousand here, sixty-five thousand there; two point two million here, seven hundred twenty-five thousand there. Once I left Switzerland, I would have every bank account number, routing number, debit card, username, and password with me in order to draw money as necessary from anywhere in the world.

In the fall, once we had the language down extremely well, it was time for the move. Our new government-issued passports, driver's licenses, and ID cards had arrived. Perry York was now Tess Beel. Her son Max's new name was Johan. I opened my new passport and looked at my name.

Ivan Janse.

Something about seeing this new name, to go along with my new physical persona, triggered nerves deep within me. It took my breath away. I thought of everything I had been through; I thought of everything that was about to come. Life had turned me into a warrior of epic proportions. I had killed. I had put everything on the line to protect those I love. I had learned to treasure more deeply, truly hold dear those things that matter most. I had learned to flip a switch and go to a place most men can never imagine going.

As we were leaving the chalet, a place we had only spent five months but I knew would live inside me forever, I caught a last glimpse of myself in a mirror. My eyes—Jonah Gray's eyes—stared at a man the world had never seen before. I wondered something.

You ever imagine what happens when a hurricane collides with an earthquake?

Nice to meet you.

My name is Ivan Jansc.

CHAPTER 17

New York City
2013

7:15 p.m.

It's going to be tight.

In 1993 my father bought a warehouse in Soho. Why did he buy it? To keep it out of a rival's hands.

Get what you need, Pop said. Always. No matter what.

When I was a kid, in the summer my friends and I used to hop from one Hamptons house to another. One night a girl named Jenny Gaynor and I hit one of the six guest bathrooms in my friend Jim Brezen's house after rolling around in the grass of his estate grounds at about two in the morning. Once the bathroom had become a steam room, and we were able to separate our naked, sweaty bodies enough to come up for a second's air, we jumped in the shower. I picked up the half-used bar of soap. The second I did, Jenny let out a shriek.

"Eeeewwww—nasty!"

"What?" I asked, dumbly, as I soaped up while gazing into her eyes—almost taunting her.

"You have no idea who used that!"

"No. I don't." I answered, never missing a beat while lathering up. "Because I don't care. You know why?"

She actually thought about it for a second.

"Why?"

I moved close to her. I reached around with my free hand, grabbed her tight, glistening ass, and pulled her body into mine.

"Because it doesn't matter who dirtied me up. All I need is a minute or two, and this soap will know exactly who it belongs to."

The world has dirtied me up.

And, fuck if I haven't made that same world my guest-bathroom bar of soap.

Golf umbrella overhead I charge east to Park Avenue. Though I need to end up more west, Park runs downtown as opposed to Madison which heads up. Because of the rain cabs are hard to come by. A black town car pulls up, no doubt a driver with a little downtime looking to make a few extra bucks.

"Where to?" asks the driver, as I jump in.

He's a stocky fella—short and thick with a cheap, black suit, a size too small, and a ridiculously heavy New York accent to match his deep voice. Looking into the front seat, I can't help noticing his white socks.

"Meatpacking District."

"That'll be twenty-five bucks from here," he goes on.

"You get me there quickly, I'll make it fifty."

No sooner than I say the words, we're on the move. The car's warm. I crack the window and hear the tire treads slosh through the street. I take the disposable from my inside pocket. I dial. All these years, and I still remember the number by heart.

"You have reached Luckman Meats."

Voicemail system as it's after hours.

"If you know your party's extension, you may dial it now. For a company directory—"

I go through the motions. Extension twelve takes me to the office of my closest friend since I'm a little boy. Tanqueray Luckman—L. L's family has been the biggest meat distributor in New

York City since horses drew carriages on dirt roads. The last time I saw L, we were running away from a cop through his family business's distribution warehouse, where I'm headed right now. As we did, I told him that was going to be the last time I'd ever see him; that I could never come back. Not to Manhattan, not to the United States. Different mothers, but we grew up brothers. I don't know which of us was more crushed by my words.

"Luckman…" his voice answers. "Hello?"

I knew he'd be there. He always works late. The sound of his voice temporarily shreds all these lost years of friendship and brings me back to the time of our youth. I see us as boys smoking pot in the high school bathroom. I get a surprising image of us having a baseball catch in the Queensboro Oval on York Avenue. I only want to say something; start explaining, rambling, rhapsodizing, justifying.

Knowing I'll see him shortly, instead I hang up.

The town car, jostled by the cobblestone streets of the Meatpacking District, slowly rolls to a stop. I depress the button and drop the window, unfazed by the water now spraying my face. I look up at the old, weathered, three-story gray-brick warehouse/office. In the center of the building is the main entrance door. To the right, windows that allude to administrative space and the like. To the left, seven wide, story-high rolled-down bay doors, a few with shutdown refrigerated trucks backed up to them.

"How'd we do?" asks my stocky new friend.

"What's your name?" I ask, my eyes still on the building.

"Dusty," he responds, with his deep, New York–accented voice.

It takes a second, but I turn to him.

"Really?"

"Really. My grandfather worked in a suppository factory."

Huh? And?

I turn back to the building. I hold out my hand.

"Here's a fifty, Dusty, for a job well done," I say. "There's another waiting for you if you give me two things."

"What's that?"

"Five minutes inside before driving me uptown. And the right to call you anything but Dusty."

I get out of the car and open the umbrella. I walk toward the front door. The front area of the property is well lit, as it's an active, 24/7 distributorship. I don't exactly have a plan. Yes, it's after hours, but people are always coming and going. And with that there is no doubt the front door locks at this hour behind whoever enters or exits.

I'm apprehensive. Something that seems warranted as a tall, lanky guy in overalls comes through the front door when I'm no more than thirty feet away.

I make a hard left. But, funny, it doesn't feel blind. It feels like instinct, like I know where I'm going.

Think.

The fire door.

The fire door I left through when I fled this building nine years ago. The one that, if I know L as well as I think I do, still hasn't been fixed. I walk around the corner, turn right on Washington, and head for the door.

It creaks open. Again, it's like all the time in between has disappeared; like I took a step outside, decided against running, turned right back around, and came inside. I leave the door open a crack, for both the sliver of alley light and so not to let it slam. I'm standing in a dark storage room full of boxes and equipment. A room that looks as though it hasn't been touched since I last came through it.

I retrace my escape route from the day I left, the day I ran through this building while missing my own father's funeral. I move through some vintage, dusty offices ripped from the set of Mad Men into a dingy hallway and find my way to the staircase leading upstairs. As I approach the second-floor landing, I hear L's voice. I stop in my tracks. I catch my breath.

"What did you just say to me? Who the hell do you think you're talking to?" L says, his voice loud as usual, "You listen to me, Jimmy! I don't give a crap if our great-grandfathers' *great-grandfathers* did business together. In fact—tell you what. You want to keep conducting yourself like this, that cute little sister of yours who keeps looking for me to take her out will get her wish. And I promise I won't be such a gentleman."

I start moving again. I take my last two upward steps, my head shaking as I move toward L's office. I'm not sure if I'm surprised by this ridiculous conversation I'm overhearing, or if I'm surprised by the fact I'm so completely not surprised.

"Oh, is that right? Tell you what, smart-ass—how's this for clear? If my cash isn't here first thing tomorrow morning, I'm coming to collect myself. And I won't just be looking for money."

At the exact moment I hear this threat—standard business practice for L—I stop dead within the frame of his open door. Standing in his usual mess of an office facing the back glass wall that looks out into the warehouse, he wheels around when he hears, feels me. Startled, maddened, his eyes and chest swell.

"Who the fuck are you?" he barks, chucking his iPhone onto his desk.

"I…uh…"

Now we both know I'm seldom at a loss for words. But there are certain moments even I can't prepare for. I've never bothered practicing this encounter. I knew it would be a futile effort.

"I asked who the fuck are you? You realize you're standing in my fucking living room?"

"I do—and apologies for sneaking up on you," I say, my European accent purposefully extra heavy. "Tanqueray Luckman, right?"

L casually reaches under his desk. He pulls out a gun. A pretty serious one at that.

"I'll ask one more time. Who are you?"

"May I close the door before telling you?" I ask, calm. "I promise it will be worth your while. And you're the one holding the gun should you not like my answer."

Without giving him a chance to answer, I close the door.

I turn to him.

For maximum effect, I lose the accent and use my natural-born voice.

"Seriously, L—a fucking Walther PPQ? Are you serious?"

L's face goes blank, his arm goes slack for a split second, then both return to normal like he's just seen a ghost. Or one of those black squiggly things out of the corner of your eye floating in the air that isn't really there.

"It's me, L. It's Jonah."

The instant I speak again, he sucks in a breath. His expression morphs from anger to fear, confusion.

"What the fuck is this?"

I open my arms, as if to say I have nothing to hide.

"It's really me."

L's trembling.

"It can't be! It's . . . you're—"

"This is crazy—I know. But it's me. Same Jonah who grew up with you on the Upper East Side. Same Jonah who missed his own father's funeral."

"Stop it! How are you—why do you sound—"

"I'm just in a different body. I mean, it's the same body, just, you know my face—*seriously*, L, can you put the gun down?"

His eyes and expression return to anger. Gun still up, he starts toward me.

"You'd like that, wouldn't you?"

"L, please, listen to me."

He's not hearing me. It's my voice, but I couldn't look more different. He's freaked. And he's coming.

"What do you want?" he snarls, rushing up to me. "Who the fuck are you? How do you know about Jonah?"

"L, please. It's me."

"Bullshit! Not possible!"

I remain calm. He puts the gun to my temple. The hard steel is cold against my skin. Our faces are close. When our eyes lock, in his

I see ambivalence. Because in mine I know he thinks—he feels— he sees me.

"Jonah Gray is dead."

"Who told you that? Morante? The FBI?" I counter.

No answer.

"Listen to my voice. I know I look different, but it's me. It's me."

Still nothing.

"They told you I was dead so you wouldn't think you were betraying me by giving up information. They told you I was dead because they were desperate and couldn't find me. And because they figured I'd never have the nerve to come back."

Gun still to my temple, he closes his eyes and starts shaking his head. Like he wants to wake up.

"No. This is insane."

"I'm sorry for this. I am. I know—"

"Now!" he cuts me off, his eyes open, alert, and locked with mine again. "Who's the first girl I slept with and what grade? You have five seconds. Four. Three—"

"Debbie Tarlow. Seventh grade."

He drops the gun. We both exhale. We hug. Neither wants to let go.

"My God, Jonah? What the hell is going on? Where have you been?"

"When did they tell you I was dead?" I respond, blowing off his questions. "I'm guessing after three months. Maybe four."

We pull back from one another.

"Close. Six. And they never said you were definitely dead. Just that they had good reason to believe you were."

"Makes sense. After all, a definitive death notice would have meant they needed to actually produce my body."

L nods. With both his eyes and extended, dangling gun, he looks me up and down.

"Wow. I mean—wow!"

"Crazy, right?"

"You're like out of a fucking Jason Bourne movie or something."

"You realize they were books first—right?"

And just like that, it's like I've been here all along.

"How about getting the gun out of my face?"

"Right—sorry."

L walks behind his desk and replaces it underneath.

"Why such a serious piece anyway?"

"Still a cash business, still dealing with old-school families. Unlike your new and improved cheekbones, some things haven't changed."

He walks back over to me.

"Where do we even begin? Does anyone even . . . I mean, are you staying? Is—"

"I can't, L. I mean, not now at least. I'll tell you everything, but right now I don't have time. The last thing I can let happen is for anyone to know about me. Being someone else, being alive, any of it. You're one of a few in this world I can trust."

"Are you still running? Are you still in danger?"

"Until Jonah Gray's name is cleared, I'll always be in danger. And I'll always be on the run."

"Where do you live? I mean—what do—where do you—"

"It doesn't matter, L. Like I said, I promise to get you up to speed. I just can't do it right now."

"You storm in after all these years as some piece of Eurotrash, and now you're gone? You're leaving?"

"I have to."

"Just like that?"

"I'm sorry. I am. But I have to."

"So then why the little coming-out party tonight?"

"What are you driving these days?"

"Serious?"

"As a quintuple bypass."

"Quattroporte Range. Burgundy. Brand-new. It's downstairs."

"I need the keys. And I promise to have it back before sunrise."

L doesn't move. He's just staring at me.

"L—look. I can't begin to imagine what—"

"No, Jonah. You can't. To leave the way you did? I know you were down to the wire. I know the whole world was looking to come down on you. But to grow up like brothers the way we did? And for you to be alive this whole time and—"

"It's not like that, L—"

"Not a word? Not a single fucking word?"

"I couldn't!" I say with urgency as I step toward him. "Not just out of concern for myself. Out of concern for you."

L nods.

"I know. I just missed the hell out of you."

"I missed you too. Every day. And I promise—maybe tomorrow, maybe in ten years—I will be back here for good. I will."

He reaches down, opens the top drawer of his desk, pulls out the keys, and tosses them to me.

"Maserati's best yet. Thing's a beast. Makes that little Porsche you used to drive look like a nursery school toy."

I catch the keys and nod.

"One more thing," I add. "I need a gun. Something small. But able to wreak havoc if necessary."

L always has a couple pieces handy. Occupational necessity when you're dealing in such a large, all-cash business within an industry that sometimes calls for a little strong-arming.

He reaches down and opens another drawer in his desk. He pulls out a compact, aluminum piece. With a rosewood grip.

"Kimber Ultra CDP II. Small enough to keep tucked away. Strong enough to keep someone off your back. Or if need be, bury them."

I jump back in the town car. The rain has tapered off quite a bit. I throw the drizzle-dusted umbrella on the seat next to me. And put my European accent back on.

"Del Posto, Brutus."

Dusty gives me his eyes in the rearview mirror.

"Sorry. Just can't do Dusty. Brutus seems to suit you."

Nothing. His eyes move back to the road ahead. I reach forward and hand him a fifty over his shoulder. He takes it.

"We good?" I follow up.

"Del Posto. Eighty-Five Tenth Avenue, I believe."

"I believe you're right."

The restaurant's about ten blocks away. I look at my watch—7:46 p.m. Which means I'm right on schedule.

The inside jacket pockets of my suit are getting fuller by the hour. The flash drive occupying about 75 percent of all my thoughts at this point has joined the inside left pocket with the disposable phone. L's Maserati keys have replaced the silver pen with the iPhone and loupe in the right inside pocket. The gun is in the rear of my pants' waistline.

I take out the disposable. I punch a 410—Baltimore—area code into it. Before hitting "send" I just look at the number. It belongs to Pavel Derbyshev. The last and only time I saw Mr. Derbyshev—the count as I like to call him because of his, well, countlike appearance—I put a gun to the back of his head then kicked him in the balls so hard you'd think I was playing in the World Cup. Derbyshev, descendant of Piotr Derbyshev, has six of the eight missing Fabergé Imperial Easter Eggs—eggs that would have been sold to my half-brother Andreu Zhamovsky had I not blown up the plan. Now, after all these years, I need to see those eggs. And learn once and for all why Galina wants them in her possession.

I remember the night I confronted him in Prime Rib, one of the few restaurants in the 410—back then, at least—for power players. His number is a private, unpublished one, but in the day's leading to my fleeing, I had gotten it from bank records. Derbyshev never knew how I'd obtained it. Which is what I'm counting on for his not changing the number. There's always the fact that I ended up saving his ass. Had the deal gone through, he would have been out both the eggs and the half a billion he thought he was getting in return. But I'm going with the fact he probably figured if I could get his number once, I'd simply get it again.

Once I was out of the country, there were a few things I would jot down in strange places. Things I couldn't risk forgetting, yet couldn't dare have on me in a more permanent fashion—like in a phone or contact book—until I was safe.

Or safer.

For example, in the room in St. Maxime there were notes, written tiny, under the end tables and in the closet right where the wall met the carpeting. One of those notes was the count's phone number. I said it over and over to myself that night driving back from Baltimore knowing it was probably one I'd need again one day. I'd even switch the first and fourth numbers any time I wrote it. This went on for each stop until we settled in Amsterdam. And I don't mean the first place in Amsterdam—I mean the gift house from Cobus. It didn't stop because I ever felt safe. It stopped because all of a sudden, when I went poking around for places in my new palace to jot them down, it occurred to be they'd all probably been engrained in my brain from the moment I wrote them down in that hotel in the French Riviera.

How's that for paranoid.

Over the years, from time to time in different parts of Europe, I would call the count's number. Probably ten times in total. Just to make sure he was still there in his palatial castle, alive. Most of the time one of his staff would answer. I'd ask if Mr. Derbyshev was in. When they asked who was calling for him, I would hang up. A couple of the times, the count picked up himself.

I hit "call" and lifted the phone to my ear. On the fourth ring a very proper-sounding woman answers.

"Good evening."

"Good evening to you. Is Mr. Derbyshev available?"

"Who might I say is calling?"

I hit "end."

CHAPTER 18

AMSTERDAM, THE NETHERLANDS
2005

Once in Amsterdam, Gaston helped us secure a two-bedroom, two-bathroom apartment on the second floor of a modest canal house. The address was 133 Langestraat, a twenty-six-foot-wide gray brick coach house. It was a solid location right near Central Station, which was the nucleus of Amsterdam. Everything scales outward from Central Station like rings scale outward from the center of a tree trunk. The landlord was a man named Olig Frindland. And what no one aside from Perry—not Gaston, not Max, no one— knew was that Olig and I also made another deal. One that gave me the top floor apartment at 251 Herengracht. It was only a couple blocks from where we would be living. And it would be my personal studio to perform all research and analysis with regard to my obsession: the missing Imperial Fabergé Easter Eggs. All I really knew was that Andreu's mother Galina wanted them, and my father had tried to warn me. But I was literally kept up at night as to why Galina wanted them so badly. Why she was willing to risk so much.

What did Galina mean when she wrote that she needed to stay true to her own?

I took a junior broker position with a firm called Oovik Premier

Property. Oovik was a small family-run firm with twenty-two commercial canal houses, mostly in the higher-rent district near Central Station, and twenty residential canal houses spread more evenly throughout Amsterdam. I applied for the position solely pertaining to the commercial portion of the portfolio and within a few days was out with my senior broker—Jan Oovik, thirty-eight-year-old son of one of the two older Oovik brother principals—learning our product, showing our space.

I remember our first showing. The address was 24 Singel Straat, an awesome piece of space overlooking the Singel Canal. The potential tenant was Henrik Heesters, a well-known European fashion designer.

"Obviously you are not to speak. Just watch, learn. Showing office space is one thing. Getting potential users to commit is another," Jan said, arms folded.

I cocked my head left like a curious puppy.

"Henrik Heesters is one of Europe's premier fashion houses," he went on, "and they are looking to possibly take this entire canal house. This is the second time they have come to see it. They will ask about the tenants occupying the top two floors—this is where you need to pay special attention. These are the intricacies that make commercial real estate a free-flowing experience, a never-ending puzzle."

I heard a car pull up out front. I moved to the window to look outside.

"These tenants can be dealt with," Jan went on. "Just listen and learn how."

"I understand you loud and clear, Jan," I say, looking out the window, "but may I offer one thought before Mr. Heesters and his team, who just arrived, step in here? Before I have the opportunity to embarrass myself?"

Jan sighed and dropped his arms to his side.

"Of course, Ivan. Please."

"Henrik is trying to hide behind his sunglasses, but it isn't working. He's discussing a couple aspects of the physical structure of the building, most notably a modification to the front door entrance. I know this because while I can't see his eyes some of his team are not as subtle. They too may be wearing sunglasses but they are pointing. And the architectural drawings they are holding—clearly of the front of the building—are marked 'Draft,' which means they have already been spending time and money planning on this space."

I turned my attention back into the building toward Jan.

"Of course, I have no idea what you have discussed with Mr. Heesters in terms of price. But you can do better. You've been speaking to me for the last hour as if this is one of many options they are looking at. While I believe that is probably the case, I'd be willing to bet this is their first choice."

"I, that—sounds—"

I looked back toward the window.

"How can—the drawings are of—" Jan continued to sputter.

"The sun's coming through them. Architectural drawings are created on vellum paper which becomes near transparent with the right light," I cut him off. "Okay, they're on their way in. Sir—I would never dare overstep and I am simply honored to be working for a family of such strong real estate minds. But with your permission, should your discussions concerning price tell me you can push harder, might I send you a signal?"

Jan was dumbfounded.

"A what?"

"A signal. I believe you are underestimating the potential tenant's desire to take your space. Which means you may be selling your own firm short, which I would hate to see happen. If I think you can press, I'll subtly play with my cuff link like this."

I showed him.

"This way I won't have to speak, which means there is no opportunity to let my inexperience show through."

There was a knock on the door.

"If you feel I am out of line, you can just forge ahead. I know I have very little idea about all of this, but I just want to help."

Seventy minutes later, following an in-depth walk-through of the entire canal house with Mr. Heesters and his team, I played with my cuff link. Jan Oovik pressed. A deal was struck to occupy the entire building for ten years. At numbers 7 percent higher than previously thought achievable.

Jan Oovik was a tall, slender guy with an equally long and slender face. He went for the tight, black suit and thin black tie on a white button-down look, always wore shiny, pointed black tie-up oxfords that made his feet look like size twenties. One showing and I made Jan Oovik look like a hero to his family. To his credit, Jan didn't forget it. He took me on as his sidekick. With each showing, with each new potential client for an Oovik property, with each commercial property potentially purchased or sold, I played the part: young, green broker with an innate sense for the industry he'd stumbled into.

Soon I displayed a desire to learn all I could about the properties in the portfolio, pretending to learn more than I had probably already forgotten on the topic over my career. I was wowing and wooing my employers and clients on a daily basis. I had them looking at real estate in a way they never had before—not as brick and mortar but as cash flow; not simply as roofs, walls, and floors but as individual entities with a need to be nurtured. I taught them to see each property—and each space within a property—as a continuously expanding opportunity that flows naturally, unpredictably like water flowing through soil. I was a young, hungry kid who had prided himself on straight living and using the experiences of those I'd read about to see the bigger picture. I brought a level of sophistication to the game these people had never seen before, sophistication I worked painstakingly hard at seeming more innate than previously learned.

We were all falling into a nice rhythm. Perry decided to take on a more casual tone to her life. She got back in touch with the skills that helped her pay her way through college and became a bartender at the uber-hotspot "supperclub," at night, a joint in the center of Amsterdam, while homeschooling Max during the day. Surprisingly, she loved it. She enjoyed the simplicity of this life as opposed to the one she had lived as a power broker in New York City. She appreciated a life where her work remained at the work-place; where when she left work—she left work.

She loved the time with Max. At night the three of us would take walks. Sometimes we'd go for ice cream and do some good laughing. Other nights we'd stroll quietly and look at the city's lights sparkling on the water, as if each of us was simply walking alone with our thoughts.

Every moment I was able to steal away to the apartment at 251 Herengracht, I took. A couple hours in the middle of the night here, a small tale to my employers about my needing to leave early for a doctor's appointment there—I did whatever I could to get into that space and perform my research about the missing Fabergé Imperial Easter Eggs. I had to know what the connection was, what I was missing about them. Yes, my half-brother's mother, Galina Zhamovsky—secret longtime lover of my father—was more than willing to go to great lengths to retrieve all eight of them currently residing in the United States.

But why?

Why would she put so many people's lives in jeopardy in order to obtain them—including her own son? What was I missing?

I had to know.

My father had been killed, and my life had been destroyed because of Galina Zhamovsky's need to obtain these eggs.

I simply would not, could not, let it go.

I had to know.

The apartment was essentially a long, narrow train-track space with uneven plank wood flooring. It was barren aside from a large, unfinished wooden Parsons table in the center that held an iMac and a lamp. There were also a couple of small, shadeless lamps scattered around the space. The place looked like it belonged to some psycho-stalker-murderer. The walls were lined with research clippings, printouts, timelines, and pictures. There were diagrams with different color arrows slicing through them. A different portion of wall was dedicated to each of the eight missing Fabergé Imperial

Easter Eggs: the year it was made, what it looked like, what materials were used, what the egg commemorated, what known history there was in terms of the egg's whereabouts before vanishing, and what documents surrounding each egg had survived. If there was information from some corner of this earth in relation to one of these eight rare treasures—six of which were sitting in Baltimore, Maryland, with a man named Pavel Derbyshev—that information was represented on these walls.

As I mentioned, Perry knew about my secret research quarters. She supported it 100 percent. She would tell me I deserved to get the answers I was looking for. Maybe she also felt me getting the answers I needed would be our ticket back to New York City.

CHAPTER 19

We roll up to Del Posto.

"Brutus, I appreciate your services tonight."

I hand him another fifty over his shoulder.

"Will you be needing me again tonight, sir?" he asks as he takes the bill.

"It has been a pleasure, and I wish you good luck. But, no, I won't."

I enter the restaurant, which is packed. The place is sophisticated but equally warm, exuding seriousness while at the same time feeling lighthearted, friendly.

I look at my wrist—8:01 p.m. A hostess leads me to the table as everyone else has just arrived. We pass the crowded bar area and enter the main dining room. The large, wide-open space is well lit yet cozy, and dominated by earth tones. A wrought-iron gated balcony, accessed by a dramatic staircase, hangs overhead with even more diners. The windows are covered with long, flowing, red velvet curtains. Tables—of which there isn't an empty one—are spaced just right, enough room for privacy, yet an overall feeling of festivity. From the moment my nostrils get inside they're filled with a mixture of savory aromas. Sauces, fine wines, olives—it's like I blinked and ended up in Rome.

I reach the table where everyone has just been seated. From our end, it's Cobus and Arnon; from GlassWell, it's Brand, Julia, a couple other members of the leasing contingent, and a few of the in-house attorneys. Scattered conversations are taking place. There will be a lot of work discussed at this meal, but from the number of cocktails already on the table, it appears everyone is also looking to unwind.

"Missed you this afternoon and evening," Cobus says to me.

Though Cobus and I are close—we're professional close, not personal close. This, no doubt, is one of the reasons our relationship has worked so well. I know the basics of Cobus's life before de Bont Beleggings: He was born and raised in the northwestern Netherlands city of Leiden, attended the University of Leiden where his father was a professor of economics. His mother worked for the city; they were a working-class family. I also know that Cobus had a gift for picking stocks, and what started as a one-man investment shop focused on the financial markets, became a portfolio with 75 percent of its holdings in commercial real estate. According to Cobus, by chance he ended up in an office building deal as a favor to a friend and because the ROI—Return On Investment—potential as well as the fact, unlike stocks, real estate was so tangible, he was hooked. That's as far as my knowledge about Cobus goes. I've never pressed, because Cobus makes no secret of the fact he likes to keep his personal and professional lives separate—something he should only know how much I appreciate. While we spend most of our lives together—all days and many nights—for business, we don't socialize personally aside from inviting the other to special family occasions or milestones.

Having been so close with my partners in my first life, have I always found his desire for such secrecy odd? Yes. Do I care? Certainly not. Because it has given me the green light to be just as secretive.

Cobus motions to the open chair to his right, between him and

Julia who is chatting with the gentleman on her right. "We have a lot to catch up on. How are you feeling?"

"Much better. Thanks. Just one of those things."

As I move to take my seat, I can't help but to notice Julia's lustrous hair. I can only see her from the back. To my surprise, the first thing I feel is how much I'd like to see her from the front.

Just as my ass is about to hit the seat two—not one, but two—white-gloved waiters appear out of nowhere to assist with the chair. Before I can say thank you, I'm offered a cocktail.

"Belvedere, rocks, twist. Thanks."

I return my attention to Cobus. I need to stay in character. I need to remain—in his eyes—driven by our mission.

"So how was your meeting with Elman?"

"Enlightening," Cobus responds, his voice a few decibels lower than normal. "The more we discussed the retail tenants, and the fact their leases all roll over so close together—"

Roll over. Expire.

"The more I realized this isn't the negative we've been factoring into our projections. In terms of worst-case scenario potential releasing downtime and so forth. In fact—quite the opposite. I see an opportunity we've been missing."

"Is that right?"

Cobus throws a large swallow of neat scotch back.

"It is."

"And what opportunity might that be?"

"Terminal five."

"Terminal what?"

"Terminal five, Ivan. Heathrow. British Airways."

"What about it?"

"Remember our conversation eighteen months ago? When we were looking into redeveloping the ABN AMRO building in City Centre? What we could do with the retail?"

I think for a second.

"The Soho House of retail," I say.

"The exact same words you used then."

British Airways' terminal at Heathrow, Terminal 5, is not your typical airport. It is a brand-snob's paradise with shop after shop of names like Cartier, Bulgari, and Prada. If you want to eat—forget Burger King or a hot dog. More like Caviar House or famed sushi haven Itsu.

"This particular submarket of Manhattan is highly trafficked and apparently starving for an infusion of retail energy. In Elman's words, the area has become a bit stale. It's prime for the strategy you outlined."

"Retail exclusivity unlike anything the market has ever seen before," I move forward. "We market the project as a retail opportunity that's half brand awareness, half company showpiece. We divide the space into seven or eight equal-size units to the inch, and invite the top global brands to make their pitch for why they most deserve a unit."

"The Patek Philippes and Bentleys and Chanels of the world," Cobus jumps in. "A fine mixture of some of the globe's classiest brands. Each, once accepted based on their pitch, given a white-washed shell to bring to life that highlights both their brand as well as their artistic vision as a firm. Each boutique becomes part marketing piece, part art gallery."

"The deal is the same for each," I come back at him. "Same per-square-foot price across the board. The number a premium, unlike rents previously seen in this particular market based on the exclusivity. Terms run no longer than twelve or twenty-four months, thus incentivizing tenants to keep their game up. And we include a clause that requires a new look every six months forcing the brands to keep their creative juices flowing."

"The Soho House of retail," Cobus reiterates. "Incredible jumping off point buzz, followed by the property becoming a retail staple in Manhattan."

"All the while setting a new standard for retail rental numbers, not to mention perhaps a whole new model we can utilize back in Amsterdam," I add. "Or anywhere else we look to conquer."

The waiter arrives with my drink.

Julia's eyes turn to it as it's placed on the table.

"Huh," she says. "I didn't realize vodka coated an unsettled stomach."

Her eyes move to me. I pick the cocktail up, slide a little through my lips. It feels cool as it lines my throat. My eyes join hers.

"Dutch thing," I respond.

"Is that right?" she asks, the corner of her mouth curling up.

Julia had changed from earlier. Tonight she's still classy, elegant, but having a bit more fun with it. She's traded in her Armani suit for a tailored, beige silk, Burberry Maxine trench dress that stops just above the knee. It has a neckline that stops just short of being described as plunging. On her feet are Burberry patent tweed T-strap platform sandals that no doubt put her head in the clouds.

"It is. For headaches—Rugby."

"Really," she replies with a cute giggle, "and let me guess what rugged Dutch men do for a sore throat—you gargle Tabasco."

"Nope—but close. We swallow sand."

More giggling.

"Nice."

The flash drive.

I need to know what's on it.

"I'll be right back," I say to Julia, as I throw back the lion's share of my remaining cocktail. "I need to look at something before I forget. I'll only be a minute. Perhaps you can order me another?"

"You got it," Julia says, knocking back some rosé champagne.

I jump up from the table.

"I'll just be a minute," I say to Cobus as I place a hand on his shoulder.

I lean in to Arnon, who is nose deep in his glass of Chianti.

"Arnon—you have your laptop handy? I need to access our cloud. There's a piece of language in the Purchase Agreement with regard to the retail I'd like to double-check..."

The perfect excuse for Cobus's ears to perk up, considering the discussion we'd just had. Arnon, who's been working like a dog to get this deal handled, didn't even look at me. He was enjoying his glass of wine too much, no doubt pondering what he was going to eat for dinner. Without a word, he handed me his coat-check ticket, his way of telling me to get his laptop from his checked briefcase.

I enter the bathroom. Big restaurants call for big restrooms. I grab a stall and close the door behind me. I sit on the toilet and boot the computer. Then I attach the flash drive.

I have no idea what to expect—but certainly not this. There's nothing but audio files on the drive. Shit. The last thing I can do, having no idea what I'm about to hear, is let it rip in a crowded bathroom with steady traffic.

Something I saw on my way in pops into my brain. I unlock the black metal door and poke my head out. At the end of the row of sinks, by the wall, there's an iPod with Apple earbuds wrapped around it. I walk over to the attendant, an old-timer who probably envisioned a beach sipping piña coladas for this period of his life, not wearing a tux to hand paper towels to the entitled for their dripping hands.

"Might I borrow your earphones?" I ask, gesturing to the iPod with a twenty. "I don't even need to leave the bathroom, and I'll only be a few minutes."

I close the stall door again and retake my seat on the toilet. I'm hesitant about the thought of putting this guy's earphones in my ears, but don't have much choice. With toilet paper I do the best cleaning I can of them, then stick the proper end in the machine and the buds into my ears. The files I notice are cataloged by dates, the farthest one out only six weeks earlier. I play the first one.

"Yes, yes, of course—but that's all irrelevant," says a guy with an Italian accent. "The issue is not if back taxes are required, it is how much. And we're not talking seven digits. More likely eight."

"Eight digits as in ten million or as in ninety million?" a second voice responds.

I recognize voice number two.

Ryan Brand.

"Not ninety. But not ten. Either way, it isn't exactly the kind of

unforeseen line item that we can just absorb without serious conse-
quences."

"When will you know the damage?"

"We don't know. We haven't gotten that far yet. The full forensic process still has a couple weeks to go. After that, we'll be given
the bill."

There's a pause.

"Look, I understand your predicament. I do. But you need to
realize we have serious financial considerations here as well," Brand
comes back. "Our portfolio has its strong points, but it also has proj-
ects such as the Waterpoint that happens to be a one-point-five-
million-square-foot financial district property that's bleeding.
Lately, it seems that for every Five Eleven Madison Avenue—one
of our best—there's a Seven Fifty-Eight Third Avenue, a building I
have dreams about blowing up myself. We're all running businesses
here. In every case, it's a give and take."

A little more banter and this call ended. I move on to the next.

"So—any word?"

"Not yet. But seems like we've been spending every waking second feeding them documents and records. Between appeasing them
and trying to actually run a business—anyway—shouldn't be much
longer."

Brand and the mystery Italian again.

Pretty benign conversation, until: "You know, I heard this tax
thing isn't your only current problem," Brand says.

"What does that mean?"

"It means that if we're going to do this dance, we need to be up-
front with one another. There's a way for both of us to get where we
need to go here."

"I am nothing but up-front with you, Ryan."

"Right. So there's nothing to the potential civil suit aimed at
you swirling in your circles. That all your employees—not just in
Manhattan but in your other cities as well—are looking to come at
you for—"

"There won't be any civil suit. I'd be careful of listening to everything you hear, especially when it comes to me. People love to talk, make shit up. You know that."

"My sources seem—"

"Sources, please. Pffft. Sources, sources, please. What fucking sources? Someone like Soto? I know you two—"

"Not Soto."

"Then who?"

"Doesn't matter. What matters is that—what matters, like I said, is that we work together here. And that means being honest with one another."

Fuck.

Who's the mystery Italian?

The next conversation is worthless. I look at my watch. It's been about six minutes. I move to number four. Also more of nothing. Next is number five.

"They've completed the audit. Not pretty," says the Italian.

"How much?" asks Brand.

"Twenty-nine million."

Brand sighs.

"Wow."

"Sorry, Ryan, but I don't think I'll be able to dance with you this go-round."

"Now let's just relax for a second, Enzo."

Holy shit.

Enzo Alessi.

World-famous restaurateur.

Annex tenant.

"You can't just bail out on—"

"It doesn't work like that, Ryan. With all due respect, I like you. You're a nice guy. But you don't exactly know as much as you think you do. Especially when it comes to things like how I operate."

"What the fuck does that mean? You realize how much I've been covering for you?"

"Don't disrespect me with bullshit. You've been covering your own ass. If there wasn't something you needed from all this as well, none of these conversations would even exist. We both know you need Alessi to make this new lease. We both know what this does to you if we walk while—"

"Look, Enzo, let's just take a deep breath. There's no need to rush right here without thinking all of this through. How long has the government given you?"

"They haven't let us know yet. They'll be giving us the drop-dead date at the end of the week."

"Then let's wait and talk then. Okay? Can you do that?"

No response.

"I need some time, Enzo. We both know your securing this lease for me is a small gesture in the big picture."

Another pause, then: "I don't know, Ryan. I will certainly think on all this further. But I can't make any promises."

"I need to unload this building, Enzo. Your lease helps me do that. Whether you plan on honoring it or not."

Fucking fuck fuck.

What did we walk into?

Why couldn't Green go to the police? Or to Spencer himself—someone, anyone?

Why'd he kill himself? Why'd he trust me?

I look at my watch again. I need to get back.

After dropping Arnon's laptop back in his briefcase with the coat check, I return to my seat. As I do, my cocktail is being set down. Cobus and Arnon are locked in conversation. Julia is in the process of taking the last sip of sparkling rosé from her flute as a fresh one is placed in front of her.

"Bread?" she asks me.

Julia leans forward and grabs a piece of focaccia. When she does, I see down her neckline at the right half of her satin and lace bra—same color as her dress—and the top half of the breast it's holding. My eyes move back to her face. Still leaning forward, hand on the bread, her eyes are waiting for mine. They now, along with her chin, drop for a split second as she processes what must be my line of vision, then bounces back up and join me again. A faint, sexy smile comes to her lips as she quickly glances around while sitting back.

"No thanks," I respond, picking up my fresh cocktail.

Julia sits back. She tears a piece of bread, puts it in her mouth. I'm staring deep into her eyes, but my thoughts are consumed with the phone conversations I just listened to in the bathroom. And the conversations I haven't yet gotten to.

"What's the story with Enzo Alessi?" I ask.

"What do you mean?"

"I mean, what kind of place does he run? Is he really the restaurateur commoners like me read about?"

"You fancy yourself a commoner, do you?"

"I fancy myself a guy much like you—someone who likes to do his homework."

"Is that what this is? Homework?"

"Alessi is a major tenant in a property we're buying. You look just like the young contemporary hotshot who frequents his places. Smart, successful, cosmopolitan, ambitious."

"Is that right?"

"Is it not?"

She tears another piece of bread, drops it on the bread plate, and opts for her flute. She tosses a sip back.

"Enzo Alessi is top of the line. You're right—I do know the hotspots and, more importantly, the people behind them."

"Why do the Alessis stand out? I mean, there are a number of hospitality groups with multiple locations in some of the world's most important cities. The Alessis always seem to be at the top of the list, on the tip of everyone's tongues. Why?"

Julia thinks for a second.

"Penthouse balance."

Not often I'm stumped when talking business.

"Excuse me?"

"Penthouse balance," she repeats. "Some people in life, business, whatever, are really good at making things work for themselves or others via balance. For example, a woman who juggles career, parenting, a little yoga here and there—balance. Or, take a small company that decides to sell quality clothes at reasonable prices and mix in fantastic customer service that one day becomes The Gap—balance."

She lifts the flute to her glossed lips and lets a bit of the sparkling pink juice slide through.

"And?" I prod.

"And—likewise—the Alessis are all about balance. Only on a level that a select few get to experience—albeit a select few willing to seriously throw down for an awesome night on the town. World class, white-gloved service. The menu? Both inventive and staple dishes with only the finest ingredients. Best paper-thin, flash-fried zucchini and spaghetti Bolognese of your life. Yet often specials include aspects that have to be flown in from exotic locales around the world. Perhaps an appetizer might be reindeer pâté from Sweden or dessert is a sorbet of mangosteens from southern India. Ambiance? Borderline scientific. Uptown for the older, more established old-money sorts and power crowd you've got the perfect blend of dark, glossed wood surroundings, crystal chandeliers, and Old World art on the walls. Downtown, in contrast, the target is a much more chic crowd. More rustic surroundings, brighter colors, and walls adorned with cutting-edge nouveau art. The hottest music from Ipanema to Monte Carlo pumps from the speakers. As the hours grow later, the music gets stronger."

She stops to take a sip of her drink.

"They hire you to handle their PR while I was in the bathroom?"

"Ask, and ye shall receive—Commoner."

"You know a lot about them."

"I'm responsible for all the leasing in the building. It's my job to know them."

"A brand built on catering to the upper-crust. Each phase of the game, top to bottom, they've got figured out," I deduce out loud.

"The list goes on and on. Take the staff. Bartenders uptown are old-school in braces and bow ties. Downtown, the bartenders are all gigantic, rail-thin women wearing next to nothing."

"Who handles the day-to-day?" I ask. "I mean—we're talking about a serious operation here. They have multiple venues in this city alone, and I know the patriarch of the family has been sick for years."

"Enzo, of course, spends a significant amount of time in Manhattan each year. Outside of Rome, New York City is their biggest presence. But you're right, he could never handle this without an amazing team. The management both organizationally as well as with respect to each individual venue has been with the Alessi family for many years in most cases. They are a very dedicated, loyal group. Which, in my opinion, must come from how they have been treated all these years. That said, it always comes back to the same person."

"Enzo himself."

"Enzo himself," Julia concurs. "It might be a decision that affects the future of the organization, it might be a color for replacing the bathroom tiles in one of the restaurants' bathrooms. Enzo always makes the final call. Because he's obsessed with staying on top."

I look past Julia's shoulder at the watch on the wrist of her neighbor.

Eight twenty-five p.m.

Two days left.

"So what was it?" Cobus asks me in the Escalade on the way back to the hotel.

I turn to him.

"What was what?"

"The language you wanted to check in the Purchase Agreement? Pertaining to the retail?"

"Ah—just wanted to confirm that the language is explicit in terms of our being able to engage a new leasing agent for the retail and not having to stay with the GlassWell leasing arm," I explain before changing direction. "Where does Feuerbach Turm stand?"

Feuerbach Turm. The office building on Leipziger Strasse we passed on in Berlin's central business district.

"Still looking like Gruden and Wayfield are going to land it?"

"Looks solid, I believe, even though Latham mentioned to me Vienna Shanks has come in to make a last ditch play on it. Why?"

"No reason," I shrug. "Just found myself thinking about it tonight at dinner as some of the discussion moved to the tower tenants. The mix of firms, years remaining on the respective leases, who has what option made me compare the tenant roster to that of Feuerbach again in my head."

I turn back to the window. Manhattan, dark made even darker by the tinted windows, glides silently by. Only streetlights and headlights pop from the black beyond the glass, like Christmas lights thrown up aimlessly in a nighttime sky.

"Until our deal is done I won't stop comparing it to others," I go on. "Especially, other properties with real intrinsic strength."

"Not like you to second-guess yourself," Cobus says.

Second-guessing? More like planting a seed.

I keep my eyes calmly where they are.

"Not second guessing. Merely doing exactly what you pay me to do. Evaluate. Constantly."

Again, I turn to Cobus.

I remember the lessons of my father and of my mentor, Tommy Wingate.

"Until I see ink, I see nothing."

Just after ten p.m. I enter my hotel room. I pull my MacBook Air from my briefcase, place it on the little round table glowing in the night light coming through the window, and boot it up. I sit down in one of the two chairs next to the table and insert the flash drive.

I pick it up at the next conversation. Not much to this one; more back-and-forth concerning timing updates, more stalemate conversation about putting the lease in place. The next one gets more interesting.

"We've discussed it. Can't happen."

Enzo.

"Can't or won't? I don't buy can't."

Brand.

"How much time has the government actually given you?" Brand goes on.

"Irrelevant," Enzo responds. "We have already been having the necessary discussions about how our operation—adjusts—to this financial matter. Unfortunately, taking this space can't work for us. It simply makes no sense. If—"

"Ah, so the plan is a little restructuring. Some fine-tuning in order to repay the U.S. government while streamlining the operation. Perhaps even scaling down a bit in the short term," Brand cuts him off.

"Precisely."

"So there's nothing to a little something I heard about the Alessi family compound in Punta del Este?"

Punta del Este. Resort town. Uruguay.

"An interesting little nugget about an addition to the family mansion taking place right now? A story that includes an underground vault with stacks of cash and all sorts of interesting documents inside? It's located on the southeast—no, wait—the southwest portion of the property if I'm not mistaken. Right by—"

"How fucking dare you!" Enzo barks.

"How fucking dare I? You blatantly rip my country off, an act that now seriously threatens the well-being of both of our firms, and how fucking dare I? How fucking dare you!"

"This is not a game you want to play, Ryan."

"News flash, Enzo. We're already playing. I need Alessi signing a lease for the Annex. I simply can't take no for an answer. Very, very few tenants make sense for this space. You know that. And I need a lease in place in order to unload the property. Something my firm is counting on me to do."

"I will slit your fucking—"

"You know, something else interesting I just learned. Turns out the word is your father, who—I truly am sorry he's so ill—has no idea what you've done; what kind of trouble you've embroiled the company in he spent his entire life building up."

"You've got fucking balls, Brand. Fucking balls. I'd be very careful. Desperation has brought down many before you and is certain to be the downfall of many more."

"You're damn right, Alessi—I got balls the size of a bison. So let's just wade through the bullshit once and for all. You've got resources. I get it. But hopefully you can listen to this conversation and hear quite clearly I have resources as well. Good ones. In high places."

"Having some people with pull looking to peek into rooms where they are not welcome for a few bucks is not resources. Having—"

"What I have, Enzo, is all the motivation I need to get you in that building. And all the artillery I need to show the U.S. government you're planning on skipping out on a certain unpaid check should you choose to not work with me."

Nothing. Someone hangs up. Enzo, I assume.

Next call.

"I need something in return," Enzo begins.

"I'd say my not getting you locked up for the rest of your life, disgraced and shamed, is something enough."

"We both know you're not going to the government, Ryan. You care about one thing—winning. And here, your winning is not my downfall, something that fucks you as well. Here, your winning is getting this building sold for the highest price you can get."

No response.

"I don't care what you think you know about my family, my company, my plans. Your silly little words and threats don't bother me one bit. You're a clueless, spineless little worm in way over his head. A worm I'll squish into the pavement with my heel when it's time. But for now, I need to focus on my firm's—reorganization. And I can't have needless outside distractions. Besides, we both know that *should* something unforeseen happen with us as a tenant, there's nothing that really prevents word getting to your buyer once you have already closed that you knew all along there could be an issue with payment. In fact, that you orchestrated the deal that put the tenant in the property knowing full well they never intended on paying. Which, of course, will never be the case with us. Simply speaking hypothetically."

"This is ridiculous."

"Is it? You say the word. This conversation, this negotiation, is over."

Brand pauses.

"What is it you want?"

"Help with my unpaid tax bill to the United States government. From proceeds of the impending sale."

"Impossible."

"Impossible is nothing, Ryan. Just ask your fellow American Muhammad Ali."

"God, you're a scumbag. Can't happen. Sorry."

"And what would prevent you from doing this? When it means you selling the building, actually reaping a huge profit for both your firm and name, and moving on?"

"You know full well why it can't happen. There are simply too many eyes on a deal like this. From beginning to end. Every last dollar will be accounted for by numerous parties, both pre- and postclosing. It simply—"

"Make it happen, Ryan. That's the beauty of being one of the forces running a private company. Get creative. Because either you help me with my little tax problem, or you have nothing to go on besides the hand you already showed me. You're so impressed with your sources? Go ask them how Enzo Alessi is at moving mountains. Let alone a little digging and reburying to get rid of a bone or two."

I upload all of the conversations to my laptop. Then I place the flash drive back in my inside left jacket pocket.

CHAPTER 20

Two years into my stint with the Ooviks I was called into Jan's office. They had received a call from de Bont Beleggings—one of the fastest-growing commercial real estate firms in The Netherlands. Jan asked me if I was up to date with regard to de Bont Beleggings's strategy.

"Somewhat," I said. "I don't know details, but I know they have made some recent purchases."

Always staying in character, I downplayed my full understanding of the situation. I knew all one could about de Bont Beleggings—just as I did all the players in Europe—as someone could who didn't reside on the inside. This conversation with Jan took me back to my days in Manhattan.

To Tommy Wingate, my mentor.

Always know the competition in excruciating detail.

De Bont Beleggings was the competition.

Little did the Ooviks know they were my competition too.

Ivan Janse was an island in this world now—one Perry and Max resided on.

An island with a mission.

"They are interested in our portfolio," Jan continued.

I wasn't surprised. De Bont Beleggings was on the prowl for commercial property. Class A office buildings, high-end commercial canal houses like the Oovik portfolio, all of it.

"They have requested a tour of the portfolio next week. Cobus de Bont himself will be attending. And my family has decided we want you to lead the tour."

I waited in front of the first property with Jan. At 9:00 a.m. sharp a black Maybach pulled up. Cobus de Bont, same black suit, shirt, and tie he wears today, got out. He was with two others, a man and a woman, who looked to be around his age.

"Cobus de Bont," he said as we shook hands. "Pleasure."

"Ivan Janse," I reciprocated.

"I know."

Shit. He knows me?

"The pleasure is ours," I went on.

All six of us introduced ourselves and exchanged pleasantries. I liked Cobus right away. His handshake was strong, confident, the handshake of a real man. And his definite eye contact never wavered. He was reading me exactly as I was reading him.

"So, Ivan Janse, what is the plan of attack?"

"I thought we'd start here and move on to Geldersekade and Valkenburgerstraat. These properties are very similar to a portion of the Dudok Portfolio you purchased last month. As you'll see, we've done some terrific renovations and come up with some very creative ideas for use of space."

"Have they translated into the rent increases you anticipated?" Cobus asked.

"Exceeded them."

We all started inside. I led. Cobus was right behind me.

"Congratulations on Concertgebouwplein Twenty-Five. Great property," I said. "I was surprised you were able to pull it off. I know The Swagerman Group was very keen on landing it."

"Not as keen as I was."

It had been less than twenty-four hours since de Bont Beleggings had closed on this property. I had gotten the word from an insider at Swagerman with whom I often exchanged market information. I'd known the deal was in the works for months.

"You seem to be pretty tuned in to my firm," Cobus said.

I stopped and faced the group. My eyes locked with Cobus's.

"That's nice of you to notice, sir. But I'd be lying if I said it was just de Bont Beleggings. It's my obligation to the Oovik family to be tuned in to every firm and every aspect of this market. Period."

I looked toward the others.

"Shall we get started?"

The next morning, as I stepped into my office, the phone was ringing. I dropped my briefcase and answered it.

"Ivan Janse."

"Good morning, Ivan. Cobus de Bont."

I smiled. He had called me directly. I knew what was coming.

"I want the portfolio. And I want you to come work for me."

My rise through the ranks at de Bont Beleggings was meteoric. I was brought in to immediately oversee a portion of the fast-growing commercial real estate portfolio, including the Oovik buildings we'd just purchased. My portion of the portfolio was far outperforming those buildings I wasn't responsible for. Rents were higher, costs were lower, occupancy was higher, turnover was lower. The buildings were running like clockwork. I was strategically working the personnel, contractors, and vendors like a never-ending chess game. Yes, I was Ivan Janse. But only Jonah Gray could become so entrenched once again in commercial real estate.

A year later, I was running the entire European commercial real estate operation. Then, eighteen months after that, Cobus and I were having dinner at Christophe'.

"I believe in fate, Ivan."

He took a sip of his scotch.

"Do you?"

I didn't respond immediately. I swirled the Belvedere and rocks in my glass, looking down into it as if the answer would appear.

"I don't know," I finally said. "I think I tend to put a little more stock in us as individuals as opposed to believing it's all some journey we have no control over."

"Meaning?"

"Meaning I like to believe we all make our luck. Work hard, push yourself to see what this life really has to offer. You just might put yourself in the position to have something really great happen with a little luck."

I knocked a sip back.

"Is that how you view this?" Cobus asked. "Your meeting me? Your time at de Bont? Us?"

I was always in character.

Where Jonah was brash and cavalier, Ivan was humble, yet confident. Where Jonah was often driven by balls, flash, and the present, Ivan was often driven by respect, privacy, and a day yet to come.

"I'd like to believe that, Cobus," I said. "I'm just a kid from The Hague who made a commitment early on in my life to work hard and see where that takes me. And it has taken me to this moment, here, working for someone like you who I believe in."

"Huh," he said, thinking. "Your work with my firm, my team, your quick rise, if you will—it validates this belief for you," he deduced.

"What it does, Cobus, is make me want to work harder each day than I did the previous one."

He raised his glass to me.

"I truly believe I was put here to help this industry, this economy, create jobs and give people great places to go to work every day," Cobus said. "Places where they can work free of mind to make their dreams come alive as mine are. Every day."

I raised my glass, toasted Cobus back, and took a healthy swallow.

"I'm a true believer that my path is predetermined, Ivan. But I equally believe that in order to fulfill what I'm hopefully here to do, God is making sure I'm surrounded by the right people. Which is why there is something I need to ask you."

"Whatever you need, Cobus. You ask, it's done."

"I need you to be my right hand, Ivan. We are prime for serious growth. I need someone with your loyalty and real estate instinct to be with me at all times. I want everyone of rank on the commercial real estate end of our firm to report to you—not just in Amsterdam, but all four markets. Ludolf Mondrian will take over your position. From here going forward, he as well as the top officers in The Hague, Rotterdam, and Utrecht will all report to you."

Cobus de Bont was a smart, savvy businessman. My face remained stone, as if I was expecting this.

Which I was.

"I appreciate the confidence, Cobus. I'll certainly do everything I can to help you take this firm to the next level."

"That level is international, Ivan. We still have some work to do here in The Netherlands. There are a number of markets and properties we need to secure in order to unequivocally be viewed as the premier commercial real estate player in this country. But that shouldn't take more than a couple years, max. It will then be time to make our move."

CHAPTER 21

At ten fifty p.m., wearing the navy Canali suit I'd been in all day minus the tie and jacket that is folded in the passenger seat, I settle into the camel-colored, leather bucket seat of L's new Maserati. The ergonomically state-of-the-art seat absorbs me like a big fat aunt or uncle giving a giant hug—soft and comfortable, yet sturdy to handle the sharp turns that come with driving such a world-class machine. I think about my old Porsche, what must have happened to it. I look quickly around the interior of L's ride, marveling at the craftsmanship. The Shiny Titan Tex finishes. The perfectly treated leather. The chrome-finished steering paddles. The name of the model—Quattroporte GTS—in relief on the dashboard.

I put the key in and turn the engine over.

Boom.

The engine roars to life.

I touch the gas pedal. The engine puffs its chest a bit as if ready to breathe fire. I let the car warm up for a few seconds, taking in the even, purring sound of such high-level engineering. Twenty seconds later, I tap the paddle and shift the car into first gear. Slowly, I pull out onto the cobblestone streets of the Meatpacking District. I head uptown toward the Lincoln Tunnel.

Conscious of the speed limit, I move through the well-lit tube running from Manhattan to New Jersey. I look at the time—10:56 p.m. The crew has a breakfast meeting tomorrow at eight a.m.—plenty of time to get to Baltimore and back. And get what I need from Derbyshev.

I put the address—one of the notes I used to keep but eventually no longer needed—into the navigation system. After a quick calculation, it spits out the route and the specifics of the itinerary: 187.6 Miles, 3 hours and 31 minutes.

I compute this in regard to my timing. Three and a half hours puts me at Derbyshev's at two thirty a.m. or so. Tomorrow morning I should be back at the hotel no later than seven a.m. in order to shower and regroup; this means I need to leave Derbyshev no later than four a.m. in order to make it back to the city with plenty of time to drop L's car and get back uptown.

As the Maserati glides onto the New Jersey Turnpike headed south, I roll the windows down. Cool air rushes through the car. I take a deep breath, filling my lungs, then look in the rearview mirror.

My eyes.

Whose eyes?

Jonah? Ivan?

Where does this all lead? Can I possibly accomplish all I have set out to?

My eyes move from the mirror to the speedometer. I'm moving right at the speed limit. No music. Instead, I listen to the sound of an airplane approaching Liberty International Airport in Newark, the passing cars, and my thoughts.

I think about Perry. How much I miss her. I think about what Max said to me in the schoolyard when I asked if his father had mentioned his mother.

"Dad said she went away. And that she isn't ever coming back."

Is she dead? Lobotomized? Dropped in some Indian or Turkish

prison under a different name? Was her memory wiped out with one of those *Men in Black* neuralyzers?

Whatever it is, I won't stop until I know. I owe it to Perry. I owe it to her son.

I think about what else Max said his father told him: "That sometimes the stars align when we least expect it. That's how I made it back to him."

Dr. Brian York.

See you soon.

As the Maserati rolls farther south, my thoughts start spinning. My mental index is like a million-blade fan on high. I stick a pen in. When I do, the blade it stops on is Andreu Zhamovsky. Where has he been? I'd like to think in jail, but between his contacts and his disregard for the law altogether, something tells me I should know better. I had tried to get information on him, but it wasn't as easy as one might think. Careful as always not to inquire when in Amsterdam, I would do so when traveling to other parts of Europe. There was no reason to try the headquarters of Prevkos—the Russian-based natural gas conglomerate he used to run in succession of his father. Because when news broke years back that I was a fugitive on the run wanted for the murder of a police officer, news was also breaking that Andreu Zhamovsky had embezzled half a billion dollars from his shareholders. And it had been me who redirected that Prevkos's shareholder money to an account in Switzerland with Andreu Zhamovsky's name on it.

Needless to say, his time at Prevkos had ended prematurely.

Using calling cards and the like from pay phones, I reached out to his home. The goal was always to find out if he was still in jail—and if not, where he was. It was useless. These people were as tight-lipped as it gets. In hopes of getting a quick answer of if he was there or not—which alone would have been helpful—I would always pretend to be someone who seemed relevant to his past or daily life. It didn't matter. His home staff, his assistants—they would never answer my initial inquiry, always moving right into a question of their own of who I was. No matter what name I gave, they would put me on hold to verify. In which case, each time, I hung up.

There'd been nothing in the news about him. Ever. To be clear, I don't know for sure he's out of jail. What I do know is: there's no telling what he'll do to find me or get those eggs one day for his mother. The question remains why.

As the Maserati merges onto I-895, I look at the clock—1:15 a.m. Detective Morante pops into my brain. At the time I fled, not only did he think I murdered the dirty cop pulled from the East River, he believed—rightly so—I was somehow tied to my father's murder as well. He just couldn't figure out how. He had no idea that the connection was a simple one—the murder a sinister message to me—any more than he had a clue that I took care of the man responsible on my own, leaving him within a millimeter of his life before I left New York City.

All over again, after all this time, it makes my blood boil. I grip the steering wheel a little tighter. I feel the white Zegna button-down covering my torso starting to stick a bit on the arms and around the neck.

I have to find Morante. For more reasons than just the obvious.

I have less than forty-eight hours.

Detective Tim Morante.

See you soon.

I must . . .

WWWWEEEEEEEOOOOOOWWWWWWWW!!!!!!

Startling me, from the grass infield dividing the two sides of the highway, police car lights come to life in unison with a blaring siren from the blackness.

No.

Fuck.

As I pass the car, which is stationary and facing me in the opposite direction I'm driving, I look at the speedometer. It reads eighty-nine mph. Thinking about Morante, getting heated, my foot must have reacted like the rest of my body. Tensed up, gotten away from me, pressed.

Think.

Add it up.

Option one. Immediately slow down, pull over, and—

Yeah, right.

A foreign license, showing my false identity. In L's car. My real identity? A global fugitive sitting somewhere on the FBI's Most Wanted List for the murder of a New York City cop. I could see the conversation now. "I see. And how is it that you know one Tangueray Luckman? Who lives in New York City? Whose car you're driving? What, exactly, takes you so far away from New York City this time of night? I'm sorry, you said you were in the States for business from Amsterdam? Now, if—"

I look quickly at my neatly folded suit jacket in the passenger seat. I think about the phones. The gun! The flash drive. The keys. The loupe.

Can I pull it off?

Probably.

But if I don't? If something seems off to this cop?

I simply can't take that risk.

There is only one option. And it isn't option one.

It's dark. To that cop, all I am is an 89 mph blur speeding away in the opposite direction. The speed gun he shot me with—all that gives him is a number. I'm moving too fast for him to have gotten my license plate, the make or color of the car, anything more than my speed. Which, already, is substantially higher than 89 mph as my foot presses down harder.

In the rearview mirror, I see the fading red, white, and blue lights start to move. He's coming. My eyes move again to the speedometer. The dial shows a top speed of 200 mph.

Get what you need. Clean up the mess later.

I scan the road ahead. Light traffic, probably as many trucks carrying overnight cargo as there are cars. My head start is more than substantial, only enhanced because of the beast I'm driving. I start manipulating the paddles and the pedals. My speed starts steadily rising. 100. 105. 110. An image from my previous life flashes in my mind—me and my old Porsche heading out to Limerock Raceway on weekends for both of us to let off a little steam.

I'm not amongst the usual weekend warriors tonight.

But I'm sure as hell ready for a race.

Cruising in the left lane, my fingers tighten around the steering wheel. I press the gas harder. 120. 130. Slicing through the night, my heart rate climbs in synchronicity with my speed. There's a car up ahead in my lane, but I've got room. I glance in the rearview. The flashing, swirling lights suspended in the black behind me aren't getting any bigger. They're not getting smaller either.

My eyes move back to the road.

Fuck!

Brakes! Downshift!

Driving the Maserati as if on a runway looking to take flight, I'm about to drive straight through the car I thought was way in front of me.

My speed is essentially cut in half. I glance in the mirror. The lights are getting larger.

Instead of honking or flashing my brights, I slam the car right. I hit the paddles. The gears shift; the beast roars. I hit the gas. Truck in front of me. Paddles, shift, roar—this time as I pull the car farther right, I look in the rearview. The lights are larger, closer. I focus in front of me. Open road. I hit the gas. The needle rises again. 80. 90. 100. 110. 120.

The lights are getting smaller again.

I pass a bunch of cars and trucks on my left. Once I do, and I've got four-lane, wide-open road, I move back into the center.

130.

The screaming nighttime air bum-rushing me is loud, hard. Like fists punching me from every direction. Realizing I can probably hear the sirens better at this point with the windows up I raise them. The more I can gauge the siren's sound, the less I have to look back.

Back in the day, because of business, I had known Baltimore pretty well. That's why I knew my way around in a basic sense when

I first met Derbyshev just before my departure from the States. My eyes move to the navigation system screen. I need to hold him off. The next leg of the trip isn't far away. Once I hit it, I can explore losing him.

140.

The siren is fading.

Or, wait, is it?

No.

Out of the corner of my eye, in my peripheral vision, a new set of lights enter stage right. And they are slightly ahead of me, about two o'clock.

No!

I move into the left lane.

The new lights slow down a bit as they curve around the ramp entering the highway. I fly by them; get a good jump.

But the chase is definitely on.

150.

A clump of cars is approaching fast. They seem to be stacked toward the left of the highway. Anticipating where my open road will lie, I slam the car right. Behind me the suspended cop lights separate. Without truly knowing what lies ahead, in terms of obstacles, they must figure this increases their odds of not losing me.

I've got some solid separation. My eyes find the navigation system screen again. My exit is coming up. Seeing this, a strategy slaps me across the face. I hit the paddles and downshift. I move left into the small patch of cars and trucks drifting down the highway like a school of fish. I coast behind a car going about seventy-five in the second lane from the left.

My eyes move to the screen.

One mile.

My eyes bounce to the rearview mirror.

The lights, still spread apart, are growing.

I continue coasting.

Navigation screen again.

Three-quarters of a mile.

Fuck. The timing is off.

I can't have them get too close.

I upshift and floor the gas. I move the beast left into the fast lane. The tires grab the road like they have teeth as four hundred and fifty horses under the hood take off like they're all in the home stretch of the Kentucky Derby. In two seconds flat, I move right again. Just like that, the car that was in front of me is behind me. Up ahead I have a good hundred feet to the next car. Beyond that, I see a car up ahead in the left most lane, a semi in the second lane from the right.

Half a mile.

Rearview mirror. The lights have grown considerably. I move my eyes back to the windshield, shift, and hit the gas. Not too much, just enough to get the beast into acceleration mode again.

80.

90.

I creep up on the Audi Q7 in front of me.

I sit tight for one more second.

Navigation system.

Three-eighths of a mile out.

Wait. Wait.

I take a deep breath.

Now.

I tear out into the left lane. The sound of my engine makes my intentions clear, I'm ready to rock. Shifting the paddles, I floor it and take off screaming down the fast lane.

110.

120.

My eyes bounce to the rearview. Just as I hoped, both sets are coming together towards the two left most lanes, behind me. Just as they do, navigation system screen again.

Quarter of a mile.

Speedometer.

130.

140.

Just as I approach the car blocking me in the fast lane, I pull the car right as hard as I can. I downshift; I pass between a few cars in the middle two lanes with my eyes on both the semi moseying down the right lane and the exit ramp just beyond it.

Rearview. The cop cars are both doing their best to fight back right across the highway to me. Eyes ahead again. I stay on my hard angle line, tires screeching. The space between the front of the truck and the exit ramp is closing. My mind, like the beast, hits overdrive. I calculate my speed and angle in relation to the patch of road I need to hit—an off-ramp that, if memory serves me right, is so sharp going thirty is probably too fast. Immediately I come to a conclusion.

Looks like I overshot.

Fuck.

Fearing this situation may be beyond my control and simply a matter of physics, I hold my breath. I pull the car even harder. As the angle I'm traveling in relation to the highway moves from forty-five to somewhere between thirty-eight and forty, I feel the beast's inside wheels actually lift off the ground. Just as they do, and what must be an inch from getting tagged by the semi, I catch the corner of the exit ramp's shoulder just where it meets the grass leading to the woods beyond. Downshifting, but applying just enough gas to give me the velocity I need to get the wheels back down, I regain full control of the car. When I do, I downshift even farther as I now brake and reduce my speed just enough to keep me from flying off the road. Once sure I'm good, I move the steering wheel into the proper position for the hard-right ramp.

I exhale.

My eyes pop back to the rearview, remembering I have two cop cars on my ass. Just as my vision hits the glass, I see one of the two go flying into the woods. The other is a bit spun around, but seems to have held the road. Just as I see the car propel forward again, the hard angle of the turn forces him out of my line of sight.

One down.

Time to refocus. Now on the Baltimore beltway outer loop, I'm not far from my destination. No doubt more backup is on the way. Now is not the time to be bashful. I accelerate again as the beast glides through the Baltimore city limits like a figure skater's blade across ice. That's when I decide it's time to let the nice woman on the navigation system start earning her keep.

Left here.

Right there.

The beast's ability to corner like it's on rails, coupled with my lovely friend's ability to "recalculate route" on a constant basis, I decide the immediate need is separation. Moving like it's on the prowl, needs to feed, the beast aggressively scours the neighborhood. With each second, the volume of the pursuing siren remains the same or loses a notch. With each turn, between the acceleration and deceleration, it seems the cop car is huffing and puffing to stay with me.

Just as I feel I'm gaining some real separation, I hear another siren approaching. That's my cue. I look at the navigation screen. Then, I punch it.

I blast off down a main drag that will take me toward Phoenix, Maryland—one of Baltimore's suburbs.

100.

110.

I look in the rearview again. As I do, out of the corner of my left eye, I sense something. I jerk my head; it's too late. A cop car—no lights, no siren—is coming from nowhere straight at me. I flatten the gas pedal, and the car lurches forward. I propel myself forward enough to avoid a complete battering, but it's still too late. The cop car clips the back of the beast. The crunching sound of metal on metal fills up the night, my ears. My hands still on the steering wheel, but my fate completely out of my hands, the beast and I are spinning. What must be a split second feels an hour. It's like I'm in slow motion until both cars stop, leaving the beast and I facing the direction we were going after a complete three-sixty.

Then, nothing.

Both cars are stalled.

The only thing I hear is hissing. I turn and look back over my right shoulder.

The hissing is steam coming from under the cop car's hood, he—still in the driver's seat—and the car about a hundred feet away.

We look at each other.

Our eyes lock. His door swings open.

Fuck.

I turn the key. Nothing. I look in the rearview. Two sets of lights now—one closer than the other—both coming on strong.

I look over my shoulder at the cop again. A white guy, approaching fast, his hand now moving to his gun. I face forward again and turn the key.

The beast roars to life.

Paddles, shift—I slam the gas pedal to the floor. I look over my shoulder again. The spinning, screeching tires spew smoke into the air as the rubber finds the road. Once it does, and the two become one, I shift again. Just as I do, through the smog I'm creating, I see the cop. He has his gun extended.

I barely hear the words coming from his mouth, then—

BOOM! BOOM!

As I'm peeling away, my head now in my lap, two shots hit the back of the beast with two loud tings. A hundred yards or so away, I look up again. Just as I do, I wince from the sound of more gunshots. Only they don't seem to be coming at me. In the mirror I see the cop standing in the street, firing yet again, only in what appears to be another direction.

What the—

Is someone shooting at the cop?

How is that possible?

Time for confusion is pushed aside when another of the pursuing cars comes screaming by him.

Fuck—he's close.

The closest he's been yet.

My breathing is getting faster. I reel it in, pounding my right fist into my right thigh as I do.

This is it.

All these years.

All this running. The deception.

The lies.

The truth.

You all want to get wild, then let's get wild.

I've got work to do.

100.

110.

120.

The third car is significantly behind the second—which I'm now creating decent separation from again. I look at the navigation screen. I'm only a few turns, and a couple miles, from Derbyshev's neighborhood. Suddenly I downshift and turn off the main drag. Doing so immediately puts me in suburbia. Narrow, winding streets lined with nice homes where families are sleeping soundly on both sides of me.

I'm calm, collected. So much so I even focus on my breathing for a few moments as I upshift again.

My breaths are even, steady, like the beast.

That's more fucking like it.

I hear the sirens. They're still coming, but I clearly have the advantage as I'm out of sight. The streets are short, choppy. There isn't much room to hit higher than sixty mph before being forced into a turn.

Left here.

Right there.

Within a few minutes, once the sirens' volume has dissipated to my satisfaction, I manage my way with the assistance of my navigation consultant to the street perpendicular to Jarretsville Pike—the street where Derbyshev's mansion sits. I scan the area, lights off. We're moving slowly, steadily through the night.

I look at my watch—2:23 a.m.

I'm actually a bit ahead of schedule.

Guess hitting 160 mph can do that for you.

Finally I see it—the beast's perfect resting spot. There's a large home with a long driveway that wraps around the back of the house. I turn in, and the beast crawls up the driveway purring quietly. Once behind the house, I shut him down.

I grab my suit jacket, get out, and gently close the door. Using my iPhone's flashlight app, I survey the damage to L's car.

The rear, left corner got smashed pretty good. I walk around the back. I clearly see the two bullet holes.

Fuck.

I scratch my head. Then I head off on foot.

CHAPTER 22

After five years in Amsterdam, my research regarding the eggs had intensified, leading me to unbelievable results. First, let me refresh your memory:

There were fifty Fabergé Imperial Easter Eggs made between 1885 and 1916. Only forty-two of them were believed to have survived the Russian Revolution in 1917. At the House of Fabergé, two men oversaw the creation of these eggs—Mikhail Perkhin and Henrik Wigstrom. Whichever of the two oversaw a particular egg, their initials were on the egg along with assay marks relating to the karats and gold and either crossed anchors for the shop in St. Petersburg or St. George and the Dragon for the shop in Moscow. Not so for the one planted on me in New York City six years earlier or, as I would soon learn, any of the eight that went missing in the Russian Revolution. These had the assay marks as well as the mark denoting the house of origin. But they were all without initials. And all eight were made by a man named Piotr Derbyshev, an expert stone carver at the House of Fabergé.

Piotr Derbyshev was the grandfather of Pavel Derbyshev, the man in Baltimore, Maryland, in possession of the missing Imperial

Easter Eggs. He—Piotr—was requested to oversee the creation of these eight eggs in particular by the Empress Maria Feodorovna herself. The woman for whom they were made.

Galina Zhamovsky—or the artist known as Ia—secretly communicated with my father through her artwork. And she wanted these eggs so badly she was willing to sacrifice even her own son, Andreu Zhamovsky, to get them. The reason I could never let any of this go—why I remained obsessed with figuring out the true story behind the missing Fabergé Imperial Easter Eggs—was not simply because they were the undoing of my life and the reason my father was dead. It was because of the message in the last piece she sent Pop.

"I must stay true to my own. Cement my legacy. At all costs."

This much I knew.

Now, here's what I have learned.

I scoured every available piece of material on the planet about the eggs. While I didn't learn anything from this in terms of what Galina could be looking for, I did learn every available detail about the missing eggs. Most notably the materials used in each. We'll get to this later.

I ultimately decided to learn as much as humanly possible about all the players connected to the *story*, if you will. I started with Piotr Derbyshev. He was a master stone carver at the House of Fabergé. He studied at the Ekaterinburg School of Art and Industry in Ekaterinburg, Russia. Apparently, the school no longer exists. I'd reached out to the Ekaterinburg City Hall online in search of something, anything, and managed to befriend a clerk. She was a seemingly lonely type looking for a pen pal, and it turned out she liked the challenge of corresponding in the English she'd been studying. She sent me everything she had on record about the school, the bulk consisting of group photos of each graduating class. And in one of those pictures was Piotr Derbyshev, allowing me to finally put a face with the name.

Next up was Maria Feodorovna. I reacquainted myself with her life, her path. Born into Denmark royalty in 1847 as Princess Dag-

mar of Schleswig-Holstein-Sonderburg-Glucksburg, she would die
in 1928 as the Empress Maria Feodorovna of Russia. She had four
sons and two daughters with Czar Alexander III, including Emperor
Nicholas II—Russia's last monarch whom she outlived by ten years.
The more I learned about Maria Feodorovna, the more intrigued I
became. She was supposed to be married to Nicholas, the heir
apparent to Czar Alexander II, but he was ill and died of meningitis
in 1865. Lore has it that his last dying wish was that Maria marry
his younger brother Alexander III, who would eventually have the
throne. I found this fascinating.

Nicholas's last dying wish was that his young fiancée marry his
younger brother.

Really?

Who does that?

In a bookstore in Amsterdam, I had picked up a book about
King Christian IX of Denmark—Maria Feodorovna's father. There
was a portrait of his vast family, one of those painted-looking ones
where everyone is looking regal with the women in frilly dresses
and the men in their military garb. The king and his queen were
standing in the center of the portrait. But one of the peripheral
players off to the side made me do a double take.

Then a triple take.

There stood Piotr Derbyshev. The same Piotr Derbyshev from
the Ekaterinburg School of Art and Industry.

Only he wasn't Piotr Derbyshev.

He was Maria's cousin.

Gustav Bjerg.

This was too fucked up. I was sure they were the same person. I
bought the book and rushed back to 251 Herengracht. I put the two
photographs side by side. Gustav was Piotr; Piotr was Gustav. It was
unmistakable. Gustav Bjerg apparently became a master stone carver under the fake name Piotr Derbyshev in order to work at the
House of Fabergé and ultimately make Imperial Easter Eggs for his
cousin—at her request.

Why?

What were they up to?

Fast-forward to our generation. Galina Zhamovsky, married to Alexander Zhamovsky, had a son—named Andreu—with my dad. And Andreu was probably, hopefully, still sitting in a Russian jail somewhere for the stunt he tried to pull with a few hundred million of his company's shareholders' dollars. He was paying for trying to purchase the eggs for his mother—without, it turned out, even knowing why.

Because Galina Zhamovsky needed to "stay true to her own."

Who was Galina Zhamovsky, really?

I hadn't been sure where to begin. While her husband and son were public figures in the business world, she was not. Whether I tried to learn about her as Galina Zhamovsky or Ia—her name as an artist—I came up empty. In fact, it was almost as if she didn't even exist no matter what I read about Alexander or Andreu. Nothing about her present, nothing about her past.

But the more I looked, one name kept surfacing. Alexander's right-hand man for years at Prevkos—a man who resigned from the company the day Alexander was found murdered in a Russian subway station.

Aleksey Mateev.

Aleksey Mateev was quoted in nearly every article written about Prevkos or Alexander Zhamovsky. Alexander was often described as the "brain" of the organization and Aleksey, the "backbone." Then, just like that, Mateev resigned after Alexander's death and refused comment. From that day in 1998 forward, I couldn't even find a single mention of Aleksey Mateev.

I was sitting at the Parsons table in my research room at Herengracht. It was the middle of the night, the only light in the room from the glow of my Mac's screen. I had one of the windows cracked for some fresh Amsterdam air. Just as I was about to give up on this particular direction, I decided to give it one more Google search for something I might have missed. There were pages and pages of all the articles I had studied. But on page twelve there was a search result I didn't recall, an article in the *Daily Telegraph* about a car accident in London. And the only witness to that accident was a man named Aleksey Mateev. The article was only three months old.

I took down the name of the journalist who wrote the article. The next morning, from a pay phone on the streets of Amsterdam, I called the newspaper.

"Daily Telegraph, good morning," a cheery voice answered.

"Joan Ellison, please," I said.

"Have a great day," the voice said as I was connected.

I took a deep breath. I couldn't decide which I wanted more: her to pick up, or not.

"Joan Ellison."

Showtime.

"Yes, Joan. Good morning. This is Detective Egerton. I work with Detective Fletcher whom you met a few months back when writing about the hit-and-run that took place on Adam Street."

I had gotten Fletcher's name from the article.

"Right, sure—the hit-and-run on Adam Street. What can I do for you, Detective?"

"There was a witness in the case, as you know, a man named Aleksey Mateev. It turns out I have come across something of interest perhaps to this case this morning, and I would like to ask Mr. Mateev some questions about my findings. While time is of the essence, unfortunately, Detective Fletcher is out of the country with his family. I was hoping you could give me Mr. Mateev's phone number and address so I can properly follow up."

There was silence on the other end. Not good.

"I'm not terribly comfortable giving out information like this over the phone," she said as I had literally parted my lips to press on.

"Of course," I said. "I understand. I can certainly swing by your office to get it from you, but in doing so I might miss out on an associated lead. That's why I figured I would call you directly and—"

"No," she cut me off, "no—you don't need to do that, Detective. Give me one second."

•   •   •

"Hello?" a male voice answered with a thick Russian accent.

"Mr. Mateev? Aleksey Mateev?"

"Who is this?" my question was answered with a question.

"I want to speak with you about Alexander Zhamovsky. About Prevkos."

"I'm sorry, I cannot help you," he responded after a brief pause.

"But you are in fact the same Aleksey Mateev who worked at Prevkos," I pressed.

"As I said, I cannot help you."

"Actually, I believe you can," I countered. "I'm a friend, Mr. Mateev. My guess is you resigned that day in 1998 because you never bought into the circumstances surrounding Alexander Zhamovsky's death. You were right not to."

"What is it you want?"

"Just to talk. But not over the phone. I would come to London." Nothing.

"I wouldn't be asking if it wasn't important, Mr. Mateev. And I give you my word our conversation will remain confidential."

"Your word? You still haven't even told me your name."

"I just need some information. I have your address. Like I said, I would be happy to come to you."

I threw in that I had his address to motivate him. My subtle way of saying I'll be coming no matter what, you can know when or wait for me to surprise you.

There was a sigh on the other end.

"When will you be coming to London?"

CHAPTER 23

The endless, twinkling stars are the main source of night light accompanied by a softly lit streetlight here or there. I come up to 5 Jarrettsville Pike. Within a second of seeing the high gates and high foliage that surrounds the count's sprawling property and castle, déjà vu overwhelms me. I could swear I was just here. It seems like mere seconds since I last saw the sharp, pointed roof of the towers, which tonight, like the foliage, are just solid, outlined shapes a darker shade of black than the night surrounding them.

I come up on the gate's main entrance to the driveway. There's a speaker and button, along with a prominently displayed camera to let any visitor know the game plan. I hit the button. From the speaker I hear ringing, like it's a phone call. At this hour, I figure the staff is gone for the night or asleep, that the count will pick up. No answer. It keeps ringing. I look around. The ringing stops.

I hear a whirring sound as the camera changes position. It stops once positioned squarely on me. I wait for words, but still nothing.

"Hello?" I say, working the European accent.

Still nothing.

"Is—"

"Who are you?" a voice cuts me off.

The man himself. The thick Baltic accent, exactly as I remember it.

I didn't give him my name then. I don't want to give it out now.

"The restaurant Prime Rib, a number of years ago," I respond, European slant on my voice.

"I'm the guy who kicked you in the balls then dove out the bathroom window."

Silence.

"I don't look like you remember me—I know. But—"

"I have already dialed the nine and first one. Police will be here shortly."

"Please. Don't. I promise you, it's really me."

Drop the bomb.

I lose the accent. And return to my God-given voice.

"It's really the Prime Rib guy. The guy who saved you from turning your family's treasures over to Andreu Zhamovsky."

There's a pause. Then: "How . . . what . . ."

Silence again.

"I know. It doesn't seem possible. And God knows what you learned about me in the news. I promise you, I'm innocent. I promise to explain all this if you'll please let me in."

"What is it you want from me?"

"I need to see the eggs."

"Why?"

"I'll tell you that once I'm face-to-face with them. And you."

Silence.

"Please, Mr. Derbyshev. I'm sorry it's the middle of the night. And I know my showing up here after all these years, looking and sounding like a completely different person who wants to come into your home is completely absurd. But I've waited a long time for the opportunity to approach you. I promise—you aren't in any danger. Nor are the eggs. I simply need to lay my eyes on them for a few minutes."

"That all sounds well and good," the count responded, "but how can I be sure it's you? How do I know you're not some mentally ill, unusually conniving, sinister animal who literally beat the necessary information out of the real man you're claiming to be to put yourself in this position to possibly just walk into my home and loot me of my family's treasures? All of this assuming I would even keep them here."

Huh.

Good point.

"Go back to that night," I reply.

"Excuse me?"

"That night when we met face-to-face at Prime Rib. I remember every second of our meeting, from when I approached you and your chauffeur slash bodyguard out front upon your arrival until I jumped in my car and took off with same said chauffeur slash bodyguard coming after me with a gun."

"Your point?"

"My point is that I'm confident whatever you may recall, I will recall as well. In the short time we met that night before—once again—I actually saved you from getting smoked by Andreu Zhamovsky, a lot happened. Both at your table as well as in the men's room. An imposter would have basic information to get into position to rip you off, not the nitty gritty of our encounter. So—ask me anything. Go for details."

His table as well as the men's room.

Possible someone who had put a gun to my head to get into this position would have asked me details like that, but not likely.

Silence.

A good thing.

He's thinking of something to ask me.

"You sat down at my table, and I asked you your name that night," he finally said. "What did you tell me?"

"I responded with a set of numbers. Which you immediately identified as your Social Security number."

The gate slowly begins to swing open.

•   •   •

As I walk toward the monstrosity of a home, the closer I get the more lights—obviously triggered by motion detectors—come on. And with each additional light, I see more of the structure against the night sky. The count's castle is even more "castle" than I could have imagined. It's like I left Manhattan, drove a couple hours, and somehow ended up in the Irish countryside. The castle is primarily comprised of dark brick and stone and has all the trimmings: cylindrical towers, coned roofs with pointed tops, a porte cochere, the works. I can't help but think I'd better look down lest I fall into a moat.

The huge, heavy wooden plank of a door slowly swings back. When halfway open, Derbyshev steps into my sight standing in the cavernous entry vestibule under the dim light of a few wall sconces. He looks older, his long face more weathered, his silver hair more silver. Nonetheless he's looking as countlike as ever—only this time in a long, red smoking jacket that seems to be doubling as a robe over his blue pajamas instead of the razor-edge sharp pinstriped suit and alligator shoes he wore during our first meeting.

He's studying my face. He looks me up and down.

"Only two types of people would change themselves as if right out of a science fiction novel. Someone very innocent or someone very guilty."

Way too loaded. Not touching that one.

"I appreciate you trusting me, Mr. Derbyshev. I appreciate you opening this door. I've thought about this moment—this night, whenever it might come—for a long time."

"You saved me from handing over my family's treasures, treasures the flesh and blood I come from crafted with their own hands, for a half a billion dollars that my accepting would have put me in jail. Please. Call me Pavel."

He turns around and heads into the house, which I take as my invitation to follow him. I step into the entry vestibule and close the door.

I follow the count inside. Suddenly the lights come up. When they do, I realize I'm indeed standing in a palace that looks surprisingly similar to what I had envisioned. Behind the count is a rich, lustrous great room. The floor is white marble so shiny and clean it looks like I can eat off it. The walls are the same red as the count's smoking jacket, robe, whatever. The furniture—all upholstered with black velvet—like the chandeliers is finished with the same gold that frames the mirrored ceiling grid topping off the room. A ceiling that looks like it's being held up by the interspaced columns made from the same marble as the floor.

"Are you hungry or thirsty?" he asks, pointing in a direction that I imagine leads to the kitchen. Or one of the kitchens.

"No, thank you," I respond. I look at my watch. "And even if I was, I simply don't have the time to spare."

"Then let's get to it."

The count starts off into, then through, the great room with me following. He glances back at me over his shoulder.

"How—if—"

He faces the direction we're walking again.

"Forget it," he continues. "I don't think I want to know."

"No," I answer, understanding he's talking about what went into this hardcore physical transformation. "You don't."

Unsurprisingly, the house is like a never-ending maze. After walking for what must be a couple minutes, we enter what looks to be a very large office. The room feels out of place. Its shell is certainly part of the home it sits in—the walls, ceiling, and moldings—but all the furniture, the iMac as well as Bloomberg terminal sitting on the huge glass desk, the multiple flat-screens on the wall are all up-to-the-minute. There are antique sculptures on pedestals; there are contemporary paintings on the walls. The space is a complete contradiction of itself. A contradiction existing in harmony.

"Welcome to my office," the count says.

He heads behind a desk and opens a minifridge sitting on a cherrywood credenza. He takes a La Croix from it.

"Might I interest you in a La Croix?"

"A what?"

"A La Croix. Seltzer water by itself is so…boring. But this La Croix? Just the perfect hint of flavor. And they have a new peach-pear flavor. It's just the right blend of—"

He stops when he looks at me, and sees my "Are you fucking kidding me?" expression.

"Please," he says graciously, gesturing to the cordovan leather sofa. "Sit. And tell me what you're doing in my office in the middle of the night after all these years."

I sit on the couch. He takes a seat on one of the leather chairs facing me. I take a deep breath.

"The night of our meeting, once I was gone and driving back to where I came from, I called your house. And you picked up. Do you remember that?"

"I do."

"I explained to you I understood, after putting it together, you didn't have just one of the missing eggs, but all six," I go on. "As we got into it a bit further, you asked me if the name Maria Feodorovna meant anything to me. I said it did. I knew by this point she was the Russian empress for whom many of the imperial eggs, including all eight that went missing in the revolution, were made. It was at this point you said something that got me thinking. Something I carried with me until a time when I could investigate the matter on my own."

"What was that?" the count asked.

"You told me Maria Feodorovna was the kind of woman who fought for the things she believed in, stood up for those to whom she'd made a commitment. That she had an eye for talent which is why she had Henrik Wigstrom, the man running the House of Fabergé at the time, give Piotr Derbyshev—your grandfather, and a man who had shown great promise through his contributions to the eggs—an opportunity to lead the creation of some of the eggs on his own."

"That's correct."

"The eggs Maria Feodorovna had her servants round up as the revolution unfolded and her castle was stormed, before all the others. She managed to save all eight, two of which were stolen soon after, not to be seen again until found in Yakutsk in 1979."

"So as the story goes, that's right."

The count shifts in his seat.

"Where exactly are you going with this?" he asks.

CHAPTER 24

In the Hampstead Garden suburb of London I walked up to a huge country-style red brick house at the address of South Square NW3. The home was gorgeous, appeared to be immaculately appointed, and couldn't have been any smaller than six thousand square feet. It was summer. The grass, trees, flowers, shrubs—every inch of foliage covering the large property was perfectly manicured. I walked up the half-circle driveway, climbed the stairs, and rang the doorbell.

A very tall man, with strong facial features that included a really large nose, answered the door. He had short, almost spikey-looking, gray hair to go with a matching gray goatee, and rectangular wire-framed glasses covering his oak-tree-bark brown eyes. He wore jeans, a white button-down shirt opened to the second button, and black casual loafers with no socks.

He extended his large hand. I shook it.

"Do I get a name now?" he asked.

"I can't give you my name, Mr. Mateev. I'm sorry. My last intention is to disrespect you. I prefer not to tell you because the less you know about me the better."

A look of disappointment glossed Mateev's face, but only for a second. The way his brows immediately furrowed showed me he was a smart enough man to get it. And after all, I had found him when he had clearly done his best not to be found. The sooner he dealt with me, the sooner he'd be rid of me.

"Like I said on the phone, I'm a friend. I just want some information and I'll be on my way."

"Come on in."

I stepped inside and followed Aleksey Mateev through the sprawling bottom floor of his home.

"Let's settle in the living room," he said as we entered the large, triple-aspect living room.

The room was white to the point it almost felt angelic. The long, wide suede couches, the lamps, the tables, chairs, the ceramic vases—everything was white. The only color was from a couple of purple throw pillows and some of the most intense purple roses I had ever seen. He held out his hand to offer me a seat.

"Anything to drink, Mystery Man?" he asked as I sat down.

"No. Thank you."

Mateev sat down as well. He crossed his legs, leaned back comfortably, and spread his arms out along the top of the couch.

"So. How exactly can I help you?"

"You and Alexander Zhamovsky must have been close. Apparently, you were next to him from the moment he was given control of Prevkos until the moment he was found murdered. That must have been a terrible day."

"Terrible indeed. Alexander was a good man."

"Tell me—how long after you resigned did you leave Russia?"

"Almost immediately."

"On your own volition? Or were you pressured?"

"Why is that of importance to you?"

It's not, really. We both know the answer, and the understanding of Alexander's death was no more than my hook to get me inside.

I changed directions.

"Mr. Mateev, I'm not here because of Alexander. I'm here because of his wife."

"In what regard?"

"In the regard that I can't seem to find any background information on her, and I need to know where she comes from. Who she is."

"Why?"

"That's complicated. And gets us back to the area of the less you know the better."

Fuck, I thought. I had to give him something if I was going to get anything.

"But I will tell you one thing. I'm quite confident Galina Zhamovsky ordered the hit on her husband."

Mateev looked puzzled.

"Galina? No—"

"Hard to believe. I know."

"Galina Zhamovsky always appeared a fine woman, a dedicated woman. She was one of my wife's closest friends for almost thirty years."

"A dedicated woman—absolutely. A fine woman—not so much. You said yourself you believed the circumstances surrounding Alexander's death were questionable. My guess is this is the reason you resigned so quickly. I'm also guessing you believed it was a hit as well—only business related."

"How do you know these things? And why now, so many years later?"

"Mr. Mateev, what can you tell me about Galina Zhamovsky? Please?"

"Of course we all spent a lot of time together, but as I said, it was my wife who was close with her, who would know the details of her life."

"Is your wife home?"

"No. She passed away a few years ago."

"I'm sorry to hear that."

He nodded.

"Mr. Mateev, you did know Galina for almost thirty years," I went on. "Anything you can remember might be helpful. Anything."

Mateev looked away from me at nothing in particular as he began thinking.

"Galina is a passionate woman. She loves her art. She loves her son. And from what I knew of her, I would have sworn she loved her husband."

"Where is she from originally?" I asked.

Mateev's eyes returned to me.

"St. Petersburg. And, if I'm not mistaken, I believe her maiden name was Romanov."

St. Petersburg.

Romanov.

The two went together somewhere in my research. And I was pretty sure where.

Back in Amsterdam, I tore into the Herengracht apartment like a cyclone. I started scanning the walls. Then I saw it. Czar Alexander III of Russia's full name was Alexander Alexandrovich Romanov.

And he was born in St. Petersburg.

The same Czar Alexander III who married Maria Feodorovna.

I started to think about Czar Alexander III, all I had read about him over the years. I also thought about his older brother Nicholas—the true heir apparent to the throne and intended husband of Maria Feodorovna—who died young of meningitis before he could ascend. In 1864, in apparently good health, Nicholas became engaged to Maria Feodorovna, or Princess Dagmar of Denmark at the time. A year later, after mysteriously starting to show symptoms such as back pain, a stiff neck, and sensitivity to noise and light, Nicholas was dead. His last wish on his deathbed: that his younger brother marry his bride to be.

Why was this so interesting?

I'd read that Nicholas had intentions for when he took the throne—intentions that were not in line with Alexander III's interests for Russia. In fact, between the years of 1865 when Nicholas was out of the picture and 1881 when he would finally take the throne, Alexander III made his vision of an ideal Russia very clear. Alexander wanted to reverse the liberalization of Russia born from his father's reign. He wanted to institute—which he eventually put into motion—mandatory teaching of the Russian language throughout the Russian Empire. He wanted an Empire of a single language, nationality, and religion.

Alexander was also with his older brother when Nicholas died in the south of France, the only one present when his dying older brother declared if he couldn't marry his beloved princess Dagmar of Denmark, his younger brother should.

Who was Czar Alexander III really?

A man willing to step up for his royal family? Or master manipulator?

Click.

It started coming together.

I remembered an article I had read online and printed out by a Russian man named Nestor Korolyev written in 1994. I easily located it on the wall and took it down. Mr. Korolyev was a doctorate candidate in history at Ivanovo State University which is located about three hundred miles east of Moscow. His thesis was based on the relationship between Nicholas and Alexander III before Nicholas' untimely death. The piece received national attention because whereas history outlines a strong relationship, Mr. Korolyev described what he believed to be a strained one. A relationship undermined by—among other things—their mother's love and preference for the elder Nicholas.

Nicholas was the popular type, a strapping guy with good looks and social skills. Alexander III was big and clumsy with a large, ugly wen on the left side of his nose. According to Korolyev, Nicholas received preferential treatment with regard to his education and gifts. Nicholas and his mother were so close they would tell secrets in the other's ear in front of Alexander III. Apparently—again, according to Korolyev—there was a solid foundation for jealousy.

Perhaps vengeance?

What did this have to do with Gustav Bjerg—Maria Feodorvna's cousin—becoming Piotr Derbyshev to make her Fabergé Imperial Easter Eggs?

Click click.

The insinuations made in Korolyev's thesis were one thing. But it was the suggestion of foul play that made the piece headline news. According to history, after Nicholas's death, Princess Dagmar—Maria—was distraught and returned to her hometown to be with her family. So distraught, in fact, her friends and family were worried about both her mental and physical well-being. So why then would she come around and marry Alexander III?

What if not only Korolyev was correct, but Maria Feodorvna was already onto Alexander III?

And had recruited her cousin, Gustav Bjerg, to help her find the truth about her beloved Nicholas?

CHAPTER 25

"Sir, I believe Piotr Derbyshev—at the least the one who worked for the House of Fabergé—is someone different than you believe."

I produce the loupe from my right inside suit jacket pocket.

"If I can just have a look at these eggs, we'll know for sure if I'm right or wrong."

The count sits silent for a second, processing what I just said. He opens his mouth about to speak, but stops himself. He stands up and walks over to one of the bookshelves on the far side of the room. In the middle of one of the shelves, between bookends separating his Keats and Nietzsche collections, is a small, unassuming gray stone sculpture no more than six inches tall that resembles an uneven *U*. He puts his hand on it, looks at me, and turns it counterclockwise.

Eight white, circular columns ascend slowly from the ground as the lights go dim. They are spaced unevenly, each one's placement as eclectic as the egg itself with regard to the collection. As the pillars rise, thin, halogen spotlights drop from the ceiling slicing through the air silently like eels through water. On top of each col-

umn is a glass case, inside each is one of the eight Imperial Easter
Eggs the world believes to be missing.

The spotlights, each placed with a surgeon's precision, eventually stop in position to maximize, highlight each egg's lustrous
beauty. The spectacle is breathtaking.

"Holy fuck," I push out in a whisper.

My eyes, mystified, drift around the room. As they do, I notice
there are eight columns, but only seven eggs. One of the glass cases
perched on top of a pillar is empty. The one missing is *Danish Jubilee
Egg*, the one that had been in my possession. That said, I'm surprised to see *Empire Nephrite Egg*—the other found along with
Danish Jubilee Egg and also auctioned off in 1979.

I point to *Empire Nephrite Egg*.

"I thought when we spoke way back when—"

"I know what you thought," the count cuts me off, "that Galina
Zhamovsky was in possession of it. All I said to you was that
Andreu and I had a mutual acquaintance in possession of *Empire
Nephrite*. You assumed it was she. In fact, it was a man named
Mehmet Nas who resides in Istanbul. And, for the right price, I was
finally able to take it off his hands."

I gaze around the room again.

"May I?"

"Please," Derbyshev responds.

I stand up and slowly walk around the room. I have seen them
in pictures, read about them online and in countless books and
papers. I had held one in my hands. But this is truly amazing. It's
like my own private showing of a museum collection. The gems,
the metals, are brilliant, transcendent. Each is like a mélange, a
dessert, of the earth's finest ingredients, plated to perfection.

"*Danish Jubilee Egg*," I say, referring to one of the missing two.

"On display at the U.S. Capitol. Has been for years. Actually,
since right around the time of our meeting."

"Is that right?" I respond, feigning curiosity.

When Andreu Zhamovsky dragged me into his sordid plan way

back when and saddled me with *Danish Jubilee Egg*, it had been on its way to the U.S. Mission at UN where it would make a brief appearance before ultimately going on display at the U.S. Capitol as a tribute to repaired U.S.-Russian relations. I was the one who made sure it got there.

Deciding I need to start at the beginning, I stop in my tracks.

"*Hen Egg with Sapphire Pendant*," I say, glancing around the room. I see it. "Ahh."

Hen Egg with Sapphire Pendant is the first one made chronologically of the eight. I notice it from the description alone; there are no visuals on record of this specific egg. I close my eyes for a moment and see *Hen Egg with Sapphire Pendant's* rightful wall space at 251 Herengracht. I locate the imperial archive invoice dated February 15, 1886 through April 24, 1886, which suggests the following description: "a hen of gold and rose diamonds taking a sapphire egg out of a nest." I open my eyes. The perceived history seems true to form, and the piece is as brilliant as it is breathtaking. Held loosely in the hen's beak is the sapphire egg. What looks like hundreds of rose-cut diamonds adorn the gold base.

As I mentioned earlier, the materials used in these eggs were the finest that can be mined from our earth, elements like emeralds, pearls, gold, silver, rubies, diamonds, and platinum. Each egg used different combinations. But only one ingredient was the same from egg, to egg, to egg.

Gold.

Galina Zhamovsky—a black widow spider who had learned to secretly communicate through her artwork—wants these eggs desperately.

Why?

What was she trying to protect?

I move my wide eyes to the glass, but I'm still inches away. I look at the count. I hold up the loupe.

He scratches his head. He grabs the U statue with both hands, and pulls it up, off the shelf. When he does each glass cube protecting the eggs at the top of each column retracts on top like a sunroof, then descends with the sides to a comfortable resting place completely exposing the eggs.

We both suck in a breath. Mine's out of amazement. His is out of fear.

"Not a *print*! I don't want even a hard breath touching that egg."

"Of course," I respond.

I put the loupe in my eye and move in. To see the precious gems on top of the exquisite gold this close—it's like looking at blinding diamond mountains sitting directly on the surface of the sun. I slowly, painstakingly, move the loupe. I don't see anything in the gold. I move my feet and begin circling with a snail's pace.

"Well?" asks the count.

"Nothing. As I look at it I'm trying to—"

Wait.

What's that.

"Trying to what?" I'm prodded.

I can't fucking believe what I'm looking at.

"Holy fuck," comes out in a loud whisper.

"Holy—what?"

"I think I found something."

It would be hard to slip a piece of paper between the loupe and egg and yet I move a hair closer.

"Letters. Words."

I stop, process.

"But they don't appear to be Russian characters."

"What are they?"

"It says, 'Intro til V.A. strong vinkel. Accepterer mig.'"

The count is speechless. He has nothing, just shakes his head. I, on the other hand, feel I know exactly what language it is.

If Korolyev was right, and Piotr Derbyshev was really Maria Feodorovna's cousin Gustav Bjerg, he would be trying to communicate with her in their native language.

Danish.

I look around the room. My eyes stop on his desk.

"Your desk, your computer," I say.

His feet start immediately.

"You know how to handle the Internet?" I ask.

He shoots me a sharp look.

"Sorry. I, uh—I just—"

"I may be an older gent, but I am living in the same year you are, young man."

"Right. Google Danish to English translation. It will bring up like a hundred translation sites," I continue. "All we do is type in the words, put English as the translate to language, and go down the list of languages we're translating from."

"Why Danish?" he asks, mid-stride.

I realize that—if I'm right—I'm about to blow up this man's understanding of his own family.

"Let's hold off on that until we know if I'm right or not."

He stops in front of his computer, sits down, and begins typing.

"Here we go."

His fingers keep going.

"Okay. Give me those words again."

"*Intro til V.A. strong vinkel. Accepterer mig.*" I repeat, then I spell each word out for him.

I take out my iPhone. I take a picture of the loupe showing the enhanced letters, making sure to get at least part of the egg behind the border of the magnifying glass into the photo.

"What are you doing?" the count snaps. "I never—"

I whip my head around to face him.

"I need pictures as evidence."

"Evidence for whom? For what?"

"What matters is that no one will ever know where these photos came from any more than where these eggs reside. You have my word. Now, the translation."

I turn back.

Get what you need.

Always.

He's trusting me. He moves forward.

"Here we go," he responds almost instantly. *"Intro to V.A. strong angle. Accepts me."*

Whoa.

We look at each other.

"Intro to V.A. strong angle. What could that possibly mean? What, or who, is V.A.?" I wonder aloud.

"How did you know it was Danish?" the count asks, disregarding my question.

I take a deep breath.

"You're not going to believe this," I start, "any more than you're going to like it…"

I take a few minutes and tell the count everything. I explain Korolyev's theory explained in his 1994 thesis. I explain everything I know about not only the eggs but about the history of the players—Nicholas II, Alexander III, and Maria Feodorovna. And why it all makes sense, when looking at the history, that the man he thought his whole life to be his grandfather Piotr Derbyshev was really—quite possibly—Maria Feodorovna's cousin Gustav Bjerg.

The count's jaw is redefining slack. His bony, pointy chin is basically resting on his desk. He has a glazed look over his face.

"Sir?" I ask. "Are you okay?"

"I…I'm…completely speechless."

It's not every day one learns he and his entire family might be Danish instead of Russian.

"I can only imagine," I respond, unsure what more to say.

My eye catches an antique clock on the wall—2:49 a.m.

Tick. Tick.

"How do you know all of this? Why?"

"Let's just say I had good reason to do a little investigation over the years. Why don't I keep going? Keep looking at the eggs so we can get an understanding of what we're dealing with."

The count thinks for a second, then starts nodding his head.

"Yes, yes, of course," he says.

He remains glassy eyed in the chair behind his desk as I scan for the second egg. I start thinking about the years each egg was made. The first was completed and given to Maria Feodorovna in 1886, five years into her husband Alexander III's reign as Czar of Russia. The next I'm about to inspect—*Cherub Egg with Chariot*—was created two years after that in 1888.

Like the first, there are no pictures available of *Cherub Egg with Chariot* and there is little known information. But there are a few pieces of documentation that suggest a gold egg, decorated with small diamonds and a sapphire, in a chariot being pulled by an angel. I spot *Cherub Egg with Chariot*, and it appears true to the description. I move toward it.

"Legend has it *Cherub* was sold by Armand Hammer at Lord & Taylor in New York in 1934," I mention, looking to keep the count's mind present. "Was your family the purchaser that day? Or did you obtain it from the 1934 buyer?"

"From the 1934 buyer," he offers up. "A man named Griff Bienemen."

I reach the egg. The piece is delicate, glimmering, exquisite. I come up on it, put the loupe to my eye, and move in. I think about the artwork Galina sent to my father over the years—and the fact whatever message she was trying to convey was never front and center, but always in the periphery. Just like the egg I first inspected.

Is Galina a direct descendant of Alexander III as Mateev may have put together for me?

Did she learn to hide messages in artwork—because she learned this was how the truth about her lineage was passed?

A truth she needed to protect by collecting the eggs herself?

At all costs?

I begin by looking at the most difficult portion of the gold egg to see, the portion toward the bottom and facing in to the back of the chariot. This time it takes no time at all; the words—again, only visible via loupe—are right there.

"G.B., V.A., *venner og fortrolige,*" I begin reading aloud. "AIII,

V.A., *venner og rivaler. Familie af hemmeligheder. P.D.-styret af intuition. Tilsyneladende klogt.*"

The count tells me I went too fast. I say it again, spelling out each word, as I take my pictures.

He takes a deep breath.

"You okay?" I ask.

"No."

Fair enough.

"Okay," he continues, "here we go. 'G.B., V.A., *friends, confidants. AIII, V.A., friends, rivals. Family of secrets. P.D. guided by intuition. Apparently wisely.*"

We both sit for a few seconds in silence.

"Right—so we're dealing with the initials of people. V.A. again. Who could that be?"

I think back on all my research, envision the royalty related walls at 251 Herengracht. I don't see anyone with the initials V.A.

But that doesn't mean things aren't getting clearer.

Much.

G.B., V.A., friends, confidants.

G.B.—Gustav Bjerg. Her cousin, the Piotr Derbyshev imposter. Perhaps he befriended this V.A., the same person who was "friends, rivals" with AIII, clearly Alexander III.

"Family of secrets."

"P.D. guided by intuition."

P.D.

Princess Dagmar.

Maria Feodorovna's name as Princess of Denmark, before marrying into Russian royalty.

Did just her cousin see her as the girl who would never be one of them?

Or did Maria Feodorovna herself never consider herself one of them? And simply the Princess of Denmark on a mission to learn the truth about the man she really fell in love with?

"What does this all mean?" asks the count.

Not looking good, Count.

"I'll need to do a bit more work on all this once I leave here. I need you to open a new Word document. For each egg, I need you to write down both the Danish words and the English translation. And be clear about which passages go with which eggs. *Nécessaire Egg*," I say out loud, referring to the next egg in chronological order.

I see it immediately. Though the exact appearance of the egg is believed to be unknown, the little documentation that exists on the piece explains it was designed as an etui containing women's toiletry items. The egg itself is gold and decorated with emeralds, rubies, and sapphires. The surprise inside the egg is believed to be thirteen diamond-encrusted pieces of a manicure set. But this has never been confirmed.

I come up on the egg. I lean in. Before bringing the loupe to my eye, I take in its brilliance.

"Did you ever open it up?" I ask. "You know, confirm what's believed to be inside?"

"I haven't. In fact, I have never touched any of them. No one in my family has. We always believed this is the only way to ensure the authenticity and value."

"Makes sense," I respond.

I put the loupe to my eye and move in. I start where I believe I will find the words, the most difficult part of the egg to see. Unlike before, there's nothing there. I keep searching slowly, methodically. I go from the bottom to the top, then from the top back to the bottom.

Nothing.

I stand upright.

"What's wrong?" asks the count.

"There's nothing there. There's nothing on this one. Unless—"

"Unless what?"

"Unless it's inside," I say, turning to him.

He sits back in his chair.

"Are you sure it isn't there? That you—"

"I checked this thing up and down. I didn't miss a micron."

The count sighs, stands up, and walks over. Once standing next to me, we just stare at the egg sitting atop the column.

"I'll be right back," he says out of nowhere.

He disappears, only to reappear a few minutes later with a pair of thin, white cotton gloves in his hand.

"Took them from the help's supplies. I'm simply too curious at this point not to look."

"You want to handle it, or should I?" I ask.

He looks down at his huge, jagged, bony hands, trembling slightly from both age and nerves. He hands me the gloves. I hand him the loupe and put the gloves on. I inspect the egg again before handling it. I want to make sure I see where the latch is to open it so I can handle it as little as possible. I identify the tiny button. Without hesitating any longer I depress it, and the top portion of the gold egg flips open.

"Wow!" I exclaim.

There's a little pile of diamonds inside, so bright it's like their shine is making up for being locked up all these years. It looks like the history is right, that the diamonds belong to a bunch of mini women's manicure items. But I don't have the time or inclination to inspect them. I care about one thing.

I take the loupe back from the count and lean in. Around the bottom edge of the inside of the top portion of the egg I see words.

"Here we go," I say.

The count takes this as his cue to get back to the computer. I take my time reading slowly, spelling it out as I go along.

"*V.A. taler om gaeld, bade gaeld og omvendt. AIII. Fyldt med skyld-folelse go bitterhed. Bliver bedomt af Lord.*"

A couple more keys tapped. Then,

"*V.A. talks of debts, both owed and reverse,*" the count says aloud. "*AIII. Riddled with guilt, bitterness. Will be judged by the Lord.*"

Huh.

With each egg the connection between this V.A. and Alexander III becomes clearer.

Who the fuck is V.A.?

And why are each of them indebted to the other?

"Any clearer?" asks the count.

I decide I owe it to the count to be straight. I explain to him everything I see, what each egg thus far means to me and why. What, to me, makes sense, and what still doesn't add up.

"What do you think?" I ask.

"That it's all too crazy for reality. That it means history as the world knows it is inaccurate."

"Yup," I say, nodding my head gently.

"But, as unthinkable as it might be, it all seems to be adding up," he continues.

This time I recruit the count to take the picture. Then, carefully, I close the egg. I remove the gloves.

"Shall we keep going?" I ask.

"Yes. Please."

Alexander III Egg is next. I notice it right away. Unlike the previous three which have a gold foundation, this egg is very different. *Alexander III Egg* is blue, with a blue enamel base and features six portraits of the Czar himself. As I come up on the treasure and lean in for a good look, it is clear where I'll be looking. The only gold on this egg is the gold paint used to outline each of the six miniature portraits.

The first two pictures produce nothing. The words lay in the gold paint surrounding portrait number three.

"Got 'em," I blurt out. "Ready?"

"Ready."

"G.B., V.A., *luk ligesom parorende. En god mand generet; jeg er ked P.D. Familie stadig forste prioritet. Hvad du mener er rigtigt. En golden son. En gron son. En golden bror. En gron bror.*"

The count, getting better with each translation, is ready to go almost as soon as I'm finished reading.

"G.B., V.A., *close like kin. A good man burdened; I am sorry P.D. Family still priority. What you believe to be true is so. A golden son. A green son. A golden brother. A green brother.*"

I sit on the arm of one of the leather couches close by.

"Interesting," I say, thinking out loud. "I always wondered why there was so much time between this egg and the last. *Alexander III Egg* was made in 1896, a gap of seven years. Perhaps this explains why."

"Perhaps what explains why?"

"'G.B., V.A. close like kin.' Maria Feodorovna's cousin and whomever this V.A. is apparently becoming closer than perhaps either he or she ever envisioned happening. And, in doing so, maybe G.B. became conflicted; maybe he worried about betraying V.A . . . 'a good man burdened.' Perhaps that's why so much time went by here, before he came back to his senses. And got back on track."

The count moves his eyes from me back to the computer screen.

"I am sorry P.D.," he reads aloud. "Family still priority."

"Precisely," I concur.

"He's apologizing to P.D.—Princess Dagmar," the count continues. "And affirming for her that in his heart family—the Princess, and her mission—still comes first. What about the rest?"

"What you believe to be true is so," I repeat, referring to the passage again. "The golden son and brother is Nicholas II—he was the apple of his mother's eye; he was the next in line for the throne and a man with values, ideals, very much in line with those of his father. Alexander III was on the short end of all that. A green son and brother. And what has green historically signified?"

"Envy."

I stand up.

"Next."

I scan the room and see *Mauve Enamel Egg*. I only recognize the egg because of historic descriptions. It is a muted, purple enamel-based piece whose real essence is in the center. Though it has supposedly never been recovered—like all the other eggs in this room—the surprise in the middle of this egg is well documented and has been photographed many times. It was sold in 1978 at

Christie's in Geneva; at the time, those in possession had no idea it was at one point in time part of one of the missing Fabergé Imperial Easter Eggs.

The egg has no gold outside, but I know—as does the count—the surprise in the middle has gold all over the base.

"I need to open the—"

"Gloves," he cuts me off.

I put the loupe back down, the gloves on, and open the egg. From the middle, delicate like a doctor removing a baby from a cesarean birth uterus, I pull out a magnificent surprise. The top is a translucent strawberry heart that opens into a three-leaf clover. On each of the clover leaves is a portrait: one of Czar Nicholas II, one of the Empress Alexandra Feodorovna, and one of their first-born daughter Grand Duchess Olga. The heart is supported on a white opaque stand adorned with laurel leaves, the stand sprouting from a base comprised of gold, strawberry enamel, rose-cut diamonds, and pearls.

I place the surprise on the top of the column next to the stand holding the egg. I grab the loupe, stick it in my eye, and move in. The topmost and bottommost rungs of gold are the thickest, the most obvious. Therefore I look for one of the thinner bands. Sure enough, I find my words.

"*Min kaere P.D., min familie,*" I begin.

The count's fingers go to work.

"G.B., V.A., *fortrolige som parorende. AIII tanket op altid af lyse vision for Rusland. Villige og i stand til at genetablere Rusland. For enhver pris.*"

Seconds later, the translation.

"My dear P.D., my family. G.B., V.A., confidants as kin. AIII fueled always by glow of vision for Russia. Willing, able, to restore Russia. At all costs."

I put the loupe down, replace the surprise in the middle of the egg, and close it.

"So what do we know now?" I ask, treating the count like the pupil.

"Reassuring her that she is still a priority, while confirming he and this V.A. are still close like kin, hence his information being reliable."

"Most likely," I respond. "And that Alexander III had an unshakable vision of what he wanted Russia to be. A vision he was going to make reality no matter who he had to, perhaps, push aside."

I look at the antique clock—3:08 a.m.

Time's running thin. I need to move.

"Here we go," I say. "Let's keep moving while we're in the flow."

I start toward the *Empire Nephrite Egg*, the next in chronological order. The one I assumed was in Galina Zhamovsky's possession. The one bought from a man named Mehmet Nas from Istanbul. There is as little known information about this egg as any of them, but according to the actual invoice for the treasure, it is a gold and nephrite egg with two rose-cut diamonds. Siberian nephrite is a semiprecious stone the czars enjoyed as part of their jewel-making arsenal, an element they tightly controlled the mining of in order to increase its value. I had learned this in my research. As well as the fact that truly beautiful Siberian nephrite is a striking, bright shade of green.

Seconds are officially starting to feel like minutes. Locating the most hidden portion of gold the words pop immediately, like I knew exactly where they'd be.

"*Min Kaere P.D., min familie. Gron son—Sort son! AIII knytte af Narodnaya Volya! Bekraeftelse taettere—*"

"My dear P.D., my family," the count comes back immediately as I start in with my photographs, "Green son—Black son! AIII associate of Narodnaya Volya! Confirmation closer—"

I stop, perk up.

"Green son, Black son," I repeat. "Fair to say he's not saying the color of his skin."

"What the hell is—"

The count moves his face closer to the screen to make sure of his pronunciation.

"*Narodnaya Volya?*"

"*Narodnaya Volya* means 'The People's Will.' It was a left-wing Russian terrorist organization responsible for the death of Czar Alexander II—Alexander III's father," I explain. "The thing is," I go on, "according to history, Narodnaya Volya was also plotting the assassination of Alexander III, an operation led by Vladimir Lenin's elder brother Alexander Ulyanov. A plot that was foiled. So why would G.B. be reporting that Alexander III was, in fact, an associate of the terrorist organization looking to cut him down?"

I look at the column with nothing on top. The one where *Danish Jubilee Egg* is supposed to be instead of on display in the U.S. Capitol. The seventh in chronological order of the eight.

"What are you going to do about *Danish Jubilee Egg?*" asks the count.

I turn and face him.

"Inspect it. Just like I'm doing the rest of them. Now let's look at number eight, *Alexander III Commemorative Egg*, and I'll be on my way."

I pause.

"Which, actually, brings me to one last question. Might you have a car I can borrow?"

CHAPTER 26

At 6:18 a.m., I pull into L's Meatpacking District Distributorship driveway and park in a far, out-of-the-way corner. With the turn of the key I bring the grumbling engine of one of the count's "weekend vehicles"—a black, 1961 Jaguar XKE, to a stop. While it's a nice, classic little antique vehicle, it's a far cry from the beast I left behind some random house in Baltimore. But I simply couldn't take the chance of driving it back, considering how many are undoubtedly looking for it.

Accessing the building through the always-open emergency exit in the alley, I make my way up to L's office. In his desk's top drawer, where I know the first thing he does each morning is drop his car keys, I leave the Jag key and a simple note reading: "Here's a loaner; far corner of your lot that never gets touched. Call your car in stolen ASAP this morning. I know you want to kill me—sorry. I had no choice. And I know you don't want to hear it, would have done the same for you in a second. This means that much."

I jump in a cab and head uptown. The blue Canali suit I've been in far too long feels heavy, creaseless. Fighting fatigue, but feeling my lack of sleep, I put my head back on the seat and stare at the taxi's ceiling.

The deal.

The coveted Freedom Bank Building.

Enzo Alessi and family. Ryan Brand.

Fuck.

Never saw this coming.

The deal was supposed to be the easy part.

My iPhone rings. Fumbling through the numerous objects in my right inside jacket pocket, I grab it and pull it out. The caller, surprisingly, is Julia Chastain.

Before answering, I look at my watch and mentally review my schedule for the next ninety minutes. The plan is hotel by 6:45 a.m. for quick shower, shave, and new suit, 7:20 to 8:00—return e-mails on other corporate matters unrelated to the target. 8:00 to 8:30, review last minute changes to the Purchase Agreement and related exhibits e-mailed to me from the attorneys about six hours ago, just after midnight. Then, meet Cobus and Arnon downstairs for breakfast to discuss said changes as well as other specifics of the deal.

"Is this an early or late start for you?" I answer.

"Depends on the morning," she responds. "But today has been like most—my first cup of coffee was at five fifteen."

"You mean you actually sleep? Not us Dutch. We save sleep for the weekends."

"Not surprised," she counters. "You all have a lot of catching up to do."

"Interesting. Is that your insight—or have you been using the euro versus the U.S. dollar as your basis?"

Raspy giggle.

"Point taken, Mr. Janse."

"What can I do for you this morning?"

"There are some security deposit specifics we still need to cover regarding a few of the tenants. I think it may be a good idea to sit down and go through these items before our respective days get going as the two teams won't be getting together until the luncheon at Alessi's."

Right. The big dog-and-pony show luncheon at Alessi's new Midtown showpiece.

"And we both know there won't be much shoptalk occurring at that function. We're really rolling downhill into this closing at this point; each minute we can find counts. I want to make sure we have the details buttoned up."

"Well, I have breakfast with my team at eight thirty, so perhaps—"

"Perfect," she cuts me off. "I'll make some fresh coffee. You meet me at my apartment at seven fifteen and we can run through this. I live Midtown on the west side—One Sixty West Fifty-Ninth Street. You'll easily be back to your hotel by eight thirty. And I'd rather not put these punch list items on hold until late this afternoon. Sound good?"

Good?

About as good as a punch in the face.

But business is business.

And I've got to sort this one out.

Now.

"Sure. Sounds good. See you soon."

After sucking down a cup of coffee I had delivered to my room and having a world-record speed shower and shave, I step off the elevator and look for apartment 22A as instructed by the concierge. I locate the proper door immediately. It's open a couple inches.

Thinking this was done to tell me to come on in, I still knock gently out of politeness.

"Come in. I'm in the kitchen," her raspy voice calls.

The apartment is bright from the newly awakened sun forcing itself in through the large picture windows in the living room. From the décor to the furniture to the artwork, Julia's home is sleek, smart, contemporary, intriguing, like the woman who lives here.

There are no moldings; the cloud-white walls and ceilings run seamlessly into each other. The floor underfoot is wide, dark planks of smooth wood finished in black. Beautifully appointed recessed lighting is throughout, some strategically placed for artwork, the rest for evening or gloomy day illumination.

I notice a bunch of photos on a shelf just a few feet into the living room. I check them out quickly, interested because I notice one of them is of Julia, Brand, and Scott Green—Houseboat Guy. The same Houseboat Guy she said she didn't really know. I move down the central corridor. I pass a small den, a bathroom, a laundry room—the apartment is not overly large, but large. Probably a couple bedrooms as well for a grand total of a couple thousand square feet worth a couple million bucks. Not bad for a young, single, hot-shot woman.

I must be approaching the kitchen. The smell of coffee is getting stronger by the step, and I need another huge cup immediately. My eyes are heavy. I'm fighting fatigue harder perhaps than I ever have in my life.

I turn into the kitchen, which is nouveau, yet traditional. The walls are comprised of perfect rows of brick-size white tiles. There's a pot rack hanging from the ceiling with shiny stainless steel cookware. The appliances are all Sub-Zero and Viking and look like they were installed this morning. Guessing not very much actual cooking goes on in here.

Standing across the room, by the sink, is Julia. She's facing out the window, which looks east out over the city, and drinking a cup of coffee. I'm surprised that she isn't exactly dressed for her day. Unless there's something underneath it—which I'm guessing there isn't—all she seems to be wearing is a black satin robe with pink lace trim around the edges that stops just below her ass.

The space is quiet now that my footsteps have stopped, aside from the faint sounds past the walls of the city coming to life down below. I squeeze my eyes closed. I see Perry. My gorgeous Perry who I miss so much, who I vow to return alive to her son. I see the exact image of the perfect physical specimen that is Julia on the other side of my eyelids. I'm praying this is a dream.

Or am I praying it's not?

I open my eyes. And as my sight spills again from my eyeballs, emotions, urges, cravings, feelings I haven't felt in three years—three lifetimes—drain from my soul all over the floor.

"So, Ivan," she says, placing her blue ceramic coffee mug on the white marble counter flanking the sink, "you ready to get to work?"

I say nothing. She turns around. She leans back casually against the counter, her hands behind her. The black satin tie around her waist is barely holding, her robe one movement away from coming completely undone. I see the top of her six-pack abs and, inside, half of each of her perfect breasts. I see the birthmark running farther down her neck and shoulder than I've previously seen.

I look her up and down, I drink her in.

Those legs.

This is wrong.

Right.

Fuck.

"You don't seem surprised," she says. "And *that* doesn't surprise me."

The coffee, caffeine. I'm craving it. Like I'm craving what the sweat on her neck will taste like once she's heated up.

No.

Stop.

"Why now?" I ask.

"Because I'm a girl who knows how to make shit happen, Ivan. And I don't know when else I'm going to get my shot with you since you're here to close a deal within a couple more days before flying back off to Amsterdam."

Cravings. Urges.

For Perry.

For gratification.

From sex. From substance.

Fuck, that coffee smells good. I know this feeling. I want it like I used to want coke. Which wouldn't be so bad right—

Stop.

I'm so tired. As I stand here, at this very moment, I have no idea where the desire, the need, for sleep begins or ends.

Damn my body might drop. Or start running.

Damn her body is insane.

Like Perry's. Which I haven't touched or seen aside from in my dreams in so long it feels like I'm about to explode.

"I'm committed to someone," I say.

"That's not what your eyes say when they lick me every time I walk into a room."

I don't flinch. But I feel my teeth clench a bit.

"No," I respond, matter-of-factly, "I'm committed. But that doesn't change whether I destroy your body right here and now in this kitchen or not."

A sexy, scandalous smile creeps onto her face.

"That's more like it, Ivan."

It's been so long. Until this moment I had no idea how much I'd been suppressing. Out of love.

Out of guilt?

I should walk away.

I need this.

Don't I?

Fuck. I can't help thinking, I need this more than I even know.

I feel myself reach for my tie, my eyes never once leaving hers. She, with barely a tug, releases the tie around her waist, the robe sliding down her back to the floor. I toss my tie onto the island, topped with the same white marble as the rest of the counters. Again, my eyes never leaving hers.

Hers never leaving mine.

I'm on autopilot.

I move on to my shirt, slowly unbuttoning from the top down. Once completely open, I remove and it toss onto the island as well.

At this moment beautifully naked Julia gently lifts herself onto the counter behind her next to the sink. She gently parts her legs, reaches down, and starts pleasing herself while I keep undressing.

"You see the color of this birthmark?" she purrs. "Think you can make the inside of my thighs the same color?"

"It's been a while," I admit.

"Which means what? This might not last as long as we're both hoping?"

"Which means just the opposite," I counter. "Which means you may not get out of here alive."

Once all my clothes are in a pile on the island, my shoes clumsily off to the side on the floor, I make my way over to her. I ease myself right in between her legs excited by the way the skin just above her knees feels against the skin of my waist. I move in to kiss her but stop an inch before her lips. Her breath is warm, faintly bitter from coffee. I finally move my eyes. I move them to the birthmark running down her face, her neck, her shoulder, her arm, and upper torso farther than I previously realized. I trace it with my finger, taste and kiss it with my lips.

I reach up with my left hand, behind her, and take a handful of her hair in my fist. I pull her head back, surprising her, arching her back. I move my eyes back to hers.

"You ready, Julia?"

CHAPTER 27

One evening, after cocktails with the owners of a half-built Class A office tower going up in the South Axis market of Amsterdam, Cobus's Maybach made its way through the city. The night was chilly, damp. Cobus and I were in the backseat.

"What do you think?" asked Cobus. "Do we really want the responsibility of finishing the construction? We're talking about the tallest building ever built in Amsterdam, Ivan."

"Diepenbrock's group is in trouble, Cobus, and we're talking about pulling the property for peanuts on the euro. We make money on this deal the second we sign the paperwork."

Cobus was nodding his head as he added, "And the construction has been spot on so far. Gropius is doing a flawless job."

Gropius & Immendorf was the German engineering firm handling the construction.

"There is a reason Diepenbrock came to you first, Cobus."

"To us, Ivan," Cobus went on. "To de Bont Beleggings. A firm you are essentially helping me steer at this point."

Cobus changed directions. He leaned forward and said to his driver, "Alex, let's head over to Keizersgracht Straat."

He leaned back again.

"What's happening on Keizersgracht?" I inquired, looking at the time on my iPhone. "I thought we needed to meet van Buuren at Vermeer at eight o'clock."

"There's no meeting with van Buuren tonight, Ivan," Cobus responded. "No dinner at Vermeer. I canceled."

"What are you talking about?"

Cobus turned his attention away from me, out the window.

"I love how Amsterdam looks passing by from inside the car. The people. The buildings. We have so much to do with both of them. It's a lot, Ivan, no?"

"What's a lot?" I responded, puzzled.

"Holding it all together. Maintaining life. Working hard, but doing it in an honest way. Really spending each day not only attacking this world, but doing it in a way one can be proud of. Doing it in a way that is—"

Cobus returned his attention to me.

"Honest."

Something strange was happening.

Fuck.

Cobus had never even used the word honesty in relation to me. Was he on to me?

I thought of Perry. I thought of Max, Neo.

"I knew from the moment we met, Ivan, that you were different. That there was more there than one could see. I just never could have imagined knowing what, well, I now know."

I was ready. I subtly moved my hand to the armrest on the door near the door handle. Before he said another word, I was prepared to open the door, tuck my chin, pull my arms and legs in tight, and roll for however long was needed until I could spring back up and head back the other way. Under my polished new façade, I was still Jonah Gray. I was still, and would always now be, a warrior who could flip a switch.

"Is that right? And what is it you now know?"

Could it be? Could Cobus have stumbled on to my real identity and turned me over?

I could feel my jaw stiffening. I was ready for combat.

His face became serious. He reached inside his jacket pocket. My hand slid to the door handle. Just as my fingertips started to grip it, he pulled out a gold Gucci keychain with two keys hanging from the ring.

"That you are one of the brightest real estate minds I have ever been around. That you are as humble as you are filled with integrity. And that this company could have never flourished this much, this fast, without you."

I relaxed again.

"Our numbers for this year are going to be extraordinary, Ivan. Do you realize this?"

"I do."

Did I ever. Cobus's foresight and positioning had put de Bont Beleggings, flush with cash and strategically aligned up the ying-yang, to capitalize big-time in the face of something like a global commercial real estate meltdown. We had spent the better part of two years kicking the overleveraged, already down, square in the teeth and taking names.

Cobus flipped me the keychain.

"What's this?"

"My way of saying thank you," Cobus said. "And also your bonus for the year. In fact, I probably wouldn't count on one next year after this."

Just then we rolled up to a magnificent five-story canal house on Keizersgracht Straat.

"A little something for you and Tess. You've earned it."

Funny. One look at the canal house reminded me of the town-house I had grown up in on the Upper East Side of New York City. The one my father was gunned down in front of.

The car stopped. I looked at Cobus.

"I'm not quite sure what to say. This isn't at all necessary,

Cobus. As you know, I'm not one much for luxury. I'm more the simple type."

"I know you are. That's why I think you'll love how the place was decorated..."

As I mentioned earlier, the ultracontemporary and immaculate interior of the home was predominantly white and state-of-the-art. We stepped into the kitchen where a bottle of Perrier-Jouët 2002 Fleur de Champagne Rosé was on ice. There was a woman in the kitchen—a fifty-something housekeeper type—who reached for the bottle upon our arrival.

"This is Laura," Cobus said. "Her quarters are at the north end of the second floor. And as part of the gift I have picked up the first year of her salary."

"Cobus, I really need to say that this is too much. I mean how—"

"Stop it, Ivan. Really. For the amount of profit you have helped this firm generate, I'm probably going light here. Especially since— I must tell you—the owner was getting foreclosed on. I had mentioned to Marco—"

Marco Oud—a banker we often deal with.

"—a little while back what I intended on doing for you and told him to keep his eyes open. Once I saw this, I knew it was perfect. I figured that little dog you adore so much would feel right at home with all of the white."

Laura handed us each a glass. We clinked, and each took a sip.

"Thank you, Cobus," I said. "This is quite overwhelming. And quite the motivator to keep at it."

I had called Perry to let her know what was happening. At three a.m., Max asleep in his new *enstig kunnen*—Dutch for seriously awesome—room, I heard the whir of our new elevator out in the hallway. I heard Perry's heels click as she made her way down the wide-plank, white, light bamboo hardwood floor. Without stopping, she entered the bedroom. The click of her heels, now absorbed by the plush white carpet, was gone.

Our new bedroom was sleek, minimalist. I was laying on our new low-to-the-ground platform bed, arms behind my head, waiting for her. Lorna Lee's "La Lune Foncée" played faintly in the background, blending beautifully with the sounds of the Amsterdam night as I had left the windows open. The lights in the room had been set to a soft glow.

Perry stopped in front of the bed. The owners of the supperclub liked the female staff—especially the hot bartenders like Tess Beel—looking sharp as a Kasumi knife. She wore Helmut Lang stretch leather skinny pants and a black, skin-tight, scoop neck Burberry matte jersey tank finished off with popping royal-blue suede, Giuseppe Zanotti colorblock platform sandals.

Another perk for Perry of her new life. All the great fashion—only now it was just the fun stuff.

"Pretty nice digs you got here, Mr. Janse."

"Glad you like them," I tossed back.

She slowly peeled off her top, enjoying me enjoying her. She tossed it aside, as well as her black satin bra. Then she kicked off her six-inch heels. She crawled up on the bed on top of me. Above me on all fours, staring into my eyes, our noses—our faces—gently caressed each other. Then we kissed deeply.

"You seem to have left something on," I whispered.

"I wanted you to peel them off me yourself."

She sat up on top of me. I unbuttoned and unzipped the leather pants. Then in an instant, I lifted her off me and I circled around back of her. Feeling both of our excitement, and only wanting that excitement to get hotter, I slowed down. My left hand enjoyed the skinlike leather covering her perfect ass. My right hand gently grabbed the front of her neck from behind and lifted her up. I put her left earlobe in my mouth. Her left hand reached back and played with my hair. Her right hand started playing with her right breast.

Finally, I reached down with both hands and slid her pants off. I dropped them off the bed.

"Did you ever wear panties when we were at PCBL?" I joked.

Perry sexily crawled forward over the silky white sheets, her torso low and her ass high, and crawled up the wall behind our new pillows. Once she was at a ninety-degree angle, she turned and looked at me, her hands still in place.

"Get over here and take care of me, Ivan Janse. Now."

Sixty sex-soaked minutes later, both of us exhausted, glistening with sweat, we were on our backs. Our legs were tangled like a pretzel as we looked at the ceiling. My left hand, reaching across my body, tickled the crease on the inside of her left elbow.

"So?" asked Perry. "You going to give me a tour?"

Both naked, we stepped out of the bedroom.

The top floor—floor five—was ours. All ours. I had grown up in luxury, then been beaten down by life, self-taught to shun bullshit. Over the course of five years, I had created this from nothing for Perry, for Max, for me.

Ivan Janse.

Jonah Gray.

As we walked down the hall, wood under our feet and the soft, white luminescence of the home's lighting system set for nighttime bathing us, Perry had her arm out. Her fingertips grazed the wall as we walked.

"I'm impressed, Jonah. You've become such a world-beater again from scratch that Cobus gave you a fucking sick house . . ."

She giggled.

"With a freaking elevator."

"Gave us a house, Perry. You, Max, Neo, me."

We examined our new digs. Our master bathroom, like the bedroom, was enormous, and connected to two his-and-her walk-in closets that were each the size of a Manhattan studio apartment and equipped with its own flat-screen and chaise for a little predress lounging. On the opposite end of the top floor was Max's bedroom, as well as his video-game room. Upon sight of her sleeping son, Perry cocked her head and smiled.

"Stairs or elevator?" I asked.

"Definitely, elevator," Perry said. "Seriously, have you ever been on an elevator naked before? How can we not?"

Just before getting on the elevator, I heard Neo's nails clicking on the floor. When he got to me, he reached his right front paw out. I scooped him up and carried him for the rest of the tour.

The fourth floor was all about work. I had a state-of-the-art office. It was tricked out with every imaginable gadget and up-to-the-second piece of technology possible in order to work from home—and correspond with people anywhere in the world—seamlessly, as if I were in the office. There were four fifty-something-inch flat-screens on the wall. The fourth floor also had a private den equipped with a fully loaded wet bar and multiple comfy chairs and couches. The last thing on the fourth floor was a gym with every piece of cardio and weight-lifting equipment one could ever need to stay fit.

Floor three was exclusively for entertaining. There was a small, cocktail type of room as well as a larger room with a long, rectangular glass table with surrounding contemporary white chairs running the length of the space. Nouveau works of art lined the white walls; a beautiful, sleek white blown-glass-and-ceramic chandelier hung from the ceiling. There was also a full kitchen on floor three—more like one you'd find in a restaurant as opposed to a home—to handle all the catering needs of whatever soiree was going on.

When we got back on the elevator, I hit the button for the ground floor.

"What about the second floor?" Perry asked.

"That's primarily Laura's space. And I'd rather not wake her up."

"Laura? Who's Laura?"

The doors opened on one, I put Neo down, and explained who Laura was. First, we checked out the living room, then the dining room. We checked out both ground floor bathrooms and ended up in the kitchen. The soft, white lights, like the rest of the house, were on nighttime setting and extremely low. There were no vivid colors, just black, white, and gray. Perry hopped up and sat on the island, letting out a quick "ooooohh!" as her naked ass hit the cold marble. After a couple of misses, I found the cabinet holding the champagne glasses. I took two out, grabbed the still half full bottle of Perrier-Jouët from the fridge, set the glasses down next to Perry's perfectly contoured thigh, and poured.

We raised our glasses and clinked.

"Do you still love it?" Perry asked before taking a sip.

"Love what?"

"The rush. The feeling of making it happen every day at such a high level. Like when we were in New York."

She looked around, extending the hand with the glass in it.

"Creating this."

"I don't know, Per. I don't really think about it anymore. All that matters to me is taking care of you and Max and Neo. And making sure the past never catches up to us."

Perry reached out and put her hand on my face.

"You really don't care about any of this anymore. Do you?"

I shook my head no.

How could I possibly?

"Thank you, Jonah Gray. Thank you for keeping us safe and helping Max and me have a new life away from his father. You are the father he is supposed to have."

I took Perry's hand and kissed it.

"Do you ever regret running with me?" I asked.

"Never. Not for a single second. Ever."

I wonder how she'd answer that question today.

CHAPTER 28

New York City
2013

My eyes open. My head's a mess. Where the fuck? Right. Julia's bedroom. The room is dark from the blackout shades, but the thin line of sunlight running around the shades' outline tells me day is in full swing. The sheets feel soft, inviting, but I need to get my shit together.

I turn on a light on the nightstand. The room, like the rest of the apartment, is smart, contemporary. The floor is wide, chocolate-colored planks of wood. The walls are the same shade of gray as the satin sheets and blanket covering the bed, and me. There's no sign of Julia. I look at the clock on the nightstand.

9:22 a.m.

Not good.

I hear my iPhone blowing up, but I don't see it. I notice my clothes neatly set on one of the gray-and-brown-striped Donghia Klismos chairs. Naked, I spring from the bed. I'm so disoriented I nearly lose my balance. I can't help wonder if no sleep even with all that's gone on—is still going on—would have been better.

I pull the iPhone from the right inside suit jacket pocket. Five missed calls from Cobus, who's calling me again. Numerous unanswered texts from both Cobus and Arnon. I clear my throat, then say a few words to no one in order to gauge the grogginess in my voice, and assess just how much effort it will take to seem I'm fully awake.

"The time got away from me," I answer.

"What is going on, Ivan?"

Cobus sounds pissed. He never—ever—loses his cool, but when he's pissed I can definitely hear it in his voice.

"Where are you? And why are you anywhere but here?"

"I've been on with Angelique…"

Angelique, my five-foot-nothing, walking piece of art of an assistant.

"I'm on my way."

I hang up before Cobus can inquire any further. I call Angelique.

"*Dag; Ivan Janse's Kantoor*—"

This is, "Hello, Ivan Janse's office," in Dutch. I'll just give you the English version of our call straightaway.

"How are we this afternoon? Any new piercings? Maybe a new tattoo during lunchtime?"

"What's up, Boss Man? What do you need?"

"Every single file, document, e-mail regarding the Berlin deal scanned and e-mailed to me immediately."

The time nearing ten a.m., I walk into the hotel and straight to the restaurant. No sign of Cobus or Arnon. I call Cobus.

"Come up to my room," he says.

I enter Cobus's suite. He's sitting on the couch, wearing his usual black-on-black uniform, finishing up a call. He motions for me to sit down.

"Where the hell have you been this morning, Ivan? What's going on?"

Just as I'm about to open my mouth, he keeps going.

"Something doesn't seem right. We're on the cusp of closing a major deal—a historic deal—for this firm, yet you're MIA. What am I missing here?"

I take a deep, defeated breath.

"You got me. I was on with Angelique, as I said, and the time got away from me."

"On with Angelique about what? What could have been *so* important with regard to any of our properties back home that you might get this sidetracked by a conversation with Angelique?"

"I was telling her exactly which documents I needed from the Berlin file scanned and e-mailed to me."

"The Berlin deal. Just as we're moving toward this close. Why?"

"Because it is my duty to always make sure we're ready for anything; that we're in position to make any play we might need to make. Something I won't ever apologize for."

"When you didn't show for breakfast, I knocked on your door. You didn't answer."

"I must have been in the shower," I counter. "Now, if it's okay with you, I've got some housekeeping to do in these next couple hours before lunch at Alessi's place. I do have other properties of yours back in the Netherlands I need to worry about."

"Good morning. And you are?"

"I'm here to see Dr. York. Please have him meet me in his office."

I know York's here. I called to make sure from the cab on my way over. Without another word, I head through the door leading from the waiting room into the office.

"Sir, excuse me, sir, you can't just walk in there like this! Please, sir!"

CHAPTER 29

It was a beautiful spring Saturday night. Amsterdam had been nuts all day with crazy drunken Scottish men in kilts and construction boots who had descended on The Netherlands for their homeland's World Cup qualifying soccer match versus Holland. The two teams had played to a zero–zero draw. The streets still had some mild activity, but the crowds had thinned out considerably since the game's completion earlier in the day. Max, Perry, and I had just had a late dinner by Rembrandt Plein and were walking back toward home. Perry stepped in front of me and asked if she had something stuck in her teeth.

A trolley passed behind her when she did. Something struck me. In the window, because of the streetlights, I saw the reflection of a large, well-built man wearing a kilt, about twenty feet behind us. And I couldn't help thinking I had caught the tail end of his going from a beer in the air to turning away—as if trying to blend in.

As if trying to seem like he wasn't following us.

A real threat hadn't presented itself in a while. I was probably just paranoid, I thought. I told Perry there was nothing in her teeth. We kept walking.

I still felt…something. I couldn't turn around; if I was right, that simply meant cover blown leading to God knows what.

I stopped short and spun Perry around.

"What about me?" I asked.

Using my peripheral vision, I could tell he was still there. Same turn away. I turned my head and looked at him. He pretended to be answering his cell phone.

"Grab Max's hand," I said.

"What?"

"Grab his hand, Per. Now. And stay close."

"What's going on, Jonah?"

"Now, Per!"

She did as I asked and we began moving. My senses told me to move toward people, not away from them. I had learned enough to know that in times of great improvisation clueless people can make very useful props. After another hundred feet or so I turned around.

Kilt Man was still on us. And he seemed to have three friends.

My right hand had Perry's left hand; my left hand helped clear our path. The simple goal being survival, I shooed people aside, their protests falling on deaf ears. I could feel Perry pulling back. I knew it was because Max was having trouble keeping up.

I needed to keep them safe.

Always get what you need. Clean up later.

I wheeled around, picked Max up, and threw him over my shoulder.

"Let's go, Tess! Keep up!"

We had trained ourselves well. Talking amongst ourselves was one thing. But talking at a level where there was even a chance someone else could be listening, we were Tess, Johan, and Ivan. We switched back and forth effortlessly between English and Dutch. As did our voices, our accents.

I couldn't hold her hand any longer. I needed to be able to use every ounce of my unoccupied physical self for propulsion, people clearing.

"Grab my shirt and don't let it go!"

Perry did as I said, and we kept moving.

"What's happening?" screamed Max.

We both disregarded him. A few seconds later, I didn't feel Perry's hand grabbing my shirt. Barely breaking stride I turned around. She had fallen back. She was caught up in a group of the drunken Scottish soccer fans who had wrapped their arms around each other and broken into raunchy song. Though it was presumably English, I remember not being able to recognize a fucking word, the accents were so thick.

Not far past Perry, over her head, I saw Kilt Man and his boys. They were closing fast.

"Let's go, Tess! Now!"

She must have seen my eyes looking over her as I screamed in her direction. She turned around. When she saw the objects of my attention she fought her way through her temporary blockade and dashed for us. Even with all I had seen in my life, I had never seen panic like the fear in Perry's eyes at that very moment.

Just as Perry got to me, gasping for air, I turned, and we continued to charge through the crowd. She had my shirt again; order restored amidst chaos. As we approached what looked like the fringe of the crowd traffic, another gaggle of boozy Scottish men in plaid dresses belted out songs, beers in hand. Unsure of what was happening, and fearful for the only two people in the world who mattered to me, I let my gut take control.

"Please!" I yelled to them in my English-with-Dutch-accent voice, "Guys—please! Those men chasing us—"

I pointed at the three surprised men screeching to a halt.

"They attacked my wife! All we were doing was—"

The terrified look on Perry's face was all it took. The team of jolly, drunken men just looking for a reason to fly into an alcohol-induced assault, swarmed Kilt Man and his boys. Not interested in sticking around to see the result, we kept moving.

Not five feet farther, before I'd even had the chance to ramp up my speed, I was completely blindsided at the corner of Amstelstraat, tackled around the waist by someone hitting me as if it was the last thing they would do in their life. I remember hearing Perry scream. Max went flying from my shoulder, and we all went rolling end over end, a mishmash of flying limbs. My face smacked, dragged against the sidewalk. Seeing the world sideways, I watched a screaming Perry go for Max. Before she reached him, two more huge, kilt-wearing guys rolled up on her. One bear hugged and lifted her into the air. The other tagged her across the jaw without a second's hesitation. Perry was in a sheer panic, fighting and flailing like an impala caught by a lion. That's when I heard the first gunshot. And the one who had cracked her in the jaw went down.

Fuck!

Was that meant for Perry? Or Max?

Who's shooting?

The crowd, erupting in a screaming frenzy, scattered.

"Johan!" Perry wailed.

"You fuck!" I growled.

I went to get to my feet as the guy who had tackled me—trying to get his own bearings—grabbed my legs from behind, pulling me down again and rolling me over.

"Mommy! Mommy!" I heard behind me. "Ivan!"

I kicked Kilt Man in the face. It was a glancing shot, but one that would have stunned most men. Kilt Man was determined. He lunged for me, landing square on my chest. We simultaneously punched each other in the mouth with our right hands. I immediately wrapped my left forearm and hand around the back of his neck and with everything I had tried to peel him off me.

That's when I heard a vehicle come screeching up right next to our commotion.

I arched my neck and took an upside-down look at the world around behind me. I saw a black van. Perry, kicking and screaming, was being carried toward it. And it looked like yet another huge guy was carrying a screaming, crying Max.

"Tess!" I cried, unable to cover the pleading in my voice. "Johan!"

A crushing fist found my face. I most definitely tasted the blood filling my mouth from the two teeth that punctured my cheek. But I barely felt it.

Whoever these people were, they were trying to take all I had.

All I truly cared for.

In what must have been a millionth of a second, I had refocused my attention on Kilt Man, looking him square in the eye. The determination I had seen was gone, replaced by surprise. I grabbed the back of his head with my right hand, and grabbed his balls with my left. My left hand squeezed harder than it ever had before. My right hand brought his face to mine, then the animal that lurked deep inside sank my teeth into the portion of his face where his cheek met his nose. Instead of letting go when the tormented, high-pitched hollering spewed into the air, I lunged my teeth in farther.

Then, I yanked my neck back, and I tore.

Kilt Man fell backward clutching his bleeding face. I spit out a chunk of his flesh, jumped up and ran toward the van. Perry and Max were screaming hysterically as the side door slammed closed. Just like that, their voices were gone. Two gunshots came from behind me and hit the van, but they didn't slow anything down. The van peeled off.

Who was shooting?

Were they trying to slow the van down, or had they just missed me?

Without breaking stride, I ran after the van. I wasn't going to catch it, but as much as my brain felt like nothing more than scrambled egg something was telling me to keep running.

What the fuck had just gone down? In a blink, I had just gone from having a nice family dinner to tasting another man's fresh blood.

Why?

Perry and Max were obviously the targets. Or were they? Was this really about me? Was I the intended target? Maybe all three of us? Maybe the goal was all three, but they were willing to settle for any two of us.

But who? Why? What could this possibly be about?

Everything about the scenario screamed "hit." The costumes, the number of guys, the surveillance—everything. How long had they been on us?

Days?

Weeks?

And why not kill us? What could the benefit be taking us alive?

Why?

For whom?

Fuck! Fuck!

My brain spinning, my legs kept churning. I simply couldn't stop. There could be more of them still gunning for me, I thought. Just because Perry and Max had been taken, that didn't mean the job was done.

The last thing I needed was anyone getting a look at or picture of me, no matter how different Ivan Janse looks from Jonah Gray, another reason my gut told me to keep moving. No matter how much I wanted to ask every single person in that vicinity what they had seen, heard, I couldn't. Plain and simple. My life didn't allow for such things.

When I returned to the house, I stripped off my shirt in the kitchen, rinsed my face, and grabbed the biggest knife I could find in the kitchen. I took a seat with it in the living room where, though essentially the length of the entire ground floor away, I could see the front door. Neo wanted up. I lifted him. He curled up next to me and soon drifted off. His eyes next opened when the sun came up. Mine had never closed.

Through the night, sitting there in the near dark, I did one thing—and one thing only. Play the entire scene over again in my head. Every time I did, I tried to slow it down. I tried to see if there was anything at all that could be a clue to what had happened, who these people were. There was nothing.

To this day, I have still not seen Perry.

CHAPTER 30

As I walk down the hallway, passing by examination rooms on each side, a man steps out of one and into my path.

"Excuse me, what's going on here? Can we help you?"

It's Perry's douche-bag husband. I remember exactly what he looks like.

"You can, Dr. York. You and I need to have a talk in your office."

"Excuse me? If you don't turn around and walk out of here right now—"

I grab him by the throat, slam him into the wall, and grab his nuts as hard as I can with my free hand.

"You'll what?"

I squeeze harder.

"Ahhhh!"

I slam his head against the wall again, then give him a quick bitch slap across the face.

"Your office, Tough Guy. Now."

I lock the door behind us.

"Who the fuck are you?" he asks.

I take the gun from my inside jacket pocket. He gasps, puts his arms up slightly from his sides. He's confused.

He's scared.

As he should be.

"I'll be asking the questions," I tell him.

I walk up to him. He backs away from me right up to the wall. I reach down and jam the point of the gun upward into his nuts.

"You feel that? That's the actual tip of a gun buried in your ball sac. You wondering right now what that might feel like if I pull the trigger? I can tell you one thing—you won't die right away. But you'll be in so much pain, you'll be begging me to kill you."

He swallows hard.

"What do you want?"

"Where's Perry?"

York's eyes can't hide his surprise.

"What?"

"Perry. Where is she?"

I think of what Max told me on the playground. I need to know where Perry is. If she's alive or dead.

"If I don't get answers, make no mistake—I am going to kill you. It will be slow, and it will be painful."

Still nothing.

"Too much time," I say.

I shatter his nose with the butt of the gun. Before he drops I grab him, prop him back up against the wall. Blood gushing from his nostrils, forming one thick stream flowing into and around his mouth, I put the tip of the gun between his eyes, which are welling with tears.

"It's only going to get worse. Where's Perry?"

He's genuinely freaked now. His breathing is ragged, choppy. He's having trouble gathering words.

And time is ticking.

"Stop crying like a little bitch," I growl. "Because if one of your assistants, or that nice receptionist, comes in here and interferes, I'm going to shut their mouth with a bullet. You got that?"

He nods yes.

"Where is Perry?"

"Okay! Okay—just, please. Just—"

I take a step back. I hold the gun down. He uses his white doc-tor's coat to wipe away some of the blood coming from his nose.

"It was a bunch of years back. This Russian guy named Andreu found me at home one night. He was asking about my wife's part-ner, this guy named Jonah Gray."

"What did he want to know about this Gray?"

"Where he was. I told him I had no idea; that he'd been either missing or on the run from the cops for all kinds of shit for a few years already. I told him I didn't have any more idea where Gray was than where my wife was. But one thing was for certain."

"Which was?" I press.

"I was sure they were together. And that they had my son. So the Russian made me a deal. If I was ever to hear about either of their whereabouts—Perry or Gray—I was to let him know. And in return he'd help, if he could, to return my son to me."

I process his words.

"That's all very interesting," I say. Then I raise my gun again. "But you didn't answer my question. Where is Perry?"

"I don't know."

"Bullshit. Where is she?" I say louder.

"I don't know," he responds, his voice growing louder with mine. "I don't! I swear! But if you'll let me just explain—"

"You'd better. Because me leaving here with you still breathing is looking less likely by the second."

"A few years ago something happened. A phone call from my brother," York continued. "He was traveling in Europe. In Amster-dam. He was sure he saw Perry. So he followed her. It was her, he said. Then he saw Max. My son. That's when he knew it was real. So I called the Russian. His first question was if she was with Gray. As much as I wanted to tell him she was, apparently they were with a guy, but it wasn't him. The Russian told me no Gray, no deal. I pleaded with him. That's when he came up with a solution that benefitted us both. He said he'd get me back my boy if he could keep Perry for himself. Because one day he was sure Gray would come looking for her. So I said yes."

The reality of the situation washed over me like typhoon-fueled wave.

That day in Amsterdam.

The van.

The abduction.

"And that's it?" I finally push out. "And just like that you hand your wife over to this Russian? Not caring what he does with her? Not asking who he is?"

Rage starts coursing through my veins, beyond my control. I step back to him and put the gun to his head again.

"Who the fuck does that? What kind of man are you? I should just kill you right now!"

Pleading, he holds his hands out.

"Please. Please. Do you have kids? All I needed was my son back home. I'm his father. It's my responsibility to know he's safe. That he's home."

"What about your *wife*? What about a commitment to keeping her safe too? The woman who brought your son into the world?"

"The woman who left me. And took my son away from me."

Fucking asshole. What woman wouldn't have left a womanizing, disrespectful, disgraceful son of a bitch like you?

I see Perry in my head. I see her laughing in a restaurant with me in Amsterdam. Then I see her in her office, in New York City, back when we were brokers before the storm broke.

I shake my head.

I need to gather myself.

Stay on course.

Tick.

Tock.

"I need his number. Andreu, the Russian. I need the number he gave you. And I need it now."

"Look, I told you what you wanted to know. Now, please, just—"

I slowly move the gun down, and push it into his mouth, killing his words.

"The number. Now. Blink twice if you understand."

He blinks twice. I remove the gun and wipe off the end on a clean part of his doctor's coat. Slowly, his arms still out at his sides, he moves behind his desk. He picks up his cell phone and finds the number in his contacts. He reads it out loud. As he does, I enter it into my phone.

"Zero, one, one—"

The country code to dial international out of the U.S.

"Seven—"

The country code for Russia.

"Four, nine, five—"

One of two area codes for Moscow; the other is 499.

He finishes it out from there, not knowing I'd have known if he was dishing bullshit digits.

The number is legit.

"I'm going to walk out that door now," I explain. "Know this. If you call the police about this or call Andreu and give him a heads-up, I will be back. Only next time it won't be here. It will be at your home."

With the gun, I point to a picture of a woman on his desk.

"Where I will sit you down with Replacement Perry and proceed to slit her throat while you watch her life run out of her. Then, Dr. York, I will do the same to you."

I step to the desk.

"We clear?"

He nods yes.

"Say it."

"We're clear."

CHAPTER 31

Back in my hotel room, I have a couple hours before the Alessi crew looks to dazzle us at their latest-and-greatest Manhattan venture. I'm rifling through Internet sites, reaching every corner I can in cyberspace about the lineage of all the players with the eggs. At the same time, I'm seeing, going over every inch, of the walls at Herengracht.

Who is V.A.?

I get it why Gustav Bjerg—Imposter Derbyshev—needed to go such a silent route with passing messages to his cousin. Had the Russian royal family learned of their true intent, they no doubt would have been executed. And being that G.B. was a man of nothing but service to Maria Feodorovna, not only was his time with her—if there was any at all—limited, but would have undoubtedly always occurred under supervision.

But who was he getting his information from? Who was V.A.?

Who would G.B. target that would be accessible?

And willing to give such damning evidence against a czar?

I begin with Czar Alexander III's closest government and church-related compatriots—Konstantin Pobyedonostsev, Count

D. A. Tolstoy, Mikhail Katkov—as well as others who supported his efforts as czar. I dig as far as I can, not just with these individuals but with their circles, their families. Nothing. I move on to those affiliated with the different Russian royal family residences like Livadia Palace, Winter Palace—still nothing. Not one person with the initials V.A.

I slam my fist on the table.

Fuck!

What am I missing?

I shake my head.

And as I do, an image of the Alexander III wall at Herengracht shakes loose from my mind.

Yes.

I see it.

But, could it really be?

I jump back into cyberspace and confirm what I believe to be true. Alexander III had five brothers and two sisters. And one of those brothers had the initials V.A.

Grand Duke Vladimir Alexandrovich.

I start digging. Vladimir Alexandrovich was a bit of a party boy it seems, but it also appears he had a deep love of the arts. So much, in fact, he was appointed president of the Imperial Academy of Fine Arts in 1880. The highest end jewelry designers—like those at the House of Fabergé—were considered masters of the arts themselves, and were very much involved in organizations such as this. Not only does the timing of their lives and careers fall perfectly into line with one another in terms of both proximity to one another as well as the timing of the eggs' creation, I learn an interesting nugget about the Grand Duke. While his brother Czar Alexander III promoted his career at certain points, according to history they were not particularly close. In fact, it appears there was nothing short of both resentment and rivalry between the two.

The kind that might very well result in spilling the beans on a murderous brother.

I need to get to D.C.

I need to see *Danish Jubilee Egg*.

At one p.m. we walk into the Alessi family's latest venture in the heart of Midtown, a very cool spot that is a combination restaurant and art gallery modeled after a similar place they recently opened in Milan. The space—operating under a partnership with a major downtown gallery owner—is massive, open, bright. Metal, industrial-looking lights hang from the ceiling, highlighting the huge, wood-and-metal sculptures set between the tables. The floor, the walls, the ceiling, the tablecloths, the servers' outfits—everything aside from the lights is white. It reminds me of my house in Amsterdam. Apparently, one of the interesting things about the place will be every couple months not only will the artwork change, but the décor will as well in a way that best highlights whatever work is being shown.

The place, for what it's worth, smells awesome. Rustic yet sweet scents from the Italian countryside. Trays with champagne and hors d'oeuvres are floating around the room. But eating is the last thing on my mind. I have work to do.

Julia's already here. Statuesque and fine as always in a black Armani suit and matching sky-high Manolos, she heads over to us. Brand is with her.

After quick, cordial hellos all around—neither Julia nor I acting like people who had torn each other to shreds just hours earlier—I turn my attention to Brand.

"Actually, Ryan, I was just thinking about something on the way over here so I am happy to see you."

"Of course. What's on your mind, Ivan?"

"The minority partner."

"Excuse me?"

"The minority partner GlassWell has in the property we're buying. What's their name again?"

"It's a family-owned firm named The Dunham Group."

"Right—The Dunham Group. It occurred to me that we have

had no contact with this company, even though they are one of the selling parties."

"Why would you? They own only a quarter of the property, and we have all decision-making authority."

"Of course," I respond, "but in a situation like this where it is clear they had such a different—philosophy, if you will—on how the property should be run, I can't help thinking it would be an important perspective to have. You know, even just a quick conversation, in terms of proper due diligence."

"Perhaps," Brand comes back, "but I'd figure such an exercise to be nothing more than a waste of time, especially this close to the finish line. In my experience, best practice is to separate the relevant from the irrelevant. And in this case— now this is just me speaking here—Dunham is simply irrelevant. Why? Because they have no say."

"Why didn't you buy them out?" I change directions. "We both know how the building performs. And it's GlassWell's bread and butter, in terms of the kind of building it is. So why?"

I want these answers. Not just for me, but for those we're standing with to hear as well.

"Good question, Ivan. And frankly you're bringing it up again makes me think we should reconsider selling it," he answers with a weak attempt at a joke—that no one finds funny. "Why do you think? Dollars. I told them what their twenty-five percent is worth. They thought I was trying to get over on them."

"And now?"

"Now what?"

"Are they happy with the number? Or do they still think they came up short?"

"Long or short, they're walking away with a nice little pile of cash. I think they're just fine with it."

Brand's eyes move from mine to over my shoulder.

"Ah—Enzo!" he says, saved. "Enzo. Please," he goes on, voice loud as he waves him over. "Please. Won't you come say hello to our guests of honor—who just happen to be your new landlord."

Enzo Alessi is definitely a presence. Dressed in a taut, custom-made navy windowpane-pattern Brioni suit, his gold tie knot thick, bold, he presents himself.

"We are very excited, and honored, to have you all here today. Ryan tells me we are in the hands of a very capable new landlord—one whom is European based, which actually makes me feel a bit closer to home."

Alessi is tall, probably six three or four, with a large head and very prominent facial features, and perfectly coiffed thick salt-and-pepper hair. And he knows how to work the crowd.

"Enzo, meet Cobus de Bont," Brand introduces them. "Cobus is the founder and chairman of de Bont Beleggings."

They shake hands.

"It's nice to meet you," Cobus says. "I'm a fan of your restaurants. And we're very much looking forward to entering this market and having you as tenant."

As I'm staring at this guy, I can't help wondering what I'm not seeing. I get it that he and Brand are working each other, but where did Scott Green come in? Why was he so scared that he'd rather kill himself than go to the police?

"Not just any tenant," I cut in, "but an anchor tenant. One locked in for a while thanks to your recent lease signing."

His eyes, and extended hand, move to me.

"Anchor tenant—I like that. And you are?"

"Ivan Janse. I work with Cobus."

"Ivan has been spearheading the acquisition," Cobus chimes in. "I'm just along for the ride."

At that moment, a waiter comes by with a tray of champagne flutes.

"Please," Enzo says, taking the filled glasses and passing them around, "A toast, if I may. To our new landlord and a nice working relationship."

"You know, your family has a lot of places to look after in a number of cities. Is that difficult?" I ask Enzo.

"We have a world-class organization, Mr.—"

"Janse. But please—call me Ivan."

"Ivan. One of the first things my father taught me is that it all starts with the right team. From myself down to hardworking men and women who clean up after hours, we're all in it for the same common goal. An unmatched experience."

"So it all begins and ends with you."

Alessi raises his eyebrows.

"If you're asking do I accept the burden of knowing our success or failure ultimately falls to me—then, yes. I take our family's name very seriously, Ivan. I gladly welcome the responsibility of making sure our establishments live up to the standards my father set years ago."

"Your father. I believe I read somewhere he isn't well," I add. "I'm sorry to hear that."

"Yes, well, he is a strong, spirited man with a lot of fight. So, why don't we all—"

"Where do you actually consider your home base? Meaning, where is the firm actually incorporated?" I barrel forward. "If I'm correct, the checks come from what is a U.S.-based subsidiary of the Milan-based headquarters, correct?"

"Perhaps this is a conversation for later," Julia tries to diffuse the situation.

"Why do you ask?"

"I'm just a man of detail, Enzo. Cobus will tell you, I like to have as much knowledge as possible when it comes to a building's tenant roster. Makes for a much easier time dealing with whatever situations arise. And I can promise you, things always come up."

Enzo, holding it together nicely, thinks for a second before responding.

"That is correct. We are a Milan-based company."

"And you handle it the way you do for tax purposes, I imagine. Meaning there must be significant tax ramifications for having separate companies in each country as opposed to having separate subsidiaries that fall under the parent."

"I'm sorry. We are a private company, so we don't discuss how we handle our tax matters. I'm sure you understand, being a private company yourself."

"Of course. Interesting. I'm just curious—how much of the corporate structure you've devised is based on the taxes as they relate to your staff?"

"Ivan, I really think this should wait until later," Julia again tries to interject.

"I'm sorry, Ivan, why is it, once again, you are so interested?" Enzo goes on.

"Nothing more than due diligence. I just like to have as much knowledge as possible about with whom we're getting into business."

"Is that right?"

"It is."

"Well, rest assured we are exactly the type of tenant you are happy to have. One that increases the value of your property."

"Well, I guess that ultimately remains to be seen when one's dealing with such a unique piece of real estate."

Cobus places his hand on my back.

"Ivan—may I have a word?"

"Of course."

"Please help yourself to some hors d'oeuvres," Enzo says, looking to bow out gracefully. "Try my son's favorite—the langoustine fritters in a lychee and dragon fruit glaze; just amazing."

Not so fast.

"Thanks for having us," I go on. "Hey, I've been thinking about taking a trip to South America. I read your family has a villa down there. Colombia maybe? Or Argentina?"

"Uruguay."

"Right—Uruguay. I've heard it's a beautiful country. I'm guessing the amount of hours you put in hardly leaves much time for getting down there."

"There's never enough time vacationing with one's family. Now if you'll excuse me . . ."

Cobus and I step aside.

"What are you doing, Ivan?"

"Learning about our tenant."

"That's you grilling our new tenant—a tenant with a fine reputation. We are both quite familiar with your due diligence practice
and techniques. This was not that. This was you being aggressive.
Why?"

Over Cobus's shoulder I see Brand and Alessi having what
seems to be an intense conversation.

Back off.

Keep Cobus where he needs to be.

To get where I need to go.

"I see what you're saying. Perhaps it was a bit more of a discussion than we needed to have right now," I concede. "Maybe I'm a
bit on edge because I haven't been sleeping well since we've
arrived."

Cobus, Arnon, and I are riding up in the hotel elevator following
lunch.

"Dinner with GlassWell isn't until eight. I believe Mr. Spencer
himself is joining us."

"He is," I confirm. "I'm going to spend a little time going
through the arrears reports for The Hague properties. I'll see you
downstairs when the car arrives."

I step into my room. After waiting five minutes, I head back
downstairs and out into the city.

CHAPTER 32

I'm so tired.

I knew these few days would be brutal, but I underestimated just how worn down—mentally, as well as physically—I'd get. I have a massive headache. Everything is amplified. The city sounds aren't just entering my ears, they're reverberating through my entire body.

I take the disposable from inside my suit jacket and dial the main number for PCBL, my old firm. I remember the number by heart.

"PCBL, good afternoon," a cheery voice answers.

"Good afternoon. I have an appointment with Jake Donald this afternoon, and I wanted to confirm his office is still on the eighteenth floor."

A brief pause.

"Actually, Mr. Donald is on nineteen."

Interesting. The Management Team floor. Looks as if someone has left the life of a broker behind.

"Ah—nineteen. Right. I appreciate the help."

"Of course. We'll see you later."

My eyelids are really heavy.

Fuck.

Before hailing a cab to go see and rock the world of my old partner and close friend Jake, I see a bodega. I move toward it, thinking
a Coke, iced tea, something with caffeine. But a little couple-ounce
bottle called "Life Fuel"—with the tagline, "Coffee, what? Wake
up! Fuel for Hours!" catches my eye.

I place two of the cherry-flavor bottles on the counter. I pay for
them, shoot one down, and put the other in my pocket. Then hail
a cab.

Steps before entering the famed Chrysler Center—where I used to
work—my mind kicks into gear. Nowadays security for large office
properties in all cities is beyond tight and starts the second one
enters the lobby. One of the keys to understanding how to beat
security in a busy building like the Chrysler Center: traffic flow.

My eyes shielded by sunglasses, I step into the lobby. Pretending
to be speaking on my cell, I stop immediately. The first thing I take
notice of is the security counter. The checkpoint is equipped with
guards checking people into the building—or granting temporary
building passes for those who show proper identification and are on
the security guest list for the day. At the moment there are three
guards working the desk. And they are completely inundated, no
doubt feeling the pressure of a line of people looking to carry on
with their days.

I put my phone away, flip my sunglasses onto my head, and
blend in with the flow of traffic heading toward the elevator bank
servicing the floor I need, deliberately never even looking in the
direction of the security desk. Just as I'm about to reach the bidirec-
tional optical turnstile—the one that will only open with the bar
code from a full-time employee or day pass—I do an about face.

Just like life, it's all about the timing.

And just like that, it appears as if I'm coming from the elevator
bank.

"Fuck!" I yell.

But not a yell like I'm at a Knicks game and I want the ref to hear, more of a what-the-fuck-was-I-thinking yell that is just loud enough for those around me to hear—including the security guards. Right on point each of the three glances up at me. I catch one's eye. I take three steps toward him.

"My cell phone. I left it upstairs. PCBL," I say, throwing my thumb backward over my shoulder.

Always own the words that come out of your mouth, Pop always said.

And if you need to look like you belong—then look like you belong.

The security guard nods.

The acrylic barrier wing panels of the high-tech turnstile swing open.

"And how might we help you today?" asks the receptionist as I approach.

The PCBL reception area has gone through a facelift since I've last been here. The walls are still the same light shade of cream lined with the same trademark black-and-white stills of the Manhattan skyline, but the space feels fresher, cleaner, more vibrant. The hunter-green carpeting has been replaced with carpet containing a smart, contemporary, cream-and-beige pattern. All of the mahogany—the wood, the doors, the furniture—has been replaced by lighter wood, most likely soft maple or birch. Lots of glass still allows the light to flow freely, evenly throughout the space. Flowers, as always, are everywhere—big, bold bouquets of vibrant, rare species that look like they've been pulled from every exotic forest on the planet.

"Good afternoon. I have a four p.m. appointment with Jake Donald."

"Very well then. Let me just ring his office."

We both wait in silence for a moment.

"Yes, Mr. Donald's four p.m. is in reception," she continues when the other end picks up.

She comes back to me.

"I'm sorry, Mr. Donald's assistant doesn't see anything on the books for four p.m. What did you say your name is?"

"I didn't give it to you. And I have to confess, I don't have a four p.m." I say, motioning to her to cover the microphone bud on the headset she's speaking into, which she does. "I'm an old college friend of Mr. Donald's whom he hasn't seen in fifteen years. I just happened to be in town and was really hoping to surprise him."

"Oh, that's so cool of you," she said, "but unfortunately I can't let you in or request someone out here unless I'm given a name. I hope you can understand."

Not only do I understand, I was planning on it.

"Of course I do. Well, it was worth a try."

Jake used to refer to a college friend he was close to but never really saw again after school because the guy lived in Seattle.

"Please just let him know that Mason Brody's here."

The receptionist relays the message. Then tells me Mr. Donald is on his way out.

I told myself I would detach upon walking into this office. I would keep my thoughts in the present and not let them pull me into the past. But my old life starts coming at me like a boxer's jabs—an image of my old senior partner Tommy sitting behind his desk, another of the old Perry tearing into someone in the very conference room off right now to my left. So much happened here. From the business, to the personal. This place is still a part of me, always will be. The moment reinforces for me that we can never escape who we are, or where we've been. All we can do as people is take any and every situation that happens in our lives, and ask ourselves what we were supposed to learn from it as we figure out how to move forward.

A door from the offices leading into reception opens. Out walks my old partner, my old friend Jake Donald. His face looks essentially the same but is older, rounder. Same as the rest of his body as he appears to have ballooned in weight.

He looks at me, then to the receptionist. He's confused.

I walk toward him.

"I'm sorry, I was told—"

"It's great to see you, Jake," I cut him off. "An old friend wanted me to show you this…"

I hold up my iPhone right in front of his face. The screen is on the notepad app, with the following words typed:

I'VE COME TO DISCUSS JONAH GRAY. IS THERE SOMEWHERE WE MIGHT TALK?

Jake is silent, motionless. I knew this would frighten him, and that I'd need to keep us moving forward.

"Everything is quite all right, but it's important we speak. Is there somewhere we might chat?"

"Mr. Donald, is everything okay?" asks the receptionist, getting it I'm not who I said I was.

"Don't be scared. You need to speak with me," I whisper.

"Yes, yes, everything is fine," Jake says to her, snapping out of it. "Of course. Right this way."

We step into the conference room.

"What the hell is going on here?" asks Jake once the door is closed. "Do I need to call security? Because you need to know I will."

"Why don't you sit down," I say.

"I'd rather stand."

"Okay. But if it's all right with you, I'm going to sit down. I've been on my feet forever." I take the chair at the head of the long conference table.

"Like nine years."

I'm hoping the soft reference to how long Jonah has been gone, and myself, might jar something loose. Which it doesn't.

"How do you know Mason Brody?"

"I don't."

"Then—how; why—I don't understand."

"I know you don't. There's no way you possibly could," I explain. "I only know about your college friend Mason Brody from you."

"We've met before?" he goes on, eyes squinting subconsciously as he searches his mind for a previous image of me.

"We have. Only I wasn't the man you're looking at."

I swallow, then continue in my God-given voice from my previous life.

"I was Jonah Gray."

My voice startles him. He literally has to grab the back of one of the conference table chairs to keep his balance.

"What the fuck? How did—"

"I mean, I still am technically Jonah. I'm just—now—"

"Who the fuck are you?"

"Jonah Gray. I swear. It's really me," I say, standing up and taking a step toward him.

He heads for the door.

"Fuck this, I'm calling the police."

"Wait. Don't, please."

He doesn't listen. His feet speed up.

"Your father's name is Ronnie Donald. He's a portfolio manager for wealthy families. Your mother's name is Florence—everyone calls her Flo—and she's a nurse. Your favorite dish on the planet is the chicken parm at Scalinatella, which we used to always share along with the tubettoni con le cozze. You love big dogs, but you're afraid of little ones, except for Neo, because he's mine."

Just as he cracks the door, he stops, looks at me.

"How the fuck do you know all this? How are you doing this?"

"It's really me. Jonah. Think about it, Jake. Think about the circumstances surrounding Jonah Gray's life when he disappeared. I had no choice to become someone else if Jonah Gray was to ever really reclaim his life. His name."

"But, still—I don't—you look—"

"Like another person. I know; I get it. I had no choice. But it's really me."

He's almost there. I take a quarter from my pocket. I start flipping it in the air.

"The quarter," he says under his breath.

"The quarter. When you were fifteen years old, on a ski trip in Vermont, you got separated from your classmates. A quarter to make a call saved your ass. You've carried one with you at all times ever since."

He takes one out of his pocket and holds it up. I keep flipping mine.

"Me. I keep one with me also. Not because it's going to do a lick of good for me on foreign soil or in the age of cell phones, but because it reminds me no matter where I find myself, no matter what situation I'm in—"

I catch the quarter.

"—I'm going to get through it. And one day, no matter what, get home."

He closes the door. He walks over to me. He studies my face.

"That's fucking insane, dude. Your face, the way they—you—"

"I missed you, man," I cut him off.

"I missed you too."

We give each other a big hug, then check each other out again.

"Don't say it. I'm fat as a fucking house."

"I . . . you . . . I wasn't going to say anything. Except for the fact you're on nineteen now. Management?"

"Management indeed. Come on, we used to both say we didn't want to be brokers forever. Four years ago they offered me a lot of stock and a lot of stress to run all of leasing, so I took it. Obviously, from my waistline, you can see how well I'm handling the stress."

"How's Tommy?" I ask.

Jake dips his chin for a second.

"He passed away. A couple years ago."

Tommy Wingate was not just a close friend of my family, the one who gave me my first shot in the commercial real estate world, he was my mentor.

"No." I say under my breath, grabbing the closest chair to me, a different one than the initial one I'd sat in. "What happened?"

"Heart attack. Right here in his fucking office."

"No way. Wow. I wish . . . I wish I had a chance to speak with him again. To tell him, you know—"

"He loved you, Jonah, and he knew no matter what the fuck

happened, there had to have been an explanation for all of it. We talked about you all the time. And when we did, all he ever said was you were the best young real estate mind he'd ever seen. And that he hoped you were safe. We both did."

I feel a slight smile creep onto my face.

"A heart attack, huh?"

"Look, I always say to people it wasn't such a bad way to go. It was fast, and he was somewhere he loved to be. Could have been worse. He could have been eaten by sharks or something."

"Where's Perry?" Jake changes direction.

"I don't know."

"You don't know? We assumed she was with you."

"She was. Until something happened a few years ago."

"Which was? Is she safe?"

Safe? I'm not sure whether she's alive or dead.

"Look," I wave him off, "it's complicated. The less you know about everything the better. And I really don't have much time."

"So, then, what is it you want? Why are you here? Why now?"

"Because I need your help."

"Help doing what?"

"Clearing my name."

"Just name it, bro. Anything."

"I need you to contact Detective Tim Morante at the Nineteenth Precinct. And tell him he needs to be on the beach behind the home at Forty-Four Mako in Amagansett tomorrow morning at five thirty a.m."

"A New York City cop in the Hamptons? Why?"

"Seclusion. Anyway, don't worry about any of that. I just need you to relay this message."

"Forty-Four Mako. Why do I know that address?"

Thinks for a second.

"Richard Plotkin," Jake continues. "Rivco's CEO who lives in West Palm Beach and never uses his houses up here?"

He was right. Rivco was a hedge fund we used to represent back in the day. And Richard Plotkin, though from Manhattan, hated the Northeast; he held this Hamptons monstrosity along with two others as investments. And told me many times way back when he'd never give any of the three up because one day each would go to each of his three children.

"Exactly. We still represent them?"

"We do. You haven't given me much time, Jonah. What if I can't find him?"

"You need to. If it's difficult, tell whomever you get they need to get the message to Morante immediately because it relates to an old unsolved case of his. And that it's urgent. Once you have the man himself on the other end, tell him five thirty a.m. tomorrow on the beach. Alone. Because someone with information about Jonah Gray will be there to meet him. If Morante asks how you know, tell him exactly what happened. Someone you've never seen before showed up in your office and told you to make this call. And that you felt you should, because you want to know the truth about Jonah as much as anyone."

"What if he asks why he should believe me?"

"Tell him you can't answer that. To believe it or not is for him to decide."

We both pause. Jake stands up, puts his hands on his head, and starts pacing.

"Fuck, Jonah, I don't know. The authorities were up our asses when all of this shit went down and you disappeared."

"I don't doubt it. And I'm truly sorry to ask you to do this. But I wouldn't unless I really need you to. As you can imagine, there are only a couple people I could possibly trust to help me, and time is running out. Besides, you've done nothing wrong. You didn't then, you haven't now."

Jake paces for another second then stops and stares at me. He let's out a long, dejected breath and sits back down.

"Trust me," I go on, "He'll believe it. He'll be there tomorrow morning. Once you relay the message, tell him you need his cell phone number. He'll ask why. Tell him the guy he'll be meeting said he'll need it to contact Morante should he feel Morante has been untruthful about coming alone. Because the man with the information about Jonah will be watching. But, you see, I won't be the one calling him. Because he can never have a direct number from me."

Jake thinks for a second.

"Then who will be?"

"You."

I walk out of the building. Just as I'm about to hail a cab, my iPhone vibrates. It's a text from Julia.

WE NEED TO SPEAK. HOW ABOUT WE MEET AT THE RESTAURANT A HALF HOUR EARLY FOR A COCKTAIL?

CHAPTER 33

New York City
2013

At seven fifteen p.m.—fifteen minutes before I'm supposed to meet Julia and forty-five minutes before the two of us are to meet everyone else for dinner—I walk into Il Mulino, the legendary Greenwich Village Italian eatery. I notice Claudio, the silver-haired Maitre d' who runs the show and used to give me a table from a simple text when most can't even get through on the phone, let alone land a reservation. He asks if I have a reservation. I want to joke with him about how an Italian fella can know so much about American football or make fun of the fact I've never seen a human wear their glasses so low on the tip of their nose. Instead, I tell him I'm with the GlassWell party at eight and that I'm early. He cordially offers me a seat at the tiny bar, which hasn't yet filled up, but within minutes will be standing room only as the evening rush is fast approaching.

The bartender asks if I'd like anything. I take a seltzer with lime. Alcohol will undoubtedly be a part of the evening's festivities. Upon this notion, I take the remaining bottle of Life Fuel and knock it back. I chase it with the seltzer.

On my iPhone I start rifling through my file on the Berlin deal.

Before this bullshit, did the Freedom Bank Building look like a good deal, a prime expansion acquisition? Yes. Better than the Berlin property? Hell, no. I need to get that building for Cobus. I owe him that.

As I look through the file, an aerial shot of the business district where the Berlin building—Feuerbach Turm—stands catches my eye. Then I think of an article I just read regarding the new zoning laws that just took effect in that particular portion of the city. I go back to one of the forecasts we were given as part of the building package. It becomes clear to me everyone involved in selling or buying the building may have missed something.

I dial a number. A voice picks up on the other end.

"Hallo?"

It's after midnight in Germany. I'm surprised to hear a live voice.

"Ernst, Ivan. I apologize for calling so late. I was expecting your voice mail."

Ernst Brecht is handling the Berlin property sale. I am well aware at this point either Gruden & Wayfield or Vienna Shanks is locked in on acquiring the building.

"Ivan Janse," Ernst responds. "Don't worry about it. Really. I've been working this late every night for a week as we're working toward a close. I'm actually happy to lift my nose up for a moment."

His English is strong; his heavy German accent even stronger.

Fuck. Is the close he's been working on for my new target?

"I must say, I'm surprised to hear from you," he adds.

"Why is that?"

"Last we spoke, I felt it was pretty clear de Bont had moved on. How have you been?"

"I've been well, Ernst, thanks. Are you telling me the property is off the market?"

Real estate is always about the dance . . .

"The property has not yet been sold, if that is what you are asking."

And I've had my share of jaunts around the ballroom.

"In that case, there's some information I could use. I was going to leave you a message to e-mail it first thing tomorrow, but the sooner I receive it the better."

"What is it you want?"

"A most likely scenario capital-improvement schedule for the next five years of major building equipment. I had requested one following a review of the offering materials, but in reviewing the file I see it was never received."

"Is that right? Hmm—I remember your request and thought I sent it on."

He had. And it had been received. But I couldn't let him think the next little piece of information I'd be handing him was the reason for the call.

"In any event, not a problem. I'll send it off as soon as we hang up."

"Thank you, Ernst, that's appreciated. And again, I'm sorry for calling so late."

"Not a problem. Business is business."

"Yes it is. Speaking of which, from what I understand there were two firms seriously interested in your property so let's just say while I'm interested in the fact it hasn't turned over yet, I'm happy you were, at least, according to the rumors in the marketplace, leaning toward the private player."

True, there were two major firms interested in the property at last notice—one private, one public. But the public firm, Gruden & Wayfield, is the one with whom they are about to make the deal.

"Because word on the street is the public player was going to look to bring in another partner at the last minute to diminish the risk. A partner that while on the surface has a solid enough reputation as to not hold up a close unfortunately has an almost equally indisputable history of failing to close as often as they actually get a deal to the finish line."

A pause.

"Yes, well, as you said yourself the property hasn't yet turned over."

I had zero indication Gruden was looking to partner with anyone, and even less of an idea what firm it was I was referring to as their potential partner. I had just described a ton of pretenders out there. But my work was done. I had planted a seed in his brain that something was up with his deal. Enough that he was at least going to give me twenty-four or forty-eight hours to see if I had any intention on coming to the table to steal the building.

"Indeed. Look forward to receiving that schedule," I finished up. "Thanks again."

Julia walks in at seven thirty p.m. on the dot, the exact second I can feel my heart racing a bit from the straight caffeine I just ingested. She's still wearing what she had been earlier in the day. Before saying a word to me, she addresses the bartender who, like every other person with a pulse in the place, is checking her out.

"Hi, glass of Chianti, please."

"Uh, we don't tonight by zee glass have a Chianti, but I have a beautiful Montepulciano zat—"

"That's fine," she cuts him off.

She looks at my glass.

"Soda with your vodka tonight? Going easy?"

"Why the request to meet early?" I change directions. "I think we're all set in terms of open items to discuss."

The bartender places her glass of wine in front of her. She takes a healthy sip and places the glass back down.

"Why were you going after Enzo today? What was that all about?"

"I'm sorry," I shrug her off. "I really don't know what you're talking about."

"Come on, Ivan."

I just stare at her, say nothing. Because I can see in her eyes, I don't need to.

Come with it.

"What you did this afternoon, that wasn't exactly how a new landlord treats their building's flagship tenant."

"We're not their landlord yet, Julia. GlassWell still is."

"What is that supposed to mean?"

I smirk at her and slowly reach for my seltzer.

"You were holding the close up on purpose today. I fucking knew it." She goes on.

I take a sip.

"Relax, Julia, take a step back. The closing was held up strictly out of business necessity. That's all. Your imagination is getting the best of you right now."

Keep her where I need her.

"Really? I'm imagining things? Like you and Alessi this afternoon?"

"This again? I told you—"

"Bullshit! It wasn't just what you were saying, Ivan, it was your eyes."

"My eyes?"

"I watched them the whole time. And they were definitely going after something."

"Again, I really wish I had something interesting to tell you, but I don't. I'm a man loyal to my boss, my firm. And in that loyalty comes an undeniable pursuit of knowledge in terms of my due diligence. At all times, at every opportunity. I make no apologies for this."

"Due diligence. Right."

She takes her glass from the bar. She's about to say something, but stops herself. She takes another healthy sip. After replacing the glass, she puts her right hand on top of my left hand, which is on the bar.

"Does any of this have to do with Scott Green? Or what happened to him?"

"Mr. Green. The attorney," I say, pretending to be catching up to her.

"Do you really think he killed himself?"

A video of his head exploding onto the wall plays in my brain.

"I have no idea," I say. "Why?"

Julia pulls her hand from mine. She looks at her watch.

"They'll be here any minute. Let me check and see if our table is all set."

Minutes later the group has arrived, and we're on our way into the tightly packed dining room. Spencer is like a deity; he can't get past one table without someone standing up and greeting him with a warm handshake or kiss. The place is in usual full-throttle form. For those willing to throw down a Range Rover lease payment for dinner, white-gloved servers are already hard at work floating through the low-lit, windowless digs, doling out perfectly prepared garlic-laden staples. The understated décor, two walls solid brick and the others off-white wallpaper with scattered, falling leaves, help keep patrons' attention solely on the Abruzzi-region inspired cuisine. We are seated at a round table in the far back left corner of the dining room. As we are, gratuitous premeal antipasti items such as spicy, sautéed zucchini and hunks of Parmesan cheese are placed down, filling the surface of the table.

As we get ready to sit, Cobus is on my left, Arnon, as usual, is to his left. A guy named Julian from the GlassWell team is about to sit to my right, but Julia shoos him away, saying we need to speak. To her right is Brand, followed by this Julian fella then Spencer.

Just as our asses hit our seats, Spencer surprises everyone.

"So, Ivan, is it?" he addresses me. "I hear you're a fiery one. A real soldier. With a passion for detail, for insight."

"I never thought of myself as a soldier before, sir."

At least not the kind you are referring to.

"But if being as thorough as I can be, sometimes to a fault, for my employer makes me a soldier, then I guess that's what I am."

"He's as fine at taking the evaluation of a property to a forensic level as I've ever seen," Cobus backs me up, realizing we're subtly discussing what happened earlier with Alessi. "I believe he always has the best interest of de Bont Beleggings at heart. Something, obviously, that is important, I believe."

The last comment, though, I can't help feeling is more for me than Spencer.

"I admire that kind of loyalty," Spencer responds.

He looks around at his crew. Then he spreads his arms as if presenting them to us all over again.

"My team—we're like family," he goes on. "We win as a family, we lose as a family. I appreciate thorough, Ivan. I do."

After ordering, dinner takes a more casual tone. Side conversations break out all around. Some are about family, others are about past professional experiences and career paths. Some are about art, others are about traveling. While speaking to Julian across the table about a trip he took to Budapest—a much more cosmopolitan city than he would have imagined—something out of the corner of my eye grabs me. Julia and Brand are in conversation, but in noticing a button of butter in the corner of Brand's mouth from a piece of bread he'd been eating, she wipes it away. Only not the way colleagues wipe butter from each other's face. The way people involved do, people close. It was as if second nature to both of them. Neither broke the conversation for a second; neither felt a need to explain why she was lifting a napkin to his face. Then, I'm guessing subconsciously, after wiping the butter away, she gently touched his face before returning her napkin to her lap.

Taking this in, my iPhone slides out of my hand onto the floor. I reach down to pick it up. When I do, I notice Brand's hand on Julia's thigh.

The thigh I'd made as red as she asked me to just this morning.

Whoa.

What the fuck?

Is she involved? Does she know everything?

Nothing?

Doesn't matter. Either way, she's tipped her hand.

It's clear which side she's on.

Isn't it?

I lift myself back up to the table. As I do, bottles of Dom Pérignon Rosé and flutes are being delivered to the table. Once the sweet, pink bubbly is poured, Spencer asks us all to raise our glasses.

"To closing this deal tomorrow," he says. "And to each of our firms continuing on their respective paths."

I look at Julia.

You know what they say about where to keep potential enemies.

SHOULD WE KEEP THE CHAMPAGNE GOING IN YOUR APART-MENT LATER? I text her.

I see her notice my message and look at her phone. She types in a message of her own, then looks at me sure to catch my eye before hitting send. Once she's done both, she looks away just as the message arrives.

YOU KNOW IT.

CHAPTER 34

At eleven ten p.m., after my usual return to the hotel with Cobus and Arnon before leaving again five minutes later, I walk into Julia's apartment. The door's been left open for me. The apartment is quiet, dark.

Fuck, I'm tired.

My head feels like it weighs a thousand pounds.

As I begin to move through the space, I reach into my cluttered pockets looking for a Life Fuel, only to remember I'd only bought two bottles, both of which I've already consumed.

"Hello?" I say as I start in the direction of the kitchen.

"Bedroom, Ivan," she responds, her voice coming from behind me, the opposite end of the apartment.

I enter the bedroom, stopping just inside the doorway. The lights are off but there's still light. It's coming from the Manhattan night through the huge window looking out, over the city as the blackout shades in effect this morning have been completely peeled back.

Julia, wearing nothing but a white lace thong, is on the bed. She's sitting up against a propped pillow, her hair falling over her shoulders, her long, gorgeous legs stretched out in front of her crossed at the ankles. She's holding a glass of champagne.

"Nice view," I say, staring at her.

"The beauty of a high floor."

I look toward the window.

"Yeah—that's nice too."

Then back to her.

"Won't you join me?" she asks. "After all, this may very well be our last private time together. At least for the foreseeable future."

On the nightstand next to her I notice another full flute. The thought of another sip of alcohol at this moment sounds about as good as a screwdriver being jammed into my thigh. Nonetheless, to keep things moving along, I walk over and pick up the glass. I extend it toward hers and we clink glasses. I take a small sip and begin to walk around slowly, aimlessly.

"May I ask you something?" I say, stopping in the center of the room.

"What do you want to know, Mr. Janse?"

I turn around and face her again.

"How long have you and Ryan been involved?"

All it takes is one twinge in her eye, one millionth of a second that her expression changes before retaking the previous one. She's doing her best to remain completely immersed in sexy mode, as if the question hasn't fazed her.

Isn't working.

"What do you mean?"

Aside from his hand high on your thigh under the dinner table?

"At dinner tonight, you wiped butter from the corner of his mouth."

"So?"

"Neither of you even flinched or changed course as it happened. Even for a second. It seemed second nature between the two of you—routine even. Almost—intimate. Like what goes on between people involved. Not just as business partners."

"Sorry, dear, but Ryan and I have always kept things professional. Not just because he's married, but because I don't play that way."

She turns the full-court press sexiness back on.

"Are you disappointed? Would fucking me again be more interesting if you thought I was with him—but craving you?"

Time to show this little girl she's involved in a dangerous game.

Whether she knows if she's playing or not.

"What about Brand and Alessi?"

Now Julia's simply annoyed and unable to keep it in.

"What about them? Why are you so goddamned interested in Ryan? Here—"

She grabs her cell from the nightstand and flips it to me.

"His number's in there. Give him a call, since it seems like he's the one you want to fuck…"

Oh, he's going to get stuck all right.

I catch her cell and gently toss it on the bed.

"I'm sorry. Really. The last thing I want to do is upset you. So, maybe it's just best if I leave."

I walk over as if I'm going to place my champagne flute on the nightstand.

"Look, Ivan. Just—let's—"

Keep it up.

"No, really. I'm sorry. I really should just go. We're hopefully going to close this deal tomorrow and then I'm off, so—"

Hopefully.

One simple word.

Something's up. Now she knows it.

Question is: what's she willing to do with that?

Where's her loyalty, really?

She's losing me.

I place the flute down. I turn back toward the door without giving her so much as a glance.

"Wait."

She grabs my wrist.

"Don't go."

I turn back around, bend down, and kiss her deeply.

"Why don't I freshen these up," I say.

I take both flutes—mine from the nightstand, hers from her hand. Just before crossing the threshold out of the room, I stop.

"I thought you said you didn't know Scott Green very well."

"What?"

I turn around.

"You said you didn't really know him. But there's a picture of him with you and Ryan right here in your own living room."

"I—" Julia starts.

She drops her chin to her chest. She regroups, lifts her head, and starts again.

"Scott was a friend. I should have told you that when you asked, but I didn't really think it mattered as I had just met you. And talking about it would have been hard. After all—they're saying he took his own life. And he was one of us. One of GlassWell."

"Talking about it would have been hard," I respond, "because it would have been emotional, you mean?"

"That's right."

Julia's voice is thick with emotion.

"Funny. Not one person I've met from your team in trying to close this deal seems to be the least bit emotional at all about Mr. Green's supposed suicide. In fact, it's as if not only no one feels anything, but he's long been forgotten. Like he's just some casualty of war or something."

"You have no idea what we all went through in the few days after it happened," she says, referring to the four days between Green's blast and our arrival in the States. "Let's just say that kind of pain, that kind of grieving, is something you look to let go of the first moment you can."

I take the flutes back to the kitchen. Once there, I place them on the island then take the flash drive with Brand and Alessi's conversations out. I look around. I hide it in the silverware drawer, under the tray that holds the separated utensils. Once it's tucked away, I head straight for the door. I get in the elevator, ride it down, and disappear into the Manhattan night.

CHAPTER 35

New York City
2013

At 2:45 a.m., my iPhone's alarm wakes me up. My head is throbbing. Only a few hours of sleep. At this rate, it will be impossible to catch up. I'm thinking, *better than nothing*. But I have no idea at this point.

At 3:10 a.m., dressed to the nines for my day in a navy Zegna suit with a mint-green button-down open at the collar, I hit the elevator. On the way down, I finally will myself into looking at the waiting texts from Julia. WHERE THE HELL DID YOU GO? A few minutes later: WHAT THE HELL IS GOING ON? There are three more in a similar vein spread out over another twenty-six minutes before she, too, must have fallen asleep.

I stop at the cash machine in the lobby then head outside. I'm surprised to see it is snowing; Halloween hasn't even come yet. The big flakes feel refreshing on my hands, face, and neck. I can't help the urge to—for one second—feel like a kid and catch one on my tongue—just like I used to do in this very city. So I do.

The city is calm. I can hear her breathing. Long breaths in—wind gently howling between buildings, a distant siren, long breaths out—the subway below, the beeping of a delivery truck backing up.

I hail a cab. Which at this time of night in Columbus Circle isn't very hard.

"How much do you make in a typical shift, Mr.—"

I look at the driver ID card in the window. The Asian face certainly matches the driver.

But you have to be kidding me about the name.

"Mr. Chew Kok?"

Melting pot. No kidding.

"I make couple hundred bucks, sir. Being driver sooo 'spensive afta gas, fees to cab company, 'cetera. Sooo 'spensive. Mr. Kok make couple hundred bucks per shift."

I reach forward with a wad of cash.

"Well, Mr. Kok, this thousand in cash should more than cover you for the rest of the morning."

Kok marvels at the cash for a second, but instead of dillydallying jumps into gear.

"Very good, sir. Where to?"

"Midtown Tunnel. We're headed to the Hamptons. But don't worry—we're not staying very long. You'll be back for breakfast."

I crack the windows just enough to feel some fresh air. We slice through the city effortlessly as we head west to east. Kok clearly knows what he's doing. He catches pretty much every light and barely once seems to speed up or slow down. As I watch Manhattan skate by on each side I think of my past—my childhood, my parents, and I think of my present. The deal I need to get right for Cobus, the scumbags who need to be held responsible for Green's death. Which, in truth, I still don't think I fully understand. Because I still don't know why he'd rather have blown his head off than go to the cops. All I know is he did.

The eggs.

Perry.

So much to do.

So little sleep.

"Kok, stop!" I blurt out.

He does, on a dime.

"Yes, sir!"

I jump out at a bodega on the corner of Third Ave and Thirty-Sixth Street just before we get to the tunnel. I buy three bottles of Life Fuel—cherry flavor again. I throw one back, ask the bodega owner to chuck the bottle, place the other two in my now over-crowded left inside suit jacket pocket, and get back in the cab.

The Long Island Expressway is empty. Some scattered headlights coming from the other side, a few distant red taillights in front of us. I'm buried in my iPhone, poring over the files and documents related to Feuerbach Turm—the building in Berlin. We had basically been a shade away from buying the property recently, therefore I already know everything about the building as if it is one of our own. But I can't take any chances. I know the numbers and all information pertinent to the deal essentially by heart at this point, but I need to be extra sure and careful if I'm going to pull this off. I double-check the projected capital improvement schedule Ernst sent me. I revisit everything from the predominant escalation clauses incorporated into the leases to the energy use projections for the next five years to the still unpaid commissions due brokers for recent deals. I revisit anything and everything related to this building in the center of Berlin's most vital corporate center.

I Google the article I had recalled having to do with the new formula for calculating not only the availability, but the pricing, for air rights over the buildings in the area. Because of zoning laws, buildings are not allowed to just keep building and building upwards.

But...

Each district has a certain amount of developable air rights in a given area, and these rights are divided by a certain formula that distributes them on a pro-rata share to certain buildings. Most owners will never want to spend the capital on building an existing property higher. That's where these air rights become interesting. They can be acquired from one property and added to another. In a situation like this, many wouldn't pay very close attention. But the way I see it—because of the new zoning and calculations—the

Berlin building will be the owner of most of the air rights in the immediate area. Which means whether the owner decides to use those rights to develop upward or decides to sell those parcels of air off piecemeal—the value of the property is greater than anyone realizes.

Just as I'm about to place a call to Ernst Brecht, I lift my head and see through the falling snow that we're turning onto Mako. Richard Plotkin's beach mansion is just minutes away. The call will have to wait.

At 5:15 a.m., the cab rolls slowly up to a gate at the end of the street, a dead end.

"You sho' this right place?" asks Kok.

"This is the right place," I say back. "The gate is there to scare people off who think they've come to a dead end and won't drive into his driveway. But if memory serves me right, there's no code; it's more about making the point than safety. All you need to do is slowly get close enough and the gate will swing open."

Kok does as I say.

The gate slowly swings open.

Kok rolls up the driveway, which stops at the four-car garage at the west end of the property.

"Wow. Now this fucking house," Kok says.

He's not kidding. The place is magnificent—about thirty thousand feet of magnificent. A shingle-style home with numerous porches and balconies, the façade is predominantly comprised of dark wood, and it is beautifully contrasted with huge white columns along the front of the exterior as well as bright white molding—the only portion of the house discernible at this time without squinting. Though on the beach the home is modeled after the more typical, huge Hamptons "farmhouses" found a bit more inland. All three floors are lined with huge picture windows, some with triangular accent windows on top of them that complement the same angles of the gambrel-style roof. The place is a flat-out beach palace.

"What's your cell number?" I ask.

He gives it to me. I punch it in to the disposable.

"Head back down the road and park out of sight, lights off," I go on. "I'll call you when I'm ready to get out of here. Won't be long."

"Here, take this," Kok says, handing me an umbrella. "That nice suit."

I jump out. Kok gets lost. I open the umbrella, thankful for it as the snow is still coming down. Not worried about anyone being around, I head toward the back of the property. The moment is eerie. Way outside of the season, there isn't a single light on in the house, on the exterior of the house—anywhere. The moonlight is muted as well because of the gray sky and falling snow. I have to use the flashlight app from my iPhone to see a few feet in front of me.

With each step the sound of the ocean gets louder, the waves more and more clearly lapping at the shore. The world is still only assorted shades of black and gray, though not for long. As I turn the corner around the back of the house, I make out three separate docks spaced evenly along the back of the property, leading from the huge pool and backyard areas over the dunes down to the ocean. I take the one closest to me.

I walk down the long, narrow dock. I step onto the snow-covered beach, something I realize I've never seen before, and walk toward the water. The waves, though really in front of me, look like rolling shadows. In the distance there is no water or sky—just darkness. The ocean is loud now, the rhythmic sound of the salty water reaching for the beach then letting go, reaching for the beach then letting go. I take in a huge breath, feeling, concentrating on the cool, crisp air filling my lungs. I slowly push the same breath back out. For sixty seconds I do nothing but stare wide-eyed into the black, existing solely in the moment, listening to the ocean, feeling her power and beauty flow through me.

I light my iPhone screen.

5:25 a.m.

I head down the beach about fifty yards then make my way up into the dunes, find a good hiding spot out of sight.

And I wait.

At exactly 5:30 a.m. I see a shadow moving back toward the house, coming around the same side of the home I had walked. The figure stops, no doubt same as I did to survey exactly where he is, what his options are.

My heart is racing.

Life Fuel?

The fact I'm about to be face-to-face with a man who thinks I'm a murderer and wants me in jail?

No doubt a combination of the two.

He starts toward the beach again and takes the same dock I took. I watch each step carefully. Once he's on the beach, near the water, he stops. It appears he's alone, but it's impossible to be sure. After a few minutes, right on cue, he seems to be putting something, most likely his cell phone, up to his ear.

The shadowy figure by the ocean becomes animated, perhaps irritated. He turns this way and that, his free arm gesturing in vain to the person on the other end of the call. All I can hear is the crash of the waves.

The shadow takes his hand from his ear. When he does, I feel the disposable vibrate in my inside suit jacket pocket.

"He swears he's alone," my old partner Jake says. "I told him you were there, watching. He didn't buy it and started to get crazy. He said he didn't come all this way in the middle of the night to play games. Sounds like he's telling the truth."

"Thanks, bro," I tell him. "I owe you one. And, hopefully, I'll see you again soon."

"In this life," Jake adds. "It better be in this life."

"In this life."

That's the plan.

We hang up. I slowly walk out of the dunes. I go at a right angle and head straight down toward the water. When I'm at the surf line, I make a hard left toward him walking along the water's edge. His back is to me. When I'm about fifteen feet away, perhaps sensing me coming up behind him, he turns around. The feeling of being face-to-face again with Detective Tim Morante is over-whelming.

This man thinks I'm a cold-blooded cop killer.

I'm not.

This man thinks I know who murdered my father.

I do.

This man thinks I'm either still running from him, or dead.

I'm back.

"Who are you?" asks Morante.

"Doesn't matter."

"Then how—"

"It doesn't matter, so don't waste your time," I cut him off. "But I do appreciate your coming."

Even through the darkness, we're close enough that I can see he hasn't aged a bit. His dark eyes, skin, and hair, his trim build, nice yet casual clothes, the shield dangling around his neck on a thin chain—it was like the guy had been kept in a bottle of formalde-hyde since I'd last seen him.

"Why here?"

"Because I needed to know we are truly alone due to the sensi-tive nature of what we'll be discussing."

"Which is?"

"Exactly what you were told. Jonah Gray. A man I believe you have some questions for. A man I can perhaps lead you to."

"And why would you want to do that?"

"That's between myself and Mr. Gray. But in order to do so, there's something I need from you as well."

"Of course there is."

He pauses.

"What makes you think I'm so concerned with Jonah Gray after all these years?"

"Jonah himself. He told me everything. How you believe he killed one of your own. How you think he knows who murdered his father. Which he does."

Morante remains silent. He turns his attention to the rolling ocean.

"I know where he's been since the moment he fled the States," I continue.

"What is it you want?"

An up-close look at *Danish Jubilee Egg*.

"Simple. You, an esteemed New York City detective, are going to call in a favor at the U.S. Capitol. Maybe you'll call there on your own, perhaps the better route is to call a favor in with your fellow officers in D.C. I'm sure someone there must be able to pull some strings on Capitol Hill. How you do it, I leave up to you."

"What am I asking for?"

"Something very small that should be easy to obtain. You have a relative from the Midwest—me, an insurance salesman named James Reynolds—who's in town this afternoon on last-minute business. Mr. Reynolds has always wanted to take a tour of the Capitol, but these tours are filled far in advance so he wasn't able to get a spot on the last one of the day at three twenty p.m., the only one he can work into his schedule as he's only in D.C. for one night."

"This afternoon? Today? What if it's out of the question?"

"Then it's out of the question. I deny you and I ever had this conversation. We both go on in our lives exactly as we were yesterday."

"We're talking about the U.S. Capitol. How do I know you're not some crazy terrorist just looking for a way in? Why would I attach my name to you—when I have no idea who you are, or why you need access to one of the most important buildings in this country?"

Good point.

One I was waiting for.

"I'm not a terrorist, Detective Morante. There's a Fabergé Imperial Easter Egg that's on display and part of the tour. It's called *Danish Jubilee Egg*. It was a gift from Czar Alexander of Russia to his wife the Czarina Princess Maria Feodorovna in 1903. I simply want to have a look at it."

"Danish—whatever—jubilee—isn't that the Fabergé Egg that

was in the news around the time everything went down with Gray?"

"It is."

"Does it have anything to do with what happened? Or why he disappeared?"

"Perhaps that's a question for Jonah, Detective. Like I said—I'm no terrorist, and I imagine security is tight to get into that building. I simply need a look at that egg."

I knew he'd need a concrete reason to feel comfortable sending me—some European he's never met before—into the U.S. Capitol. What could be better than a direct connection to the one who got away?

The one he thinks I can lead him to?

He looks again toward the water.

"Tell them I'll be there for the three twenty p.m. tour. That you know it's short notice, but it will mean the world to you and a nice return favor for someone the next time they're in New York City. Once you have confirmation, call Jake and let him know."

"Why should I take you for your word? If I do this, how do I know you'll lead me to Gray?"

"Something tells me that's a chance you're willing to take. If I get what I want, I'll have Jake call you and tell you what time my return train pulls into Penn Station. I'll take you to Gray from there."

As Kok barrels back west on the LIE, dawn moves into full-blown day.

"Hallo?"

"Ernst, Ivan."

I need that building in Berlin.

"Mr. Ivan Janse. I had a feeling I might be hearing from you again in short order."

"I have a number for you."

"Really."

"Really. And it's a nice one. But before I give it to you, I need to know two things."

"Which are?"

"How close you are to finalizing a deal with Vienna Shanks, and that I have your word until we have agreed on terms, we keep this quiet. The first paperwork, should we be able to come to an agreement, will be the Purchase Agreement. Understood?"

Ernst thinks for a second.

"I guess there's no harm in talking, Ivan."

"So we are clear?"

"We are. As far as putting a deal in place—"

He doesn't say the name Vienna Shanks, because it's Gruden they're making the deal with. Something he doesn't think I know.

"We are handling the final language issues in the Purchase Agreement. Now, what number are you thinking?"

"Three hundred and five euros per square foot."

The number is a good one, and I'm sure higher than the figure Gruden & Wayfield has on the table. It's definitely higher than what I had previously offered, but then I wasn't coming in to steal the target from under someone's nose as I am now. As always, I left myself considerable room the first time around. And, as always, I've done the same now.

"That puts the value of the property at three hundred and six million euros," I go on, "I'm guessing a better number than you are achieving with Vienna Shanks. No?"

"I can't comment on the other deal, Ivan, but I will tell you the three hundred and five euros number is a solid offer. Do you have room there if we need to inch up?"

Bastard.

But can't blame him for trying.

"I don't."

I actually believe I do. Because poor Ernst—and everyone pursuing this property—has overlooked the air rights situation. Something that in my estimation has everyone significantly undervaluing the property.

"And, not to make it harder on your end, Ernst, but I need to know if we're the new buyer in no more than twenty-four hours."

"Why so fast? For a building you just recently walked away from?"

Because this is the deal we should have gone with in the first place, had this strictly been about business. Cobus took me in and let me reclaim my life and get back where I needed to be. Now he's about to make what could be the biggest deal in his and his firm's lives—his first in a market outside The Netherlands. Like so many deals before, Cobus has put his faith in me. I owe it to him to make this deal. Especially now that I'm about to kill the one for the Freedom Bank Building.

"I'm not at liberty to say. But what I can say is that if your side accepts, we're ready to move forward."

"Then let me pass this along. I'll keep it quiet. And I'll be back to you."

I stop talking and turn my attention out the window. We're still far enough outside the city that the passing landscape is scarce, a random warehouse or big-box-anchored mall here or there. Everything is covered with a couple inches of snow, which has stopped falling. Many of the trees, still lush with foliage yet draped with thick, white powder, look like they might topple over from the weight.

My mind moves to Scott Green. And the houseboat. And his brain dripping down the wall. And why he didn't call the cops—he called me.

Why was he so scared?

What am I missing?

It couldn't just be the conversations I heard. If that was all there was, anyone with even a bit of sense would have gone to the powers that be at their firm and washed their hands of it from there.

I need to go through it all again. I shift my sight, now I'm looking out the opposite window. What's the first thing that comes into my mind when I think of this—whether it wakes me during one of my small stretches of sleep or pops into my head out of nowhere like right now?

The rambling.

The drunken fucking rambling.

I start to go though it all again. I close my eyes, take myself back to the houseboat. I can feel the warm interior. I can smell the weed and booze.

Go there, I tell myself, actually softly saying the words to myself.

"Go there."

I remember the awkwardness of the situation, my surprise at seeing this seemingly conservative man I barely know out-of-his-mind loaded. Once we got past the niceties and his bumbling explanation about his surroundings, we moved into the living room. From there the rambling carried on and only got crazier. There were comments about me being someone he felt he could trust, comments about his upbringing in Maine. He spoke about being a corporate trial attorney. He spoke about being the first in his family to make it to the big city.

As if thrown inexplicably back in time, I'm sitting there again, listening, staring down the barrel of a gun.

"That's why I did it to myself when all the darkness began," he says, almost in a whisper. "Talking—you know—darkness. But it makes sense. I know how to do it. One was elsewhere, the—covert, but I learned how to do it. I—for proof."

The pen.

I see the conversation again about the silver pen he offered me, without a reason for doing so.

"I know that you and Mr. de Bont are headed to New York in a few days," I remember him saying. "Just make sure you, when you're there, just be sure to pay attention. When it's time, just—just make sure the pen is straight. You know, straight forward. Straight. Because you'll think you're done. But looking closer is—to look closer—"

I had found the pen's rightful home, which had led me to the flash drive and the "proof" he was referring to. But what was he talking about making sure it was straight forward? What did that mean?

"Because you'll think you're done," I watch him say again.

Was there more in the study?

Right under my nose?

CHAPTER 36

New York City
2013

8:02 a.m.

T-minus less than nine hours before we're scheduled to head back to Amsterdam.

As I walk into the hotel to meet Cobus and Arnon for breakfast, I down another shot of Life Fuel. Then I dial my office from my iPhone.

"*Dag; Ivan Janse's Kantoor.*"

Again—I'll give it to you in English.

"Angelique, Ivan."

"What's up, Boss Man?"

"I need you to call Willem and change our liftoff time to tonight. Eight p.m. New York time."

"You got it. What's the problem?"

"No problem. Just the usual housekeeping bullshit that sometimes delays a close. You know the drill."

"That I do. Been living in your world for a few minutes."

"One more thing, Sunshine, tell him we'll be heading to

Moscow before returning to Amsterdam. And that I'll need a car waiting when we land."

Cobus and Arnon are already seated. The place is bustling with high-energy types all ready to take this city by the balls. I sit down.

"Gents," I begin, "How we feeling this morning?"

"Well, Ivan," says a smiling Cobus, "in fact, better than well. Because this morning we get to go over to GlassWell and sign this deal, then I get to return to my family who I haven't seen for three days."

Cobus turns to Arnon and continues.

"We were just settling in. So, Arnon, we all set? Any missing estoppel certificates from the tenants or anything to worry about?"

"I'm happy to report that after a Herculean effort by everyone, all the docs are in order," Arnon responds, turning to me. "Is the property ready for transition from your side?"

Fuck.

So much to do. My head's spinning. I don't know if I need sleep or more caffeine.

"Everything is officially ready for transfer," I squeeze out, thinking I might choke and vomit on the words. "The software that keeps all the tenant records, the property management records—it's all ready for transfer into our system."

"And the building personnel?" asks Cobus.

"The concierges, the porters—we're ready to transfer their employment from GlassWell to de Bont Beleggings USA."

De Bont Beleggings USA is the U.S. subsidiary we had set up just for this deal.

"The security contract, the messenger center contract—it's all ready to go. But—"

We all sit in silence for a few seconds.

"But, what?" asks Cobus.

Here we go.

I take a deep breath.

It's time.

"But, we can't make this deal."

Silence.

It's like the world—including Cobus and Arnon—freezes for a second. Then they look at each other and back to me.

"Excuse me?" asks Cobus.

"We can't make this deal," I reiterate. "It's simply not in the best interest of de Bont Beleggings."

Cobus, composed as always, places the coffee mug he's drinking from on the table. He leans forward.

"Ivan, what are you talking about? We're making this deal. Today. In a matter of minutes, you, Arnon, and I will be walking out of this hotel, getting into a waiting car, and traveling just a short way to GlassWell's headquarters so we can sign the final papers. You know all of this. We *are* making this deal. In a matter of hours it will be complete. Thanks to you."

"Again, Cobus, making this deal is a mistake. It is not in—"

Cobus, frustrated, cuts me off.

"Arnon, please, will you excuse us for a few minutes?"

Arnon, looking more like a frightened child than our chief in-house counsel, scurries off.

Cobus pauses, collects his thoughts, then speaks.

"Ivan, you've been acting strange since the moment we touched ground here. Yesterday when you said you were late to breakfast because you had been on the phone with Angelique, I know you were lying. I know you spoke to her for thirty seconds tops. I need to know what's going on. And I need to know right now."

Fuck.

Decision time.

I never wanted to drag Cobus into any of this. I wanted to kill this deal, land Berlin, and explain it all on the plane home.

Which I may be able to do yet.

But not until I have all the answers.

Tell him everything?

Tell him nothing?

Tell him something?

"Berlin is the better deal."

"Nonsense."

"Cobus, Berlin is the better deal. I'm serious. I wish I had known sooner, but I know now."

"There's more, isn't there? What aren't you telling me?"

Give him something.

Keep moving forward.

Damn my heart is racing.

"Okay, it's not as simple as just the numbers or anything so elementary. There's more. I just can't tell you. Yet."

Or ever?

Because when you're a ghost, when no one can ever be given a reason to look directly at you for one second longer than necessary, you have to clean shit up on your own.

My father, who I've learned to feel closer to in his death than in his life, taught me well.

"Anyway the *more* is not important. What's important is making the best deal, the right deal for your firm."

"Is that so? We have a signed Purchase Agreement, Ivan. We're in formality mode at this point. The lawsuit that will come our way will be a heavy one. And one that will come at us fast and hard."

"There won't be a lawsuit," I counter.

"Oh, is that right? And how can you be so sure?"

An image of Brand pops into my head.

Followed by a movie of me with my hand around his neck squeezing so hard his eyes look ready to pop from their sockets.

"I'm sure, Cobus. You'll have to trust me on this."

Cobus collects himself and leans back in his chair.

"Okay, Ivan, let's be clear about exactly where we are, and exactly what is going to happen. There's been a lot of time and money spent here."

"Not nearly as much as we're talking about should this deal go through," I cut him off.

"Let's assume I'm fine to learn what *more* means later on. Which I am. You mentioned Berlin is the better deal. I'm assuming you've been spending some of your time seeing if that deal is still alive for us."

"It is. I can make it happen. I can land it."

Cobus, surprising me, stands up. He grabs his chair, slides it around closer to me, and sits back down. He puts his arm around me. He moves in close and quietly speaks into my ear.

"I trust you, Ivan. I trust that you believed the deal here in Manhattan was the right one—for the right reasons—and now you don't. I believe we can still land the Berlin target because you're telling me we can. I trust you, Ivan, because you've never given me a reason not to. So tell me—"

"Tell you what?"

"This is about much more than just real estate, isn't it?"

I can't hide myself swallowing.

I can feel perspiration forming under my collar.

Shit, I'm tired.

I want more caffeine.

"Excuse me!" I say to the first waiter who passes us. "May I have an iced coffee?"

My eyes meet Cobus's again. He's waiting for an answer.

I don't give him one.

With the quickness and subtle grace, precision, of a panther, Cobus surprises me and grabs my wrist so hard it feels like he can break it if he wants to.

"Everyone has secrets, Ivan. Everyone. But you'd better look me in the eye and promise you have not put yourself or me—my family, my firm—any of us in harm's way. Can you do that?"

I'm Cobus de Bont's right-hand man.

I'm a warrior on a silent mission. A warrior with unfinished business.

I'm loyal.

To many.

To whom?

Careful, Cobus.

"Of course," I respond.

Wearing an aura I've not seen him in before, he eases up. In posture, in expression, he eases up.

"I need a few more hours," I continue. "This deal is wrong. Berlin is right. But I want to finish the job of undercutting Gruden and getting a signed Term Sheet in place before we notify Glass-Well we'll be walking away. I would hate to lose focus and lose both deals. But you need to let me handle this my way. All I need is a few more hours. I need until this evening."

Cobus, surveying me in a way he never has before, stands up, moves his chair to its original spot, and sits back down.

"Once we're on that plane tonight, and we're headed out of New York, I'll tell you exactly what happened, why GlassWell is not the firm we thought they were. But to do so now would simply be wasting time."

"Call the office," Cobus says. "Tell them we need to push back liftoff until this evening."

Check.

CHAPTER 37

Back in Murray Hill, I ring the doorbell of Scott Green's townhouse. Nothing. Just as I'm about to ring again or knock, or both, the door opens. It's Anne Green.

"Good morning, Anne. May I come in?"

"Of course. I was wondering when I was going to hear from you again."

I step inside and she closes the door behind me.

"Did you ever hear of a man named Enzo Alessi?" I ask her.

"Of course. The restaurateur family. I know they just signed a new lease in one of the GlassWell properties. The building that is in the process of being sold."

"That's right. Ryan Brand, who heads up acquisitions for Glass-Well, is the one who put that deal together. The flash drive I took from your husband's office upstairs? It contained recordings of conversations between Ryan Brand and Enzo Alessi. Conversations that revealed the two were working together for all the wrong reasons."

"I don't understand."

"The details of those dealings are not what's important. I have a feeling your husband taped these conversations by tapping Brand's phone because he was being threatened. Because he knew what they were up to and was not going to allow the deal to happen. Because he was a good man. And they are both pieces of shit."

"How do—why?"

"Anne, can I have another look at Scott's study?"

We step into the office upstairs, which is exactly as I left it. The people coming by to sit shivah have all since gone. The home and office, while comfortably warm temperature-wise, feels cold, lonely. Like the walls and everything in between them feel as cheated as Scott's grieving widow. Life can be heard going on, though faintly, past the study windows. In here, death is what hangs in the air.

Knowing I have Anne's blessing to roam, I head straight for the desk. I take a seat behind it, and my eyes go straight for the pen I had replaced, the pen Scott had given me. I remember the line about pushing it straight forward, but also remember other words from that moment.

"That's why I did it to myself when all the darkness began . . . I know how to do it. I learned how to do it. I—for proof."

Had he taped himself as he had the other two?

Why?

My eyes search for the phone and find it under the desk's mess. I pick up the handset. I examine it, from every side, thinking perhaps there's a recording device. I start taking it apart. Once it's in pieces, I pick up the base from the desk and do the same. I determine that I have nothing. And, more importantly, that if there was something of note here, I would have no idea as it would probably just look like one of the other parts I can't identify.

My eyes move back to the pen. The slim holder it rests in has a small ball at the end fitting into a socket attached to the base. I reach forward, and push the pen forward. The ball smoothly rotates in the socket until the *D* on the top of the pen is pointing straight ahead at the opposite wall.

At a photograph of Anne Green.

She looks at the picture I'm now staring at.

"It's from a few years ago. We were in Miami for a wedding."

I stand up and walk over to the picture. Anne joins me for the up-close examination. I study it, remembering my past has taught me to look closer when it comes to pictures, art, anything. Convinced there's nothing I'm not seeing, I take the picture from the wall. On the back, written small toward the bottom of white backing of the photograph by the frame, I find something: www.-VivRecord.com.

"What is that for?" asks Anne.

"Let's find out," I respond.

I replace the photo back on the wall, head back behind the desk, and sit down. Anne settles in behind me looking over my shoulder. The PC monitor on Scott's desk hovers above the mess. Down below is the tower, or CPU. I reach down, press the "on" button and listen to the whir of it booting. In seconds the monitor comes to life.

I hit the browser and type in www.VivRecord.com. Within seconds, the purpose of the site becomes clear.

"It's an audio file storage site," I explain to Anne. "One for the purpose of recording and storing telephone conversations."

My eyes find the "login" button, which I click on. The username is already there: "DavidWendy."

"What would your husband have used as his password?"

"Try Brewer. It's the town in Maine where he grew up. He used it as the password for everything."

I type it in.

Done.

We're in.

"What are we looking at?" asks Anne.

"A log of all the calls your husband recorded, calls associated with the number 917-555-6676."

"That's his cell phone number. You mean he was recording his own phone?"

"It appears that way."

I point at the screen.

"If you look here, it gives the date and time of each call, and next to it is an indication of whether it was an incoming or outgoing call. Here," I go on, "you can play it back or download it as an MP3 to either be archived or e-mailed."

The calls go back about four weeks. All incoming and outgoing calls were recorded so the log is a long one. I start by playing back random calls when the recordings began.

"Hi, honey, it's me," begins the first one. "Listen, I know we're supposed to meet Laura and Harlan tonight, but—"

"Me," Anne says.

I move on.

"Scotty! Big Bri here—"

"His friend Brian May," Anne fills me in. "Law school buddy."

"Look, may be a few minutes late to the Garden so messenger my ticket to my office, and I'll meet you in the seats probably about halfway through the first quarter. Lakers coming to town—love it!"

We move on.

"Scott, it's Ryan."

Ryan Brand.

"You need to call me back."

He hangs up.

I take the number the call came from, Brand's cell number, and put it in the search box. The call log we're looking at has now been reduced to those coming from and going to this number. The majority of which are incoming.

"Scott, Ryan. Look, I don't think you'd be foolish enough to try and hold this deal up in any way, but in case you're thinking it may not be—uh—it may not be something the firm should see through, you may want to talk this through with me. Call me back."

"What deal is he talking about?" asks Anne.

"The one between GlassWell and the Alessi family. Your husband was on to them. And I'm pretty sure it cost him his life."

I hit the next one. Then the next. The calls become more heated in nature. And more and more it becomes clear Scott Green is not only having cold feet about allowing such a deal to happen, but he's being threatened that if he fucks with it he'll pay.

"What, Ryan?" starts the next one.

"What, Ryan? That's how you want to speak to me? I left you a message in your office to come find me."

"I was busy today top to bottom."

"I don't care. If I say I need to speak with you, then you need to find me."

"For what? So you can hear me tell you I'm okay with all of this? That I'm willing to be party to this?"

"Well, aren't you?"

Green doesn't answer.

"Hello?" continues Brand.

"I have to go," Green says.

Then he hangs up.

"That's why I did it to myself when all the darkness began . . . I know how to do it." I again remember Green saying to me, "One was elsewhere, the . . . covert, but I learned how to do it. I—for proof."

Covert. Elsewhere. Once Green overheard them, and Brand started threatening him, he must have used some kind of spyware to tap Brand's phones. While he was able to use something like VivRecord.com to record himself, the other conversations must have been housed elsewhere. That's why those needed to be passed by flash drive.

Next call. Then another. Then another.

Each more contentious in nature.

Each more threatening toward Green.

I play one from a week ago.

"How we looking?" asks Brand in an even voice. "You getting all the contracts in order?"

"I don't think I can do this," Green says after a pause. "I'm going to go and speak with Gary..."

Gary Spencer.

The Big Boy.

"I'm going to tell him everything."

"No, you're not," Brand counters. "You know why?"

Green says nothing.

"Because if you do anything but see this deal through and carry on as though life is just rosy, I will act on my promises. You have the pictures. Don't ever doubt me."

"Why are you doing this?" asks Green. "Why are you doing this to me?"

Because he's a greedy lowlife who fell in way over his head.

That's why.

I hear a sniffle back over my shoulder. I look up at Anne who, trying to remain strong, is suppressing a cry that on the inside is much bigger than she's allowing me to see.

"You all right?" I ask.

"No. What kind of animal is this guy?"

"The worst kind," I answer. "One without a soul."

"I'm doing this because GlassWell needs this deal," Brand goes on, "and because I'm not going to let you fuck it up over something you have all wrong."

"Something I have all wrong," Green says, showing some fight still. "You so sure about that?"

The recorded conversations between Brand and Alessi.

"Don't fuck with me. I am a man of my word. Remember what I told you will happen if you decide to make up stories."

"What's that?" responds Green angrily, losing patience. "That if I tell GlassWell or the cops what happened, you go away quietly because the order to kill my family if you're outed has already been put in place? Huh? Isn't that how you put it, you sick fuck?"

No doubt a last-ditch effort to get such a damning threat confirmed on tape.

A threat—perhaps more a promise—Brand made to Green offline.

In person.

Brand doesn't bite.

"Like I've already said, Scott," Brand comes back, his voice still calm, "you need to reel in your imagination and keep the story-telling in check. It's liable to get you into trouble at some point."

Then, he's gone.

Turns out Green wasn't scared for his own life. He was scared for his family.

Silence behind me. I turn around. All the color has rushed from Anne Green's face. She's covering her mouth.

I close the browser and open Green's e-mail. I do a search for all those from Ryan Brand, but nothing unrelated to business dealings comes up.

Pictures.

What pictures?

If something was received via e-mail, it wouldn't have come directly from the scumbag. My mind moves to anonymous e-mail services. I start scrolling back through e-mails looking for anything that seems odd. The first thing that catches my eye is an e-mail from the address Bobbi@GunBroker.nl. 'nl' is the e-mail suffix for the Netherlands; 'GunBroker' speaks for itself. To spare Anne, I keep going without stopping or opening it. Then I see an e-mail that came in a week ago from a source called FlazMail.

I open the e-mail. It has three attachments. I open the first one, a photograph of a doctor—or dentist I'm guessing from the chair in the center of what appears to be an examination room. The dentist, dressed in dress pants and a button-down shirt with a white smock-type thing on top is on the far side of the room, half-turned toward a counter with a canister of tongue depressors and the like on top. The picture gives a good shot of his face. He's writing in a chart. The photo is clear. The subject seems to have zero idea he's on camera.

"David," I hear over my shoulder. "Our son."

I open the next attachment, another photo. This one is of a twenty-something brunette seated in a restaurant—brasserie I'm guessing from the décor—at a table with another woman. They're having coffee. Both seemingly unsuspecting of a photo being taken.

"That one," Anne says, pointing, "that's our daughter. Wendy."

I open the final one. It's of Anne Green. She's accepting a package. The person making the delivery, standing right in front of her, snapped this shot. Anne Green never knew it.

"Oh, my God, that's right here, at our home," Anne says. "We have to go to the police."

Green wasn't kidding. Brand had made it clear if the truth got out, Green's family would pay. These photos drove that message home.

"It's definitely time for the police, Anne, but I'm going to have them come to you. You are to tell no one about any of this—no one—except a man named Detective Lovell. When he comes here, and he will come here, you show him everything we just looked at—the call-log website—"

I bring VivRecord.com back up, and minimize the window so it's ready to go.

"—and the e-mail and photos we just looked at. Got it?"

Anne nods yes.

"Detective who?" I test her.

"Lovell."

"That's right. Until he's standing here in front of you, in this study, not a word of it to anyone."

The disposable vibrates in my pocket. It's Jake. I pick up.

"You're all set for three twenty p.m. Go to the Visitor Center. James Reynolds will be on the list."

CHAPTER 39

Amtrak Acela number 2155 from New York's Penn Station to Union Station in Washington, D.C., is tearing down the East Coast. The ride is smooth, steady. First Class on any luxury train line is sure to be emptier than coach, and even more so during the middle of the day such as the 11:00 a.m. I'm riding on. Essentially alone aside from a few other scattered folks in the car, I take out both phones. I put them on the small table in front of me. First I check the iPhone. There are numerous texts from Julia.

WHAT'S GOING ON?

WHY DID YOUR SIDE DELAY THE CLOSING AGAIN THIS MORNING?

IVAN—WE NEED TO TALK.

CALL ME NOW.

Leaving Julia alone for now, I find the number Perry's husband gave me for Andreu. I pick up the disposable, dial the number, and hit send. It's ringing.

"*Zdravstvuj?*"

I pause for a second before speaking. The sound of him both angers and excites me.

"Been a while, Andreu," I say, making sure Jonah Gray's voice is coming from Ivan Janse's throat. "Sounds like your stint in jail was a pretty quick one. Whose dick did you suck to get out?"

"If by whose dick did I suck you mean who'd I pay off—what's the difference? It's nice to have a couple bucks. Isn't that right, my half-brother?"

"We may share some of the same blood, but make no mistake. We're far from family."

"Anyway, that's all in the past for me. Unfortunately for you, jail very much remains in your future should you ever try to return home. Is that hard? Any harder than knowing that scumbag of a man who fathered us was murdered in cold blood, like the animal he was?"

The words sting. My father was a lot of things, but he was far from the kind of man who deserved to die the way he did. Gunned down in his own front doorway.

"I'm coming to Russia, you fuck. And I'm going to be there sooner than you know, so keep your phone close. I'm going to give you—and your slut mother—something you both want. You're going to give me Perry."

"I knew even if it took years it was only a matter of time before you came looking for her, Jonah."

"Looks like for once you were right about something. Because that time is now."

I get off the train and head right for the public restroom. I take the second to last stall, close and lock the door. I've done my homework. Once at the Capitol there are no restrooms available until after one has gone through security. Therefore the gun in my pocket might be an issue.

I remove the piece and place it on the ground, behind the base of the toilet, out of sight. I step back, look at it from every angle possible—sides, crouching, on tiptoes, the works. Then I take a leak. I exit the stall, wash my hands, and leave.

As I step out of Union Station, I swig down my last Life Fuel and toss the empty little bottle in a garbage can. The sky is gray, the air is cold but a refreshing slap in the face. I head up Massachusetts

Avenue. Twenty minutes later, my iPhone's GPS system has me staring at the U.S. Capitol.

The Capitol Visitor Center, the new main entrance to the U.S. Capitol, is located beneath the East Front plaza at First and East Capitol Streets. I review the game plan in my mind as I head there, going over the map of the property, and the sequence of events exactly as they will unfold from the moment I step through the front doors until I exit them again. I suck in a breath and cross the threshold. The security area is tight, buzzing. There are tourists of all ages, lots of cameras and lots of passes and badges hanging around necks. I wait for a few minutes in line to check-in.

"James Reynolds," I say when my turn comes, my best Midwest accent in play. "I'm here for the three twenty tour."

The serious-looking woman in the U.S. Capitol garb checks her computer. She has both the glasses and the black, beehive hairdo to suggest she's had a bit of trouble leaving the sixties behind.

"Reynolds, James, yup, right here," she says.

Morante. Nice.

They don't usually ask for ID, something else learned from my homework. I'm ready with a story in case, but don't need it. The agent hands me my pass. I get in line for screening and again wait my turn.

I step up to the conveyer belt that will be carrying the contents of my pockets through the X-ray. I take a bin. I place everything in from both cell phones to the loupe to my keys to my shoes and lay my suit jacket on top. My belongings start their trip through the tunnel. When they do, I'm invited to step into the magnetometer—same type of screening machine used at the airport—which will X-ray my person.

"Is there anything in your pockets?" asks an older fella also proudly wearing his U.S. Capitol uniform.

"No."

"Hands above your head please," he goes on.

Within minutes I'm through security, as are my belongings. I place everything back into its rightful pocket. I look at the Perregaux—3:18 p.m. Right on time.

I step into Emancipation Hall, the centerpiece of the new Visitor Center opened in 2008. My eye immediately catches the plaster cast of the Statue of Freedom standing in the space—a replica of the actual statue sitting atop the building. The space is wide open, bright; the colors are predominantly lighter shade earth tones. Despite projecting a feeling of both history and dignity, Emancipation Hall also feels fresh, modern. My group is comprised of about fifteen people, some whom I recognize from the security process.

The tour begins in the Orientation Theatre with a thirteen-minute film entitled "Out of Many, One"—a piece about our country's struggle to create the world's first truly representative democracy as well as the remarkable building that houses the U.S. Congress. But I don't hear a word of it. Our tour will last about an hour. I'm thinking solely about what takes place at minute thirty. That's when I'll be breaking off from the tour and heading back to the same place the tour begins—the Visitor Center. More specifically, Exhibition Hall. This way any of the people I'll have been with, who might recognize me, will still be off somewhere in the Capitol. By the time they return to where they started, I'll be long gone.

At 3:50 p.m., once the group has already been to the Crypt of the Capitol and is coming toward the end of their time in the Rotunda before heading to the National Statuary Hall, I literally stop in my tracks as we collectively take a turn. As the rest of the people following our guide make a hard left to turn a corner, I simply do an about-face and head right back where I came from. I retrace my tracks, stopping for a second to pretend I'm looking at something on the wall to unzip my fly and pull a pair of latex gloves from my underwear. Within minutes I reenter the Visitor Center and make my way to the lower level where the Exhibition Hall is located.

Though I have never been here, I have full knowledge of all that exists within these walls. The main purpose of Exhibition Hall is to tell the story of the U.S. Congress and U.S. Capitol. It does so with original documents and artifacts, utilizing computer interactives, touchable models, and videos. Exhibition Hall also hosts all kinds of other interesting documents and artifacts that are significant in our country's history, such as the display entitled "Instruments of Change" dedicated to highlighting events or material pieces that signify moments that have affected the lives of U.S. citizens and the direction of the nation. Whereas *Danish Jubilee Egg* used to reside in the Rotunda, it now rests in the portion of Exhibition Hall dedicated to the "Instruments of Change," symbolizing our sometimes-contentious yet today sound relationship with world superpower Russia.

I know exactly where the famous treasure is, but more importantly I know everything about its display case, a specially designed glass pedestal showcase with a pull-out deck made by a company called Wilhelm & Odo. Two columns hold up a deck that is encased by a large rectangle of glass. In order to open and close the case, the deck slides out along with the back wall of the rectangle's glass. It does so with the turn of a key.

The sixth key on my keychain.

Wilhelm & Odo is based in Hamburg, Germany.

My weekend trip to Hamburg Cobus asked me about at Annabelle's party had nothing to do with old friends. It was to meet with folks at the Wilhelm & Odo headquarters. I had been in previous discussions with them fronting as a man about to open a high-end jewelry store in The Hague, Copenhagen, and other locales throughout Europe. In doing so, I explained to them I was only interested in going with their display cases, in particular one model—the exact model in the U.S. Capitol holding *Danish Jubilee Egg,* a nugget I kept to myself—if I'd be able to have one skeleton key for all the cases, no matter what location I was in. They said this was no problem. I also told them I'd like to know if they were fine with me picking up the same display case used when opportunities arise—something their competition made clear to me was fine so long as I committed to an initial order of a certain amount of cases. Because of the economy and these size orders being far and few between, they went for it.

I had figured because of security concerns there would be further conversation about my needing a more universal skeleton key

because of this—one not just able to work on those made specifically for me—but there wasn't. They basically told me that though not
something they publicize, any skeleton key for a certain model
works across the board. For them, they had me on camera in their
headquarters, they had my name—Lars Hildengird—which I'd giv-
en them over the phone. The fine folks over at Wilhelm & Odo
had no reason to see me as anything but an honest entrepreneur
and a big sale, not someone looking to get one over on them. That's
when I asked if I could borrow a skeleton key for a week or so since
I'd be traveling and looking at a few used cases.

I spot the case and enclosed treasure. A funny feeling washes
over me, a mixture of anticipation and concern. We can't yet
speak—*Danish Jubilee Egg* and I—as we're too far away, but we're
eyeing each other. Like two old friends about to be reacquainted.

The space is populated, but traffic is not heavy. As expected,
there are security guards standing at strategic posts around the hall.
Looking the part, walking with the gait, posture, and speed of someone who belongs, I stride toward the security guard closest to the case.

"Yes," I say while putting on the latex gloves and speaking with
a full American accent, albeit with pitch lower than that of my
God-given Jonah voice, "I need you to accompany me to the
Fabergé egg case. We'll only be a second."

My father always told me to own every single word that rolls off
your tongue.

Be the fucking words. Live them.

Make everyone see exactly what you need them to.

Get what you need. Clean up the mess later.

Now. More than ever.

Go get it.

"I'll be opening it for no more than sixty seconds. I just need
you to stand in front of the area until I reclose the case. Understood?"

I turn and take a few steps toward the case, knowing full well I
won't be followed. I stop. I turn back.

"What's the problem?"

The security guard, a young, serious, tall and thin clean-shaven white guy doesn't budge. Not because he's looking to be a hard ass, simply because he's confused. I walk back toward him.

"Sir, I'm sorry, who . . . who are—"

I hone in on his tag.

"Security officer—" I say, going with "officer" as opposed to "guard" to offer some respect, "—Mitchell. We need to do this quickly. The fewer people in the hall the better, hence the reason for handling it now."

"Handling what?"

"Not your concern. Your job, as always, is simply to *secure*. Leave the work surrounding the artifact to me."

"Sir, I have no idea about any of this. My boss—"

"Your boss? You mean Chad Daniels?" I say stepping to him, cutting him off. "Oh, wait—that would be the Director of the Visitor Center, the individual your boss reports to. Your boss would be Anne Marie Maxwell. Now, what do you think happens when I have to explain to Ms. Maxwell that you questioned me and refused to move on this? What do you think happens then?"

I anticipated some push back, hence the research of information such as personnel in order to be nimble, but my operational window is small. The key to pulling this off is converting this guy quickly.

I look at the Perregaux, then around the room before back to Mitchell with a look that says "don't fuck with my job, bro." I turn back toward the display case. I stop when he still hasn't moved.

"Fuck this," I say, taking out the iPhone, "We'll get someone else over here and you can go fight for your job."

I pretend to dial. I lift the phone to my ear.

"Wait," Mitchell mutters, "Wait. Okay."

I put the phone away.

"Good choice. Now let's get to it."

I step behind the case. Mitchell stands a foot in front of it, hands clasped down in front of him as he scans the area. I survey the lock then take my keychain from my right inside suit jacket pocket. A few eyes are looking in our direction, but not many. I place the proper key between my thumb and index finger, and slide it into the keyhole.

Nothing.

Keeping my composure, I jiggle it a bit, hard enough as to engage in a bit of force, but delicate enough as to not draw attention.

Still, nothing.

I remove the key. I take a deep breath. I reinsert the key. I try again.

Nothing.

Fuck!

I start to jiggle harder, then harder.

Mitchell turns around. He sees I'm having an issue. His expression grows concerned.

"Sir—"

"Hey!" I say sternly, pointing straight at him with my free hand, "don't you *dare* turn your back on the people you're supposed to be securing."

Work with me, Mitchell.

Because you have no idea where I'm willing to go.

"Turn your ass back around, now! Or I promise you you'll never work in this building again!"

I turn the key one more time. It turns all the way, releasing the lock. I start to slide the display deck and back glass wall of the casing toward me. I stop, as if to say "until you turn back around, dipshit, I can't get this over with."

Mitchell turns around, reclasps his hands.

I slide the deck fully out. A few more eyes now. People thinking, "interesting—one of the artifacts is actually being handled."

No time to waste.

Not a second.

It feels like ages, it feels like only seconds, since I've last seen, held this rare tribute to true artistic beauty and craftsmanship. I take in the mostly smooth blue-and-white enamel surface, the tiny, intricate human faces, and graceful gold vines. I quickly scan the finely cut emeralds, diamonds, and rubies.

How are you, old friend?

You are still as breathtaking as the moment we met.

I look for all parts gold, for the place most likely to hold the writing I need.

I take the loupe from my pocket. I start with the gold vines where they are thickest. It is immediately clear this is not where I'll find what I'm looking for. I move to the base, made of the same materials as the actual egg it holds and topped off with three golden lions each on its hind legs. Below the lions is a thick band of gold. Nothing.

More eyes in our direction. A few folks actually start coming closer to see what I'm doing.

"Please," Mitchell has to say to someone, "you can't come any closer. We'll only be another few moments."

I look at what's happening. Then, out of the corner of my eye, I notice one of Mitchell's counterparts across the way looking toward us curiously.

Tick.

Tock.

I throw all my attention back to the egg. Finally, around the bottom of the base, is yet another thick gold band. Here, I find the writing.

"*Mijn beste PD, mijn familie—*"

This portion of the writing is followed by a skull and crossbones. Then, "*Bevestigd. X2. Moordenaar!*"

Translation will be later. For now—it's all about the picture. I take out my iPhone. I take the necessary pictures, which again garners the attention of Mitchell.

"Necessary for the Historian Procedural Sequential Protocol," I say, conjuring up such nonsense on the fly as I place my loupe and iPhone back in their respective pockets. "It's a very important step in the proper preservation of such artifacts."

Mitchell's look says all I need to know.

Huh?

Wha?

Danish Jubilee Egg back properly in its place, I close and lock the case. As I do, I notice Mitchell's coworker approaching. I emerge from behind the case.

"I'd hold that thought until later," I say just as coworker is about to open his mouth. "I'm guessing Ms. Maxwell isn't a big fan of you guys standing around playing with yourselves when you're supposed to be securing one of the most important buildings in the world."

They look at each other.

"I'm actually on my way to see Ms. Maxwell right now," I go on, my eyes now on coworker. "You still sure this is the best place for you to be standing?"

Own the words.

The moment.

Always.

Both return to their posts.

As I exit the U.S. Capitol headed back to Union Station, my pace brisk, I'm already Googling a Dutch to English translation site on the iPhone. I flip back and forth from the first site that comes up and the photo of the writing on the egg until I have all the words entered. I hit "translate."

"My dear PD, my family—

Then the skull and crossbones—or the universal symbol for poison.

"—Confirmed. X2. Murderer!"

Holy shit.

There it is.

Imposter Derbyshev is confirming for his cousin what she must have always known. The true love of her life, Nicholas I, was murdered.

X2. Times two.

As was, it appears, both Nicholas I and Alexander III's father—Czar Alexander II.

Legend has it Czar Alexander III had clear designs—right or wrong—on how Russia was to be run. And he wasn't going to let his father or brother stand in the way of that vision.

These eggs show this isn't just legend at all.

The premise of Nestor Korolyev's doctoral thesis is true.

Which means history is false.

I drop my arms to my sides, but keep my pace up as to make sure I'm on the Amtrak 2122 leaving Union Station for New York Penn Station at 4:25 p.m.

I'm in complete shock, but finally I get it. I understand why Galina Zhamovsky was willing to ruin as many lives as possible, including my own, in order to corral the missing eight Fabergé Imperial Easter Eggs and stay "true to her own." Galina Zhamovsky's maiden name is Romanov, as I learned from Mr. Mateev, and she's originally from St. Petersburg. Galina Zhamovsky is a descendant of the royal Russian family. And she knows the only way to ensure history remains as is, is to get those eggs for herself so no one can look close enough to actually see the truth.

Too late.

I enter Union Station. I find the Arrival/Departure Big Board and see my train's gate. I bury my nose in my iPhone again, as now I'm busy forwarding every photo taken of the writing on the eggs from my iPhone to the disposable.

My phone's blowing up. It's Julia.

"So, how was the tour, James?"

I stop and look up.

"Detective Morante," I say, surprised. "I uh . . . the . . .I wasn't expecting you."

"I know. Don't take this as a sign of my not trusting you, but I figured, why wait until you get in touch with me?"

He's thinking I wasn't going to reach out, hold up my end of the bargain. He's wrong. The only one who truly wants Jonah Gray brought to justice is ultimately the one most needed to clear his name.

I look around.

"I'm guessing you're on the 2122. Figured we'd ride back together," he goes on.

"I am."

"Great. Then we'd better get moving."

We begin walking. My phone vibrates again—Julia. I immediately silence it.

"Get a good look at the egg?" Morante asks.

"I—what?"

I could give a shit about the chitchat. I'm more concerned with the bathroom we're walking by.

"If you'll excuse me," I go on, "I need to stop in the restroom. I'll only be a moment."

There's a gun I need to retrieve.

"Good idea," Morante says.

We hit the bathroom together. I head right toward the stall I need, which is occupied.

Damn.

I need to make a split second decision. I opt for a urinal. Downside: I'm only feet from Morante. Upside: I can see the stall I need in the mirror. I take my sweet time. The feet I see between the bottom of the stall door and the floor have bunched pants around them, and don't seem to be moving. I pee and just stand there for a bit longer, lingering. Morante is already washing his hands. I can only stand here for so long. Finally, I zip up and head to the sink. Again—I take my time, thinking Morante will head on out and wait for me in the concourse. No such luck. He's waiting for me. I lather up, my eyes glancing in the mirror at Bunched Pants. No movement. I lather up a second time and rinse. Still nothing.

Fuck.

Not good.

I grab a towel and dry my hands. I join Morante. As we head for the exit I hear a toilet flush. I can't just turn around. I get my last chance to sneak a look when we drift left with the gentle curve of the hallway leading out. I look out of the corner of my eye and my peripheral vision just gets a glimpse of Bunched Pants exiting the stall.

Go get it.

I take a few more steps, then—I stop.

"Something wrong?" asks Morante?

I put my hand on my stomach. And make the face of someone who just ate bad cheese.

"I'm not sure," I say. "Perhaps my lunch is not agreeing with me."

I look at the Perregaux for full dramatic effect.

"We're going to be close as it is," I continue.

I take a few more steps. Then I buckle over as if a surge of severe abdominal cramping has set in.

"Oh, not good," I push out.

Before he can even respond, I make my move. I hightail it back to the bathroom.

"I'll hopefully only be a second," I hurl back over my shoulder.

As I fly into the bathroom, I pass Bunched Pants who's on his way out. I hit the stall, close, and lock the door.

What if Morante followed me in?

Using my foot I flush. I had a good enough jump that an immediate puke would have already happened by the time he's in here. Damn Bunched Pants. Christ, it stinks in here. I hold my breath as I reach down, behind, the bowl thinking about what must have just happened in here to create this kind of foul. Thankfully, my hand finds the piece right where I left it.

Placing it in the rear of my pants' waistline I stand up. Holding my breath, as if I might actually taste the germ-junked air, I flush with my foot again. I unlock the stall door and step out.

"You okay?"

I step to the sink. I wash my hands, then rinse my face and mouth out.

"Actually, yeah. I am."

CHAPTER 39

WASHINGTON, D.C.
2013

We settle into First Class. The train is more crowded than earlier, but we're able to find seats that are pretty secluded.

"Do you mind if I complete some correspondence?" I ask.

"Please, go ahead. We'll have plenty of time to chat."

I finish forwarding all the photographs taken of the writing on the eggs to the disposable. But what happens from here will have to wait as to bring the other phone out now will only raise suspicion. Next, I text Julia.

TIED UP. DEALING WITH A PROPERTY MATTER IN AMSTERDAM. WILL MEET YOU IN YOUR OFFICE IN A COUPLE HOURS. WE'LL CLEAR UP EVERYTHING THEN.

My mind drifts to Scott Green. A man who killed himself to do exactly that—kill himself. Get these animals off his back. What incentive was left for them to hurt his family if he'd never suffer for it? He found a small window in the trip to Amsterdam to do it. A tiny window he also used to dish off the necessary information to me—a good candidate because I was an unlikely candidate. One Brand would never see coming. I would be there, across the Atlantic, on their home turf. And Green was running out of time

to foil this deal, but, more importantly, save his family. In that one
fateful night, summoning me and giving me that pen, riding a hope
and a prayer, he accomplished both. Scott Green was a fucking
hero. Like me, in his own way, a warrior.

Now it's up to me to finish the job.

The train starts moving. My eyes drift out the window as we
slide past the platform.

"So, I did what you asked. Now where can I find Jonah?"

"I don't know."

I turn to Morante.

"He won't be letting me know until tomorrow," I add.

"Where has he been all these years?"

I don't answer.

Morante starts to shift in his seat.

"Look, you told me you can me lead me to him when you
returned from D.C. Now—"

"I did. And I will. But things change. Like I said, now I won't
know where he is until tomorrow. As soon as I know, you'll know."

"This is bullshit. I swear, if you're fucking with me—"

"I'm not."

Morante is about to speak again, but stops. He's gathering his
thoughts.

"He killed that detective. The one they pulled from the river," I
start in, perking Morante up. "Only he did it in self-defense."

"What are you talking about?"

"Jonah trusts me. We've spent a considerable amount of time
together these last years. I don't know if it was for my insight or if it
was simply cathartic for him, but he told me what happened, what
led to his fleeing New York City. He told me everything."

"He murdered my fellow officer."

"How do you know it isn't my version?"

"The self-defense crap you just spilled? Because everything used
to dump and hold the body down in the water came from his
father's townhouse—the one he grew up in—on the Upper East
Side. That's why."

"I'm not saying Jonah didn't panic, detective. That he didn't try to cover up what happened. What I'm saying is that your fellow officer was up to no good. He was shaking Jonah down."

"What do you mean shaking him down?"

"*Danish Jubilee Egg*. The one I came to see today. Jonah is the only reason that egg ever made it to the U.S. Capitol where it was scheduled to go on display. And that happened because he kept it out of your guy's hands."

Morante shakes his head.

"I don't get it."

I take a deep breath.

"Try and stay with me."

Morante nods.

"*Danish Jubilee Egg* is one of eight Imperial Fabergé Easter Eggs that went missing during the Russian Revolution. There was a family—is a family—out there who desperately wants those eight eggs."

"Why?"

"Not important right now. You—like the rest of the world—will know the answer to that soon enough. Anyway, as I was saying, this family I'm referring to found a way to get their hands on this particular egg—only that plan got fucked up and *Danish Jubilee Egg* ended up in Jonah's briefcase. Literally. He had no idea why."

Morante thinks for a second. He shakes his head.

"Why didn't he go to the police?"

"Because he couldn't. The world was looking for this thing. Jonah had no idea where it came from and he would have looked like nothing more than an accomplice who'd grown a conscience. Besides—"

"Besides what?"

In case you've forgotten, this hadn't exactly happened at a time I was in the cops' good graces. They were sure I'd been part of a white-collar crime that went down not long before and they wanted me to pay for it. Truth is, I had nothing to do with it. But the way to start addressing that would not have been to show up with the missing rare artifact in the news for having been stolen.

"Nothing," I back off. "Let's just say there were a number of other things working against Jonah. What is and is not pertinent—I'll leave that up to Jonah."

"Wait. So, what does this have to do with the detective?"

"The detective was given the task, most likely for a handsome payday, to get it back and into police evidence to then be retrieved by the people trying to steal it. Only little did they even know this guy—your *detective*—was probably going to keep it for himself to extort the fucking extorters. Quality guy."

"Not possible. He was one of us," Morante says, lifting his chin even higher. "And one of the best."

"What he was, Detective, was a scumbag who got greedy and got himself killed. Would you like to know how you might start believing me?"

"Try me."

"Grand Central Station has eyes everywhere—something I'm sure you know as well as anyone, Detective. Has for years—well before any of this went down with Gray."

"Of course."

"And that footage is not only recording in a continuous loop, it is archiving in a continuous loop. I can give you exact dates, Detective. Exact dates and exact times to go back in time and look at the cameras by a certain bathroom in Grand Central. A certain bathroom where you will see your detective entering, then waiting for, Jonah Gray who he knew would be there."

Morante is in a near trance from my words.

"You have got to be kidding me."

"Far from it. I can also tell you where he waited for Jonah outside of Grand Central with duffel bags filled with millions in drug money from the streets—money he was going to use as payment for the egg. I'm guessing there are plenty of exterior cameras that must have picked this up. You see, Jonah had goaded the son of a bitch into thinking he was going to play ball. But he was never going to turn *Danish Jubilee Egg* over to him or anyone else. Never. And that, Detective, is what got your boy killed."

As the Acela slashes up the Eastern seaboard, I tell Morante everything. All that went down from the moment Jonah saw Pangaea-Man until the moment Jonah killed him by accident when the car they were riding in nicked the curb. I also told him that it was not Jonah who actually disposed of the body. That in the moment, someone had offered to cover. And Jonah didn't have the luxury of time to stick around and ask questions.

"What do you mean? Then who?"

I thought of Mattheau—my father's longtime chauffeur who had covered for me, given me the assistance and room to escape. I have no idea where he is. Alive, dead, in New York City, another continent—zero idea. But Mattheau was a good man who had looked out for me. I can't take the chance of putting him in harm's way.

"That . . . that I'm not sure of. You'll have to take that up with Jonah."

My stomach is in a full-out riot as I recount all of these moments. It's not like I haven't relived each second before—just not to the detective I barely eluded when the world turned upside-down on me. I can't believe I'm actually talking to him. I'm staring in his eyes, but all I see are white backdrops—oval-shaped, white, backlit backdrops in his head projecting images from my life, one after the other. Vintage Perry in our Manhattan office before this ever happened appears in the left eye. Perry behind the bar at supperclub in Amsterdam pops in the right. Tommy pops in the left. My father in the right. Jake of old in the left, fatter Jake I just saw the day before in the right. I see the chalet where my transformation happened—and Max and Gaston, then Perry again—in the left. I see an image of me and Detective Morante speaking in front of my father's townhouse just minutes after Pop's head was blown apart. The slideshow goes on and on, the soundtrack of Morante's voice behind them. It's like a scene ripped from the fucking *Twilight Zone*. If only this guy knew.

We finally pull into Penn Station. I've certainly given Morante more than enough to run with in beginning to see the truth, beginning the process of clearing my name. I look at the Perregaux. Time is mad tight. I still have work to do. And a flight out of here in a couple hours.

"So, when will I be hearing from you?" he asks as we ride the escalator up from the platform.

"According to Jonah, should be tomorrow," I answer. "Soon as I know, I'll get in touch with Jake. He'll tell you where to meet me and we'll go from there."

"Uh-huh."

Uh-huh.

I don't care for "Uh-huh."

We ride a bit farther up in silence.

"So, you've made it pretty clear you don't feel comfortable giving me your name, but you still haven't mentioned anything to me about your relationship. How you know Gray. Why you're here. Anything."

I turn to him.

Because, Detective, I'm a ghost.

And that doesn't change for you or anyone else until I can safely walk the earth again as Jonah Gray.

"That's right," I say.

Something is happening, telling me to be on alert.

Though I'm not sure what.

"Why is it such a secret?"

He then adds a chuckle to his words.

"I mean, you two meet in a Turkish prison or something?"

We hit the landing. I pretend to be unsure of where I am.

"Let's see," I say as we keep walking side by side, stride for stride. "Where would I find a taxi stand?"

"This way. Seventh Avenue," he replies.

"Ah."

We slightly shift directions. But our pace remains the same. We head up yet another escalator and exit onto the sidewalk on Seventh Avenue between Thirty-First and Thirty-Third Streets, right under the main entrance to Madison Square Garden. Off to my left I see the taxi stand line.

"I appreciate your efforts today, Detective," I say, as I get in line. I extend my hand.

"And as soon as I know, you'll know," I continue.

He shakes my hand.

"I'd better."

He looks at his watch.

"You know, probably best for me to take a cab as well since my car's up at the precinct. Mind if I wait with you?"

Not good.

React.

Now.

"Actually, I'm on a really tight schedule," I shoot back, now looking around wildly. "Ah! That. The One Line I think it was," I say.

I jump off line and start heading to the subway entrance on the corner of Thirty-Third and Seventh for the 1, 2, and 3 lines.

"I believe we took that train yesterday. Anyway, Detective, thanks again."

"You sure? The line moves really fast," he says to me.

He isn't waiting for my answer. He's jumped off the line too and is coming my way.

"I'll be in touch," I go on, disregarding his words.

I turn and get moving. My walk becomes any faster and it will officially be a run. The street is busy. I'm weaving the best I can, rubbing shoulders, excusing myself without looking back. I'm working the crowd, every muscle in my body clenched and ready for, absorbing incidental contact.

I look over my shoulder.

Morante's working the crowd just as I am. He's coming.

Fuck!

What did I say?

What is he thinking?

Once I hit the stairwell down into the subway, I stop with the charade. I start taking the steps two, three, four at a time, full speed. I avoid people coming up the best I can, but a few aren't very lucky as they get my lowered shoulder or I crush their toes.

Once officially in the station, the last thing on my mind is a MetroCard or paying. Like a track star, I hurdle the turnstile and take off down the platform for the Downtown One line. All of a sudden I hear a programmed woman's voice come over the intercom throughout the station:

"Ladies and gentlemen, there is an Uptown One Train to South Ferry approaching the station in four minutes."

I keep going without breaking stride. The platform is crowded. I have no idea if Morante is keeping up with me or not. I look over my shoulder. Nice. I don't see—wait—no, there he is. He's caught in the crowd but still coming. I slow back down to that place between a walk and a run as I have good distance.

In my last life as a commercial real estate broker in this very city, one thing was as much of a constant in my life as anything.

The New York City subway.

I don't care of you're rich, poor, black, white—there is simply no more efficient way of getting around this city for people who actually care about being on time. When you're a powerhouse rainmaker with the biggest firms in the country waiting on you multiple times a day, like I was, the subway system becomes your best friend.

I hear the station woman's voice again:

"Ladies and gentlemen, there is an Uptown Two train to Two-Hundred and Forty-First Street approaching the station in one minute."

One minute.

Shit.

Without having to look, I know exactly where I'm going. At this particular station the Two and Three lines, both express, share another platform that requires me to go down another staircase—coming up on my left in about thirty yards—then take yet another one back up.

Making that train is going to be tight. But without a second's hesitation, I take off. I've undoubtedly just made it clear to Morante I have something to hide, but getting caught in his clutches without his first being forced into investigating some of what I've told him is not an option. For him to catch me now means everything unravels. For him to catch me now means too many others avoid exactly what it is they have coming.

And I'm simply not having that.

I bail from the platform like someone, well, running from the cops, and start barreling down the stairs. As I do, something unexpected pops into my brain. It's the chalet. I see Perry. And Max. And Neo. And Gaston.

Once I get to the bottom of the stairs, I run through the tunnel that heads back across Seventh Avenue underground. To keep going straight would take me to the Uptown One—a local train—as well as an exit back up to the street. To make a right halfway through the tunnel takes me up to the express lines.

I hear the rumbling of a train approaching overhead. Then I hear some screaming and commotion coming from behind me. I turn for a split second.

"Police! Please, move aside! Please!"

Morante hits the bottom landing of the staircase. And he has two officers with him dressed in blues.

Fuck.

When did he call for help?

Were we still on the Acela?

Or were these guys by chance in the station?

Our eyes meet for a split second. I turn and bounce up the stairs like I have springs on the bottom of my shoes.

The train is coming. Rumbling.

Louder.

Louder.

I'm almost there.

I see the chalet again.

Only I'm not seeing Perry, Max, Neo, or Gaston anymore.

I'm seeing the surgeon who transformed me.

"Ladies and gentlemen, there is an Uptown Two train to Two-Hundred and Forty-First Street approaching the station."

The Two Train and I surface on the platform at the same time. I keep running. Until this thing stops and the doors open, I need to keep moving. Even then, I need to keep moving. I have to time this just right. Or I'll be stuck either in the station, or on the subway car with Morante and two more officers.

I'm dodging people left and right. As I do, the train comes up on my left, then past me. I look over my shoulder. I see Morante yelling something as he pursues me, but he can't be heard above the braking train.

The train is slowing down. Finally, it stops. The doors open, but I keep running. People file out of the train into my path slowing me down, but no doubt Morante is experiencing the same obstacle.

The surgeon.

I see him again in my mind.

He's saying something.

Realizing I can use the influx of people now on the platform to my advantage, I crouch while still moving as fast as I can on low, crooked legs.

I keep moving.

Keep moving.

Then—

I break left, through the crowd, and onto the train. Channeling my last life, I truly feel I've timed it right. The doors start closing. I feel the air returning to my lungs.

The doors bounce open again.

No.

Fuck!

Standing up again, I look out through the subway car windows at the platform in the direction we came from.

Why? Why did the doors open?

Is someone holding a door open for someone else to make it?

Is there a hold-up up ahead?

My heart is racing. My chest feels tight.

The surgeon.

I see him again.

Only now, I can hear him too.

Like a narrator; my life, the film.

"No matter how we change the way we look, there is one thing we can never change. Our eyes. And there will always be a special few that no matter what you have done to conceal your birth face will always be able to recognize your eyes."

"No," I whisper, "it can't be."

I see Morante and the officers running into view. He's spotted me. Preparing for war, I pull the gun from my waistline. He keeps running toward the subway, toward me, only now he has his iPhone up to his face.

I'm trapped.

"My guess—" I hear the surgeon in my mind say again, "those people will not let you know they have identified you until it is too late."

Realizing Morante is trying to get a photograph of me, I lift my free hand in front of my face. When I do, through my fingers, I see someone running full speed slam into Morante sending both of them flying just before he jumps on board.

I'm as baffled as I am relieved.

The doors close. We start moving.

What just happened?

Did he get a clear picture?

I move to the door to look through the glass. Just like that—my last image of Morante—sprawled out on the platform. He's gone, as we pull out of the station into Manhattan's underground maze.

CHAPTER 40

At Forty-Second Street, I transfer to the One Train, take the One up to Fiftieth Street, exit, head above ground, then head West toward Sixth Avenue. My nerves are jacked. I'm riled up. I'm pissed, amped, freaked. But I remain calm, cautious. Morante may have a halfway decent picture of me, he may not. Either way—that's all. He doesn't have a name, he doesn't have a single piece of information about where I've come from, how I got here, where I'm staying, anything about me. No matter what he thinks he may know, what his gut's telling him—I could give a shit. So long as I stick to my plan, I'll be long gone by the time he starts making heads from tails. Hopefully, he'll start going on all the information I gave him on our ride back from D.C. Or he'll make this about finding me instead of finding the truth. I can only hope for the former. Truth is, who knows?

I look at the Perregaux—6:44 p.m. I keep my gait strong, purposeful. The evening air is raw, the dimming gray sky helping ease crisscrossing New Yorkers into night. My mind is spinning from everything happening. I'm wired. I'm exhausted. I see a bodega. I grab three Life Fuels, down one on the spot, and put the other two in my pocket. I keep moving.

I take out both phones. I Google NYPD Precincts on the

iPhone. Once a comprehensive list comes up I go with the Thirteenth Precinct on East Twenty-First Street. Yes, Lovell was in Scott Green's office, but I'm guessing he's from the precinct closest to Green's home. I dial the number into the disposable and hit send. I replace the iPhone in its rightful pocket.

"NYPD," a gruff, female voice answers.

"Hi, I'm looking for Detective Lovell," I say. "Is he in?"

"Let me see. Give me one second."

I wait.

"I'll transfer you."

I wait again.

"Lovell."

"Detective Lovell, I'm going to speak for sixty seconds. So I suggest you begin writing."

"What? Who is this?"

"I'm guessing you were following up on Scott Green's suicide as a matter of protocol, making sure there was no foul play due to the odd nature of the circumstances. His conservative history, a loving family, alone in a houseboat in Amsterdam, all of it."

"Who is this?" he asks again.

"Scott Green did in fact kill himself. But he was driven to it. He sacrificed himself to save his family. You want to worry about how, or do you want to worry about my name?"

"Wait—wait—"

I hear fumbling around. He's grabbing a pen and paper.

"Okay. Tell me what you know."

"Go to Scott Green's home. His wife, Anne, is expecting you. You are the only one she is going to speak with. Tell her you want to see everything on her husband's computer in his study. Make sure she shows you the VivRecord.com account. Then, make sure she shows you the e-mails with the photo attachments."

"Viv what?"

"VivRecord.com," I repeat, then spell it for him. "It's an audio file storage site. One for the purpose of recording and storing telephone conversations."

"Got it. Anything else?"

"Yes. After that, go to the home of a Julia Chastain," I continue, giving him her address. "In the kitchen, under the tray holding the silverware in the silverware drawer, there is a tiny flash drive. On that flash drive are conversations between Ryan Brand, a colleague of Scott Green's, and Enzo Alessi, the man on the other end of the conversations you'll be hearing on Scott's home computer. A man the U.S. government is very interested in. Got it?"

"Flash drive. Conversations. Ryan Brand. Enzo Alessi. Got it."

"Julia Chastain is also a colleague of Green and Brand. Unlike Anne Green, Ms. Chastain is unaware you will be visiting, and I'd keep it that way. She's fucking Brand—a married man—and she may or may not be involved in all this. I'll leave that up to you to determine."

There's a brief pause. I figure Lovell is finishing up his notes.

"Got it. Anything else?"

"You have a busy evening ahead of you, Detective. Good-bye."

6:54 p.m.

I walk into the GlassWell headquarters building, stop at the security desk, and get my temporary badge. I head upstairs and straight to Julia's office. I let myself in and stop in front of her desk.

"Where the hell have you been?" she yells at me, jumping from her chair. "What the hell are you fucking people trying to pull, Ivan?"

"Sit down, Julia."

"Excuse me? Really? You think you're going to—"

I take the gun from my pocket. I point it at her face.

"Sit down. Now."

Her arms still at her side, like her elbows are attached to her sides, her hands flare out.

"Holy shit, Ivan. I . . . I—"

"Sit down now," I say again.

She does.

"What the hell are you doing, Ivan?"

"Where's Brand?"

"Ryan? I . . . I don't know . . . I mean, he probably—"

"Get him in here," I cut her off. "Now."

"I . . . I'll try. I mean, he may be—"

I drop a fist to the desk. I lean forward.

"I'm guessing with his deal cratering the way it is, he's available. And if he's not—I don't care if he's in fucking Dubai. Find him. And get him in here. Now."

She tries his office. No answer. Then she calls his cell. He's in another colleague's office just down the hall. He's on his way.

"What's going on, Ivan?" asks Julia. "Why are you doing this?"

"Did you know?" I respond with a question of my own.

Nothing.

"Did you?" I press.

"Did I know what?"

The door opens.

"Janse, what are you doing here? We closing this deal or what?"

"Close the door," I say.

He does. Then I show him the gun.

"Sit down. Now."

He looks at Julia.

"What don't you understand about sit down?" I growl.

I step to him and put the gun to his head. I hear a scared shriek come from Julia behind me.

"Okay," he concedes. "Okay."

He takes a seat facing Julia's desk. He sheepishly turns to me.

"What's going on, Janse?"

"Fuck off, you lowlife. I'll be asking the questions as well as making the statements. If I want to hear from you, I'll ask. Understood?"

He nods.

Standing to the side of the office, where I face both Julia behind her desk and Brand in front of it, I drop the gun to my side.

"I want you to both know that I get it. And that while you

almost pulled it off, this is all happening because—well—you didn't—"

"You're not making any sense, Ivan," Julia says.

"I know Alessi was strong-armed into leasing the Annex with a promise from you to help pay his tax bill with GlassWell funds. As much as I know he has zero intention of honoring that lease, which we all know destroys the property's financial viability."

"What?" says Brand, doing a terrible acting job.

"You heard me."

Brand's expression goes from fake surprise to fake serious.

"You're delusional, Janse. Do you realize what you're saying? What you're doing?"

On the contrary, Ryan Brand.

Do you have any idea who you decided to fuck with?

"What are you talking about, Ivan?" Julia chimes in. "That's crazy."

"Ah, so you two want to play games, is that right?" I ask. "Is that right?"

The video of Green blowing his head off plays in my head.

I calmly walk over to Julia.

"Let me ask you something, Ryan." I go on. "You ever seen a head blow up? Like what must have happened when Scott Green took his own life?"

Neither says a word. Then, I grab the back of Julia's head like a cantaloupe with my left hand, gripping it tight.

"Open your mouth," I tell her.

"Ow! Ivan, you're hurting me," she says, her words rife with shock.

"You have no idea what pain is, Julia. Now open your fucking mouth. Or I'm going to open it for you."

Brand stands up. I point the gun straight between his eyes, no more than a few feet away from me. He stops dead in his tracks. I see him swallow.

"Sure you want to play hero?"

He sits.

I return my attention to Julia.

"I'll say it one last time. Open your fucking mouth."

Adrenaline and caffeine are coursing through me so violently I feel my veins throbbing. I'm boiling.

Finally Julia listens.

And I jam the gun in her mouth.

"Open wider!" I demand.

Tears are flowing from Julia's eyes. Some of them are mixing with the snot bubbles under her nostrils and running onto the shiny metal in her mouth.

I move my eyes to Brand as I keep talking.

"That's right, Sweet Julia—take it deeper."

I push it in farther.

Fear is pouring from Brand's eyes.

Fear of what happens next.

"What do you want?" he says quietly, almost in a whisper.

"What's your bigger fear right now?" I go on, disregarding his words. "That Julia will actually feel pain—maybe die—or that no matter what comes from all this, it's a guarantee your wife, your kids, everyone you have ever known in your entire life is going to learn all about what a piece of shit you are?"

He's about to say something, but stops. Now I see something else in his eyes. An understanding.

"I have the conversations between you and Alessi. All of them. Green may have been afraid of you fucks, but you underestimated him. He had more fire in him than you realized. And now you're all going to pay for what you did."

Brand says nothing. He looks at Julia.

"Because of what you did a life was lost," I go on, "a family was ruined."

"Look, I—" Brand starts, "it—I never wanted any of this to happen. Really. It just—everything got so, so—"

An image of my father goes off in my brain like a firework. I look at Julia. She's a crumbling mess, her makeup running everywhere.

"And Julia," he continues, "Julia, I mean, Julia knew we were pushing him but, but, I mean—she had nothing to do with how, you know, how—"

My eyes are reaching deep into Julia's. She's genuinely scared for her life. I take the gun from her mouth. I step away. Sobbing, she collapses forward into her own lap.

"This man—this was a simple, family kind of man. A man his kids were lucky to grow up with. A man whose wife loved him. Because of you—because of your fucking selfishness about your fucking building you took him from all of them. You took him from himself. Who the fuck do you think you are?"

I walk toward Brand. I look at Julia, waving the gun in her direction.

"I keep wondering if you knew about all this, or if you got pulled in because of the guy you're fucking— behind his wife's back, apparently," I go on. "And you know what I decided? I have no idea. Nor do I care. If you really knew nothing, the cops will come to that conclusion. And I promise you—they're coming to look. Right in your backyard."

I stop in front of Brand. I look down at him.

"Get on your knees."

"Oh, God," I hear from Julia behind me between sobs. "Ivan, stop. Don't."

"Please," begs Brand. "Please."

"On your knees. Now."

"I—look—"

I put the tip of the gun to his knee.

"Three, two—"

"Okay! Okay!" he says, jumping from the chair.

He does as I order.

Now I put the point of the gun to his temple.

"Was it worth it?" I ask. "The threats? The following and taking pictures of this poor man's family? Was it worth it, all in the name of business? Was it worth driving this poor fucking man to blow his own fucking head off because he felt this was his only fucking option?"

"Please! Please! I didn't follow him or his family or send those pictures—it—I wasn't responsible for that."

Alessi sent the pictures. Not Brand.

I glance at the Perregaux.

Enzo Alessi.

See you soon.

"But I know that doesn't make any of this right. I never wanted for this to happen! I swear! I swear! The whole thing—the whole thing just got so out of fucking control..."

I take a step back, gun still pointed at his head.

"Take out your phone."

"What? Why?"

"Just take it out."

He does. I grab it from him. It's an iPhone, and it's locked.

"Code."

"One, one, one, seven."

First I go to the Alarm Junction app. Alarm Junction is the firm that handles security for all the GlassWell properties. These days, everything can be handled for these types of systems remotely via applications or the web—real-time monitoring, camera angle adjustments, cameras being turned on and off, everything. The system is very much like the one we use in The Netherlands. And because we've been in the process of buying the building, and have scoured every aspect of this target up and down, I'm very familiar with what I'm looking at. I even have the username and password I need tucked in my brain, but it isn't necessary as Brand's already logged in. With only a few taps and touches, I turn all the security cameras at the Annex off.

"What are you—"

"Shut up," I cut him off.

Next I go into the contacts and find Enzo Alessi. I text him.

I NEED TO SEE YOU IN YOUR OFFICE. NOW. IT'S URGENT.

"Ivan," I hear Julia say behind me through chokes and sobs, "Ivan, please. There has to be—"

Her words may as well be in Japanese. Done with her. I put the gun back to Brand's head. Thirty seconds later, I get the return text from Alessi.

WAS ABOUT TO LEAVE, BUT WILL WAIT FOR YOU. WHAT'S UP?

I drop Brand's phone to the ground. With three quick, hard stomps I destroy it.

I lean down. And whisper in his ear.

"Boom."

Brand starts crying.

"The biggest mistake you made? Trying to fuck a guy like me. Trying to fuck a firm like de Bont. Thank your lucky stars, Ryan Brand. Had you actually succeeded—had you actually sold us that building—you'd be leaving here today in a body bag."

I snap back up and kick Brand square across the face with everything in me. In agony, he rolls onto his back. Blood is coming from his nose, from his mouth and cheek. That's when I drop my heel into his face again for good measure, causing both of them to scream.

I lock eyes with Julia.

"The Spencers treated you like family," I say. "Some sister and daughter you turned out to be."

Then, I'm gone.

CHAPTER 41

After stopping at the hotel and grabbing my belongings, I have my car stop at the Freedom Bank Building before heading east across town to the Queens-Midtown Tunnel. Before opening the door to get out, and going upstairs to see Alessi, I get a text. It's from Ernst Bjerg.

YOU NEED TO CALL ME, IVAN. 305 IS GOOD. APPARENTLY, NOT GOOD ENOUGH.

"Right on cue," I say to myself.

One thirty a.m. in Berlin. Ernst, though pushing it, has the green light to make a deal.

Sensing eyes on me, I look up. The driver is staring at me in the rearview. I turn and look out the window at the Freedom Bank Building. At the Annex.

"Why am I here?" I ask myself. This guy—these fucks—they're all going to get what they deserve for what they've done. Their families, their careers, they've all lost more than they even realize yet. I should be on my way to the airport.

Right?

Damn, my chest feels tight. My skin feels warm under my suit. My nerves are shredded.

Yet those same nerves are as steely as ever.

Yeah, they'll all get what's coming. But will they ever really feel it? Scott Green blew his head all over a room after dealing with what must have been days, weeks of pure anguish. Alessi, Brand, Julia if she needs it—they'll all load up on high-powered attorneys, and it will be ages before any of them face any music. When they do, will they even really feel it? Once all the charges through fancy litigation and maneuvering have been watered down? Will they ever really *feel* it? Will they ever feel even an ounce of the pain Green did?

A flash goes off in my brain—my father's gunshot-riddled body on a gurney.

Then another—the starburst of Green's head, brains up on the wall.

I should go to the airport.

I look at the Perregaux.

"Sit tight," I say, gathering myself. "I won't be long."

The Annex, like I mentioned, is like its own property affixed to the main building. Therefore it has its own entrance, one much less complex and with less security than the main property. People who work exclusively for the Alessi operation come and go with a card-key access system. They wave their card in front of the card reader on the wall next to the entrance. So, I'll just wait until someone exits—hopefully—so I can slide in.

Seven thirty p.m.

I'll never make wheels up. I dial Cobus.

"Ivan."

"I figure you know, but I wanted to mention that I have made it clear to GlassWell we're not closing. They get it. As I said they would."

"And Berlin?"

"Working on it."

The door opens. A great-looking, tall, slender woman with dark everything exits the Annex draped in a tight-fitting, chocolate-colored Armani overcoat. I act as if I'm simply a guy on the street talking on the phone, perhaps waiting for someone, as I watch the door. She gives me a quick up and down, smirks, and moves on.

"So why the call, Ivan? You could have told me this when you arrived."

"I, uh—"

She's ten feet ahead down the sidewalk, her mind most likely already on wherever it is she's going, when I sneak the toe of my shoe between the closing door and doorframe. I slide inside.

"I need a little more time. There's one more stop I need to make."

Cobus pauses.

"Ivan."

"Cobus."

"I sent Arnon back commercial. I decided this was probably best once I learned you decided we will be returning to Amsterdam via Moscow."

Damn.

"Cobus. If I—"

"As you know, these flights are not as easy to change—either time or destination—as you are treating them. Nine p.m. Ivan. We're wheels up at nine with or without you. My advice? Make it."

I bypass the elevator and head up the central, spiral staircase. Because of the time, the space is pretty empty.

"Hi, I'm here to meet with Enzo," I say to a guy coming down the staircase. "Third floor, right?"

Look like you belong. And you do.

"Fourth floor," the guy says back, barely giving me a thought. "Front corner on the left."

I let myself into Enzo Alessi's office. The space is more Old World than I would have imagined. The desk is an old, traditional flattop mahogany piece. The oversize windows are adorned with heavy, navy hanging drapes that match the carpeting. The accompanying furniture—the couches, chairs, coffee table, end tables—all have ornate, curved moldings.

Alessi is standing behind his desk. He's decked out in a custom Brioni suit, minus the jacket, talking on the phone. The knot of his shiny, lilac necktie is huge, tight. He's talking on the phone. I close the door behind me.

"I'll have to call you back," he says into the phone when he sees me.

He hangs up.

"Ivan, I believe. Can I help you?"

"We need to talk," I say.

"How did you get in here?" he goes on.

"Front door."

He takes a glance over my shoulder toward his office door, like he's expecting someone else to walk in. Like Brand.

"Unfortunately, I don't have time. I have a very busy night ahead. Perhaps if you'd like to sit down you can call my assistant tomorrow and we—"

"I think you should reconsider," I say.

"Excuse me?"

"You heard me."

His cordial demeanor, expression, hardens.

"And why is that?"

I take the gun from the back of my waistline, under my jacket, and make sure he sees it as I reposition it in the front of my waist-line, just off center enough to remain covered. I walk back, around Alessi, behind him and his desk, over to the first of the huge windows. We're only on the fourth floor, so people in the buildings across the street—if any remain at this hour—can see in. I draw the blinds closed.

"Because you're the reason GlassWell's deal to sell the Freedom Bank Building and Annex is officially dead."

"What are you talking about?"

I move to the next window.

"The conversations between you and Ryan Brand? The ones that led to GlassWell's in-house counsel blowing his own head off in Amsterdam?"

I draw them as well.

"You have no idea what you're talking about," he goes on.

He looks to the door again.

"Brand isn't coming," I enlighten him. "Just you and me."

I move to the last window, now off to his left and in front of his desk. He returns his eyes to me. He reverses his demeanor, his strategy.

"Look, I think there may be a terrible misunderstanding happening here," he says. "And perhaps I can spare a few minutes. Why don't you sit down? Can I make you an espresso?"

I don't answer. I draw the last set of blinds, I walk to the front of his desk and face him.

"Put your hand on the desk," I say, calmly.

"Excuse me?"

"Put your hand on the desk. Now."

"Who the fuck do you think you're talking to?"

I take the gun out. I point it between his eyes, just inches away.

"Hand. Desk. Now."

He hesitates, but obliges. I casually take a pair of scissors from the desk. And without hesitation, with all the speed and force I can muster, stab Alessi's hand, securing it to the desk. He lets out a primal scream. I silence it with a fist across his jaw. He's dazed, confused. Blood is coming up through the wound, trickling over the sides of his hand onto the desk. He's still standing, but his torso is laying on the desk to the side of his maimed hand.

"You talk a big game, like some big fucking man when it comes to threatening people. So act like a man. You make one more noise, the first bullet I let go is into your balls to let you bleed out a bit. The second one burrows into your temple and ends your life."

I take a fistful of tissue from a Kleenex box on the desk. I ball it up and jam it in his mouth, his eyes popping like headlights beaming to life when I do.

"Other hand on the desk," I continue.

He's hesitant. He knows what's coming. He shakes his head "no," grunts.

This fear, this moment, this anticipation.

This is for you, Green.

"Fine with me, motherfucker!" I say, and start around the back of the desk.

His free hand reaches for the sky. He starts making whatever noise he can behind the tissue to get my attention.

I stop.

"On the table," I repeat.

He does as I say. I come back around. I put my gun back in my waist. His eyes watch every inch of my deliberate movement. Slowly, I reach for, pick up the letter opener on the desk. I hold it down at my side. His eyes can't move from the letter opener.

"I suggest you remove me from the memory of this little encounter—perhaps blame it on Brand since he did, after all, text you to meet him here. Understood?"

His eyes move from the opener to my eyes. He gives me no indication he's with me on this last request. I lean forward and place my free hand and fist holding the opener on the desk so we're face-to-face.

"Otherwise, I find your son who enjoys the langoustine fritters so much, gut him like a fish, and spill his insides over your head. So I'll ask you one more time—understand?"

He nods "yes."

"He had a family. And you? You literally scared him to death. Why? So Brand could steal from his company to help with your tax bill and we'd end up with this building even though you were going to bail to Uruguay. I've seen the pictures you sent him on behalf of you and Brand. The cops are probably looking at them as we speak, while they review the conversations you and Brand had."

He closes his eyes, absorbing the gravity of all that's happening—what I'm telling him.

"That's right. You have no idea how it's all about to come crash-ing down on you. So I have to ask you—"

He opens his eyes again. I stand back up. I hold the letter open-er in the air. Both of our eyes look up at it.

"Was it worth it?"

I drive the letter opener into and through his other hand. He's stuck to the desk, but his back and neck arch. A primal concoction of gurgling and screaming gets squashed behind the tissue. Every thick, throbbing vein in his neck looks like it might burst. Blood comes up, around the letter opener, coating his hand.

"Get used to that position, asshole," I say, "considering what the U.S. government is about to do to you."

As the car rolls down the Van Wyck toward the private jet FBO ter-minal at JFK, I take out both phones. On the iPhone I go to my contacts and locate Nestor Korolyev—the dude whose doctorate thesis at Ivanovo State University was based on the relationship between Nicholas and Alexander III's relationship before Nicholas's untimely death. And the foul play he believed had taken place. Before this trip, through some simple Googling, I'd learned Dr. Korolyev had gone on to do some more research and had become a teacher. Today, he's a professor at the same university where he wrote the thesis. A couple months back I called him in his office, pretending to be his wireless carrier reaching out about a potential security breach involving his mobile number, which I ended up with as a result of the call. Today, with that number, I'm about to let him change the history books.

I enter the Russian mobile number into the disposable, setting up a text. I attach the first photo taken with the writing from the eggs—the one of *Hen Egg with Sapphire Pendant*. Then I type a mes-sage.

INTERESTING DOCTORAL THESIS. HOW DOES IT FEEL TO BE RIGHT?

I hit "send."

I send another set of texts.

MORE PICTURES TO FOLLOW IN ORDER FROM THE MISSING FABERGÉ IMPERIAL EASTER EGGS. THE EIGHT WERE MADE BY A MAN NAMED PAVEL DERBYSHEV FOR MARIA, ONLY HE WASN'T REALLY PAVEL DERBYSHEV. HE WAS A MAN NAMED GUSTAV BJERG, AND HE WAS MARIA'S COUSIN. GO CONNECT THE DOTS. HE WAS HER SPY. AND THE EGGS WERE HIS WAY OF GETTING HER PROOF OF WHAT SHE BELIEVED; WHAT YOU BELIEVE. THAT'S WHY IN THE CHAOS OF THE REVOLUTION THEY ARE THE ONES SHE MADE SURE OF SAVING. GO SET HISTORY STRAIGHT. GOOD LUCK.

I forward the rest of the pictures. Then I break the disposable in half, and crush each half under my heel. I open the window and toss one of the halves to the side of the highway. A few miles farther I do the same with the second half.

I look at the recently dialed numbers on the iPhone. I tap one.

"Ivan."

"Ernst."

"Ivan, look, the three oh five is close, but we really need to—"

"Three ten," I cut him off. "That's the best I can do."

"Three ten," he repeats.

"Three hundred ten per foot. Take it or leave it. And I need to know yesterday. Understood?"

He probably would have done the deal at three hundred five per foot, but I decide to make it a no-brainer. Because as far as I'm concerned, I'm still buying the building cheap.

"Understood. I'll be back to you."

In the throes of all the chaos once again surrounding my life, an image comes to me bringing comfort. An image that makes me think of all the years past, an image that reinforces the urgency of me finding strength in the moment, an image that reminds me the future is far from surety. I hit Face Time on my iPhone, and dial a number.

"*Dag Ivan. Hoe is uw reis?*"

"*Dag Laura,*" I reply.

I'll give it to you in English.

"My trip's going well—thanks. How's my favorite boy?"

"I'll get him for you. You can ask him yourself."

I can tell Laura's in the kitchen. She places her iPhone on the island. The live feed image goes everywhere before settling on a shot of the ceiling. I hear her in the background calling for Aldo. Suddenly she reappears and picks the phone back up.

"Look who I found," she says, the two of them on the screen, their faces side by side.

"How's my best guy?"

At the sound of my voice Neo visibly becomes excited. He cranes his neck forward and licks the screen.

I smile.

CHAPTER 42

Exhausted, but still riled up, I board the de Bont Gulfstream. I drop my things and walk over to Cobus, who's sitting on the couch with a cocktail, legs crossed, looking very relaxed. As usual, he's dressed impeccably tight in his usual black uniform like he's just started his day as opposed to finishing it. He doesn't say a word. Just stares at me.

I look out the window, into the night. Airport vehicles move in all directions amongst the different colored lights lining the runway and the signs that make no sense to civilians. I take a Life Fuel out, down it, and place the empty bottle on the table. Then I take my suit jacket off and lay it on the couch.

I look back at Cobus. He's still staring at me. He hasn't moved. I don't think he's blinked.

"May I bring you a drink?" asks Aimee, our perky, blond flight attendant, as she picks up the empty Life Fuel bottle.

I'm so frayed, I'm flying. I'm soaring as I'm sinking. My mind and body can't decide who's coming, who's going.

"Get him a Belvedere on the rocks with a twist," Cobus says. "A double. Bring me another too."

"I, uh, I'm not sure I need that right now," I respond.

"Trust me, you want it. For the conversation we're about to have, you'll need it."

Using just his eyes, Cobus encourages Aimee to run along, then for me, motions to the couch. I sit down.

"Cobus, I know this has all—"

"Stop."

"Stop?"

"That's right. Stop."

"Why?"

"I'd like you to slow down for a second, breathe, and have a sip or two of your cocktail. Then we can get down to business."

This, actually, sounds good. I look out the window again. I put my hand to my chest. My heart is literally racing. After all this time, I made it back to New York City. Now, I'm leaving again. I feel a certain satisfaction for what I accomplished. A lot of years of research and planning gone right. I feel equally disappointed I may have fucked this deal up for Cobus. I feel undeniable sadness I still don't have Perry back, that I have no idea if she's safe.

"Here you are," says Aimee, placing two coasters down followed by our drinks on the table.

"Aimee, we're going to need complete privacy," Cobus says. "Please don't reenter the cabin until I call for you."

"Of course, sir."

Aimee disappears. I hesitate, but can't resist how cool, refreshing the cocktail looks. I pick it up and knock a bit back. Cobus doesn't budge. He's staring at me again. Seconds later, we begin taxiing toward the runway. I decide to try and break the ice again.

"Cobus, I would have never killed this deal unless it was best for us. Unless it was right. You'll understand this once—"

"Why do you think you ended up in Amsterdam?" Cobus cuts me off.

"Excuse me?"

"You heard me. But perhaps I should ask the question in another manner. In a way you won't have to think so hard in order to come up with an answer, as I assume that must become extremely exhausting."

"I'm not following."

"Why do you think Gaston chose Amsterdam for you, Jonah?"

The second he says my name—my real name—every hair on my body stands on end. I can feel all the blood in my body rush south. My hands start trembling. Fear swallows me.

"What are you talking about?"

Gaston Piccard.

Pop's Swiss financial consultant and my springboard to a second life.

How does he know Gaston?

"Who?"

Immediately, my mind starts strategizing, starts preparing to go that place I've learned to go.

I'm trapped in the air.

I have a gun.

Cobus, like nothing out of the ordinary has just happened, picks up his cocktail, leans back again in his chair, and takes a healthy sip.

"You heard me, Jonah. Jonah Gray. Gaston Piccard suggested Amsterdam was the place for you to restart your life—you and Perry. Max—"

What doesn't he know?

What am I missing?

"Did you ever stop to ask why? Or was it simply that he was a trusted member of your father's inner circle? And that's all you needed to know?"

"What the hell is going on?"

"What's going on? After all these years, you and I are about to get acquainted. That's what's going on."

Instinct has kicked in. Adrenaline and caffeine—survival—flowing, I grab my jacket and in one quick motion I grab my gun. I don't point it, I just rest it in my lap.

"What's that for?"

Cobus hasn't flinched. He takes another sip, then swirls the lowball, the ice cubes jingling as they hit the glass.

"Just so we're clear," I say. "Ivan Janse respects you. As a businessman and as a friend. Jonah Gray, on the other hand, doesn't fuck around."

"Is that right?"

"That's right."

"Actually, Jonah. I know that about you. In fact, I'm surprised by how big your balls are. I mean, high-speed midnight chases with the police? Tackling all this other shit while we're here for three days to close a deal—*and* finding the time to sleep with Julia? It's no wonder your eyes look like that. Like fire's about to shoot out of them."

"How do you—when—"

"Now, why don't I tell you a little something about me," Cobus goes on.

He throws down the rest of the drink and puts the glass on the table. He leans back in his chair again, only now he's less relaxed. His posture is more serious.

"Have you ever noticed that I'm always the first one off our plane?"

The question surprises me. I'm thinking about it, but have no idea.

"If I'm not the first person off my plane—ever—everyone else on that plane dies. Pilot, flight attendants, Arnon—you. Doesn't matter. Before anyone has a chance to leave the aircraft—they'll all be dead. You know why?"

"I—"

I have no idea what's going on. My head's spinning one way, the interior of the aircraft the other way. I shake my head "no."

"Because if I'm not the first person off the plane, those literally watching my back at all times know I'm dead. And that one of the people on board is the reason. Doesn't matter which one. The fact that someone like me is dead is a much bigger deal than the collateral damage."

I can feel myself squinting from the confusion.

"I'm not following," I say.

"What I'm saying is that you should probably put your little gun away now. God forbid something happens to me, you won't only have killed yourself, you will have signed off on the death of everyone else on this plane."

I don't move. Cobus leans forward, resting his elbows on his knees, his chin on his hands.

"That's not a request," he continues.

His face becomes more serious than I've ever seen it before. It's like I'm looking at a different person.

"Put the fucking gun away, now."

This is the first time I've ever heard Cobus use profanity. No matter what's going on, it's clear that something is taking place bigger than perhaps I realize. Obviously, I'm not going anywhere right now. So in formulating my best strategy, going along for now seems to be the best choice. I do as he says.

Cobus's expression softens, but not much. He sits back again in his chair.

"You have nothing to be afraid of," he goes on. "In fact, quite the contrary. You know why?"

I don't even know what fucking language he's talking anymore.

"Try me."

"Because I swore to Gaston you'd be in good hands."

"Let's, for sake of discussion, say I do know Gaston," I say. "How do you two know each other?"

"Gaston Piccard, as you know, is one of the preeminent bankers in Switzerland. Agreed?"

"Agreed."

"Gaston has a very high-level clientele. You know because you—your family—have been clients for years. In fact, your father, Stan, and Gaston were very close, so close Gaston trusted your father with information about the clients he represents—and how he represents them."

Cobus pauses, staring on a forty-five-degree angle at the table as he chooses his words. Then he moves his eyes back to me.

"Information you used to bribe him into creating your new identity. Ivan Janse."

A sliver of clarity.

"So you've known since the beginning? You've known about me since I've been in Amsterdam?"

"I knew about you the second Gaston agreed to assist you. I knew the plan would be for you to end up in Amsterdam from the moment the surgeons began working on your face. This gave me more than ample time to get specific plans in place to watch you."

"Watch me? I don't get it. Why watch me?"

"Because there is a side of Gaston Piccard's business he wants people like you and your father to see—the side of wealthy families from around the world and governments who trust him with billions of dollars. But there is another side of Gaston's business that accounts for just as much, if not more, of his net worth. A clientele of a more unsavory type."

My mind is sprinting, I'm processing.

"What do you mean unsavory?"

"What do you think I mean, Jonah?"

Sure, Cobus has a lot of information, but not sure what any of this means—what's real, what's not—I let the use of my true name roll down my back. I stay in character as Ivan.

"What? Like white-collar crime types? People who know how to manipulate markets, steal from corporations, things like that?"

"Things like that and then some. That, my friend, is why Gaston needed you looked after. Why he needed eyes kept on you. Should something have ever happened to you, and it became public knowledge there is a connection between him and a global fugitive like you, both sides of his business would have blown up in his face. The legit side because wealthy families and governments can't be associated with a financial advisor who harbors and assists the FBI's Most Wanted. The other side because criminals and the like can't be associated with a financial advisor on the authorities' radar."

"So why Amsterdam? Why did Gaston call—"

Before I complete my sentence I feel a tingling in my midsection.

Am I looking at a man, a self-made real estate magnate, named Cobus de Bont?

Or some kind of different animal altogether?

Cobus leans forward, then reaches out, picks my cocktail up, and downs the entire thing. He puts the glass back on the coaster and stands up. For a few seconds he does nothing, just stares down at me. He slowly removes his suit jacket and carefully, neatly, places it on the chair next to the one he's sitting in. Then he reaches up with both hands and begins undoing his necktie.

"You remember why I wear these same clothes no matter the circumstances?" he asks. "You remember the name of my affliction?"

"Solar something," I answer. "Solar…Urli…Urtlit…Urticarial. Solar Urticarial."

"That's right. Solar Urticaria."

Once the knot of his tie is undone, he pulls it around, off his neck, and lays it on the suit jacket. He reaches to his waist, and untucks his shirt with both hands all around. He starts to unbutton his black dress shirt from the top down.

"Cobus, why the undressing?"

He disregards me. He keeps going. Once the first few buttons are undone, and the two sides of the shirt begin to separate, I see something underneath on his skin. It's black. It's ink.

"What the fuck," I think out loud in a whisper.

"The reason Gaston called me, Jonah, is because I'm his best kind of client. I'm both sides of his business. Gaston reached out to me because he knew I had the ability to keep you safe should you run into trouble. Something in both of our best interests. Little did I know you'd be somewhat of a handful at times."

He's completely unbuttoned. The shirt hangs open. Cobus drops his arms to his side.

"Who do you think was responsible for the gunshots fired at the van when Perry and Max were abducted? Who do you think ran over that guy on the subway platform just a few hours ago before he cornered you? The guy you rode back from D.C. with?"

The strip of skin running north to south between his hanging shirt sides is covered with squiggly black lines I can't make out. They are thin, tight. It appears as if there's more ink than skin. He removes the shirt and neatly places it on top of the tie and jacket. He stands back up.

"You're good, Jonah. A badass motherfucker, actually. But you're alive because I've made sure you remain out of harm's way. I've stayed out of sight on the periphery of your life only stepping in when absolutely necessary."

I barely hear him. I'm mesmerized by what I'm looking at. There isn't a hair on Cobus's body. He's lean, but ridiculously muscular. I can see every box in his stomach, every striation in each muscle from his shoulders to his arms and down his torso. And he's literally covered in black ink. Letters, numbers, names—it's all neat, orderly, tight like there was a fear from the very beginning running out of skin one day would be an issue. It starts on his neck, right where the top of his collar sits, and goes right on down to his waist. Some of the writing is cut off. I'm guessing it goes below the waistline as well. I think I even see some sort of map on his right shoulder.

"But, how . . . if . . . how did you know to—"

"I never wanted you so close. At least, that wasn't the plan. Amsterdam was the place for you. I could put a team together easily to keep an eye on you. I didn't give a fuck what you were doing. You were working for the Ooviks. You and Perry were re-creating your lives. Everything was cool. Then you started taking trips everywhere. Copenhagen here, Prague there—it was getting too hard to keep track. That's when I decided to make a play for the Oovikses' portfolio. And make a play for you. Someone else? We probably go in another direction. But you? You . . . you were like—what's that my Jewish friends call something like this? Two souls who are supposed to—"

"*Bashert,*" I finish his thought.

I grew up on the Upper East Side of Manhattan. He thinks he has Jews to quote?

"Yes! *Bashert!* I wanted to be real estate, you are real estate. Why do you think Gaston made you see the light when you were talking about pursuing a different career with your second act? Anyway, that's when I decided keeping you close was the only way to go. For a multitude of reasons."

"You bought me a house."

"You earned that house."

"To keep eyes, and probably ears, on me," I finish my thought, deducing what really went down.

"Eyes, yes. Ears, no. I never gave a fuck what you were doing. I get it from the apartment at Herengracht and the weekend trips it was about Fabergé eggs and whatnot, but I never really got it nor did I ever care. Whatever you were going to do you, I was responsible for not letting you get caught if you got too close to the edge. Or killed. Simple as that."

"Who are you?" I ask.

"You'll never have my name. And you don't want it. There are a number of large organized-crime syndicates in this world. Let's just say one of them answers to me."

Exasperated, stunned, I point at him.

"What is all that?"

"Insurance. Dirt. Bargaining power. Though few can get to me—or even know my true identity—there are a lot of people who want me brought down in this world. I'm very careful about who I get in bed with. But when I do decide to deal with someone, there's nothing for buying loyalty like showing them their name next to an account number I know they use for money laundering tattooed to my body. Or maybe their name next to an address that represents a safe house where a certain missing person is buried in the concrete foundation. My connections run deep—in business, in government, in the underworld. No one will ever get to me, and they know that.

This—what you see—is my way of letting those I allow into my world, whether they like it or not, know there is no turning back. And they'd better be looking out for my best interests. Because it doesn't matter whether it's the authorities or another crime syndicate. There isn't a database in the world that can bring down the house more than my body should it fall into the wrong hands."

I continue to scan his naked torso in awe, confusion.

"Which name do you think I've written for you? Ivan Janse or Jonah Gray?"

My eyes move from his body, meet his.

"Hint. Your little secret has to do with both."

From Cobus de Bont's right-hand man to casualty of whatever war this guy's fighting. Just like that.

In a blink.

"So, de Bont Beleggings—what?" I change direction. "It's all bullshit? Just some front company?"

"Oh, no. Not in the least. De Bont Beleggings is the complete opposite. And the accomplishment outside of my children of which I'm the most proud. The world has changed. Once it became clear I would be taking the reins, I knew I would need a life to hide behind, a legitimate cover with legitimate business dealings. In line with the story you know, I started with a securities trading shop and built from there. But when we fell into the commercial real estate game, for the first time something really stirred inside me."

Cobus grabs his shirt and starts rebuttoning it.

"I was born into this world, if you will," he continues. "It was all my family knew, all we had for earning money, sustaining life. We had friends, we had enemies. So if I had to be in that world, I was going to become the master of that world. That's just my nature. But I always wanted something more, something for me. That's what I found in real estate. I was instantly fascinated by the complexity of this world—and I loved the challenge. I always knew my best bet for keeping myself out of harm's way would be a seriously legitimate business. Only once the real estate world came my way, I decided I wanted an empire. Because in all my working life nothing had ever made me feel like a success in this world more than growing my portfolio of buildings."

"Why are you telling me this?" I ask. "Why now?"

He starts tucking his shirt in.

"Because in learning how to best keep myself where I need to be, I have become, well, you know. Like you, Jonah. Real estate is in my bones whether I like it or not. Survival is one thing, but I have learned more than anything I want to thrive. I want to *win*. I have built up a legitimate empire for my family. My wife, my kids. Because of real estate, my children will not have to live the kind of life I've led."

He reaches for his tie. He wraps it around his neck, and begins tying it.

"Why am I telling you this? Because without a care in the world—no matter our history, or how I've trusted you and made you my guy—you fucked with my livelihood. You treated a few-hundred-million-euro deal—I now see—as nothing more than a means to an end. A return home. I trust you so much, you said New York over Berlin I believed New York over Berlin."

"Cob—whoever you are—it's not like that. I really believed this was a deal we could—"

"I don't doubt that. But do you think the Freedom Bank Building is special because of the Annex? Or a scary property because of the Annex? One that's probably not the best choice for a firm's first venture in a foreign market?"

I don't answer.

"The day you taught me about signals in a meeting, Jonah— what the touch of a cuff link can mean, what a request for water can mean—is the day I knew you were not like anything I've ever met. I've put all my faith in you, which means I'd expect you to realize you've taught me more than you know. Without thinking de Bont is anything but my family's everything, you chose *you* over the hand that feeds you."

He puts his jacket back on. Looking just as he did when I boarded the plane, he hits a button and requests Aimee. She appears, he orders a fresh round of drinks, and she's gone again.

"Why am I telling you this?" he says again. "You needed to hear—and see—that Cobus de Bont might be someone who will tolerate what you pulled. I, on the other hand, will not."

In the moment, I'm overwhelmed. Yet, surprisingly, at the same time I'm comfortable. Relieved. Better sense tells me I should fear whoever this is. But I don't. Because to me, this is Cobus de Bont. And if he wanted me to think of him as anyone else—All-World Mobster, Gangster, White-Collar Motherfucker, whatever—he would have told me his real name. He would have given me more to go on to remember him, fear him, certainly after he just told me more than he's probably told anyone before. Then he would have killed me.

Cobus de Bont has been looking out for me.

Because Cobus de Bont needs me.

Not just me alive.

Me.

"Berlin is still—" I start.

"I don't care. I want—"

"I didn't finish," I cut him off. "You want to know how we still end up with Berlin? Or you want to spend some more time telling me how big your balls are?"

Cobus juts his lower jaw toward me. He's thinking about what he just heard. Then, as Aimee appears with our drinks, he starts laughing. Cracking up like I've never seen him crack up before.

"Berlin will still be ours," I say.

"Why?"

"Because I still have a chip. And I'm finally about to get my chance to use it."

I lift my drink from the coaster and extend it toward Cobus. He obliges by lifting his as well. We clink. We drink.

"After the shit you pulled, I can only imagine one thing that would give you the nerve to take us to Moscow," Cobus says. "But I want to hear it from you."

"Perry."

"Perry," he repeats. "And Max? Or Johan?"

"He's not with her. He's in New York. He's safe."

I lift my glass toward him again, toasting him.

"We'll be watching, Jonah Gray. As always, I'll have the man-power to step in if we're needed. But do you have a plan?"

"Look where we are," I respond. "I always have a plan."

Same plan as always.

Go fucking get it.

Worry about the mess later.

"Why didn't you just kill me?" I ask.

"Excuse me?"

"When Gaston called you all those years ago. Why didn't you just kill me?"

"Because of Gaston himself."

"He told you not to?"

"To be clear, if I tell Gaston to take a crap, he asks how big. Gaston Piccard doesn't tell me anything. He asks me."

"So, he asked you?"

He takes a healthy sip.

"That's right. He did."

"Why?"

"Because he said he owed it to your father. Because your father, apparently, wasn't just a close friend, your father built his career. Sent him his first big U.S. clients, as well as some others in Europe, which allowed him to take off. According to Gaston, if it weren't for Stan Gray his professional life simply wouldn't have happened. In his words—'looking out for Jonah is the least I can do for his father. Jonah says he's innocent. I owe him—them—the chance to prove that. And get his life back.'"

I stare him in the eye.

Animal to animal.

"You happy he made that request?" I ask.

Cobus looks at his watch.

"Get some sleep. You need it."

Sleep. Right.

"I'll wake you when we're forty-five minutes or so out. God help you from there," he says.

Said with the most devilish smirk I've ever seen.

CHAPTER 43

Moscow, Russia
2013

An immigration officer boards the plane and we clear customs. My gun in the rear of my waistline, I step off the de Bont Gulfstream at Moscow Domodedovo Airport in a fresh suit, and into the waiting black Mercedes E Class. In the few moments between the two, as I breathe the biting Russian air, I notice the weather is sunny and freezing. I'd barely slept. It's two p.m. in Moscow. Between the eight-hour flight and eight-hour time difference my body is even more out of whack than when we left New York. The driver is a tall older guy, bald with a thick mustache, wearing a gray overcoat over his uniform. He asks where we're headed, his strong English wrapped in a Russian accent. I tell him to sit tight for a moment as I dial Andreu's number.

"*Zdravstvuitye.*"

"I'm here, I'm in Moscow," I start. "Where is she?"

"Ah, Jonah. Wow. You weren't kidding."

"Where is she?" I repeat.

"You have what I need?"

"You only get what I have once I have Perry. So I suggest we get started."

He pauses.

"Come toward the heart of the city. When you—"

"I want somewhere secluded," I cut him off, "and you'd better have her with you."

"And I want somewhere crowded," he comes back at me. "Because I don't trust you for shit."

"Fuck that. I'm on your turf, which means—"

"That's right, Jonah!" Andreu barks, "You're in my city now. So if you want to see Perry again, you'll do things my way."

I take a deep breath and accept I'm going to have to follow Andreu's lead.

"Where am I going?"

"Near Red Square is a mall called the TSUM. Across the street is a restaurant called Vogue Café. I'll meet you there in an hour."

He hangs up.

Talk about feeling out of place. Not being able to read the street signs or billboards is one thing. Not even recognizing the symbols that are in fact the letters of the Russian alphabet is another. As we approach the nucleus of Moscow, traffic is thick. The roads and intersections are like runways, seemingly ten-lanes wide on each side. At some of the intersections I can't see from one corner to the other. The architecture in the heart of Moscow is massive and old, yet wildly eclectic. There are blocky, austere structures that along with the wide roads scream Stalin. There are the famous ornate Orthodox cathedrals. Coming up on Red Square, I can see the colorful, swirling turrets atop the Kremlin, but we veer off and stop in front of a brown, six-story building on Petrovka Street.

"The TSUM," my driver says.

He points across the street.

"Vogue Café."

The place even for lunch is a scene, an apparent hotspot for the pretty people—something that doesn't surprise me once I see the 'Vogue' in Vogue Café is in the same typeface as the magazine with the same name. The space is clean, stylish, understated Euro-chic. The cream-colored walls, dotted with traditional sconces, are adorned with black-and-white as well as color photos of models from the magazine. The square columns have mirrors up and down them. A fire burns in the fireplace.

Immediately, I see Andreu at a table by himself toward the rear. He looks the same aside from his hair having seriously grayed. Slicing through the eyes on me, I move through the dining room toward him. When I get to his table, I say nothing.

He looks up at me, a forkful of grilled octopus nearing his mouth.

"Can I help you?"

Andreu is dressed tight as always—perfectly tailored navy suit, white, open-collar Purple Label dress shirt underneath, brown leather Gucci shoes and belt.

"Where is she?" I say, Jonah Gray's voice coming out of Ivan Janse's body.

He drops his fork, moves back in his seat.

"What the fuck?"

"Where is she, Andreu?"

He looks me square in the eyes. Processing what's happening, squinting his eyes, he leans toward me.

"Jonah?"

He looks around the room, then back at me.

"How the—holy shit."

"Let's get to it, Andreu."

He looks around again.

"I'm alone," I say, addressing what's clearly on his mind.

He leans back in his chair, and for a third time focuses on me.

He takes out his iPhone, dials a number, and hits "send." He asks the person on the other end what sounds like a simple question in Russian; I'm guessing if I was followed inside by anyone. Once he receives an answer he says nothing, just ends the call.

"You have what I need?"

"Show me Perry and you'll find out."

Staring at me, he thinks silently. Then, *"Tee-Pyehr,"* he says casually.

Four well-dressed big dudes, sitting two each at a table close by, stand up and come toward me. Fast. I crack the first to reach me in the jaw. I reach back to grab my gun. All it does is assist one of the guys coming up on my back in restraining me. From behind he grabs my backward-reaching arm as well as my other. Then one of his comrades returns the favor, tagging me across the face. I twist and turn as hard as I can to break free. Diners scatter. Dishes, glasses, and silverware from the surrounding tables go flying. The dude who hit me steps to me again. This time I kick him square in the balls, just as another fist from one of the other guys lands on the other side of my face. Fending them off is a losing cause. Before I know it, my arms still tightly secured behind my back, two of the guys are each grabbing one of my legs and lifting me up.

Andreu stands up. He starts for the exit, his goons following him with me in tow. Just as we cross the threshold out of the restaurant, an Escalade comes screeching to a halt out front. I'm immediately tossed in the back. His goons get in with me.

"Where are we going?" I ask.

"So, Jonah," Andreu says from the passenger seat, blowing me off, "this is how it's going to work. We both know *Danish Jubilee Egg* is still in the U.S. Capitol, therefore I'm assuming you've brought me a little present from Pavel Derbyshev. Which you'll need to hand over in order to see Perry. Understood?"

"Fuck off, Andreu. Perry first. Or no deal."

"Wrong answer."

One of the goons lands a hard right to my jaw again. Another, sitting on the other side of me, lands a nasty left to my ribs.

"We going to do this my way?" Andreu asks.

Bluffing, I have no choice but to stick this out.

"No Perry, no dealing. Last time I say it."

The fists keep coming.

I have no idea where we're going.

What I do know is the ride there is going to be brutal.

CHAPTER 44

Moscow, Russia
2013

My eyes open. My head snaps back from the smelling salts. My vision adjusts to my surroundings. I rack my pounding brain to recall what happened, where I am. My chest is tight. My heart, too big for its cavity. Every muscle in my body aches. I'm naked. The air is frigid. I try to move. My arms are handcuffed behind the chair. I am strapped so tightly I can feel the blood trickling down my wrists. My legs are equally overpowered. I look down. There is an iron cuff around each ankle. They, too, are shackled together.

The room—a cold, dank basement of some sort—finally comes into focus. The windowless walls are made of large, gray bricks. Thin, jagged streams of dirty water snake down them resembling human veins. The low ceiling, also gray and coated with dripping moisture is made from the same solid stone under my feet. The space is poorly lit; a single dim lightbulb is all that shines from above. In the far corner, where the wall meets the ceiling, is a single, small basement window a body couldn't even squeeze through. Aside from me, and the clouds that appear and disappear in front of my face with each breath, the room appears empty. All I hear are my thoughts and the occasional droplet of water falling from above if it manages to hit a puddle.

I could have been here ten minutes or ten days. I have no idea. Just as I ask myself why I feel so alone—even though someone has awakened me—I hear steps behind me. They are hard steps, shoes hitting rock. Each is slow, deliberate. Out of the corner of my right eye, a shadow enters my field of vision. I turn to look. The pain in my neck is excruciating. Just as I move my lips to speak, a crushing fist blasts through my jaw. Immediately, I feel the devastation. I have bitten off a piece of the side of my tongue. It swirls in my mouth with shards of ruptured teeth and blood. I spit out the absurd stew, the chunky goop hitting the floor with a splat. It feels like a bomb exploded in my mouth. My eyelids are heavy. They only want to close. My soul only wants to shut down. Maybe even die.

A hand from behind reaches over me and grabs my chin like a vice, pulling it back as far as it will go. I groan in agony. My eyes stare at the ceiling. A drop of filthy water hits me dead center on my forehead. Seconds later, my torturer's blue eyes meet mine from no more than two inches above.

"*Gereed om te spreken? Of jullie nog denken jullie wipen enigerlei handeling held?*"

What language is that? I think, his spittle spraying my skin. And why do I understand it? Given my restrained circumstances, my reflexes still function, and I attempt to shake my head. As I do, my assailant repeats himself. This time I hear it in English . . .

"You ready to speak? Or you still think you're some kind of action hero?"

. . . As I recall why I now process everything I hear in two languages.

He gently traces my face with his fingertips, like a blind man seeing something for the first time.

"My God, Jonah. Look at you . . ."

My thoughts are distorted, but I recognize the voice. Andreu Zhamovsky, my dear half-brother. My head slowly bobs back up.

Then in an instant, bright, beautiful colors flash across my mind. There are jewels—splendid green emeralds, luscious red rubies. There is gold, silver. Subconsciously or consciously, I can't be sure, I squint from their sheer brilliance. I look forward. I could swear *Danish Jubilee Egg*, the one of the eight missing Fabergé Imperial Easter Eggs I had been saddled with years earlier in New York City, is suspended in midair. I think of how I had kept it—a true, rare treasure—out of harm's way. I smile.

"I have something you want, Jonah. And we both know what you have to give me first to get it."

My mouth fills with blood again. Instead of spitting it out, afraid of the ensuing pain from such force, I part my lips and gently push the deep red liquid down the front of me. Its warmth feels strangely comforting against my raw chin, my freezing chest.

Shoes on rock, the pacing footsteps behind me have restarted. Only now there are more than one pair.

"You're hard-nosed, Jonah. A real animal, you know that?"

I don't answer. Someone slaps the back of my head.

"You going to answer me, mister?"

Mister. I grin in my near delirium. The word, even for a second, returns me to my youth. Returns me somewhere safe. As if my minutes on this earth truly may be numbered.

"Mister, I ain't a boy, no, I'm a man," I push out, my voice weak, "and I believe in the promised land."

Andreu sighs.

"You surprise me, Jonah. And you disappoint me. A simple exchange is all it takes for us both to be happy. Instead, it seems you've accepted your unfortunate fate. Scripture?"

"Springsteen, you fucking coward." I utter through clenched teeth, some fight left in me yet. "Why don't you uncuff me and face me like a man."

The pacing stops. Silence. After a few seconds Andreu speaks again.

"This is your last chance, Jonah. Either give me what it is I want, or you leave this room—this world—without what you came for."

This is bad. I know it. But even though I'm rocking all this on a bluff, risking one of the most important things in the world to me at this very moment, I know in my gut it's the right move. Not just because I have no other choice. Because Andreu wants what he thinks I can give him all too much.

"This, actually, is your last chance," I respond. "You're a lying, deceptive, disgraceful soul. You can't be trusted. You first show me you have what I came all this way for. You don't like it? Drop fucking dead. You and that black-hearted excuse of a human being you call Mother."

Footsteps come rushing up behind me. They don't sound like the ones I'm associating with Andreu; it must be whoever's with him. I open my eyes as wide as I can. Just as I do my chin is grabbed and yanked back again. In one swift motion a vodka-soaked rag is crammed into my mouth. The burning of my torn-up flesh is off the charts. A guttural scream pours from my lungs only to be muffled. My nose immediately clicks into overdrive. My nostrils flare as they hungrily draw in air.

"You're a fucking dead man, Jonah Gray. Today. In this room. You're about to die a brutal death."

He's bluffing.

He's got to be.

A clear plastic bag is pulled over my head. Trying to move is of no use. I simply can't. My heart is racing so fast I think it might explode. The unmistakable scratching sound of duct tape pulling away from its roll fills the room, though I can barely hear it. The plastic is thick. The noise seems distant. The tape is being wrapped around my neck, securing the bag to my skin. Moments later, breathing my own warm, recycled breath solely through my nose, the bag starts crumpling in and out. It won't be long until I'm dead.

He's bluffing.

He's got to be.

I'm trapped. All of the things I have ever done, warranted or not, have caught up to me. A tear forms in my right eye and gently rolls down my cheek.

Slowly, Andreu walks around and faces me. He's wearing a perfectly tailored black pinstriped suit with a white, open-collar button-down underneath, no tie. An enormous, mountain of a man accompanies him. His friend is wearing expensive gray pants, equally expensive black, leather shoes, and a white, skin-tight, cotton tank top. His head is the size of a boulder, each feature from his rounded nose to pointy ears, huge. He has a slight underbite, his front teeth roll white chewing gum like knuckles kneading pizza dough. His massive, chiseled arms and shoulders are covered with black hair so thick it is like fur. Without a word, he holds up a safety pin. For what seems like an eternity they both just stand there, taunting me. My ragged breathing begins slowing, I can feel myself fading. He drops the pin to the floor and approaches me. Then he buries the sole of his right foot in my face so hard I can feel the bridge of my nose, the orbits of my eyes crumbling.

My heart. It's . . . it's . . . what's happening?

I fall backward. The back of my head cracks against the gray rock. Blackness.

I start to regain my sight. It's like being on an airplane and trying to see through the clouds while you're ascending. I see the ceiling above. It looks to be speckled with beads of moisture. I can't keep my eyes focused on anything because, though still shackled, I'm violently bouncing around the floor.

"What the fuck is he doing? Is that a seizure?"

I want to clutch at, grab my chest. The pain is so severe, like an elephant is sitting on me. My chest is reaching for the sky as quickly as my back is slamming on the cold floor. Too much caffeine, too much Life Fuel, too fast.

"Please! Help him! Help him!"

Is . . . is that—

I'm so hazy. My mind is playing with me.

"Please!" I hear again.

Perry?

"He's having a heart attack or something! Please!"

The pain radiating from my chest is hitting every cell in my body. It's the only pain I feel. The beatings I just took are a distant memory.

My teeth are gnashing uncontrollably. My restrained arms and legs are contorting from stiff unnatural position to stiff unnatural position. My eyes are rolling back in my head. I'm seeing black and light alternating as fast as my heart rate. I'm fading.

"Jonah!"

Perry.

Like God has decided enough, my flailing starts to subside. I'm able to breathe again. I suck in air as if I've just nearly drowned. I can feel, taste the blood and saliva filling my mouth. My body's insane thrashing is morphing into a slow writhing. I hear the rustling of the popped plastic bag necklace I'm wearing—a plastic bag that nearly helped end me.

"Leave him alone, you sick fuck!" Perry screams. "What's wrong with you? He needs help!"

Still on my back, Andreu's face appears above me.

"Good thing you didn't die. If you had, I'd have no use for her."

I hear the chair I was sitting in propped back up. Mr. Mountain grabs me under my armpits and picks me up fast, hard, then drops me back in the chair.

Finally. After all this time, after all the questions and heartache, I lay my eyes on Perry. She's sitting across from me, about twenty feet away, in the same kind of metal folding chair I'm in. Her wrists are cuffed in front of her. Her ankles are cuffed as well.

She's crying. There's terror in her eyes. She's in jeans, a plain white t-shirt, and Nike running sneakers—the same ones she was wearing the day she was taken from me. Thankfully, she looks unharmed. And, as always, she's the model of simple, pure beauty.

My left eye's field of vision, vertically, is much less than my right, meaning it must nearly be swollen shut.

"Did he hurt you?" I ask. "Did he lay a hand on you?"

"What do you think I am?" Andreu snaps. "Some kind of animal?"

I ignore him. My eyes are squarely on Perry.

"Jonah," she says to me tenderly, shaking her head "no." "Holy shit, Jonah—"

"Did he hurt you?" I ask again.

My words are barely audible. It's like a grenade went off in my mouth. My altered tongue, teeth, and cheeks are figuring out how to work together.

"No. Physically—no."

In this answer I also hear yes. Emotionally—yes. For taking her son away.

"Max is okay," I tell her. "I saw him. He's fine."

Perry drops her chin to her chest. Tears of gratitude start flowing.

"Now let's get on with it," Andreu breaks in. "I believe you have something for me."

I move my eyes to Andreu.

"I do."

"Well? Where is it? Because until I have what I want you may think you and your little—"

"I have a message for your mother," I cut him off. "She lost."

"What did you say?"

"You heard me. She lost. The message contained in the eggs? The truth she wanted to keep from the world? Not going to happen. In fact—history is probably being rewritten at this very fucking moment."

"What the hell are you talking about, Jonah?"

"You and your mother—you fucking assholes lost. And I fucking won."

Battered, exhausted, I can't keep from starting to laugh.

"Still want those fucking eggs—Brother?"

Andreu pulls a gun out and charges.

"No!" Perry screams. "Stop!"

Just as he reaches me, the basement window glass behind him, in the far corner, shatters. Both he and Mountain Man drop in an instant.

Andreu is faceup while Mountain Man is facedown. Both are screaming, squirming in pain. The back of Mountain Man's bare right shoulder is a shredded mess of blood and flesh. Andreu is gingerly clutching his right knee. Blood is soaking through his pants. Mountain Man starts to get up. Another bullet tags him in the back of his other shoulder, inflicting equal if not more devastation. Mountain Man, primal noises pouring from him, is down for the count.

A door behind me blasts open. Three men, all huge and dressed casually in jeans and such, come around me where I can see them. One immediately tends to freeing Perry. Another picks up the gun Andreu was holding then gets to work freeing me. The last guy puts an iPhone up to my ear.

"Hello?" I manage.

"Do you want them left alive or dead?"

It's Cobus.

I look at Andreu. He's struggling, suffering. He doesn't deserve to live. And his mother deserves the anguish of knowing she got her own son put down like a lame racehorse.

I look at Perry. Through tears and chokes, she's focused on working with the guy assisting her to get free. She's being so brave, doing everything she can to hold her shit together. I have no idea what these last years have been like for her. What she's endured. What it must feel like to be kept from your own son, the beautiful boy she brought into this world she only wanted to be there for and protect every day.

My eyes move back to Andreu.

"The little one, the guy who got it in the knee," I say, "He deserves to die."

Andreu, through the searing pain he's experiencing, looks up at me. His eyes are filled with forced courage yet rich with defeat. His eyes are still challenging me yet pleading with me to show mercy.

"But, I'm no murderer," I go on. "I just want to leave him with a reminder that if I ever hear from or see him again, he won't be so lucky. Something that will remind him every day. I'm thinking cutting off the middle finger on each hand."

"Ah, Jonah, wait. Please," Andreu pleads while trying to mentally manage the pain he's in. "Please. If—"

The guy working on me wheels around, steel-toe-boots him dead center in the face, laying him out, then returns his attention to me. Working with some kind of sharp, thin utensil, he unlocks the cuffs around my wrists. The metal eases away from, out of the wounds it's been sitting in.

"Then," Cobus goes on, "where are we going?"

This is a kind gesture from my boss—whoever he is. He knows Perry should be with her son. I look at her. It breaks my heart to know what I've put her through. It would kill me to now have to let her go again. But she needs to be with Max. Whether that's in Amsterdam or New York City.

I think about Morante. God, I hope he's going to search for the truth, not me. In my heart, I believe I've laid the foundation for clearing my name. But until that time comes—until Morante constructs the walls and roof that sit on that foundation—can I even consider going back and reclaiming my life?

Our life is now in Amsterdam.

Our life will always be in New York City.

"Home," I say. "It's time to go home."

AUTHOR'S NOTE

SPOILER ALERT: This author's note contains information that will give away key elements of the plot of The Deal: About Face.

In *The Deal: About Face*, contemporary fiction collides with historical fact.

It has given me great pleasure to weave day-to-day past experiences in the commercial real estate arena into this fictional drama. That these experiences might please and enrich others makes this journey even more rewarding. Yet while *The Deal: About Face* is contemporary, occurring in today's world just as we know it, there is also a historical element that commemorates rare treasure. The fabled Fabergé Imperial Easter Eggs stand among the world's most celebrated artistic achievements. If not for others and their diligent research and writings, a bevy of which I found online as well as in books and articles, it would have been impossible for me to incorporate these mesmerizing antiques into the story.

The eggs populating this novel are historically true to form in everything from name to description. As described in the book, fifty bejeweled Fabergé eggs were commissioned by the Russian royal family between the years of 1885 and 1916, as gifts from the czar to the czarina and other family members. It is also a fact that after the Russian Revolution, only forty-two of these prized antiques ever resurfaced.

This is where fact ends and fiction begins. While in *The Deal:*

About Face the errant eggs are discovered, in reality the eight missing since the early twentieth century are still unaccounted for. They were neither found underneath a home in eastern Russia, as the book suggests, nor anywhere else for that matter. Rather, everything surrounding the lost imperial eggs in *The Deal: About Face* and all the other events described were created purely for entertainment value—including any and all material that suggests the history surrounding Czar Alexander III, Maria Feodorovna, or anyone else associated with the Russian royal family is anything other than history describes. If any names, situations, or sequences of events that mirror true life have arisen as a result of my approach to telling this story, this is truly a circumstance born of coincidence.